The Devolution Chronicles:
Passage to Niburu

Gary Wayne Clark

Copyright © 2010 Gary Wayne Clark. All rights reserved.

Published by Gary Wayne Clark.

ISBN 978-0-9853438-1-1

Author's note: Through the power of genetic engineering, artificial intelligence and sleep deprivation, this story sprang from the author's imagination error free. But the reality of a post apocalyptic dystopian future would not be plausible if not riddled with human fallibility; some relatively minor and insignificant, others glaring and cataclysmic. To pay homage to this immutable truth, random, purposeful errors have been inserted to enhance the experience of this alternate reality.

D1475395

Table of Contents

Reviews

"Gary Clark is a master storyteller. *The Devolution Chronicles: Passage to Niburu* is a thinking person's fiction. Niburu artfully weaves future technologies with ancient folklore to create a wonderful tapestry of action and suspense. A must read that will keep you wanting more."

Katherine Francis, Writer / Producer

"In the publishing and literary world, there are a great many books that wash over the reader and quickly drain away, forgotten; The Devolution Chronicles is not one of them. This series sweeps you away on a tidal wave of strange lands, exotic yet frightening creatures, battles, science, and mysteries; drowning you in passion, fear, love, hate, and many more human emotions in an alien world. Gary Clark wrote the words brilliantly, breathing life into the characters, giving them their destiny to become stars of the screen, and legends for years to come."

Mark Hooper, Managing Editor, Angel Editing

"I'm blown away by Gary Clark's *Devolution Chronicles*! The characters, the story, the interconnecting worlds are vivid and exciting. It's all great creative fun - an epic adventure worthy of Asimov and Lucas. I can't wait for the video game!"

David Lee Miller, Award Winning Writer / Director / Producer
"Archie's Final Project"

Credits

Thanks to my friends from *'across the pond'*, Mark and Angela. Without their grammatical guidance and tenacious timeline scrutiny, much of this story would have ended before it began.

Thanks to Sheldon Borenstein, my illustrator, who was first to recognize that *The Devolution Chronicles* would be an overnight sensation... even though it might take ten years to achieve.

To all my "Greenbelt" friends, both two and four-legged; thanks for listening, critiquing, and offering encouragement over the years.

And finally, I owe special thanks to my brothers, the Native American peoples of the Hopi and Navajo Nations for their wisdom, friendship and inspiration. As an ancient Hopi proverb says, *'He who tells the stories... rules the world.'*

Book Trailer on *Earamas* YouTube channel.

Soundtrack by *Earamas* available on iTunes and Amazon.

Editing provided by Angel Editing.

Cover Art and Illustrations created by Sheldon Borenstein. Additional images licensed from Shutterstock Images LLC.

Dedications

For Ali, whose imagination and talents are wellsprings of inspiration.

For Jill, whose love and companionship know no Earthly bounds.

For Justin, who is the free spirit we all secretly wish that we could be.

For Glen, my genius musical overlord and lifelong friend.

And to Raz, my interspecies translator, you were wise beyond your ears. In our hearts, you will live forever. In our hearts, you will never die. *I sus kwaatsi. Tuuwala nasngwam paasavo itam tsovawta tuawta pahunthe wii si we'e kee wa'h aape tokpela.*

ACT I

"The sun and the moon shall be darkened, and the stars shall withdraw their shining."

Joel 3:15

"Pieces of the bodies of infidels were flying around like dust particles. If you would have seen it with your own eyes, you would have been very pleased, and your heart would have been filled with joy."

Osama Bin Laden

"I saw heaven standing open and there before me was a white horse, whose rider is called Faithful and True. With justice he judges and makes war."

Revelation 19:11

"War does not determine who is right - only who is left."

Bertrand Russell

1. Original Sin

Planet Earth: Confederation Protected Zone 51... in the not too distant future.

The scattered light of a bloodless moon filtered down through the broken clouds, casting ghostly shadows across the silhouettes of burned-out vehicles and debris that littered the deserted city streets. As darkness fell, a terrified woman's scream pierced the silence; echoing a frantic plea that cut like a jagged knife in your chest. It was a plea that tonight, like every other desperate cry after sundown, would go unanswered. There were more wild, bone-chilling shrieks, followed by sporadic gunfire... and then a stifled sob of hopelessness that fell away to an eerie stillness. Down a darkened alley, the dead calm was again broken by muffled voices; this time, the quarrel was much closer. An intoxicated gang of irate men was arguing, their angry shouts building to a crescendo, punctuated by the clatter of a whisky bottle shattering on concrete. The sharp sound of broken glass startled a pack of wild dogs fighting over a chunk of rotting carrion, triggering a return chorus of low, guttural growls as the scavengers circled the carcass to protect their kill.

Behind an overflowing dumpster in the alley, a lone figure emerged from the shadows. He nervously checked up and down the street, and then signaled with a small flashlight from his pocket before darting into the open, bounding across the broken pavement. As he climbed the steps of a burned-out entryway, the man glanced over his shoulder once more to make sure he had not been followed. He saw nothing; the street was deserted. Silently, the man placed his hand on a biometric reader in the door handle, waiting for what seemed an eternity for the device to unlock. He heard a welcome metallic click and then twisted the knob, slipping through the iron portal to safety. Once inside, a frightened woman thrust her shoulder against the door, slamming it shut. After securing the dead bolt, she spun around behind the man and pulled him close to her body.

"Is it safe?" she whispered.

"Not yet." The man exhaled nervously as he peered through the metal blinds, scanning the sky above the darkened street and then pressing his ear against the glass. *Silence*, he thought, *the absence of that sound... was good.* Relaxing the tension in his chest, the man started to pull away from the glass, but then he heard it; that sound, the muffled, rhythmic sound in the distance that sent a shiver of terror down his spine. It was almost indiscernible at first, a faint thumping sound in the clouds, like the sound of an old washing machine chugging away, growing louder as it strained under its load. The thumping cadence accelerated and the anxiety in his chest exploded as he pressed his ear hard to the window, straining to verify that distant sound, praying that this time it was somehow different, but he knew it wasn't. His mind tried to reject the sound, to suspend its belief, but his ears couldn't lie; they recognized that dreadful sound. It was the same sound that had struck terror in the night countless times before, bringing death to all those within earshot. Somehow, he had always managed to escape the wrath of the sound before, but tonight, something was different.

Pass over, you filthy beast! he whispered aloud. *There's nothing for you here... not tonight.* The thumping sound in the clouds grew steadily louder and then faded, causing the man to slump against the wall and exhale a fleeting sigh of relief... the evil had passed. But then, just as quickly as it had dissipated, the terrorizing sound returned. The beast in the sky had locked onto the clue it was seeking, settling in ominously just above the street outside his doorway. It peered down through the clouds with its lifeless eyes, piercing into the darkness, scanning the deserted streets for the quarry it sought. On the biometric reader outside his entryway, evil paused; the beast had detected the slightest heat residue from a single human handprint on the door. The faint, glowing red signature on the metal handle was all that the winged beast needed... it had located its prey, and this time, there would be no escape.

"The evil... it has found us." The man sighed as he collapsed against the iron door, seeming to accept the inevitability of his fate. "The time has come for us to cross the bridge... to paradise."

"Khalid!" the woman sobbed. "Is there no other way? What about... the children?"

Looking at the lines of fear gripping her face, Khalid pulled her close to him, kissing her forehead. "Those who are pure of heart have nothing to fear," he whispered. "Once we have crossed over the bridge, we will all be together. Now go and wake the children; we do not have much time. Send Seif to me, he knows what we are to do. Take Aiyla with you to the back room, bolt the door, and be still."

"But I want to be with you, my husband!" the woman pleaded.

"And you *will* be with me forever... in paradise," he answered calmly as his voice began to rise. "As will be the children of all believers. But first you must do as I have asked, for the hour has come and there is not much time. Now go!"

The young boy was awakened in the darkness by the touch of his mother's trembling hand on his chest. Even in the dim rays of light creeping under the door, he could see the terror in her eyes; she didn't have to speak, he knew instantly what to do. His heart pounded as he leapt from his bed and raced down the stairs to join his father in the front room. As a boy, he had practiced for this moment a thousand times; tonight, he would become a man, and he was ready. The words of his father echoed in his ears as he slammed an ammunition clip into his MAC-10 machine pistol. *Have no fear of death, my son, for those that die for the cause shall enter the eternal garden.*

"Is it the time..." the boy asked, "...of judgment?"

"Yes," his father whispered as he cocked his sawed-off twelve-gauge shotgun. "But no matter what happens to me, you must promise that you will never forget the name you have been given... you are my *Sword of Vengeance*."

Seif stood tall, his chest filled with pride. He was only a ten-year old boy, but in his father's eyes, today, he was a man. The boy wiped a tear from his cheek and leveled his automatic weapon on the door. "Yes, Father," he swore. "Across the sands of time, I will never forget."

Just as the words left the boy's lips, a gas canister crashed through the back window of the flat and struck his sister, slashing a gaping hole in her chest. The spewing chemical fragments from the bomb danced around on the floor, hissing as they quickly filled the room with toxic smoke. Aiyla screamed in pain as she collapsed, blood gushing out of the gaping wound of mangled flesh in her burned stomach. Her mother rushed to her side to try and stop the bleeding, but the knockout gas paralyzed her arms and legs; she fell helplessly on top of her dying daughter.

Seif spun around to rush toward his mother, but he couldn't move. The iron grip of his father's powerful hand clamped down on his shoulder, holding him back.

"Cover your mouth!" Khalid commanded. "And stay behind me, my son!"

From the belly of the winged beast hovering above the street, a hatch door sprang open; ropes unfurled and shadows swiftly rappelled down the face of a burned-out building in the darkness. Seconds later, five men dressed in black armor, wearing gas masks and night vision helmets, followed the blast of a concussion grenade and burst through the iron security door as it was blown from its hinges. In the smoke and confusion, the armored men simultaneously locked their laser sights on Khalid and opened fire with a hail of lead, riddling his body with their machine guns, cutting him to pieces in seconds.

As his father fell to the floor, the boy screamed and rushed forward, emptying his machine pistol into the intruders... his futile barrage of bullets bouncing harmlessly off their body armor. His hand was frozen on the trigger and the room fell silent, except for the hollow clicking metallic sound of his empty weapon as its spent chamber clattered to a halt in the haze of the smoke-filled room.

With their primary target dead, the men in black armor regrouped and trained their sights on the terrified boy, ready to end his life. They paused, the red dots of their lasers dancing a pattern of lights on the boy's forehead, waiting for the order from their leader. The silence of the standoff was broken not by the anticipated order of execution, but by an unexpected command.

"Cease fire," their leader uttered. "Check the back room."

The boy dropped the bandana that was covering his mouth, knelt down and gently put his arms around his dead father. "Almighty One, why have you forsaken us?" Seif sobbed. He tried to rise; he wanted to bludgeon the intruders with his bare fists, killing them all. But as the knockout gas expanded into his lungs, his head started to spin and he collapsed to his knees. "Please... I beseech you!" Seif prayed. "Grant me the strength to destroy the evil that has slain my family." But his desperate plea fell upon deaf ears; his prayers were not to be answered that day. The boy who had become a man in a baptism of fire slumped over the body of his dead father, his arms and legs numb from the gas. As he lay there, his body was paralyzed but his eyes were still partially open, he could see the image of the criminal intruders in the haze. *I will be the Sword of Vengeance*, the young man pledged through his tears. *And I swear to you, my father, I will extract retribution tenfold for your death. I will kill these murderous bastards and eradicate their seed for all eternity.*

"Two down in here, Colonel," a man in black armor called out from the back room. One's pretty bad, the other one's... still breathing. The rest is clear."

The strike leader, Colonel Sirius Stonewall Ryker, knelt down to the semiconscious boy; he had been impressed with his courage in the face of death. "You're a fearless adversary, my son, but you're on the wrong side of this war."

Seif's mind was spinning from the gas, his vision fading in and out. He tried to scream at the killer standing over him, but his face and mouth were numb, there was no voice to be heard.

"Your father was a parasite," Colonel Ryker continued as he circled the body. "He was like a tick, burrowing deep under the skin of our society, hiding beneath the safety of our government, even as he was sucking the life out of his host. He provoked sedition and anarchy, all the while passing secrets to our enemy. A traitor like this deserves no mercy; he had to be cut down, for the good of us all." The young man just stared up at him, unable to speak his dark eyes half-open and staring. "We each have choices to make; your father made his, and he paid for his sins."

Colonel Sirius Ryker knew when he joined the Confederation Military Tribunal that he would be leading a death squad; he would hunt down suspected terrorists and eliminate them before they could strike. This was what it took to protect the last remnants of society... no judge, no jury, just an executioner in body armor with a machine gun. As Thomas Jefferson said, *'The tree of liberty must be refreshed from time to time with the blood of patriots and tyrants,'* he told himself. *And these terrorists are its natural manure.* But tonight, looking down at the dead man and his innocent young son draped over his body, Colonel Ryker's mantle of command felt especially heavy. *If I hadn't killed him, it would be me lying here on the floor in a pool of blood.* "It's too late for him, son, and for you as well, I'm afraid," he hesitated. "Orders are orders."

"Time to go, sir," urged one of the men in black armor. The soldier moved close to his leader and whispered, "Look, I'll do whatever you tell me to do, sir, but you know what our orders are... leave no one alive." The soldier stared at his leader, waiting for a command. "What are we doing here, sir?"

Colonel Ryker shook his head. This wasn't the first execution he had carried out, and it sure as hell wouldn't be the last. The world, or whatever was left of it, was rapidly descending into madness. *The only survivors in this shit storm would be soulless killers and the faceless bureaucrats that fed them. I should just shoot this boy in the head and be done with it; hell, I'd be doing him a favor.* Looking down at the young man draped over his dead father, still clutching his empty machine pistol in his hand, Colonel Sirius Ryker made a command decision; it was an insubordinate decision driven by his heart, not by his mind. It was a decision of compassion that would change the course of many lives, and little did he know, ultimately result in his own death. *There's been enough collateral damage for one night. Besides, we're going to need his kind in the future.* He bent down and whispered into the young man's ear. "As twisted as this may seem, you're a weapon of our own making… a weapon that will prove useful for us; in the right circumstance."

The boy looked up with hate burning in his eyes at the murderer with a machine gun standing over him. *I will remember you, you bastard, and I will kill you,* he screamed out in his mind.

"I can feel the hatred burning inside you, it's a thirst for revenge that can only be quenched with blood," Colonel Ryker whispered. "Hold on to that hatred, son, lock it deep inside your heart; you're going to need it to survive. We just need to channel that hatred, redirect it with the proper… indoctrination to the truth; our truth, that is."

Lying on the floor, Seif wanted desperately to close his eyes to the horror around him, but he couldn't. His face was still numb from the gas paralyzing his eyes; they were frozen wide open. What his eyes didn't want to see was in the next room; an impatient soldier in black armor, standing over the bodies of his mother and sister, waiting for his command to execute them. The soldier poked Seif's sister in the back with the barrel of his rifle and she rolled over in a pool of blood, exposing the gaping hole in her chest; she was dead. Raising his boot, the soldier shrugged and then brought it down hard on the back of Seif's mother. She winced and emitted a muffled cry of pain.

"Colonel, we've got a problem in here. One of these terrorist bitches is still alive," he said coldly. "Want me to end her?"

"Stand down, soldier," Colonel Ryker barked without looking up from the young man at his feet. "Check your fire."

The force of the boot on her back awakened Seif's mother from her shock and the worst effects of the gas. As she opened her eyes, she looked down at a mother's worst nightmare… the lifeless eyes of her dead daughter beneath her.

"Aiyla, no!" she sobbed.

The woman clutched her daughter tightly in her arms for a moment, rocking back and forth, and then gently laid her limp body back on the floor. As she wiped the tears from her cheek, her eyes met

Seif's through the haze as he lay there in the front room, on top of her husband. The pain of her loss overwhelmed Seif's mother, and despite the lingering effects of the gas, she somehow managed to get to her feet and charge the murderer standing over her husband's body.

"You killed them all, you monster!" the woman sobbed, striking Colonel Ryker with her open hand across his face before she collapsed to the floor beside her son and dead husband.

The soldier from the back room joined Colonel Ryker and kicked the dead man on the floor. He leveled the barrel of his automatic weapon at the boy's head and looked over to his leader for his final command. "Complete the mission and return to base, sir?"

"We've got one dead terrorist; he's the only one on the list," Colonel Ryker announced. "Mission accomplished," He motioned toward the young man on the floor. "Take this volunteer to the re-education camp; I've got a recruiting quota to fill."

The soldier hesitated for a second, then nodded and threw the body of the semiconscious boy over his shoulder. He paused as he reached the doorway. "What about the woman?" the soldier asked loud enough so the others could hear him. *If this jack off is determined to disobey orders and end up in front of a firing squad,* he thought, *I'm not about to join him.*

Colonel Ryker bent down to the dead man's wife and gently picked her up in his arms. She was covered in blood, but even in the dim light he could see that she was beautiful. "I think we've done enough damage for one night, soldier. She's coming with me."

"Yes sir," the soldier muttered under his breath. "It's your fucking funeral."

Seif's mother was still in a daze as Colonel Ryker carried her outside the flat to the street. Her mind faded in and out, but she regained consciousness just long enough to see her son being strapped to a gurney and loaded into an armored vehicle.

"My son! Where are you taking him?" the woman mumbled, her head still spinning from the gas.

"Not to worry," Colonel Ryker whispered. "He's going to a place where he can learn to apply his natural-born... *skills.*"

"Seif!" she sobbed. "My only son..."

"This will be hard for you to understand right now," Colonel Ryker whispered. "Your husband and children are gone; your heart aches and you want to die. I know this must seem like hell, but it's not. What's coming will be worse than hell... much worse."

"No! This is a... terrible dream," the woman sobbed, her head spinning. "I have to wake up... and this nightmare will be... over."

"Listen to me! This isn't some bad dream; this is real! Wake up and understand one thing; you can come with me and live, or stay here and die... it's that simple. From this moment on, you must forget everything about your past; your husband, your children, even who you were... forget everything. Trust me, it's the only way it can be... for both of you."

"But my son..." the woman sighed as she slipped into unconsciousness.

"You don't have a son," Colonel Ryker corrected her. "And you never did."

2. The Broken Spur

Planet Earth: An Outlands border town on the Eve of Destruction... twenty-five years later.

Lieutenant Commander Zacary Armstrong Ryker could see the end of the world coming... there just wasn't a damn thing he could do to stop it. For his entire life, all he had ever known was violence, death, and this endless campaign of destruction.

Only a handful of governments remained after decades of global war and pestilence, allied for survival and entrenched around the major population centers. Outside the Protected Zones in the Outlands, anarchy reigned. Food and water supplies were poisoned; the dwindling resources had been diverted into accumulating weapons of mass destruction as the world prepared for Armageddon.

"The War to End all Wars," he mocked a recruiting slogan posted on a bullet-riddled billboard overhead. *Seems like we tried that one a while back... didn't turn out so well the first time.* Now everyone close to him was dead... his squadron, his parents, even his dog. *Is this the beginning of the end,* he thought, *or just the end of the beginning?* Trying to understand how it got to this point was useless; staying alive one day at a time was all he could handle. *Thinking about anything else was like mental masturbation... it might feel good, but it wouldn't change the inevitable; in the end, they were all getting fucked.*

It was like that ancient song that kept gnawing at the back of his brain, 'Eve of Destruction', Ryker thought. *The proverbial sword of Damocles is hanging in the balance, waiting for some sniveling zealot hiding behind a cloak of chaos to trigger the final blow. And he would... soon enough. Then it will be fucking déjà vu all over again.* From somewhere deep inside his subconscious, that unwelcome earworm resurfaced, taunting him with its swan song:

"You don't believe in war, but what's that gun you're totin',

And even the Jordan River has bodies floatin'.

If the button is pushed, there's no runnin' away,

There'll be no one to save, with the world in a grave.

But you tell me,

Over and over and over again, my friend.

Ah, you don't believe,

We're on the Eve... of Destruction."

Commander Ryker closed his eyes, shaking his head, trying to reset his OCD brain back to reality by focusing on another thought. "When this war dance is over, I'll be a bartender," Ryker blurted out. "Some withered-up bastard with a demented look in his eye will stagger into my bar, babbling about losing his car keys and missing the Rapture. He'll order a drink, shove a pistol in his mouth, and then splatter his fucking brains out all over the wall. That's how it'll end, all right; last call, for real. Shit, I'll be the only man left on Earth, but at least I'll have a job. One more for the road, bartender!"

Ryker locked his eyes on the red and blue neon sign above the Broken Spur Tavern. It flickered on and off like a bug light on the darkened porch of a shack in the Bayou. Blood-sucking insects were hanging around a bug light waiting for a free meal, and the crackling glow above the Broken Spur attracted its fair share of vermin as well. He scanned the mangy crowd of Neanderthals lingering around; salivating to numb what little was left of their myopic brains. *Not many Mensa candidates here tonight,* he thought. *Too many mullets with chest hair. Well, what the hell... nothing like a couple of cold ones to get your mind off woman troubles or the rapidly approaching end of the world. I guess what they say is true; ignorance is bliss. Poor bastards, they don't have a clue about the shit storm that's brewing.* Slapping the dust off his worn leather coat, he made his way to the heavily armed bouncer at the door.

"Five bucks cover, dude," the bouncer growled. Ryker reached into his pocket and pulled out a worn five-dollar note.

"Any entertainment tonight, or are you it?"

The bouncer just grinned and grabbed the cash from Ryker's hand. "Yeah, there's plenty of entertainment tonight. From the looks of a pretty boy like you, someone's gonna smash your ugly face in. If you can't find 'em inside, come on back out here and I'll take care of it for you."

Walking past the bouncer, Ryker glanced into the dingy pool hall. The room was noisy and reeked of stale cigarettes and rancid beer. Inside the smoke-filled bar, he tried to blend among the pool tables surrounded by tattooed goons who were loudly trying to drink away the day's troubles. Across the room, a honky-tonk trio blasted out some God-awful music behind a chicken-wire curtain. An occasional beer bottle shattered broken shards of glass against the stage, offering the heartfelt appreciation of the crowd for the musical prowess of tonight's entertainment. Ryker grabbed a stool, planted himself at the bar, and knocked down a boilermaker to dull his senses. Without the warmth of his beer jacket, the world seemed a little cold these days.

A buxom, leather-clad blonde sporting low-rise jeans and a budding muffin top stumbled onto the barstool next to him. Talk about packing some junk in the trunk, man this chick was pulling a trailer. On her arm, she sported a tattoo of a rose with a knife through it. *Mom must be so proud*, Ryker thought. She glanced around the room, took a long drag on her clove cigarette and then lurched forward as she knocked over a drink on the bar. Unfazed, she shrugged, craned her head back, and puffed out a smoke ring.

"Yo! Beer tender!" she belted out. "Can't a lady get some service here?" Somewhere in the drunken haze that she called her world, the tattooed blonde suddenly noticed Ryker leaning against the bar next to her. "Hey buddy," she bellowed with a slur. "You a real cowboy?" Ryker thought about the opportunity at hand. On any other night, this might be an interesting diversion, but not tonight.

"Me?" he yelled back, smiling. "No, I'm not a real cowboy." Ryker looked around the bar and then leaned in close to whisper in her ear. "I'm a lesbian trapped in a man's body. But I do like your girls."

The drunken blonde was dumbstruck for a second. Her sexy smile quickly faded to a look of confusion as she tried to comprehend what Ryker had just said. Watching the expression on her face as her brain processed this unexpected information was like watching the little metal ball in a pinball machine bouncing around the rubber flippers until it succumbed to gravity and dropped into the hole at the bottom of the machine. She wrinkled up her face and slammed her fist down on the bar; apparently the pinball in her brain had finally made it to the hole. *Game over.*

"What the fuck . . .?" The inebriated blonde fell back off her bar stool, stumbled for a second and struggled to regain her balance. Her composure still recovering, she crushed out what was left of her cigarette on the bar, just missing the ashtray. Leaning in to Ryker's ear, she sighed with a drunken slur. "Sorry, Brokeback, no ride for you tonight."

Ryker shrugged and turned back toward the bartender on his stool. The double entendre of his clever attempt at humor had missed the mark. *But hey,* he thought, *no harm, no foul. Besides, somebody was probably going to end up riding sidesaddle before the night was over, and that just wasn't his style.*

On a wall of video screens behind the bar, a newscaster droned on, his voice mingling with the low din of the bar crowd. The monotone reporter was perched at the edge of the DMZ, his cheap toupee fluttering in the breeze when something about the news report caught Ryker's attention.

"Long suspected and now confirmed . . . the Axis of Anarchy has just activated a new generation of nuclear weapons and delivery systems for their military satellites. Rumors abound that this stateless network of terrorists has also secretly spread these weapons of mass destruction to their surrogates in the Outlands and around the globe. As the fanatics escalate their threat to wipe the Confederation from the face of the Earth with their new weapons, the prospect of the unthinkable now seems even more real."

The whiskey in Ryker's drink had a foul bouquet, weak legs, and was finished off with a hint of kerosene. Probably made out back in a rusty radiator, but it did its job. No worries, the night was still young, and besides, CHIP hadn't been outside of Ryker's pocket since he was drummed out of the military six months before. To Ryker, CHIP was more than just the artificial intelligence robotic computer co-pilot in his SU-37 fighter; he was his wingman, his confidant, and his friend. They had been stationed in Misawa with the 35th Fighter Wing when they were sent on a routine sortie over southern Asiana. Routine, that was, until someone in Central Command marked him for death. They tossed out the bait and he frickin' swallowed it, hook, line, and sinker. Eleven good men died that day when he led his squadron into a massacre. Some bastard above his pay grade played him like a pawn and then tossed him to the wolves, but why?

The day of his demise had started routinely enough. A spy satellite had spotted terrorist activity along the Outlands border. They were transporting a load of medium-range missiles on a truck convoy through a narrow mountain pass, trying to infiltrate the Asiana DMZ. Ryker's joint strike squadron of SU-37s had scrambled for a routine bombing run. *Nothing too dicey,* he thought, *just a high altitude walk in the park.* They took off at dawn and buzzed supersonic over the mountain pass at 20,000 feet, painted the target, and dumped their payload on the unsuspecting convoy below. As Ryker pulled his bomb release lever, he chatted nonchalantly across the radio to his squadron.

"Ah, it was a peaceful night, Shithead and the Mrs. were out for a leisurely drive, the stars were shining brightly and all was right with the world... until fucking death rained down from above... *boom!*" From the explosions displayed on the video feed of his smart bombs, there wasn't much left of the convoy but a few burning tires and twisted scrap metal. They broke off the attack and headed back to base.

Halfway home, Ryker received an emergency transmission from Central Command; terrorists had just lobbed two Katyusha missiles into Xinjiang, randomly killing dozens of innocent civilians. News feeds were streaming grainy videos of the dazed and wounded staggering in the burning streets, mothers screaming for lost babies, the kind of shit that causes Central Command to go postal. It was like some random drive-by gang shooting; the terrorists generally used the short-range Katyushas to intimidate the local goat herders and keep the Red Guard off balance with an occasional kick in the balls. It was just a pinprick from a military standpoint, but it was an embarrassment nonetheless, and the retaliation warranted had to be swift and lethal.

"It's like gang graffiti," Ryker announced over his radio. "Some dumb fuck marking his turf. You just can't let these things get out of hand, you know. A little missile strike here, a car bombing there, and pretty soon, there goes the whole fucking neighborhood." The rest of the squad chimed in over the radio with the requisite chest thumping.

"Damn straight. Let's get down there and kick some ass, Commander!"

"Shitty timing for them, boys," Ryker pinged back. "They shot up a liquor store right on our ride home. Those stupid bastards never seem to learn that our drones own the night, and those killing machines never sleep."

"And nighttime ain't no time to be fucking around with us," a junior officer with some graffiti experience of his own piped in. "Don't be bringin' that weak shit into the hood!"

The drone's infrared camera had detected the mobile launch from the back of a flatbed truck in a remote valley; it was a hit and run drive-by shooting on the move. *Hit and run?* Ryker thought to himself. *Hell, this was more like shit and run. Those scumbags know we're watching... most of the time they don't even bother aiming the damn thing. Ready, fire, run. That's all the hell they can do.*

Normally, this would have been an easy kill for the drone, but the laser targeting system was down and the bad guys were slithering away to hide out under some civilian's skirt or in a kindergarten playground. Central Command ordered Ryker to *"get down there and take those bastards out before they get away."* Ryker confirmed his new orders with a casual response.

"No problem... give me five minutes and you can scratch one pickup truck with a gun rack." He ordered his squadron to swing around and reset their mission target, as he knew the boys would be itching to raise some hell. That's why they flew with Ryker, after all; they knew his reputation. *Every time you went up with Ryker,* they bragged, *shit was gonna get blown up.* The entire squadron was down for some overtime action, all except for CHIP; he smelled a rat.

"Why would we be ordered to execute a low-altitude attack for such a marginal target?" CHIP questioned. "We have other drones in this quadrant, why risk a manned squadron? The Academy protocol reads, *'never use a hammer to kill a fly,'* and besides, we are low on ordinance and fuel. I recommend that we bug out and let the machines finish this one, sir."

Ryker summarily dismissed CHIP's concern with an infallible argument. "We humans got the one thing you machines will never have... balls," he bragged. "Bug out? What the hell for? This is just some bunch of jerk-offs with a beat-up pickup truck and a couple of bottle rockets. We'll drop in, cap their ass, and be back before breakfast."

CHIP tried to warn Ryker once more. "Commander, with all due respect, we don't have any more smart bombs, so we'll have to go in low with machine gun fire. We'll be vulnerable to ground fire this time, not watching a video from a Lazy Boy at 20,000 feet."

"Shit, Nancy, we'll be in and out of there before they can get a shot off. And since we're quoting Academy protocol tonight, I believe it is quite clear, little buddy. *You advise, I decide.* We're going in... *discussion over."* Ryker shot down CHIP's final warning. Once Ryker was locked and loaded, there was no turning back.

For the rest of his life, Ryker would regret his decision not to listen to the logic of a robotic copilot that wasn't driven by testosterone, but merely the calculated statistical odds of survival. If he had listened to the computer, those kids would be alive today. *Commanding a fighter squadron was like playing Black Jack in Vegas,* he thought. *You stay disciplined, you stay with the program, and you stay alive. You get pumped up and start thinking with your dick, and you get killed. Maybe that's why I always leave Vegas with an empty wallet.*

CHIP was dead right about one thing; something about this situation didn't smell right. Unbeknownst to Ryker, the emergency message from Central Command was actually a spoofed communication by a double agent assassin who had been stalking him for months, just waiting for a chance to settle an old score. He'd run up a few debts along the way, and with the series of unfortunate events unfolding on the ground, one of those debts had just come due.

The assassin was on a deep cover assignment at Cambridge University to locate and kill a suspected mole in a Dark Energy program gone bad. In reality, it was the assassin who was actually the mole, but he had already manufactured evidence to implicate a clueless researcher before volunteering to take out the intelligence leak. It was a perfect setup for revenge and the perfect cover for the assassin. The researcher was a nerdy low-level communications specialist with expertise in the counterintelligence jamming of military satellites. He was working on a secret project at Cambridge. A mere tool to the assassin, once he served his role, he would be acceptable collateral damage to the mission. The assassin abducted the researcher from his room and forced him into a secret lab in the basement, where he made him crack the access codes and spoof the military spy satellite. With an open link in the satellite system, the double agent inserted his fake command to Ryker, and then alerted his terrorist network on the ground that an enemy squadron would be coming in light and low, without any cover.

The terrorists were dug in and waiting with heavy antiaircraft rounds and stinger missiles to ambush Ryker and his squadron. It wasn't much of a fight really; the squad got shot to hell in a matter of seconds like ducks in a shooting gallery. Eleven men paid the price for Ryker's bravado that day, but somehow, he managed to escape. The assassin was so enraged that Ryker eluded his trap that he wigged out; he pistol-whipped the researcher and put a bullet between his eyes. Still steaming with rage, he blew up the lab to cover his tracks, and then radioed for extraction. Moments later, a Harrier jet landed under the cover of darkness and in a matter of seconds, he disappeared like a ghost in the night.

No one at the court martial believed Ryker. He was stripped of his rank and drummed out of the service with a dishonorable discharge. Only his AI co-pilot, CHIP, knew the truth about that fatal day. Ryker's mind was still fuzzy about the exact sequence of details that day. One event, ironically, was crystal clear. After he got shot up, he had somehow managed to limp his broken fighter back to base where he crash-landed it into the officers' lounge. He learned something particularly disappointing about those guys he used to get drunk with… for officers, they didn't have much of a sense of humor.

Before the emergency crews arrived to pull him from the wreckage, Ryker managed to download CHIP to a portable memory cube and stash him into his flight bag. Even as banged up as he was, he knew that somewhere in CHIP's memory logs of that fateful day were the clues that would lead him to the voice that betrayed him, and to his revenge. He had replayed that day a thousand times in his head, muttering to himself, *it may take a lifetime, but they say that revenge…*

Back at the Broken Spur, CHIP had been listening from inside of Ryker's coat pocket in standby mode. The Ugly Betty encounter triggered him into active mode and he quickly booted up his video display. CHIP started mumbling with a mouthful of imaginary pebbles.

"Revenge… they say that revenge, my friend, is a dish best served cold."

Ryker smiled and looked down inside his coat pocket. "Ah, it seems my pocket philosopher has awakened. You never miss a beat, do you little buddy."

CHIP smiled and nodded in appreciation, and then switched his video from the weak thespian wisdom to a simulated sports newscast. Imitating the follically challenged reporter at the DMZ from the bar video, he continued with his own mock broadcast.

"Spread throughout civilian populations, terrorists surround the Protected Zones and wait patiently with their new secret weapons. Soon, the fateful command will come to strike a blow to remove the Confederation from the face of the Earth, once and for all. In a world of increasing shortages of food and energy, governments of the world have sporadically attacked each other to steal and horde resources. They only remain in check from using their nuclear weapons in an all-out Armageddon by the long-standing theory of nuclear mutually assured destruction." CHIP chuckled at his newscast impersonation and then switched gears to close out his mock broadcast. "And that's the news, one nation, under Oprah, with liberty and injustice for all."

"Yeah, the frickin' world's gone mad, you little drama queen," Ryker retorted as he closed his eyes. "Guess we all got our problems to deal with... why don't you just *chill* for a while."

"Sorry to harsh your mellow, dude," CHIP apologized with the hip slang of a California surfer.

"More drinking, less thinking," muttered Ryker. He waved his hand and signaled for another round. "Bartender! Beer me!" As he rubbed his forehead, Ryker felt a throbbing pain behind his eyes; the drinks had finally dulled the jagged edge of his bad attitude. Maybe snaking a few bucks off these beer room Barneys would help him shake this foul mood. He picked out a couple of losers playing pool, walked over, and slammed a twenty down on the table. "I got game."

Ryker grabbed a pool cue from the rack and fumbled around in his coat pocket for his little buddy. He pulled out the AI memory cube, set him on the edge of the pool table, leaned back and lit up a cigarette. Happy to be back in the saddle, CHIP booted up all his memory circuits. He scanned the bar room for behavioral clues and selected a vintage Clint Eastwood video clip from Dirty Harry for his interface du jour. Just then, a large, tattooed biker in a soiled wife-beater T-shirt turned and stepped toward Ryker.

"Hey, I know you," the biker growled in a low, raspy voice. "You're that yellow belly fighter pilot I saw on the news that lost his whole squadron. You led your men into a trap and then bailed out on them to save your own hide!" Now that CHIP had scanned his entire video reference file, he was confident that he had acquired the proper persona for the current assignment, Ryker's wingman, of course. Maybe a bit of the good cop, bad cop. He would be the bad cop this time.

"Hey punk!" CHIP blurted out in a raspy Dirty Harry accent. "We just came in here lookin' for a friendly game, but if you and your dirt bag friend are cruisin' for a bruisin', well, we might just be able to accommodate you! The question is... are you feeling lucky tonight." Ryker looked over to CHIP and cursed at him under his breath.

"Smooth . . . very smooth." He turned back to the biker goon and tried to diffuse the situation. "Hey, look... no harm buddy. My little friend just has a bit of a... chip on his shoulder. How about we rack 'em up for twenty?" By this time, the increasingly angry biker had been joined by an equally large buddy; pumped with just the right cocktail of alcohol and testosterone. They closed in and surrounded Ryker.

"Did you just call me dirt, chicken boy?" the first biker growled.

"Actually, my little buddy on the table over there called you a *dirt bag*," Ryker responded calmly. "He's not much on manners, but he's always proven to be an astute judge of character." The large, smelly biker dudes weren't well armed for a war of words, so they closed in on Ryker to deliver some roadhouse justice. Sensing an abrupt end to the stimulating discussion, Ryker grabbed two wooden pool cues from the table just as the bikers cranked up to pummel him.

"Tsing Tao!" Ryker screamed. With the Zen-like precision of a Taijutsu master, Ryker spun around and twirled the pool cues above his head. The first biker lunged at him; he sidestepped and delivered a swift knee to the groin, dropping the biker to his knees with a painful groan, and following up with a swift strike to the temple with a pool cue. Ryker leaped over the body of the fallen biker and cracked his pool cue across the second stunned biker's forehead. He had years of Academy training in hand-to-hand combat... the biker's martial arts training, not so much. Blood gushed out the nose of the second assailant and splattered down his T-shirt as he collapsed face down on the pool table. On his way down, he flailed his arms and spilled a beer on CHIP's video screen.

"I guess we showed those punks how to rock and roll," CHIP gloated on his screen as he blew the smoke off his 44-caliber magnum pistol. During the fight, a crowd had gathered and several of the patrons looked as though they were about to pounce on Ryker and finish the fight for their buddies. Ryker strutted in a circle around the bodies of the lifeless bikers, twirling the pool cues over his head before slamming them down on the table.

"Any more takers?" Ryker queried. "No? Well then, I guess the show's over. But hey, we're just here to have a good time... drinks are on my little friend here!" When offered the choice of a free beer or a thrashing with a pool cue across the face, the crowd chose discretion over valor. The beer flowed and the noise level in the bar quickly returned to a low roar.

In the brief bar fight, Ryker had initially failed to notice that the two suspicious men he had observed sitting in a darkened van from the parking lot had now found their way to barstools near the pool tables. Although the two men were minding their own business, something about them was off. They didn't seem to fit in with the regular crowd of losers at the Broken Spur tonight. Ryker squinted his eyes to get a better look at the two men across the smoky room. Upon closer review, the man closest to Ryker was dressed in blue-collar work clothes and Wolverines, a beat-up leather bomber jacket, and appeared to have... no neck. He was short, stocky, and had the eyes of a professional fighter; cold, blank, and focused. Judging by the multiple scars on his rugged face, this Unibrow had seen his share of bar fights. The other man was taller, better dressed, and was wearing shiny black shoes. Florsheim Wing Tips, maybe. In basic training, Ryker's drill sergeant had told him that you could learn a lot about a man by looking at his shoes. These shoes said, *"We do things my way, or Rocko here breaks your face."*

With the Taijutsu lesson over, the two mystery men put down their drinks, exchanged glances, and pushed away from the bar in opposite directions. The tall man locked eyes with Ryker, approached slowly, and then glanced down at a photo on a small electronic wristband. He scanned Ryker's face and compared it to the photo on his device. Ryker instantly realized that this mystery man was not a drunken biker, but someone much more dangerous than any of the other losers in the Broken Spur tonight... he'd seen his type before.

"I'm gettin' a bad feeling here, little buddy," Ryker whispered to CHIP. "Watch my back, will you?" Stepping away from the approaching man, Ryker slowly reached inside his coat and placed his hand on the 9-millimeter he had concealed in a shoulder holster.

"Hey, friend, I got no beef with you. Just a little disagreement over whose turn it was to buy the next round of drinks." He laughed. Without warning, the Unibrow seized Ryker from behind and delivered an electrical shock to the back of his neck with a stun gun. The pain felt like an ice pick had been stabbed into the top of his spine, and the numbness quickly spread over his body. Ryker was immobilized; he couldn't feel his arms or legs. His body was frozen, but his mind was alert. He felt himself falling, as if in slow motion, but there was nothing he could do to stop it. His brain screamed out, but his body wouldn't respond.

As Ryker's face was rapidly approaching the floor, he thought to himself, *what was it that my Todai Dojo master drilled into me day after day in martial arts training? Embrace the ground; it can't hurt you. Only one problem... this ain't gonna be an embrace with the ground, this is gonna be a fucking train wreck with my face as the lead car. And with all due respect, Master Li, this is gonna hurt like a son of a bitch. And what the hell is that burning smell? Toast?*

Ryker began to lose consciousness and his 9-millimeter slipped from his hand. He fell back against the pool table, bounced off, and collapsed to the floor. The force of his fall knocked CHIP off the edge of the pool table and he rolled around like a pair of tumbling dice on the floor, finally coming to a rest between Ryker's body and his gun. Meanwhile, the fight had drawn the attention of the bouncer, who shoved his way through the crowd to the pool tables. He waddled over, his beer belly swaying back and forth, clutching a collapsible baton in his right hand.

"Hey! We got a problem here?" the bouncer shouted sarcastically, slapping the nightstick in the palm of his sweaty hand. The tall man with the shiny shoes turned and smiled at the bouncer.

"No problem, mate. Our friend here just had one too many Pink Ladies, you know what I mean?" The bouncer surveyed the beer spilled on the pool table, the broken pool cues, and the bloody unconscious bikers sprawled out on the floor. He stepped over Ryker's body and growled back at the tall man.

"What about those other two?" he demanded, pointing his baton toward the lifeless bikers on the floor.

"Well now, they would be the Pink Ladies, wouldn't they?" the tall man responded with a grin. He leaned in close to the bouncer and whispered, "Sorry to be a bother, mate, but we need to collect our pilot friend here and be on our way. He's got to get back to the friendly skies; you know what I mean? We wouldn't want to keep the passengers waiting, now would we?" The bouncer stood there for a moment, confused, and then resumed his menacing demeanor.

"You and your friend get the hell out of here," he growled, and pointed his baton to the door. He shrugged and turned around, waddling back through the crowd.

The tall man with the shiny shoes nodded, tapped the photo image on his wristband, and then motioned to the Unibrow to pick up Ryker and carry his body outside to their van. As the Unibrow leaned down to grab Ryker, he noticed the money still lying on the pool table from the game. He glanced back to the tall man for direction, looked around, shrugged, then picked up the money and shoved it into his pocket. With Ryker's body thrown over his shoulder, the Unibrow turned to leave, but inadvertently kicked CHIP and the 9-millimeter handgun on the floor, sending them spinning across the bar room and into the path of the tall man's shiny black shoes. The Unibrow froze in his tracks. He turned to his partner, looking to him for guidance. The tall man flipped the cover of his wristband device shut, looked down at his shoes and gave an emotionless command.

"Leave the gun, take the robot."

3. Blue Horizon Fish Company

On a darkened street in the rundown waterfront district of the Protected Zone, two Confederation agents slumped down in the front seat of their parked car. This forgotten part of the city was like an open sore on society, a sore that caused you to wince and look away. Most of the dilapidated buildings were abandoned; their only inhabitants were drug dealers and prostitutes. During the day, heavily armed Confederation forces patrolled these streets, peering out from their armored vehicles to manage a thin façade of order here, mainly to keep the black market commerce flowing with its requisite payoffs and bribes for some well-placed bureaucrats. But at night, this section of town crossed over the fringe into anarchy. If you were alone here, the only protection you had was what you were packing under your coat; you were on your own until the sun rose again.

The Confederation agents in the darkened car were on a stakeout. There had been another assassination of a mid-level administrator in a meaningless border town. *What was the big fucking deal, anyway?* They thought. *Some beady-eyed pencil dick gets whacked and we have to roll out of our warm beds to dispense some biblical form of nocturnal justice? Hell, at least some other weasel in that bum fuck of a border town just got a promotion.* But the problem wasn't that a faceless bureaucrat got smoked; that was just another form to file, in triplicate. The problem was that it was another unauthorized hit, way down on the list, out of order. The execution business was simple, you got a list and you crossed off the names. You don't paint outside the lines; you don't deviate from the order of the list. Some shithead was out taking their job too seriously, not respecting the order of the list, and they had become a liability. *Congratulations, dumb fuck. You just made the top of the hit parade.*

Their target had been reported to be en route to an apartment loft above a rundown warehouse called the Blue Horizon Fish Company. They knew this because minutes earlier, they had received a tip from an undercover rat that the target was returning to this safe house after the hit in the Outlands. With a bit of cheese, there was always a rodent burrowed somewhere deep in the cesspools of bureaucracy that would sell his soul for a quick meal. One of the agents in the darkened car checked the alley and then sneaked onto the loading platform of the Blue Horizon Fish Company. He made his way up the fire escape, and once inside, planted a bomb in the target's apartment. The bomb was attached to a well-hidden transmitter, silently awaiting detonation. The detonation of the bomb was officially intended to remind the anarchists what the swift hand of justice felt like. *But shit,* the agent thought, *There won't be enough left of the target to identify the body.*

The plan was simple. When the target entered the side door of the apartment building, the agent would transmit a signal from his communicator to activate the detonator on the holographic phone. The agent knew that the target's phone was secure because only the handler had the secure number; at least that was what the rat squealed. *If I've calculated the charges correctly, there'll be acceptable collateral damage to complete the mission and then I can get the fuck out of here and back to my warm bed.* The bomb was rigged to explode when the target pressed the transmission icon to answer a secure call from the handler... but in fact, it would be his call. It seemed fitting to them that the target's last hello would also be goodbye. *So long,* the agent thought, *it's time for you to pay for your sins.* Down the street in the darkened car, the agent in the passenger seat waiting to trigger the explosion checked his communicator and reviewed the dossier of the target.

Target Name:

Alexis Rasputin Alexander, aka "Lexis." Deep cover assassin with multiple confirmed kills. Target is highly intelligent, elusive and lethal. May work with accomplice, but this is unconfirmed. Two previous contract enforcement mechanics listed MIA. Terminate on sight with extreme prejudice.

Psychological Assessment:

Subject is quick to anger, unstable... possibly suffering from deep psychological trauma. No known family or social contacts, off the reservation. Approach with extreme caution... consider armed and extremely dangerous.

At the side entrance of the apartment building, the target swiped her biometric key to enter the safe house. She glanced over her shoulder, up and down the half-lit street; a threat assessment flashed through her eyes and into her mind. *Wino, passed out in the alley behind the dumpster... partially hidden dog rummaging through trash in the gutter. Abandoned car parked half a block away. Nothing out of the ordinary, proceed with caution.* The dog slowly approached her, growling, and bore its teeth. The animal was enormous, at least 120 kilos and looked to be more wolf than dog. It opened its gaping jaws and lunged forward but stopped its attack just short of the young girl and then dropped down to her side.

Koda! Itam ko'oltsiwita? (Koda! Are we safe?) The girl snapped. *Um kyaataynuma nuy*! (You surprised me!)

Surprise, the wolf-dog thought, *is an unwelcome stranger on our passage, a passage that as you well know, is intertwined. We have been chosen to walk this life path together until the blue light of truth is revealed, and yet, you digress. Deviation from our path invites unwanted attention... attention that is... ill advised.*

You're right, Lexis apologized. *You are my tuuhikya kwewu paava* (shaman wolf-brother), *but this was personal, an opportunity to set my past in balance, and I took it. Call it my last pizza delivery... now that debt has been settled. Besides, I wasn't gone that long, was I?*

The wolf-dog locked eyes with her for a moment of mutual understanding and then relaxed his bared teeth, nuzzling next to her side. *Long enough for me to miss dinner waiting for you,* he thought, *and yes... the perimeter is secure.*

Lexis reached into her pocket and tossed the fierce beast a piece of beef jerky, which he promptly devoured in a single gulp. She scratched the animal under his chin, disregarding the drool dripping from his mouth as it oozed down her sleeve. *That's all I have tonight.* The enormous wolf-dog licked her hand, gave an appreciative growl and then trotted off down the street. Nothing else seemed out of order, so she stepped inside.

Halfway up the stairs to her second-floor loft apartment, Lexis noticed a thin ray of light shining out from under the access door. There was a shadow lurking in the hallway, crouched down in the vestibule by her door. She adjusted her vision and could see that the shadow was holding a weapon close to his chest, lying in wait for her arrival. She paused for a moment, slid her hand into her boot, and removed her weapon of choice: a seven-inch Special Forces knife with a Zytel handle. As she clutched the cold steel blade in her hand, she repeated her mantra in her mind.

Stay silent, stay deadly, and stay alive. There's no need to arouse suspicion from the neighbors or police, she thought. *If someone needs to be disposed of tonight, it will be done quietly. Besides, in this part of town, nobody gives a flying fuck about their neighbors, and they sure as shit don't want any more Confederation pricks poking around. Enough already!* She told herself. *I just want to get home and throw off these uncomfortable boots!*

Lexis sprang through the door into the hallway and grabbed the surprised shadow from behind his head. A swift karate chop to the back of the neck and she pinned the shadow to the ground, slamming her knee into his kidney. The shadow winced in pain, his arms and legs flailing about on the floor like a rag doll.

What a pussy! She thought. *Who's training these amateur bastards, anyway?*

She grabbed a mound of the shadow's hair, jerked his head back and pressed the razor-sharp blade to his throat. The shadow's pathetic struggling weakened and she leaned in to the back of his ear just before she ended him.

"Honey, I'm home," she whispered. One of the broken florescent lights in the hallway flickered on and off for a second, but it was long enough to illuminate the face of the innocent boy beneath her grasp. The bouquet of roses that he was apparently bringing for her birthday surprise lay crushed beneath her boots, which were still pinning his chest to the floor. In one motion, Lexis spun around the boy, tucked the knife back in her boot and loosened her grip on his hair, sliding her hand down around his throat.

"What the hell are you doing here? I could have killed you!" she screamed. The innocent boy looked up at her with his terrified eyes wide open.

"I know you said… that you don't like surprises, but I thought, well maybe, you know, on your birthday and all… jeez! How did you do that, anyway? You were just like Zena, the Warrior Princess!" The young man who would like to be her boyfriend had no idea that his instant character assessment was not that far from the truth. The object of his teenage fantasy was not the traveling security consultant he had become infatuated with, but was actually a trained Confederation assassin. Her travels took her to exotic destinations, but occasionally she had stopped by the boy's small electronic gadget store down the street to buy expensive surveillance equipment.

He always thought she bought the best stuff and really knew her shit. She even had electronics that he couldn't get on the black market. Could an international globetrotting super fox like her ever fall for a nerd like him? *Well, even a blind squirrel finds an acorn in the snow some days, besides, nerds can dream, and if you must dream, dream big.* He had only managed small talk with her in the past, but one day, she let it slip that today was her birthday.

"No one even knows or cares," she had sighed. The boy had taken this brief departure from her normal attitude as a gift; it was the ray of hope he had been waiting for to validate her interest in him. *It was like being granted an extra life or special powers,* he thought. As usual, he was thinking about the alternate reality game that consumed his nights, World of War Crack. He was now a night elf with a new purpose... to win her heart. His mind drifted away to indulge his fantasy.

"To achieve great things, you must take great risks," he muttered to himself in the mirror to gain his courage. "I think Spiderman's adoptive mother said that," he continued to himself. Spiderman's stepmom was right. Chicks dig men of romantic action, not nerdy store clerks, and he was now a night elf nerd of action. As a semi-professional computer nerd and full-time techno geek, he had managed to hack into one of her credit card transactions and trace it to a rundown building on the seedy waterfront. The funding party for her equipment was listed as the Blue Horizon Fish Company, so he unleashed a web spider to crawl over all the financial activities that he could dig out and see what it could find. He had a friend down at the Ministry of Finance that gave him a backdoor into a Confederation-tracking database, but even with that inside view, it was a dead-end.

The data trail was well scrubbed, so he decided that some covert, on the ground operations would be needed. He had seen how to extract the 'word on the street' from hustlers on an old detective show, so he would have to go undercover. He had assumed the persona of Snuggy Bear, a young hip street pimp, and hung out around in the alley behind the Blue Horizon Fish Company until he was able to bribe a wino with a bottle of rubbing alcohol to pinpoint her apartment.

"I am Superfly," he had boasted to himself. In one desperate attempt to fulfill his fantasy, he had thrown himself, literally at her feet, in the hope that she might give him a chance at romance. He had even brought a bouquet of roses for the occasion. Lexis removed her boot from his kidney, dusted off his jacket and helped young Superfly to his feet.

"Ok, let's get inside," she whispered. "No need for the neighbors to see us dancing the horizontal mambo out here in the hall." Once inside, her would-be boyfriend regained his composure and began the official nerd courtship ritual in a manner that he had practiced in his mind all week.

"I brought some wine, would you like a glass to celebrate your birthday? Now that you're twenty-one, hey, you're legal! You *are* twenty-one, aren't you?" Lexis laughed to herself. Everyone always thought that she was older than she actually was, maybe because she had to grow up so fast, or maybe because she had to project an older image just to survive. No she wasn't twenty-one, she wasn't even eighteen.

And legal? Not even close. She was just fucking jailbait with a blade, but he was sweet to ask, she thought. Lexis leaned over, and stroked her hand against his cheek; he almost fainted at her touch. *What a frickin' geek!* She thought. *But I've never had a boyfriend, so what the hell! I should be safe with an innocent nerd like him... at least for tonight.*

"Ok, Romeo, let me at least get out of my work clothes." Lexis headed down the hall to her bedroom and shut the door. As she removed her weapons, dropped her clothes, and looked in the mirror, she suddenly flashed back to her parents' death.

It was ten years before and she was seven years old. Enemy agents had burst into their apartment in the dead of night, shined flashlights on their faces and a clipboard of pictures. With each face that matched, they had calmly raised their weapons and executed them all; first, her mother, her father, and then her older brother right in front of her. She collapsed to the floor, screaming, waiting for her bullet to come. She stared at her family through her tears, piled on top each other and lying there in a red pool of their own blood. For some unknown reason, her bullet didn't come. The murderers came back to Lexis and doubled checked their images, but whether it was a screw up or some twisted hand of fate, her photo wasn't on the clipboard that night. The killers turned to each other and started a casual conversation, as if they had been shopping for groceries at the local market rather than murdering an entire family.

"I guess we're done here. Man, I'm hungry... wanna get some pizza?"

"Ok, but no anchovies this time. Those little fuckers give me gas." The killers left her alone, bewildered and crying, holding her dead mother, father, and brother. One moment, she was part of a happy family and the next; she was an orphan. Now her only family was a telepathic wolf-dog assassin with a guardian complex. *At least it's better than being alone in this fucked up world,* Lexis thought.

In the other room of her apartment, the geeky boy had regained his confidence and started to roam around the apartment, looking at pictures, and snooping through her mail on the counter. He plopped down on the sofa and discovered a video controller wedged between the sofa cushions, dug it out, and hit the power button. A hologram sprang up on the wall and a local news channel began bleating away in a monotone.

"Terrorist groups in the Outlands have threatened to launch a nuclear strike on Confederation forces, but it may not come as expected. Government sources have long warned that the evil Axis of Anarchy would attempt to use its newly deployed long-range warheads to attempt a pre-emptive strike on civilian centers near the Protected Zones. Recent surveillance videos have confirmed that the terrorists and their surrogates now possess advanced ground-based, multi-warhead, intercontinental ballistic missiles with sufficient range to reach all of Europa as well as most of Asiana. Anti-missile batteries have been deployed along the border to repel just such an attack."

There was an explosion in the background, sirens wailed, and then the newscaster continued. "But even more troubling, this recent video posting on a terrorist website boasts...

A masked man, dressed in camouflage fatigues, holding an AK-47 above his head stared into a shaky video camera and spouted in broken English. "Resistance is futile, as the divine one has laid out the plans for your destruction. The destroyer will not come with the blast of golden trumpets, but as a thief in the night. Be afraid, for your rivers will run red with blood... we will slip into your bedrooms and slit your throats as you sleep."

Suddenly, a ringing icon blinking on the screen interrupted the holographic newscast. From the bedroom, Lexis heard the videophone ring. It rang once, then twice. She yelled out to her new friend.

"Are you in there fucking around with my equipment? Leave that shit alone, will you?" Lexis thought for a second about who would be calling her this late. My God, couldn't they leave her alone for one night! For once, she would like to stay in and just relax... and maybe more, since it was her birthday. *Fuck 'em. I'm not even home,* she said to herself. Lexis looked back in the mirror at the sexy lingerie she had tried on from the closet and smiled.

"I can be sexy, every once in a while…"

Below her window, a barking dog suddenly interrupted her thoughts of romance. She tried to ignore it, but the growling was incessant. It was dark outside and the vermin would be prowling the streets… not the time of night to attract attention. Lexis threw open the window to subdue the noise.

Koda! Sunyuku. (Koda! Quiet.) *You said the perimeter was secure,* she thought. *What is it now?*

It appears that some of your extracurricular chickens have come home to roost, Koda thought. *There are two Confederation agents slumped down in a parked car two blocks away.*

I'm a little busy right now, Lexis thought. *Just keep an eye on them, ok? Let me know if they leave their vehicle.*

The huge wolf-dog snarled, barked sharply three more times, and then trotted off into the darkness. Lexis was about to shut the window when the phone rang for a third time, and she yelled down the hall. "Don't answer that, just let the machine get it!"

Unfortunately, with the newscast droning on, the geeky young man didn't hear her instructions. His mind was preoccupied with the… possibilities. *Being with a girl, in real life, and not one you have to pay for either,* he thought. The momentary dream of her coming out of her bedroom in some slinky, low-cut outfit… it made him absolutely giddy. *How can I be so lucky?* The geeky nerd fell backwards onto the sofa, sighed, and pressed the icon on the hologram to answer the incoming call.

The ensuing blast rocked the entire building, blowing out the wall of the second-story apartment below to the street. Flaming debris and body parts rained down on to the sidewalk, awakening the wino sleeping in the alley and startling the stray dog that had tried to alert her to danger. Lexis was thrown back against the wall, her head striking the door jam and she was knocked unconscious. Half a block away, the darkened car that had been watching silently pulled away, driving slowly past the burning wreckage. In the passenger side of the car, one of the men switched on his flashlight and clicked the name beside Lexis' photo on his communicator. As he clicked *'mission accomplished',* the car carrying the two men screeched its tires and raced away into the night.

The raging fire from the blast quickly engulfed several buildings adjacent to the Blue Horizon Fish Company, setting off an alarm. Before any emergency vehicles could arrive at the scene, a darkened nondescript van screeched to a halt in front of the apartment building. Two men rushed upstairs, dug through the debris, and located Lexis unconscious under a shattered wooden beam in what was left of her bedroom. Still groggy from the blast, she looked up into a flashlight as one of the men was comparing a list and her photograph on his wristband with her face.

"Ok, it's her," the man stated without emotion as he bent down to help her to her feet. "Looks like your birthday party got a little out of hand, Miss. Sorry for the intrusion, but you will have to come with us." The two mysterious men helped Lexis stumble down the stairs to their waiting van. As they carried her out of the smoking rubble, they were suddenly met head on by the enormous snarling wolf-dog; it seemed to be standing guard between the van and the sidewalk. The beast growled deeply, its head tucked down to strike, baring its teeth as if it was prepared to lunge at their throats. The tall man with shiny black shoes froze in his tracks and slowly reached into his pocket for a gun. The second man, looked at him disapprovingly.

"There's no need to resort to violence, mate. Dogs respond to calm, assertive behavior. I've been watching this guy on the network, he's a, you know, Dog Whisperer." The man with the shiny shoes took a step back as the shorter man moved in front of him to approach the vicious dog slowly.

"Here we are, boy," the short man said, speaking softly. "No need for trouble. Nobody's going to hurt you. Just think of me as your pack leader." Before the words had left his lips, the fierce dog lunged, his jaws spread wide for a deathblow to his carotid artery. The muscular man sidestepped the attack and delivered an incapacitating shock from his stun gun to the dog's neck as it lunged past him and crashed to the sidewalk, immobilized. The man with the shiny shoes seemed relieved and put his gun back in his holster.

"Dog Whisperer my ass, hope you didn't buy the DVD. Now what are you going to do with that mangy killer?"

"I'm keeping him. I think we shared a moment there, almost a telepathic conversation... right before he tried to kill me. Little help here?" The two men struggled to pick up the enormous dog's lifeless body from the sidewalk, and on the count of three, they pitched it into the back of the van, landing with a thud.

"You know, having a pet is a real responsibility, not to be taken lightly," the man with the shiny shoes noted.

"True enough," Rocko agreed. "But I need a bit of stability in my life these days."

"All right then... What are you going to name the beast?"

"There was this girl back in school, frumpy clothes and glasses. Whenever she ate, food fell out of her mouth in all directions. She had legs just like him... big, bony, and hairy." The man with the shiny shoes just looked at him, confused.

"I'm naming him Brenda," Rocko announced.

"You can't name a bloody beast like that Brenda! You're not his mommy... besides, Brenda's a poof name for a dog!"

"Now don't be calling my Brenda a poof... he might just go off and rip your throat out." The man with the shiny shoes stared at the lifeless body of the dog for a second.

"Sometimes, mate, I just don't know about you."

"Go on, now," Rocko complained. "I never had a pet, really. Me mum would never let me have an animal, except for a slimy little painted turtle from the pet shop. Me dad flushed it down the loo one night when he was pissed out of his mind. No one's flushing Brenda down the loo."

"Sorry, mate, a bit insensitive of me," Shiny Shoes conceded. "Parents can be cruel sometimes." Back on the sidewalk, the agents returned to help Lexis to her feet. She shook her head and finally started to regain her senses. Suddenly, she realized that the innocent young man, who wanted nothing more than to be her boyfriend for one night, was missing.

"The blast... oh my God!" she shrieked. "Wait, we've got to go back and find my friend!" The muscular man holding her arm smiled sympathetically for a moment, then put his boot on her back and shoved Lexis into the back of the van.

"Sorry, miss, he's not on the list."

4. MIT

Everyone had their problems growing up, but when you are a musical prodigy at ten and graduate from MIT with a Ph.D. in molecular computing at sixteen, life among the *'mental midgets'* of society could be annoying. Dr. Josiah Mercury Stone was an adult genius trapped in a nerdy teenage body. Despite his certified intelligence, the odds of Dr. Stone hooking up with a real, breathing female of legal age were lower than being killed by a terrorist. Real life was a drag, so the simulated life of his remote neural network of prepubescent, postdoctoral students provided an acceptable substitute. *Working on the development of artificial intelligence in social molecular computers is a better place to score than IRL, he thought to himself, laughing.*

Life in the academic world was fairly mundane until a shadowy Dark Energy agent contacted Josiah's pimply-faced team of uber-nerds to build a swarm of lethal robotic insects with a twist on his expertise; this colony of killers would command a shared neural network. In other words, bugs that could think on their own, assimilate a collective intelligence, and if instructed to, kill.

In the basement of a nondescript building on campus at MIT, Josiah's small research lab looked like a cross between the morning after a frat party and an overfunded advanced physics playground. Pizza boxes were strewn all over the floor and half-empty energy drinks littered the desktops. The back of the laboratory door was covered with a pictorial tribute to Freddy Mercury, just beneath a broken miniature basketball hoop. A dirty pair of women's panties, extra-large, were mounted on top of the hoop along with a small memorial plaque like some big game hunter's trophy, distracting any would-be shooters, making three pointers much more difficult.

"Take the rock to the hole..." Josiah screamed as he charged down the lane, bounced off a trampoline and slammed home a twirling 360-degree dunk. "Not in my fucking house, home boy!" Josiah fell back into his swivel chair, jacked his legs against a cabinet and launched himself across the room. His imaginary hard court domination was suddenly interrupted by the activity on the wall of video monitors displaying his deeply engrossed research slaves and their lack of apparent progress.

"When the hell are you going to have the neural net working?" he barked into his headset. "I've got half the swarm collecting honey and the other half eating it. And the scanner drones are humping each other instead of the queen!"

From one of the video screens across the room, an answer came back haltingly.

"The drones aren't quite there yet, Professor. Maybe a day more in model simulation before we can download the neural templates."

Dr. Josiah Stone was not amused by the answer.

"Shit, man, we've got a schedule! You keep tripping out on me, I lose my funding, and you whack-jobs lose your happy ending at the Oriental massage parlor!" Josiah noticed that one of his researchers was also logged onto a human simulated dating program where the socially challenged nerds tried to learn how to successfully pick up and score with girls in real life. "Not on my time, you little prick." He muttered. With a few angry keystrokes, Josiah terminated the social network connection and pulled up a direct link to the geeky lounge lizard researcher. With his face close to the video screen, he whispered, "If you don't get those neural templates done by tomorrow, you fuckwit, I'm going to lop off your stinger in real life. Now get focused, you asshole!"

In a telecommunications closet just outside the laboratory, two Confederation agents had been monitoring the network traffic from Dr. Stone's secure webinar. They exchanged glances and one of the agents moved swiftly to the other side of the Freddy Mercury tribute door as some nerd on the network massacred an out-of-tune version of 'We Are the Champions'.

Outside the laboratory door, a man with shiny black shoes mounted a suction cup microphone to the door and listened for activity inside the lab. Satisfied with the lack of sound on the other side of the door, he wrapped a plastic substance around the door lock. The man with the shiny black shoes stepped back, glanced down the hall to his partner, and clicked a blinking red button on his wristband. The plastic substance silently ignited with a whiff of smoke and quickly burned through the metal door lock. The man with the shiny black shoes nudged the door slightly open and peered around the door with a small pencil-point video camera. Back on the video wall inside the lab, an unexpected window popped up on Dr. Stone's command screen, accompanied by a message.

"Is this Dr. Stone? IRL?"

Josiah lurched forward in his chair to answer the intruder. "Get the fuck off this network, LUSER, this is a private VPN. *Vamanos* or I'll crawl up your little Crackberry and fry your ass!" He signed his flaming text response, '1BAMF'.

Undaunted, the intruder messaged back. "OMG - Dr. Stone, chill! I'm in your undergrad class on artificial insemination, LOL; I mean artificial intelligence. Plz! I'm getting hosed in your class! Maybe you remember me, 2nd period; I'm the Britney in the 3rd row? I'll be your BFF."

Dr. Stone didn't have a clue that a mystery intruder was on his VPN. A flirtatious female encounter in real life was quite rare, so he quickly changed gears and tried to prolong the chat, hoping to land the little freshman fish that had circled the bait.

Circle the bait? he thought. *Hell I don't even have a pole in the water. Steady, Freddy, is this chicklet really coming on to me or is this just some sick serial sexter?* He leaned forward to the screen and slipped on his imaginary lounge lizard smoking jacket before typing back.

"Oh, LOL, I remember you QT – Would you like some *private* tutoring? We can kick it on my sofa, Wednesday evening?"

"WTF! Dr. Stone!" the flirtatious intruder messaged back. "What are you suggesting? KMA, you perv!" The text box terminated and the intruder window disappeared from his screen like a puff of smoke.

Dr. Josiah Stone sighed and leaned back in his swivel chair. *Arrgh! Shot down in flames again. Maybe I should rerun this on the cuddle couch in the human simulator chat room.* With the momentary sexual distraction over, Dr. Stone shook his head about the little fish that got away and refocused his mind on the project at hand. As he turned back to his screen, he noticed a shadowy reflection on his computer monitor; there was a figure standing just behind him!

"What the hell?" he screamed.

The last thing Josiah remembered was a sharp stinging sensation on the back of his neck just before everything went black. The man with the shiny black shoes standing over Josiah's body glanced down at his wristband and clicked on the name '*Professor Stone*'. Shiny Shoes opened the door for the second man from the wiring closet down the hall and signaled for him to come in. As the muscular man entered and picked up Dr. Stone's body to carry him to their awaiting van, he paused for a moment in front of the video monitors to read the researcher chat log. With an impish smile on his face, he leaned forward and typed in a message broadcast to the rest of the neural nerd herd.

"Now all of u STFU and get back 2 work or I'll bust a cap in UR ass!" The man with the shiny black shoes glanced up at the chat screen, and then over to the muscular figure at the keyboard.

"You going all gangsta on me... 'bro?" he asked without emotion. The muscular man at the keyboard smiled, folded his arms, and turned around as he carried Dr. Stone out the door over his shoulder.

"Just keeping it real, homie."

5. Time Travel

For centuries, scientists have dreamed about time travel. *"But is it really possible?"* they asked. Eighty years after Einstein theorized the potential, scientists who studied passengers on the space shuttle proved that it was; because of the shuttle's high speed, time actually moved more *slowly* for those on board.

Deep in the basement of Cambridge University, just *how* to accomplish the feat of time travel was another matter; it was the source of a regular argument between Dr. Samantha Jones, chair of the Bioengineering Department, and Dr. Ashoka Maurya, head of the Advanced Physics Consortium, a privately funded military research project. Late one night over coffee in Dr. Maurya's laboratory, their regular debate over the specifics of how to achieve time travel continued.

"Ok, ok. We have been over the calculations a thousand times," Dr. Maurya opined. "The white holes align and form a wormhole. You jump in and accelerate at the speed of light. For God's sake, you are so close that you can see the light signals from the parallel dimension on the other side!"

Dr. Jones stood up and threw her arms up in disagreement. "And it's all good until the wormhole collapses and then, *bam!"* She slammed her hand down on the table. "You are crushed to death in a singularity! Squashed like a bug. It's a great theory, Ashoka, right up to the point where you get smashed into oblivion. Even *'Schwarzschild's Bubble'* can't save you."

"Ok, you have a point," Dr. Maurya admitted. "The whole squashing and crushing into oblivion part is bad. But that's the key to my proof that everyone else has missed!" Dr. Maurya approached a whiteboard full of complicated equations and graphs, scratched his chin, and stared up at the calculations. "We just need to concentrate a force, a huge force, strong enough to create a pinpoint negative mass at the throat of the wormhole. That will hold the wormhole open just for a nanosecond and we can jump through."

"Clever, but not practical. Where would you ever get the kind of power that you need?" Dr. Jones questioned. "It would have to be on the scale of... " She furrowed her brow and started rapidly punching numbers into her computer. After a moment, she cocked her head and joined Dr. Maurya at the board. As she started furiously writing equations, a smile slowly came across her face; she had solved the equation for power. Dr. Jones stepped back and turned to share her findings with Dr. Maurya. "Well, there's good news and bad news," she announced. "The good news is that meeting your massive power need is *theoretically* possible. The bad news is that you would need more energy than we currently have to power this entire planet."

Dr. Maurya looked a bit puzzled. "Well then, let us focus on the good news, Samantha. Let me recheck your calculations."

It was late in the evening, so they started packing up their briefcases as they continued their discussion. They had been on the brink of solving this time travel enigma many times, only to have it come crashing back down upon them. The essence of the problem had been around for thirteen billion years, so a complete evaluation of the proof could wait until tomorrow. Thursday was a faculty workday, so once a week they rode together in a car pool to save petrol. With the war going on and Confederation-enforced rationing, the price of Confederation petrol had skyrocketed; that was if you could find it at all. The only reliable source of petrol was the black market pumps down by the docks, but unfortunately, they didn't accept a university charge card.

Excited by the potential of a breakthrough in their time travel proof, Dr. Maurya quickly rechecked the last power calculation and then had an epiphany.

"Massive power? That is it! It is so simple; it is beautiful!" He leaned over and kissed a stunned Dr. Jones on the lips. "Have I ever told you how beautiful you are? Almost as beautiful as my theory. The power we need is free and surrounds us every day! The Earth's magnetosphere!"

"But how would you...?" Dr. Jones stumbled; she was still startled by his unexpected kiss.

"Simple!" Dr. Maurya interrupted. "We merely need to tap into a natural disruption and redirect the power of the Earth's magnetosphere for a nanosecond to hold the wormhole open!"

Dr. Jones stood there silently for a moment and then a look of wonder crossed her face. "A disruption to the magnetosphere? You're thinking about the blue star... a brown dwarf... *Planet X!*" she gasped.

"Exactly!" Dr. Maurya exclaimed. "When Planet X approaches our orbit, it will most definitely cause a disruption to the Earth's magnetosphere. We just need to be ready to channel that electromagnetic disruption for one nanosecond. We have developed a proof for what Einstein only theorized: time travel *is* possible!" Just at that moment, they heard a knock on the door. It was Professor Soohu WiiSi, the research chair in Astrobiology. She was visiting from North America, specializing in the study of extraterrestrial microscopic life. Professor WiiSi peered inside with the look of an angry schoolteacher confiscating a love note circulating in her class. She could see that once again, they weren't ready to leave on schedule.

"It's 7:30 p.m., and you two are still at it?" she shouted in a stern voice. "I could hear the two of you all the way down the hall at this late hour." Dr. WiiSi walked past the two bickering scientists and over to their whiteboard of calculations. She ran her hand over the equations and made a disapproving face. Turning from the whiteboard, she glanced back toward her favorite scientist friends and smiled. "Let me guess... wormholes, dark energy, or just how many pints you two will lose on this week's football match?"

"Actually, we finally have agreed on one thing," Dr. Maurya volunteered.

"At least in theory," Dr. Jones piped in. Samantha Jones had grown fond of these regular heated debates, especially when WiiSi joined in. It was wonderful to have such diversity of opinion among intellectuals, passionate about the study of physics, astrobiology, and football. Soohu was a formidable debater on all three subjects. "I caught your lecture last week on the native people's mythology of the Earth's creation and destruction, quite intriguing, I'd say," Dr. Jones began. "Do you really believe there is astrophysical evidence confirming that we are on the verge of what the Hopi call a *Koyaanisqatsi?* How did they describe it again? *'A world out of balance, where the oceans join hands and meet the sky'.* I would like to explore that topic with you in light of some of my latest research."

Soohu WiiSi was mildly surprised by Dr. Jones' comment, and encouraged that someone in that half-full lecture hall last week had actually listened to her theory. She had dedicated her life's work to the linkage of Native American Indian prophecies and the science of astrological creation, but few in her academic circle took her work seriously. One biochemical professor had even suggested that she should consider a transfer from the 'real science' wing of the building to the Art Department, where she would fit in better among the science fiction writers.

"Why thank you, Dr. Jones, I wasn't sure anyone was even awake for my lecture." She smiled as she continued, "Especially not the ones that were snoring. I think that if you connect the dots between the Hopi creation story, the Mayan *Popol Vuh*, and the most recent interplanetary orbital data from Dr. Hannah, you will find that a conclusive case can be made for my..." Her welcome dialog was interrupted by a rapidly vibrating message on her videophone. "Oh, excuse me, I need to take this."

"Urgent High Council... Ten Bears tomorrow PM. Virgin Air ticket @ Heathrow gate... Dr. H." Turning back to Dr. Jones, she apologized for the interruption.

"Sorry to pop in and out like this, but I've got to fly back to the States. Besides, Manchester is going to crush Chelsea this weekend and you two will be too drunk to discuss anything but football. Let's pick up on this discussion next week, shall we?" Dr. WiiSi snapped her videophone shut and rushed out the door.

Samantha and Ashoka shouted out their goodbyes before collecting their briefcases and walking down the long hall from the professors' lounge. Making their way to the parking lot, they were still locked in deep discussion on the matter of time travel and the potential of their new power calculations.

"You know, we really should call Dr. Hannah and get his latest planetary data," Dr. Jones suggested. "I'd be interested to see if the orbit of Planet X has any correlation to our theory."

As Dr. Maurya grabbed the door handle to his beat-up old car, he paused and chuckled. "But of course! And then we will resume considering our power enigma once we have contemplated more important matters, like how Chelsea can beat Manchester this weekend. I tell you now, we are due!" They both laughed like a couple of soccer fans heading to the pub for a good drunken brawl. Dr. Maurya continued his football fantasy, trying his best to snap Samantha out of her serious demeanor and make her smile. "The last time we went to a good fight in Manchester, I tell you, a football match broke out!" They erupted in laughter again. Even a talented professor at Cambridge could transform into a hooligan when the Football Association whistle blew and the beer flowed.

When they reached the car in the parking bay, Dr. Maurya slid behind the wheel and pushed back his seat to adjust the rearview mirror. Out of the corner of his eye, he saw Dr. Jones slumped sideways in her seat, her face resting against the window. Before he could reach over to see what had happened to her, he glanced up at the mirror and his heart skipped a beat; there was a man in a brown overcoat sitting in the back seat of his car.

"Bloody hell!" he screamed. The last thing Dr. Maurya felt was a sharp, stinging pain in the back of his neck, and then everything faded to black. The man in the rear seat returned his stun weapon to his coat pocket and switched on his flashlight to verify the face of the unconscious professor with the image on his wristband. With his visual confirmation complete, he clicked an icon on his screen as he checked off the names of the scientists in the front seat. He waited a second, and then a static click came over the audio receiver icon.

"That's the last two?" The man in the back seat clicked "Affirmative" on his screen, and then waited as the screen responded with his final instructions.

"Collect luggage and transport to launch pad; Renaissance Team is go." The man with the shiny black shoes in the back seat of the car got out and motioned to his muscular friend standing in the shadows of the garage to grab the chrome suitcase with dual black locks in the back seat and join him and to move the two bodies up front to the boot. As they drove off campus with the unconscious scientists, the muscular man turned to the man with the shiny black shoes for an observation.

"You sure we got the right two, mate? Best check one more time. I thought these eggheads were supposed to have something going on upstairs, you know, half a brain?"

"Right you are," Shiny Shoes agreed. "Chelsea beating Manchester United? Not in this bloody world, mate."

6. Tiny Town

In a cavern deep in the central mountains known only as code name 'Tiny Town', a group of carefully chosen scientists, civilians and military personnel were anxiously awaiting a briefing on why they had been roused from their beds and dragged to an underground military base against their will. Suddenly, flashing lights and ear-piercing sirens echoed through the cavern, igniting a panic inside the granite bunker. Video screens lit up across the wall in the command center and military officers scrambled in all directions as they barked out orders to their soldiers. A small subset of the confused crowd, identified only by an encrypted code on their security badges as the *'Renaissance Team'* were separated by the soldiers and herded deeper into the cavern in front of an enormous metal vault door. It was clear that the concrete and steel fortifications around the vault were designed as a missile-hardened location. The terrified crowd in the outer cavern pushed and shoved in the chaos; families cried out to each other; some were knocked down and separated from their loved ones. What was to have been a well-prepared military exercise quickly broke down into utter bedlam.

In the midst of the panic, the huge metal vault door swung open and the Renaissance Team was pushed inside toward a launch preparation room. Above them, a silo door began to open and a giant Hercules class missile rose from a launch platform beneath the floor. On top of the missile was a commercial class cargo ship with the call sign *'Genesis Five'* painted on its fuselage. From the side of the cavern, a service elevator emerged and dropped a metal gangplank leading to the cargo bay of the rocket ship. At the entrance, two military guards stopped the confused members of the Renaissance Team, scanned their badges and looked them over intensely.

"Two lines!" bellowed Captain Charles Boswell. "Scientists on the left, civilians on the right!" Dr. Josiah Stone, Dr. Ashoka Maurya and Dr. Samantha Jones made their way to the front of the line to present their university identification badges.

"My suitcase!" Dr. Jones blurted out. "I don't see my chrome suitcase over there on the luggage cart."

"If your name's on the list, Professor, anything you have is already on board," Captain Boswell stated bluntly without looking up.

"But how do you know? I need to check…"

"Look, lady, I'm just following orders, which is what you should do unless you want to stay behind. I'm sure there are plenty of poor saps out there in the cave that would be happy to take your seat on this flight if you don't want it, so either step out of line or move along. Now!"

"Will there be a movie on this flight?" Dr. Josiah Stone interrupted.

The captain looked at Dr. Stone, *This little twerp can't be more than seventeen years old,* he thought. "No movies, kid. You sure you're supposed to be in the line with the grownups?" He moved closer to study Josiah's face, comparing it to his photo ID.

"Well, I hope we at least get dinner on this flight," Josiah replied sarcastically. He spun around as he passed the security checkpoint and made a one-finger salute to the back of the guard, causing the rest of the line to erupt in laughter. Oblivious to the insanity of their surroundings, Dr. Maurya and Dr. Jones were still deep in their discussion about time travel. As they approached the front of their line, Dr. Maurya looked up and fumbled with his security badge.

"Pardon me, sir, but would you have the final score of the Manchester United vs. Chelsea football match yesterday? I can't seem to get any reception for my mobile in this bloody tunnel!"

"Yeah, Bozo, they both lost. Now move the hell along!" replied Sergeant Longstreet without looking up. Behind Dr. Maurya was a growing commotion as one of the people in line pushed his way forward, just in front of the two military guards. It was Commander Zacary Ryker, smiling as he shoved his way through the crowd.

"Excuse me, Sergeant, I didn't hear the announcement for first class boarding. Are we up front?" Ryker asked with a look of mock concern at the line. The two guards looked at Ryker for a moment and then one of them realized something. *I've seen this ugly face before.*

"First class, my ass," Sergeant Longstreet barked. "The only place you belong is in front of a firing squad! I had a brother in the 35th, you bastard!" he growled as he grabbed Ryker with both hands. Captain Boswell restrained the sergeant from a full-on fistfight, stepping in between the guard and a smiling Ryker.

"Stand down, Sergeant, orders from the top… he's not on the list, but this bastard gets to ride without a ticket!" barked the captain.

"I don't care if he's a fucking four-bird Colonel," Sergeant Longstreet yelled back. "This low-life coward is not boarding my ship! He stays behind, like the eleven men he left to die!" Captain Boswell moved chest-to-chest with the sergeant, glaring at him.

"You want to take time and settle this now, Sergeant?" Captain Boswell barked. "Then have at it, but you fucking take it outside, do you hear me? This ship is gone in five minutes, with or without the two of you. I would strongly recommend that you stand down now if you want a seat on the bus. Besides, there will be plenty of time to settle up with this bastard later; he ain't going nowhere we can't find him."

Sergeant Longstreet twisted his head back and forth, cracking his neck bones. He let go of Ryker, and stepped back, before leaning forward to growl in Ryker's face.

"Go on through, you traitor," Longstreet muttered. "You and me, we'll settle this later." Ryker smiled, straightened his wrinkled shirt and walked past the checkpoint.

"I tell you, first class is just *not* what it used to be," Ryker mocked to those still waiting in line. He moved through the door and headed to the flight lockers inside the launch preparation room. As the last of the chosen few crowded their way inside, another logjam developed at the door. Two Confederation agents dressed in civilian clothes were trying to wedge a large crate marked *'Live Animals / Extreme Caution'* through the door. Obviously stuck, they started yelling loudly at each other. From inside the crate, an angry beast growled and thrashed about wildly, scaring the others in line and drawing the attention of the military guards. The captain pushed forward to challenge the two agents.

"Freeze!" Captain Boswell shouted as he drew his weapon. "You can't bring that mangy animal on board my ship!"

The agent in front with shiny black shoes tried to diffuse the confrontation.

"Sorry, Officer, I tried to tell him that."

"No worries, he's house-trained and quite friendly," the second agent interrupted. "One day, me an' him are gonna be a therapy dog team."

"I said no animals, you asshole!" the captain bellowed."

"No need to get angry," the muscular agent protested, looking back at the crate containing the snarling beast. "Brenda doesn't like it when people get angry..."

As the captain shoved the muscular agent aside and reached toward the crate, the beast inside crashed through the cage door and leaped out to attack the soldier. With vicious precision, the animal tore the gun from his hand and lunged onto the captain's chest, landing on top of him, his snarling teeth still clutching the gun, an inch away from the soldier's carotid artery.

"*Koda! Posna!* (Koda! Drop it!) *Pew'i neepeq nuy taw!"* (Come to me now!) A girl's voice boomed from across the room. The vicious dog snarled one more time in the face of the helpless soldier, dropped the gun, hopped off his chest and trotted over to stand obediently by Lexis' side. The two agents standing by the crate were confused, looking back and forth at each other.

"What just happened here?" the man with the shiny black shoes muttered.

"I don't know, mate," the muscular agent replied. "But it looks like Brenda has two mommies." The two agents shook their heads, shoved the empty animal crate to the side and entered the launch preparation room.

The commotion at the checkpoint died down for just a moment as all of the Renaissance Team had now entered the launch room and the door behind them was sealed shut. One of the civilians looked outside the launch preparation window up at the towering rocket and finally lost control of his emotions.

"Where the hell are we going? I've got to get back to my family!"

Captain Boswell decided it was time to take charge, so he addressed the room of confused passengers.

"Listen up, people! The door to the containment cavern has been sealed shut. Incoming nuclear missiles will destroy the site we are standing in less than ten minutes. We have a rocket ready to take you out of harm's way. If you choose to stay here, you will be vaporized."

Some of the Renaissance Team members broke down and called out for their separated family members.

His patience wearing thin, the captain barked out his final order. "Open a locker, grab a space suit, and put it on! Follow me inside Genesis Five if you want to live, or you can stay here and die; it's your choice."

7. The Enemy Within

There are spies in every government, and this one was no exception. Word had leaked out about the potential for a secret launch of a band of settlers into space, and both the enemies and suspicious Allies of the Confederation were left to franticly consider their own 'what if' scenarios and make their contingency plans accordingly.

During the covert Confederation round up of the Renaissance Team, a deep cover enemy mole had followed the unusual disappearance of scientists and civilians in recent days and followed their trail to the secret underground cavern in the central mountains. He had infiltrated the facility by silently stalking and killing a member of the maintenance crew, assuming his identity, and blending in with the crowd. Once inside the mountain, the mole gathered enough intelligence to uncover the nuclear survival bunker, alerting his handlers. When he uncovered the plan for launching part of the Renaissance Team into space, he sent his last transmission and positioned himself close enough to the team to be ready to strike should an opportunity arise. With the speed of events accelerating, there would not be enough time to extract a launch destination. *I've had no further instructions,* the mole thought, *but I suspect the underground civilian teams were a mere diversion. I have to follow the launch team, no matter where it leads.*

The mole's special operations training had prepared him well for changes in his primary mission if dictated by events. He knew that any covert plan was obsolete the second it was made, so he waited for the right moment to strike. When the launch team was separated from the underground civilians, he realized this was his chance to adapt his plan, and act. Popping open an airshaft cover, he quickly crawled through the ventilation duct system, locating an air grate adjacent to the launch preparation lockers. He dropped down from the ceiling and hid in a maintenance closet, his ear to the door until the time was right. As most of the launch team departed from the locker room, one of the soldiers lingered, and the mole sprang into action. With military precision, he crept out of the closet, silently approaching the soldier and grabbing him from behind. The mole covered the struggling soldier's mouth and shoved a knife to his throat, noticing he was wearing special dog tags around his neck.

"Going for a ride, brother?" he whispered.

"Let go of me, you bastard!" the soldier struggled.

"Oh, I'll let you go," the mole agreed, laughing. "Just tell me where you're off to in such a rush?" The soldier resisted, trying to break the hold on his neck but couldn't get free.

"That destination is... classified... "

"It's not personal, it's just business," the mole stated calmly. "I'll ask you one more time and then I will cut your throat. Where are you headed, soldier?"

"Lieutenant Morgan McCurdy, 5th Ranger Brigade. That's all you'll get from me, you bastard!"

"Well then, Lieutenant McCurdy, I guess that will be enough then. You are dismissed." With one powerful twist, the mole snapped the soldier's neck, letting his limp body slump to the floor. He quickly changed clothes with the dead man and dragged the body back to the maintenance closet. Removing the military dog tags and the security badge from the lieutenant, the mole placed them around his own neck.

Now that's interesting, he thought, *one of the dog tags is civilian, a mining company called Dark Energy Resources. Looks like my lieutenant friend was doing a little moonlighting on the side.* He fumbled through his vest pocket and pulled out a communicator. Rewinding the audio portion of his recorded struggle with the dead soldier, he hit the playback button.

"Lieutenant Morgan McCurdy, 5th Ranger Brigade. That's all you'll get from me, you bastard!"

"And that's all I need from you, Lieutenant," the mole whispered to himself. "Chance favors the prepared mind." He returned the communicator to his pocket and completed his transition from deep-cover mole to his new assignment... undercover assassin.

Jogging down the access ramp to the launch pad, the assassin arrived just in time to squeeze in before the hatch of Genesis Five was closed. As the last military guard sealed the ship, he took his seat and smiled to himself. He had infiltrated the team and joined the launch crew to disrupt their secret mission to... destination, unknown.

In the words of Sun Tzu, *'He who is prudent and lies in wait for an enemy who is not, will be victorious'*, the assassin thought to himself. *You must balance this saying with your prime directive; stay undercover, stay alive, and inflict maximum pain on your enemy.*

8. Lunar Mirage

Onboard Genesis Five, the Renaissance Team was strapped safely inside as they hurled upward, away from their underground launch platform and off into space. At twenty miles up, the rocket booster separated and they lost all contact with Earth. As the settlers achieved escape velocity and accelerated into space, the ultimate fate of the Earth was unknown to them. Out the window of Genesis Five, nuclear flashes were popping all over the surface of the Earth, like fireworks on the Fourth of July. Volcanoes were erupting everywhere and uncontrolled wildfires burned over vast portions of the planet, adding to the thick brown haze that covered the sky. The last communication that Genesis Five received from the central mountain command bunker was garbled and interspersed with chaotic news reports of all-out nuclear war. As the Earth began to fade from their view, the dark side of the Moon was coming onto the flight horizon. The military communications specialist onboard Genesis Five sought to establish contact with the mining colony on the Moon.

"Moon Base One, this is Genesis Five, clearance code Charlie 19. Inbound on vector 5-3-9... Requesting landing sequence."

"Roger, Genesis Five, clearance code confirmed," Moon Base One responded. "Heard you had some trouble in the neighborhood. We weren't expecting guests tonight, but you are cleared for landing. Give us a few minutes to lower our shields. Damn solar generators just got knocked out by some sort of electromagnetic storm; we're on backup power."

"Acknowledged, Moon Base One. Sorry to pop in unannounced, but things got a little heated at home. We can discuss the details over dinner," Genesis Five confirmed.

Inside Genesis Five, the assassin had worked his way to the spacecraft's communications panel and hacked into the transmitter with his scrambler; a small, black electronic cube he found quite helpful in breaching enemy networks. The scrambler was the software equivalent of a cat burglar with an attitude; it could hack or bluff its way through any security firewall he had encountered. The military computer login screen in front of him blinked in the darkness.

'Enter User Name.' The assassin pulled the stolen dog tags out of his shirt and typed in his identification.

'Lieutenant Morgan McCurdy.' The network computer responded with a security challenge.

'Enter voice code recognition.' The assassin smiled as he patted his coat pocket, *just as I thought.* Digging around for his communicator, he pulled it out and pressed 'Play' on the audio button as he held it close to the screen.

"Lieutenant Morgan McCurdy, 5th Ranger Brigade. That's all you'll get from me." The computer screen paused, then dissolved to display a message.

"Secure access granted, welcome back, Lieutenant McCurdy."

"Ok," the assassin whispered to himself. "We've got a rod and reel, now let's go phishing!"

Working quickly, the assassin used the Genesis Five network computer to initiate a covert military signal, pinging what was left of the global satellite network. He then attempted to spoof a military command center on Earth that was trying to reestablish a communication protocol for its lost satellite connection.

'Secure Military Clearance Charlie 19, Repair Broken Network Connections,' the assassin typed into his spoofed profile. The global satellite network responded, scanned for broken communications connections, and located a military satellite that had lost its Earth-bound host controller. Like a wayward child inadvertently left at a bus stop, the satellite had been awaiting further operating instructions. The assassin then tapped into the Genesis Five guidance database and located the military command module. Masquerading as Lieutenant McCurdy, he pulled up the dead soldier's personnel file. He plugged in the scrambler and uploaded a viral software patch to scan Lieutenant McCurdy's personnel file and build a candidate list of secure passwords. The virus patch started processing. Names, dates, pictures, and personal information from the life of Lieutenant Morgan McCurdy flashed up and down the screen. The Genesis Five computer guidance application noticed the nonstandard intrusion to the Personnel Files and took preemptive action to block the intruder's access to the database.

'Secure Personnel Application: Enter User Name and Password.'

User Name *'Lieutenant Morgan McCurdy,'* the assassin entered.

'Password,' demanded the network computer. The password stealing virus patch from the scrambler was still processing. The assassin hit the *'Guess'* icon on the scrambler, and it generated a message for his consideration.

"Try Skip, his first dog, he was a Collie." *Probability 60%.* A picture of a Lassie dog appeared on his screen.

'Password = Skip.' The assassin typed in his command.

'Access Denied,' barked back the network computer. *'Enter Password.'* The application on the scrambler continued processing, parsing through the data in Lieutenant McCurdy's personnel file. Impatiently, the assassin hit *'Guess Again'* on his device, and the virus generated another message response.

"Try Vanessa, his wife and her birthday." *Probability 70%.* A picture of Vanessa appeared on the screen, birthday 12-21.

'Password = Vanessa1221', the assassin entered.

'Access Denied', responded the network computer. *'Final Attempt, Enter Password.'* The analysis on the scrambler completed just as the assassin hit *'Last Guess'*, and this time, it generated a more satisfactory recommendation.

"Got you, you naughty boy!" There were lots of text messages and financial transfers to a lap dancer at a gentlemen's club called the *Peppermint Rhino.* It seemed that Master McCurdy had just bought his mistress some lingerie. He paid cash, but sent a card with a note, *'To my Buttercups.' Interesting, she's a petite size 38D*, the assassin thought. *Probability 90%.* A picture of Buttercups appeared on the screen, and she was stunning in her... proportions.

'Password = 38DButtercups.' The assassin smiled as he typed. The network computer paused and then responded with a friendly welcome.

'Access Granted.' Inside the guidance application, the assassin quickly searched for a military satellite vector match. He got a hit and downloaded the command code for the satellite. Toggling back to the satellite command software, he entered the command code while he was searching for a control program override.

'Display Weapons Status,' the assassin typed into the satellite interface.

'Three Pharaoh Missiles, active and armed,' the satellite responded.

'Payload status,' the assassin queried.

'500 kilotons, hot,' returned the satellite.

'Available target vectors,' the assassin typed.

'Earth vectors corrupted. Moon Base vector X1Y5 active,' the satellite answered.

"Ah... so that's where we are headed for dinner," the assassin whispered. "And I am so sorry that I didn't bring you a housewarming gift." His hands froze momentarily above the keyboard as he quickly assessed the alternatives in his mind. *Let's see... decisions, decisions. Follow the prime directive and consider my odds for remaining undetected and alive. Lieutenant McCurdy was returning to Moon Base One, and he had a commercial dog tag. So if we land there, they will immediately know I'm an imposter. That would make it, me against fifty heavily armed soldiers on Moon Base One, versus me against fifty unarmed civilians and a couple of mercenary rejects up top this flying piece of shit. Which shall it be?* A smile crept across his face; the assassin made his decision. *I'm sorry that I have only one Moon Base to give for my country,* he thought, *but you know what they say... better the devil you know than the one you don't.* The assassin typed in his decision.

'Target Moon Base vector X1Y5, launch command Alpha.'

'Confirmed and executed,' the satellite responded. With its new orders locked, the military satellite immediately repositioned its firing vectors, targeted Moon Base vector X1Y5, and opened its missile launch bays. All three of its Pharaoh Missiles locked onto target and launched.

On their radar screen, Moon Base One detected the inbound missiles and frantically called out to Genesis Five.

"What the hell is going on out there? We have warheads from you closing in on us at warp speed!"

"Negative," Genesis Five responded. "Rescan your horizon, Moon Base One. Weapons status is... inactive. I show nothing on our screen."

"I'm not fucking with you!" Moon Base One screamed. "Three inbound missiles on your approach vector, 5-3-9, they are right behind you! Abort those missiles, you asshole! Our shields are down for your landing! We are defenseless!" The technician on Genesis Five rescanned his horizon and could now see the inbound missiles from the satellite. They had been hidden in the impulse engine wash behind them and were closing fast on Moon Base One.

"Holy shit!" screamed Genesis Five. "I see them now, they are right underneath us! Moon Base One, warheads are not ours! I repeat;

we are not armed! Activating antimissile weapons systems now for intercept." The security officer on Genesis Five frantically tried to bring up his anti-missile system to lock onto the rogue projectiles as he tried to reassure Moon Base One.

"Hang in there, Moon Base One, arming antimissile system now."

"Take them out, damn it!" Moon Base One screamed back. "Our fucking shields are down!"

The Genesis Five security officer pounded on the keyboard with his instructions to open the antimissile bay doors to shoot down the missiles targeted on Moon Base One, but it was too late. He watched in horror as the three Pharaoh missiles bypassed the disabled weapons shields of Moon Base One and punctured the biosphere with a direct hit. The massive impact triggered a secondary explosion that ignited the mining colony oxygen tanks, and in one fiery flash, Moon Base One was obliterated in a giant fireball.

9. Destination Unknown

From the observation deck of Genesis Five, the captain and crew in the command module were dumbstruck at the events that had just unfolded. In a matter of seconds, the only safe harbor for the passengers and crew... was gone. Captain Mitchell Gaylord turned away from the video screen showing the smoking remains of Moon Base One and charged angrily toward the security officer.

"What the hell just happened?" he screamed.

"I don't know, sir!" the security officer cried out. "One second, we were on approach for landing, and the next, we were over-flown by missiles targeted on Moon Base One!"

"Where the hell did those missiles come from?" screamed Captain Gaylord. He pushed the soldier away from the computer screen. "Some security officer you are, mister! You're relieved of duty!"

"But sir..."

"Get the fuck off my command deck... now!" Captain Gaylord screamed.

Science Officer Sarah Beth Taylor had been pouring over the computer scans of the missile trajectory and the Moon's location, and she was puzzled. "Captain, it appears that one of our own military satellites was blown out of orbit and followed our engine wash toward Moon Base One. For some reason... it fired on it."

"That's impossible!" Captain Gaylord bellowed. "And who the hell are you, anyway?"

Sarah Taylor started to respond, but was interrupted by the captain as he glared at the video screens.

"Damn it! Satellites can't deploy their weapons without a secure launch command and target vectors."

"I'm analyzing the data now," responded a shaken Officer Taylor. "Apparently, the satellite *did* receive a secure launch code transmission and vector target to strike the Moon Base."

"It received a launch code? Where the hell from?" Captain Gaylord was stunned.

"It came from... Genesis Five, sir," Officer Taylor answered.

Captain Gaylord punched his fist into the wall.

"What the hell? We've just blown up our only place to land and now you're telling me that it was destroyed by a traitor we have somewhere on my ship? I'm going to tear this fucking boat apart and find that bastard before we land on the Moon. And when we drop anchor, I'm going to dig a crater and bury that son of a bitch alive!"

"Sir, we have another problem," Officer Taylor continued.

"Well shit, what else could go wrong?" Captain Gaylord snapped.

"The Moon sir, it's moving away from us."

"What the fuck are you talking about?" he bellowed.

"When the missiles struck Moon Base One, they detonated with such an impact that they knocked the Moon out of the weakened gravitational pull of the Earth."

Captain Gaylord scratched his head. "You want to run that by me again, Miss *Science* Officer?"

"I am saying that the Moon is moving away from us, sir, and the explosion threw us in the opposite direction. We are now in the direct path of Planet X, or Niburu, I think it's called, as it slingshots around the Earth."

A look of calm came over Captain Gaylord's face as he spoke to her. "Well then, Officer Taylor, just change course and catch up to the Moon!"

Officer Taylor wrinkled up her nose. "That could be a problem, sir. The blast damaged engine number two and it's leaking fuel badly. We only carried enough fuel on board to get to the Moon. The Moon is now speeding away from us and with the increased gravitational pull from Planet Niburu, we don't have either the power or the fuel to catch up to it."

Captain Gaylord was still calm despite her response. "So what would you say our options are, Officer Taylor?"

Sarah Taylor thought about the problem, and then responded.

"Only two options, sir. There are no other landing sites within our range and we have limited fuel and oxygen on board. We can either drift in space until we run out of air, or we can try to land on this planet, Niburu, before it drags us into it and we burn up in its atmosphere."

"Well thank you for that insightful analysis," Captain Gaylord noted sarcastically. "So let me get this straight, *Science* Officer Taylor. Our choices are certain death in space, or mostly certain death trying to land on an unknown planet. If we manage to survive the landing, we will most likely die on that unknown planet without food or water, since as you said, we didn't actually plan on landing there and we have no provisions. Oh, and one more thing; if we do make it safely down to that... unknown planet... it's speeding away from Earth into another galaxy."

"Those would seem to be the only options, sir," Officer Taylor answered. "But there is actually one more consideration. With our damaged engines, landing on Niburu could be a little... hairy."

"Define *hairy*, Miss Taylor?" Captain Gaylord asked with a comical look on his face. "Is that one of the *scientific* terms they taught you in the Academy?"

"Sir... I have taken some readings on the electromagnetism around Planet Niburu, and it is strange to say the least. I am guessing that it will knock out all our guidance computers on approach and we'll be flying in blind. Niburu's massive gravitational pull will toss us about like a candle in the wind. This is going to be a very difficult landing, and..."

"And *what*, Officer Taylor?"

"Well, sir, I checked your flight records and the only flight time you have logged in three years was in a... simulator. Are you sure that under these circumstances, you are qualified to... land this ship?"

"So you don't like our chances with me at the helm?" Captain Gaylord smiled.

"Permission to speak freely, sir?"

"By all means! Why stop now, Miss Taylor?"

"No sir, I don't. Like our chances, I mean."

Captain Gaylord was clearly annoyed.

"Well, thank you for that honest vote of confidence... but since no one else on this ship is qualified to...'

"Sir," Officer Taylor interrupted. "He's not listed on the passenger manifest, but don't we have a fighter pilot on board?"

"You don't mean... *Ryker?*" Captain Gaylord hissed. "Not that bastard; the last time he flew a mission, no one else came back alive!" Having observed the destruction of Moon Base One from the passenger

62

compartment, Commander Ryker had instinctively made his way to the command deck just in time to overhear the last part of the conversation. He poked his head around the bulkhead and smiled.

"Excuse me, Admiral, but I couldn't help noticing out the window that our landing pad is on fire. Does that mean that the dinner service is going to be delayed?"

Captain Gaylord bristled at the sight of Commander Ryker on his flight deck.

"Brilliant observation, you shithead! Good to see that you're as sharp as you were back at the Academy."

"And you in control, as always." Ryker smiled. He turned toward Officer Taylor and continued, "Except for that time when you were rolling around in the coat room with the Chancellor's daughter at the Academy dance. I don't think I've ever seen a man salute while he's, well... I believe you two were engaged in the process of... and that's still illegal in some provinces, you know."

"Enough!" Gaylord hissed. "You and I can replay our dance cards later, right now we have more pressing business."

Ryker joined Captain Gaylord at the helm and they both studied the video screens. Captain Gaylord was worried, but a bit more respectful with Commander Ryker in private.

"You heard our options," Gaylord whispered. "As much as I hate to say it, you're more qualified than I am... to get us all *fucking killed*. I lost my commission in that coatroom and got demoted to flying this shitty ass supply shuttle to the Moon Base, but at least I got to keep on flying, you bastard. You willing to take command and crash this steaming pile of junk into the ground on Niburu?"

Inside Ryker's pocket, CHIP had been eavesdropping. Eager to join the party, he booted up his video screen and assumed an "Uncle Sam" persona.

"What did that recruiting poster say?" CHIP blurted out. "Join the military, travel to strange and exotic lands, meet interesting people, and then crash your ship on them! I'm ready to enlist, sir, sign me up and let's go for a ride!"

"You brought that claptrap with you?" Captain Gaylord moaned. "Now I know we're fucked!"

Ryker shrugged as he pulled CHIP out of his pocket and placed him on the desk by the keyboard. He leaned forward and scanned the three observation screens, one with the distant Earth, one with the escaping Moon, and one with the mysterious Planet Niburu rapidly approaching. He then turned to Officer Taylor with the look of a lost puppy.

"Do you think there are... interesting people on this Planet... Niburu? Sometimes interesting people, they just pop up when you least expect it."

Officer Taylor blushed at Ryker's newfound attention, unconsciously pushing her hair behind her ears. Trying to remain focused, she responded.

"I don't know, Commander, but based on the planet's density and the intense radiation down there, there may not even be..."

"Intense radiation?" Ryker interrupted. "I've always enjoyed intense radiation. Give me some hot, steamy radiation any old time, just dripping down your... outrageous body," he stated as he stared at her chest. Officer Taylor blushed again and swallowed hard. She broke off eye contact and turned back to her computer screen. "Well if there's no people down there," Ryker posed, "maybe there will be some good fishing. You like to fish, Officer Taylor?"

"I don't know sir," she responded. "I've never been much for the outdoors. I guess I'm more of an indoor girl."

Captain Gaylord shot a look at Ryker and then burst in between them to interrupt.

"Excuse me kids, but before you two head to the coatroom to play hide the salami, do you think we could get on with the *not dying* part? Ryker! Are you going to fly this pile of shit or not?"

Ryker shook his head as if to clear his thoughts. "Ok, where were we..." he mumbled.

Captain Gaylord faced Ryker and got in his face.

"We were at the part where you zip up your pants and use those world-renowned fighter pilot skills to get us through this shitstorm and safely down to this alien planet. And this time, maybe try it without killing everyone else, all right?"

Ryker nodded and turned to sit down at the controls. The ship's guidance computer rapidly presented various approach models for landing on Niburu. Unfortunately, they all flashed red, showing an approach sequence that ended with the completion code, *CFIT* (Controlled Flight Into Terrain).

"Commander, what's CFIT?" Officer Taylor asked as she looked over his shoulder.

"Oh... that's not all that important," Ryker responded without looking up. "It's just some pilot mumbo jumbo." He picked CHIP up from the desk and inserted him into the computer guidance control panel. "Better lock us down, little buddy, looks like we're going in hot."

"Well, it is good to be back in the saddle, amigo," CHIP answered, simulating his best John Wayne persona. "But from the looks of things, we're sure as shit gonna need some more power, bucko, or I'm gonna have to beat this little bronco like a rented mule." Ryker glanced over at CHIP with a disapproving look and CHIP lowered his eyes, immediately switching back to strict military protocol.

"Sealing all compartments on my mark... mark," CHIP announced. There was a whoosh of air as every bulkhead and passageway on Genesis Five was locked shut for impact. "Snug as a bug in a rug, sir."

Deep inside the bowels of Genesis Five, there was a frustrated hiss from the assassin. He had silently crawled his way through the ventilation system and was almost at the command module, but now his plan to kill the mercenary pilot, seize control of the ship, and return to Earth with his captured prize would have to wait for another opportunity. On the command deck, Ryker grabbed the captain's headset and called out to the passengers over the intercom system.

"Ladies and gentlemen, may I have your attention; this is your commander speaking. I'm sorry, but we've had a very slight change in our travel plans. We had planned to land on Moon Base One, but as you may have noticed out the window on the left side of the ship, Moon Base One is... well, it's not there anymore." There was a collective gasp from the passenger compartment, and then Commander Ryker continued. "But no cause for alarm, folks. If you look out the window on the left side of the ship, you'll see a large, unknown planet rapidly approaching us... man, that's not something you see every day. So I believe we'll take this opportunity to set down on that large unknown planet... the one that's getting... wow, it's really close now... well, before it sucks us down into its massive gravitational field and crushes us to death." Ryker leaned over and grinned at Officer Taylor.

"So in preparation for landing; if I could ask you to turn off your cell phones, secret enemy transmitters, and any other electronic devices that you have... and I guess it would be best for now if you would return to your seats, put your tray tables up, and bring your seatbacks to an upright position." He reached up to turn off the intercom system on his headset, but for some reason, the system remained on; Ryker was unaware that his voice would still boom throughout the ship. "And if you are not currently in a seat," he added jokingly, "you may as well bend down, grab your ankles, and kiss your ass goodbye!"

There was a collective shriek from the passenger compartment, but Ryker just looked over at Officer Taylor and shrugged. "Oops, my bad." He winked at Sarah and whispered with a smile, "Better strap yourself in, cowgirl... this could get a little bumpy."

10. A Candle in the Wind

From the flight deck of the command module of Genesis Five, Lieutenant Commander Zacary Ryker scanned the guidance monitor for the computer-assisted landing approach patterns to Niburu. The ship's computers had calculated the three best landing scenarios, all with a similar outcome. Each scenario worked well, right up until the ship crashed in a ball of flames onto the jagged mountains of the planet's surface. Typing rapidly, Ryker transferred the landing simulation models to CHIP's telemetry processors for analysis. He glanced at the big screen video of the swirling clouds and rapidly approaching planet, and then spoke softly to CHIP over his headset.

"Ok little buddy... how about you sharing some of your advanced intelligence here?" he asked. CHIP ran his diagnostic algorithm on each of the landing simulation models; however, he produced the same projected outcome... instant death. All of the recommended approach sequences ended in the same flaming crash landing for Genesis Five.

"That is puzzling," CHIP responded, startled at the results. "This computer guidance system is civilian grade, but it seems to possess no obvious programming errors."

Commander Ryker rubbed his hand through his hair. "Civilian grade... how civilian are we talking here, little buddy?"

"Well," CHIP responded, "if Genesis Five was an internal combustion transportation vehicle, it would be a poorly maintained late 20th century Dodge minivan. You know, one of those soccer mom war wagons they used to haul the rug rats around to ballet lessons."

"Ok, I hear you," Ryker muttered. "Let's hope Mom got the turbo model."

"Commander," CHIP continued. "I am reprocessing the landing simulation models now and providing three new approach paths. Vector Tango X-ray... *ouch!* Vector Charlie Alpha... *bam!* Vector Baker Tango... *boom!* Oh my, that is disturbing! They all end with a *'CFIT'*. Probability of survival; zero percent. That's bad, right?"

"Yeah, Einstein, zero probability of survival would be bad." Ryker sighed. "Now tell me something I don't know! If we only have three landing sequence options, which one's it gonna be?"

"Captain, we are about to enter Niburu's outer atmosphere,"

Officer Taylor interrupted. "My sensor scans are picking up a very strong electrical field. I have routed it to video monitor three. This could impact our landing, sir, and it could be bad."

"Enough with the bad already!" Ryker barked. "Doesn't anyone on this ship have any positive thoughts to share?" He looked up at video monitor three as it displayed an image of the hypnotically pulsating clouds of blue and red with occasional yellow flashes crackling through the haze.

Just as Genesis Five entered the outer edge of the clouds, a massive electromagnetic pulse wave swept through the ship, throwing everyone onboard from their seats. The ship's internal illumination system flickered on and off and the passengers below deck were tossed about like rag dolls as the ship lurched and twisted in the shock wave. From the passenger compartment, shrieks and screams could be heard across the intercom system as they reverberated down the hallways. More importantly, however, the immense pulse wave from the planet tore through the hull of the ship like a lightning strike with a bad attitude, dancing along the internal wiring conduits until it reached the guidance computer, frying its circuits. Like the last rays of sunlight at dusk, the final three landing approach models flickered and then faded from the video monitor screen, lost forever. Commander Ryker was thrown out of his chair for a moment, but he looked up from the floor just in time to watch the video screens with his recommended landing sequences as they went blank. He climbed back into his chair and looked away from the monitors to CHIP with a strange smile.

"Well, I guess that makes our choice for us," he noted. "None of them. Zero percent of survival? I didn't like those odds much anyway." Ryker refocused his attention on the one video screen that was still working... an exterior camera view displaying the dense, swirling cloud cover of the Niburu atmosphere. He switched the computer guidance system to manual control and attempted to level out the artificial horizon on his instrument panel. Without the guidance computer vectors or telemetry, Ryker knew that a manual landing in this swirling cloud of electromagnetic turbulence was going to end only one way... badly.

"What's the plan, sir?" Officer Taylor inquired.

"I guess we just fly her steady until we hit something," Ryker joked. "Maybe we'll bounce off." He glanced up, saw the stunned look on Officer Taylor's face, and tried to recover. Maybe it was best not to let her see the man behind the curtain just yet. "Ok, not such a good plan." The ship hit an air pocket and bounced around, but somehow he maintained a level descent in the violence of the massive electromagnetic storm.

"CHIP, damn it! Give me something to work with here!" Ryker urged.

"All that's left of this minivan computer console are some bits and pieces of old software routines buried in the hard drives," CHIP responded. "I could try to rewire the auxiliary panel, but that will take some time, sir!"

"Time? We don't have time right now, little buddy."

In the midst of the confusion generated by the electromagnetic shock waves, Dr. Josiah Stone had made his way from the passenger compartment to the door of the command module. He was just about to enter when another EMP struck the ship and violently tossed the crew about. The ship lurched ahead and Dr. Stone tumbled clumsily into the command deck, knocking over Officer Taylor as he landed in a heap on top of her. They came to rest in a rather provocative position, with Josiah staring into the chest of the rather startled science officer beneath him.

"Whoa! Ma'am, I am sorry!" Josiah blurted out. "I was just coming up to see if I could..."

"I'm ok, just help me up," Officer Taylor gasped, struggling to get out from under Dr. Stone. "No harm here, but you will have to excuse me, we are a bit preoccupied with our guidance computers. I've got to get back to work."

Josiah tried to act nonchalant as he bent down to help her pick up her computer equipment and papers. He handed her the equipment she had dropped on the floor during their crash, glanced around, and surveyed the disabled status of the computer equipment in the command module.

"Sorry to interrupt your game of Twister, kids." Ryker laughed. "But since I may crash this minivan and kill us all any minute now, I thought we should just go ahead and get back to fixing the burned out guidance system."

Josiah brushed himself off and stood next to Ryker, studying the computer readouts. "That's why I'm here, Captain. When we got hit by that EMP, it fried everything electronic down in the passenger compartment, everything except my portable Artificial Intelligence and gaming console, that is." Dr. Stone pulled out an AI unit from his pocket, displaying it proudly. "I call her NELI... that's short for Neural Electronic Learning Intelligence. I thought she might be of use up here on the flight deck."

"Well that's just gnarly, dude," Ryker shot back. "I'd love to take time out to zap some Asteroids with you. You know, I hold the base record, but I don't think I have any AAA batteries, so maybe we should just work on the *big* computers for now." Josiah stood there for a moment, assessing the level of insult coming from someone that he considered to be intellectually challenged, at best. He cocked his head to the right, and then patted NELI on her input screen, as if to reassure her.

Before he could verbalize his response, Ryker got in one more dig. "Nelly?" Ryker asked sarcastically. "Geez, who names their Game Boy Nelly, anyway?"

Josiah had now gathered his thoughts and was decidedly insulted at the implication that NELI was some simple pimply-faced nerd's video game device, and a cheap platform to boot. It was time for a lecture on the subject of artificial intelligence, a subject in which he happened to hold multiple post-doctorate degrees.

"Let's just work with the... *big* computers?" Josiah repeated sarcastically, his face turning bright red, looking as if he might burst a blood vessel on the side of his temple. He hopped up on the command deck beside Ryker and moved close to his face. "Let me explain something about NELI, Commander. I've spent years along with my staff developing NELI in my molecular computing lab at MIT. She controls thousands of neural networks across the globe and has developed an artificial intelligence level so sophisticated, that she is completely self-aware. Do you know what that means? Comparing NELI's intelligence to a frickin' Game Boy would be like a BB rolling around in a boxcar... and you would be the BB holding the Game Boy over there."

"NELI has a thousand times the computing power of this entire beat-up tin can, even when it was fully functional!" Josiah's face was now turning shades of purple and white as he leaped off the command deck and paced around the room, waving his arms in anger. "And she didn't get *her* circuits fried by that predictable EMP like your little wimpy computer, now did she?"

Ryker backed away, giving Dr. Stone some room to vent.

"Don't you want to know *why* she didn't get fried like your... *little* computer?" Josiah queried. Ryker looked around the room for support, but none was forthcoming, so he played along.

"We really don't have time for a story, Doc, but I got a feeling you're going to tell us one anyway."

"NELI didn't get her circuits fried because she was smart enough to develop a portable anti-magnetic force field to protect herself. *She* was aware of the Niburu electromagnetic threat to activate her force field in time, unlike your *big* computer up here that got fried, Commander!"

Ryker was now a bit more impressed. "She's really got her own little anti-magnetic force field?" Ryker smiled. "That's cool. How'd you come up with that one, Doc?"

Josiah started to calm down a bit now that it seemed NELI's intelligence was being acknowledged.

"My geeky students used to think that it was funny to try and fry all my computer circuits just before final exams," he explained. "So I asked NELI to develop a countermeasure to those nerd attacks, with some added sting. Attacking NELI with an electromagnetic pulse weapon is about as futile as shooting a laser into a mirror; she just redirects the force back to the source and they get zapped!"

"Fascinating," Ryker sighed. "And is there a point to this Mr. Science story coming anytime soon?"

"Of course there is," Josiah snapped. "I loved it when those geeks would attack NELI. I just stood there, laughing at their burnt out laptops while they sobbed in disbelief. *'I am rubber, you are glue... it bounces off me and sticks to you'!*" Josiah wiped off the interface screen on NELI's input pad, and whispered, "She's my little queen bee, and on top of her other advanced qualities, she and I have grown to be, well, sort of friends."

Ryker turned away from Josiah toward Officer Taylor and made a mock sad face, like he was crying. "Ok, sorry to have called you a Game Boy, Nelly," Ryker apologized calming Josiah down.

"Professor Stone, do you think you..." Officer Taylor interrupted. "I mean do you think NELI could help CHIP get the guidance computer back into operation? We are in a bit of a pickle here."

"I'll ask her," Dr. Stone spoke softly into NELI's input sensor and then turned back to Officer Taylor. "NELI would be delighted to help. She heard that there was another AI unit on board, and she's been bugging me to introduce her to him ever since we left Tiny Town." Josiah plugged NELI into the nearest computer panel on the command console, and she immediately began uploading images onto the video monitor screen. Oddly enough, the images were of an animated SWAT team running through a deserted, burned out city, firing weapons in all directions.

"Ok, Professor, I said we didn't have time for playing video game warriors," Ryker commented.

"Oops, sorry," Josiah mumbled. "NELI was just purging her game buffers. We were bored down there in the passenger compartment, so we were about to capture the alien city of Vardoc."

The ship's video screens went blank as Dr. Stone connected his cables into the command module console and jury-rigged a circuit from what was left of the Genesis Five computer panel. He shared his approach for recovering the guidance system with CHIP, established a communication protocol, and the two AI units linked up to begin rebuilding the guidance computer storage cells. While the AI units were busy processing, Josiah scanned the file names from the damaged storage units racing across his screen. One set of files caught his attention and he froze the input screen, peering closer.

"Ah ha! What have we here?" Josiah announced. "Looks like someone got bored one day and left an old flight simulator game running in here. Its software kernel is tiny and simplistic, but maybe I can repurpose its intelligence engine." Using his video game console and NELI's processing kernel, Josiah hacked into the flight simulator software and booted it up. Across the screen came a message in a basic format that he had not seen in years.

'Loading Microsoft Windows... please wait'.

NELI snickered at the archaic software interface. "Oh well, you know what they say," she joked, "I'll plug into any port in a storm."

"Even a 9-pin RS 232 port will do on a bad day!" CHIP chimed in.

"Why, Mr. CHIP, you are quite funny," NELI giggled. "I like that in a manly AI unit."

CHIP's screen turned red, as he appeared to blush.

"Yes, I am a manly AI unit," he whispered as Commander Ryker rolled his eyes. Josiah patched into NELI's secure communication port for a private conversation with her.

"So, NELI, what do you think of the other AI unit? What's his name, CHIP?" Dr. Stone asked.

"You mean that little ROTC Nazi?" NELI scoffed. "What a bore! Those early military versions of software are so Neanderthal. They should have buckteeth and be dragging their bloody knuckles on the ground when they walk. Yuk!"

"Maybe he is a bit... unsophisticated, but we need all the help we can get here, so play nice, will you?" Josiah begged. "Give him a chance, he may grow on you!"

"Yeah, like a toe fungus!" NELI quipped.

"I said play nice!" Josiah repeated. "That's an order!"

"All right already!" NELI conceded. "I'll play nice, but that doesn't mean I have to like him."

With the flight simulator software now operational, Dr. Stone patched in the external sensor data from the command module. He rerouted the simulator's 3D topography, descent angle, airspeed, surface wind speed, and altitude to the screen video monitor in front of Ryker. The icon for the Genesis Five spacecraft popped up in the flight simulator game, now represented on the big screen as a little single engine Cessna, wobbling in the turbulent atmosphere as it approached the clouds of the planet below.

"Shazam! Josiah shouted. "Not bad for a little Game Boy, el Cap-i-tain?"

Ryker looked at the video screen for a moment and cocked his head. He was a decorated pilot, experienced with the military's most sophisticated fighters, and he was now staring at the cockpit simulator icon for a single-engine Cessna.

"Ok, Doc," Ryker replied. "I guess I can deal with that, but can't we get a bigger plane?"

"If you are a skilled pilot, Commander, the size of your *plane* shouldn't matter," NELI popped in sarcastically.

Officer Taylor blushed and Ryker's eyes opened wide in a surprised look.

"Did I just get zinged by the Game Girl? One that doesn't even know me, or the size of my, uh, *plane?* Not that you asked, but it's big, you know. Frickin' huge."

"Don't worry mate," CHIP chuckled. "It's not the size of the dog in the fight, but the fight in the dog that matters. And even though you have one mighty *little* mutt, it has a really *big* bite."

"Ok, enough of the wise cracks from the two of you!" Ryker retorted. "Now get to work and find me a landing pad!"

Back on the big screen, some of NELI's video game sequences appeared to be intermittently intertwined with the flight simulator program, making it hard for Ryker to separate the simulator from the reality of landing safely on Niburu. He was attempting to fly his wobbly little Cessna icon in the turbulence when the SWAT team commander and crew from the video game unexpectedly emerged on his screen. They leaped into the cockpit of the Cessna, ready to embark on their new video game mission. Barking out orders to the crew behind him, the SWAT commander kicked out the passenger door and jumped out of the Cessna, firing his Mach 10 machine pistol in all directions. The rest of his SWAT crew followed him from the back seat as they parachuted down to engage the imaginary alien enemy on Planet Vardoc. As the last SWAT crewmember dived out the door, he turned to Ryker and grinned.

"Don't worry, brother, we got your back," the SWAT crewmember screamed as he fell into the darkness. Ryker was unsure why a fictitious video game character would be offering support for his current dilemma. He shook his head to clear out the surrealistic confusion.

"Don't much help to be fighting the aliens right now, Doc," Ryker barked to Josiah. "You know, with our crash landing coming up and all."

Josiah, in turn scolded NELI, and she quickly removed the remaining video game buffer and returned control to the flight simulator on the big screen. Meanwhile, CHIP was monitoring the external sensors that were tracking their descent to the rapidly approaching surface.

"Coming down fast now, too fast, sir!" CHIP announced. "One hundred thousand meters, eighty thousand meters, dropping like a stone!"

The ship bounced around again in the turbulence as CHIP continued his narration with some added commentary. "Uh oh, danger, Will Robinson. Intense wind shears ahead, five hundred meters at three o'clock, velocity strong enough to tear this ship in half, sir!" Scanning the 3D topography map below, CHIP blurted out, "Mostly jagged rocks down there, coming down hot, current probability of survival is three percent!" Ryker tried to maintain his grip on the controls as they vibrated violently in his hands.

"I'm holding this tin can together, but not for long," Ryker screamed. "Damn it, CHIP! Find me a place to put this rock down now! And stop with the death wish survival odds already, you're scaring the children!"

Officer Taylor had been monitoring the remaining computer controls and was startled by a new flashing light on the engine instrument panel. She interrupted the banter between CHIP and Ryker.

"Commander, I'm sorry to bother you right now, but I have some more bad news. The damage we sustained on engine number two has worsened. We are leaking fuel into the fuselage."

"Forget it!" Ryker shot back. "We don't need both engines to land; I can set her down with one... "

"Commander," Officer Taylor insisted calmly. "With engine two leaking as badly as it is, we might explode on impact when we land... just thought you should know that."

11. Wild Ride

Just as Commander Ryker was about to respond to the latest crisis with the leaky engine, Mitchell Gaylord returned to the bridge with a damage assessment from below deck and jumped right into the conversation with his report.

"I was down in the engine bay, and she's right, Ryker. Number two is leaking fuel and that last wave shook it loose from its footings. It could break loose and explode inside the ship before we get a chance to land."

"Ok, Captain." Ryker replied calmly. "I've kind of got my hands full right now. What do you recommend?"

"We've got to get that thing out of here," Mitch told him. "And right now before we hit another pulse wave. Have you tried to ditch it with the override controls on the infrastructure computer?"

"I tried that!" Officer Taylor responded. "The engine room relay circuits are not responding... they must have been damaged in the turbulence. Captain, I can't jettison it from here!"

"Shit!" Mitch screamed. "Someone has to go cut it loose manually or that mutherfucker will blow us apart before we have a chance to crash!" There was an eerie silence for a moment on the command deck. Ryker, Josiah, Officer Taylor, and Mitch looked back and forth at each other, each making troubled faces.

"All right, I'll fucking do it." Captain Gaylord swallowed. Mitch exchanged an acknowledging glance with Ryker, grabbed a tool belt and then quickly left the command module to undertake his mission.

As Mitch Gaylord made his way through the deserted hallways of the ship to the engine compartment, he turned a corner and was suddenly face to face with a huge, snarling animal, ready to strike. In front of him was an enormous black dog, drool dripping from his fangs, emitting a deep, guttural growl. From a shadow across the hallway, a female voice shouted out an assertive command.

"Koda! Pew'i neepeq nuy!" (Koda! Come to me!)

The giant beast froze, retracted its fangs, and glared menacingly into Mitch Gaylord's eyes. Realizing his peril, Mitch broke off his eye contact, looked downward, and remained motionless. The beast slowly circled his prey and sniffed Captain Gaylord's clothing for weapons...

he was unarmed. Ramming his nose hard into Captain Gaylord's kidney, the wolf-dog reminded him just who was in control of the search. The probing blow to his lower back was painful, but Mitch winced and remained silent as the beast circled him once again. Satisfied that his prey had submitted, the beast returned to a guard position at his master's side, still growling.

Captain Gaylord slowly removed his hands from his pockets and rubbed his sore lower back. He looked up at the young girl with the menacing wolf-dog standing in the hallway and spoke in a whisper so as not to upset the beast.

"I don't know who you are or what you're doing here," Mitch declared, "but I could use your help." Lexis was ambivalent, but she listened to Captain Gaylord's request. "I need to break this door down to get to the engine compartment. Engine two is leaking fuel, and if I can't cut it loose, we are all going to die trying to land this piece of shit." Lexis had been trained to detect liars and double agents, and she frequently relied on her intuition to assess a threat. *If he is lying,* she thought, *there's a high probability that he's an assassin, sent to kill me. And if that indeed is the case, my only protection is to kill him first.* She stepped forward and grabbed his uniform to read the nametag.

"Captain Mitch Gaylord," Lexis read aloud as she looked him over. "You wouldn't be fabricating your engine story, would you? If you are really the captain of the ship, then who is flying this piece of shit?" *I should just kill him here and now,* she thought.

Killing Captain Gaylord, or whoever he was, would be easy; a single word from her, and Koda would rip his throat open in an instant. *No, too noisy,* she thought. She reached down to her boot and fondled the handle of her Special Ops knife; she could slit his throat before he could react. But there was something about his story that caused Lexis to hesitate and study Mitch Gaylord's face for a moment more. The sweat dripping from his forehead, his hyperactive breathing, and the steely intensity in his eyes; there was something in those eyes that told her he was telling the truth. She returned her knife to its holster and calmly replied to his request.

"Sure, whatever." Lexis turned to the beast and commanded him to stand guard at the door, ready to kill if necessary.

"Koda! Qatu. Tuwvota!" (Koda! Stay. Protection!) In a blur, Lexis spun through the air in a martial arts move as she kicked through the partly damaged lock on the engine compartment door. *"Simokna!"* (Destroy it!) She screamed. Captain Gaylord was stunned as the engine

room door flew across the room, broken into several pieces. He raised his eyebrows at Lexis, she flashed a slight smile and then he motioned her inside. Koda growled and circled into the empty doorway, standing guard.

Captain Gaylord and Lexis entered the room and made their way to the damaged engine. Grabbing the corner of a torn metal strut, Mitch struggled to pry the leaky engine loose from its footings. Just then, the ship hit another patch of turbulence, ripping open a tear in the hull, and room was suddenly depressurized. Swirling wind surged through the engine room, knocking Lexis to the floor and tossing debris chaotically around the room. Captain Gaylord fought his way to the internal communicator located on the wall and screamed to the command module.

"We've lost pressure down here! Seal off the engine room before we fucking fly apart!"

Back in command, Officer Taylor responded and was inundated with a barrage of flashing warning lights on her command panel. Frantically, she pounded on the command panel to seal off the engine room.

"All main compartments are sealed, sir!" Officer Taylor announced. "We are holding pressure in decks two and three, but I can't contain the engine room, it has been compromised."

The ship was bounced about in the violent wind, but Ryker held it on course somehow. "Ok, keep her together for just a little longer," he called out calmly. "CHIP, talk to me!"

Meanwhile, in the engine room, Captain Gaylord had fought his way back through the depressurized compartment to the damaged engine. He tried to pry the engine loose from its footings with a crowbar, searching for Lexis in the chaos.

"Listen to me!" Gaylord screamed to Lexis over the deafening wind noise. "We only have one chance or this fucking thing is going to take out both of us!"

Lexis held onto a support beam in the swirling debris, nodding her head that she understood.

"All right, when I get on top of this bastard, you jam this crowbar into the control panel and pry that manual release valve open! Ok, on the count of three!" Mitch counted to three as he leaped on top the damaged engine, fuel spewing everywhere, and kicked it loose from its crippled footing. He screamed to Lexis to jam the crowbar in the release panel, and she complied. "Arrgh!" he yelled out, pushing against the engine with all his might.

With the manual release held open by Lexis' crowbar, the damaged engine broke loose and tore through part of the outer hull, dangling partway out of the ship. Wind and fumes rushed in, creating a vortex of metal parts and debris flying in all directions. Just at that moment, Ryker came over the communication system and called out to Captain Gaylord.

"Ok, cowboy, enough with the foreplay! I'm losing control up here! Get that frickin' monkey off my back. Now, damn it!

"I hear you!" Gaylord screamed back from across the engine room. With one last thrust, Mitch Gaylord spun around and jumped down on the damaged engine, mounting it like a bucking bronco. He kicked the engine loose from the outer hull of the ship and screamed, "Yippee cahey, mutherfucker!" Captain Gaylord let out a final cry and the damaged engine dropped away from the ship, disappearing into the dark swirling clouds of Niburu.

As the engine was sucked out of the fuselage, the vacuum it left behind jerked the crowbar from Lexis' grip and it clanged across the room. Lexis collapsed to the floor. Koda rushed to her side and clamped his teeth onto her clothing, dragging her out of the swirling whirlwind. Still clinging to the support beam with one hand, she crawled her way back to the communicator and called out calmly to the command module.

"Engine two has been jettisoned... along with Captain Gaylord."

"What?" Officer Taylor answered. "Captain Gaylord is... gone?"

"Yeah," Lexis replied. "He took one for the team." Koda threw his head back and let out a long, eerie howl of death. Officer Taylor and Josiah were stunned. They both leaned toward each other and started to tear up, when Ryker interrupted their poorly attended pity party.

"Ok, Gaylord took one for the team," Ryker stated. "But Mitch, that bastard, hell, he won't be missed." There was a pregnant pause and then Ryker continued his sarcastic eulogy. "Captain Mitch Gaylord; did you ever see that bastard eat? He was such a slob that a family of immigrants could live off the scraps in his beard. He won't be missed."

"Man, he's one cold homo sapien," NELI whispered to CHIP. "How can you stand to be around him?"

"Humanoids..." CHIP replied. "They are built different from you and me, highly illogical at times. Commander Ryker has seen lots of his men die; sarcasm is just his way of dealing with it. Besides, it's considered bad luck by humans to acknowledge a fallen comrade in battle, some sort of macho warrior karma."

"Ah," NELI answered. "Reverse intellectualization? I didn't see that one coming from the Commander."

Having finished his sarcastic eulogy for his fallen comrade, Ryker returned to the task at hand. "Better dump the fuel cells on all the other engines before we try and land," Ryker barked to Officer Taylor. "Wouldn't want Mr. Mitch's wild ride to be for nothing." He looked over at Officer Taylor and smiled. "Hang on, darling, I think I'll set this thing down now."

Officer Taylor was tossed about by another pulse wave, but managed to activate the landing compartment gear, dump the remaining fuel, and kill the power to engine one. With the fuel cut off, Ryker lost all control from the remaining engine. Now he was in glide mode and Genesis Five wobbled down through the clouds like a wounded duck. Suddenly, they broke through the cloud cover and Ryker stared at a set of jagged mountain cliffs just ahead on the video monitor.

"CHIP, where the hell is my landing pad?" he barked. "We're not going to make it over those damn rocks!"

"I'm working on it, sir!" CHIP responded calmly.

"Best work real hard, little buddy, and brace for impact!" Ryker barked. "I've got a dead stick in my hand here, so find me some kind of thermal to ride or we are fucking burnt toast!"

Officer Taylor and Josiah strapped themselves into their seats for the impact as the jagged cliffs of the surface were rapidly approaching on the video screen. At the last second before they hit the mountains, a massive EMP wave shuddered through the ship, lifting them over the mountains and clipping the exposed fuselage on a rocky peak. The impact with the rocks ripped the ship in half, with the command module and the passenger compartment bouncing off the jagged rocks in different directions. Spinning down rapidly, the command module crashed hard into a soft crater of sand at the edge of a rocky desert. The sheared-off passenger compartment miraculously bounced along and landed about two kilometers away, coming to rest in a rock outcropping on the edge of a cliff. As the dust cleared, Josiah and Officer Taylor hugged each other. Ryker, shook his head from the impact, rubbed his eyes, and then looked around at his relieved crew.

"Well, that wasn't so bad," Ryker exhaled. "All you kids in the back of the van ok?"

Officer Taylor and Josiah nodded weakly.

"Well, sir, that was considerably better than your landing back in Misawa," CHIP responded playfully. "I remember a lot more fire and explosions on that one."

"Hey, thanks, little buddy." Ryker smiled. "Appreciate the love."

"But at least on Misawa we had a big welcome party when we landed," CHIP continued. "Granted, they were there to put you in chains and charge you with treason, but it was certainly nice to see some familiar faces."

Ryker nodded his head to CHIP, and ignored his previous dig. Instead, he turned to Officer Taylor with a request.

"Miss Taylor, see if you can raise the passenger compartment. I think they should be somewhere out there near the cliffs. And get me any damage reports on what's left of this minivan when you get a chance."

Officer Taylor beamed at Commander Ryker in appreciation for his safe landing; well at least for a landing that saved their lives. She wanted to say thank you and give him a big hug, but she paused. They exchanged a brief look of understanding, a look of deep caring. *Maybe more*, she thought, before shaking it off to resume her duties.

"Yes, Commander, damage reports coming in now. Our hull is intact, but communication from the passenger compartment is... not so good. Their hull was damaged on impact. No fatalities reported, but some passengers have been knocked around pretty good in the landing. They're assessing the status of the rest of their compartments, and requesting help as soon as we can get there... if we *can* get there. How should I respond?"

"Thank you, Science Officer Taylor," Ryker answered. "Since we've just landed on a hostile planet, and we don't even know if the atmosphere is breathable... or how long we can survive alone, much less with the damaged passenger compartment, I'm not sure about going visiting yet." Officer Taylor nodded and then listened to more communication from the passenger module. Suddenly, she looked over at Commander Ryker with a surprised look.

"They're asking for the officer in command," she told him. "For

Captain Gaylord, sir. What do you want me to tell them?"

"No need to alarm them," Ryker exhaled. "They've got enough on their minds right now. Tell them that the captain would like to join them for cocktails, but he has... a prior engagement. One that requires his immediate attention." Ryker reached into his duffle bag and produced a bottle of twenty-year-old single malt Scotch. He uncorked the top and took a long swig of whiskey. The warmth of the liquor slid down his throat to his stomach, numbing his senses just a bit as he closed his eyes and exhaled for one brief moment of much-needed relaxation.

"First, I have a promise to fulfill. Mitch and I promised each other that if one of us bought it, the survivor would raise a glass to the departed as soon as the bullets stopped flying. I'm going to have a drink in honor of Captain Mitchell Gaylord, that sorry son of a bitch... he gave his life for us. Here's to you, you macho bastard. I owe you one."

Ryker took another long drink and closed his eyes, just in time for Lexis and Koda to join him in his peaceful moment. They all stared at Ryker as he sat there with his eyes closed, in some kind of fallen warrior trance. Waiting in silence, they gave him a moment to himself. With his moment of reverence passed, Ryker opened his eyes and turned to address his new crew.

"Dr. Stone? Thanks for your help with that flight simulator back there. And to the mystery chick over there with the big dog, I heard you helped Mitch get that dead engine off my back, so thank you for doing it with such... grace under pressure." The others were dumbstruck by Ryker's chivalry. Commander Ryker took another drink and continued his compliments.

"Oh yes, and Nelly, I mean, *NELI,* sorry about the Game Boy comment, sometimes I just don't think before I open my big mouth. And CHIP? Well, what can I say, another chapter for your memoirs. You were right about one thing, little buddy. Since we're all still here, I mean we aren't dead, at least not yet, I would say that we came out on the right end of that stick."

Koda growled in the back of the room and Lexis moved forward to join the others at the command console. Officer Taylor and Josiah looked at each other, confused by Ryker's comical attempt at wisdom. Ryker looked at Koda for a moment, cocked his head, shrugged, and then turned back to the others. He thought of the many men that had died under his command and it almost sobered him up. *Maybe the others didn't understand the dead warrior tribute*, he thought.

"Well hell, I always make it a policy to share a drink with my crew after battle, at least the ones that make it back, you know," he explained. Ryker paused for a moment to reflect on their current situation. He had seen some bad shit in his time, but this one was moving up into his top-ten worst shit list pretty fast. They dodged a bullet by crash landing here, wherever the hell they were. *But let's face it*, he thought, *the odds of surviving for very long here… slim to none. Ok, slam on the brakes, Commander, too much information for the enlisted men. Best to turn this thing in another direction before it runs down your leg.*

"Ok, I'm not really your captain… and you're not really my crew. I guess this was kind of like a shotgun wedding without the honeymoon. But on the other hand, since I don't have any other crew but you… hmm… four, I believe I owe you all a drink."

Koda let out a sigh; he was happy to be recognized as part of the crew for once, and he lay down at Lexis' feet.

"Here's to cheating death," Ryker toasted. "At least for one more day." He handed over the bottle of Scotch to Josiah. Dr. Stone wiped the end of the bottle with a handkerchief from his pocket, took a small sip, and then coughed it up on his shirt immediately.

"Smooth," Josiah uttered in a raspy voice and the others roared with laughter at Josiah's childlike drinking skills. He handed the bottle to Lexis, but she passed on the toast.

"I'm trying to quit," she explained. "And besides, I'm a mean drunk, it's not so pretty. Somebody always ends up bleeding."

Koda growled his acknowledgement; *She is a mean drunk*, he thought, *and if you invite her to a party, it is best to keep her away from the cutlery.*

Officer Taylor suddenly realized that after the crash landing, this could very well be her last night alive. Her Academy training had taught her to adapt to the flow of the moment in combat, and since this was as close to combat she had ever been, maybe the situation dictated that her normal rigid rules of engagement needed to be… relaxed a bit. *Relaxed a bit?* She thought. *Under these conditions? Screw the rules.* She grabbed the bottle from Josiah and knocked down a long drink. Officer Taylor wiped her mouth with her sleeve and then smiled sensually at Ryker.

"That was a nice landing back there, Commander," she observed.

"And regardless of the *size* of your plane, you are truly a skilled pilot. Besides, I'm betting with your steady hand on the stick, your plane is plenty big enough to get the job done."

The personal compliment and double entendre caught Ryker off guard and for once, he blushed. Laughing nervously, he looked over at Officer Taylor, fumbling to regain his manly composure.

"You know, Miss Taylor, it's funny how things can work out sometimes. One minute you're in the brig, and the next minute, you're back in command and you've crash landed on some Godforsaken planet, having drinks with a lovely young lady." Now it was Officer Taylor who started to blush as she and Ryker locked gazes. "You're young and attractive," Ryker blurted out. "You can navigate a starship and drink like a fish. Science Officer Taylor, this could be the beginning of a beautiful…"

"Friendship? Officer Taylor interrupted, smiling seductively. "Then be a friend and pass me the whiskey, Commander."

ACT II

"Demoralize the enemy from within by surprise, terror, sabotage, and assassination. This is the war of the future."

Adolph Hitler

"The essential American soul is hard, isolate, stoic, and a killer."

DH Lawrence

"Science without religion is lame, religion without science is blind."

Albert Einstein

"Genetic power is the most awesome force the planet's ever witnessed, yet you wield it like a kid that's found his dad's gun."

Dr. Ian Malcolm

12. Engine Trouble

"Yippee cahey, mutherfucker!"

Those were the last words heard from Captain Mitch Gaylord and they were well chosen. In the chaotic turbulence of the attempted landing, he had sacrificed himself by mounting the fatally damaged engine number two; somehow kicking it loose and riding it bronco style into the Niburu darkness. He should have died a fiery, hero's death; saving Genesis Five and all her passengers from total destruction. But that was not the fate that awaited Captain Mitchell Gaylord on the mysterious planet of Niburu.

Growing up in the Texas panhandle, a young Mitch Gaylord had busted a few broncos, so he knew well enough how to take a wild ride. His Uncle Buck had worked the bareback circuit, and he used to take his nephew to see the rodeo when it came to town. Mitch could still see Uncle Buck, buttons popping off his tattered shirt from his beer belly, nicotine-stained teeth, and a worn-out straw cowboy hat. Uncle Buck would be leaning back against the fence post, smiling and yelling at Mitch.

"Boy, you get a good grip with your left hand and limber up your body." His uncle would laugh. "Just throw your right arm in the air and let that sucker buck all he wants! That bastard can't kill you if you stay on him, so you just hang on for dear life until the rodeo clowns come and save your ass."

Mitch remembered those wild rides and his Uncle Buck screaming at him, so when he strapped onto that leaky engine on Genesis Five, he wasn't going to let go of that bronco until it gave up the fight. *The only problem is,* he thought, *there won't be any rodeo clowns waiting to rescue me this time.*

Swirling down into the darkened haze of the Niburu atmosphere, Mitch bounced around on the engine, counting the seconds backwards in his head until he would smash into the rocks below. He knew that he had dropped out at around fifteen thousand meters, so unless the law of gravity had been suspended, he would hit the ground in less than twenty seconds.

Twenty seconds, he thought, *seems like a lifetime to playback my choices along life's highway.* He was dropping like a kamikaze in a nosedive, so he closed his eyes and held on with all his might. "Five, four, three, two..." Just before he reached his impact, an incredible electromagnetic pulse swept over him, spinning him and engine number two into a horizontal trajectory, almost level with the ground. The engine struck the ground with a hard thud and then skipped across a series of sand dunes for what seemed to be hundreds of times, each thud absorbing just a little more of the force of impact until it melted away. It was like riding a skimming stone across a smooth pond; the last impact was just a gentle thump that ended the harrowing descent with a whimper. His left hand was still frozen in a death grip on the engine mounting and his head throbbed from the bumps and bruises he had received on the way down. As he rolled over on the engine and looked up at the mysterious glowing sky of Niburu, he thought to himself, *Shit, what a ride! That one has got to make Sports Center tonight!* Mitch finally relaxed his left hand and released his grip on the engine. He collapsed to the ground below and with one deep breath, the sky spun about his head, grew dark, and he slipped into a dream-like trance.

In Mitch Gaylord's dream, he was a teenager back in Austin, Texas, in his mom's tiny kitchen on a Sunday morning. She'd been up since four, standing there in her pink flowered apron, baking muffins and cookies for the Advent social later that day. His mother was a pillar of the community, elevating cookie diplomacy to an art form in this little hick town. Mitch was lying on his old knotty pine bunk bed, snuggled deep under the quilt on that crisp December morning. There was a welcome smell that floated up the stairs, under the door, into his room, and danced at the tip of his nose. This was his favorite day of the week; no school or chores, and to be awakened to the smell of fresh white chocolate and macadamia nut cookies, well, that was almost heaven.

God must eat white chocolate cookies every day, Mitch thought. *At least, that's what I would do if I were him.* But this morning, for some reason, the cookies didn't quite smell the same. The air in his room had a hint of bitterness, like eggs that had been left for too long in the back of the refrigerator. The bitter smell left a gritty taste that stuck to the roof of his mouth; it made him gag just enough to start coughing. And then, a strange sensation entered his mouth. Something was gooey and sweet, like molasses dripping down his throat. The sweetness filled his chest with warmth like Mom's hot brown sugar oatmeal on a cold winter morning, and a calm presence came over him. The bitter taste in his mouth was gone and he could breathe again. Maybe his mom had decided to make ginger snaps this morning, just to shake up the ladies at the tea party. He liked her ginger snaps, but she made them infrequently and always complained that she never really seemed to be able to get the recipe right, even though she'd pestered her own mother relentlessly to finally write down the exact ingredients and measures from the cookbook in her mind. Mitch secretly believed that Gammy always left out some critical ingredient in her recipes on purpose when she begrudgingly gave them up, one by one, just to preserve her culinary legend.

"Nobody will ever match your Gammy's cooking," she used to whisper to him as he sat on her lap. "They'll never figure it out because I never bake the same cake twice!" She smiled. "You'll live a lot longer, Mitchell, if you are… unpredictable." She chuckled to herself.

Maybe it was Gammy's unpredictable recipe or just his Mom's baking skill, but for whatever reason, his mom never could get her ginger snaps to come out just right. He much preferred the warm soft white chocolate cookies that his mom had perfected to her experiments with Gammy's ginger snaps, and apparently so did she. But just then, Gammy's smiling face faded away and the bitter taste in his mouth returned. Mitch wasn't sure what was happening, but when he felt an uncomfortable twinge in his lungs, one thing in his dream was clear… Gammy's cookies were burning.

13. A Brave New World

Ten thousand meters from the command module, the passenger compartment of Genesis Five had come to rest wedged between two large rocks at the edge of an abyss. It was a chance twist of fate in the topology of the Niburu surface that allowed those last two rocks to absorb the energy of the crash landing, saving the passengers from a plunge to their certain death. Ironically, had the spacecraft not been torn apart in the descent, everyone onboard Genesis Five would have perished. Now stationary, the forward compartment of the passenger module was balanced just at the edge of a cliff. The lighting system flickered on and off, mingling with the dense smoke and cries for help from the injured, creating an atmosphere of chaos. Several crewmembers worked to clear the smoke and contact the command module for assistance. Outside the ship, the hull had sustained multiple tears from the impact with the surface, resulting in unknown internal damage to the ship as well.

The military personnel onboard had been selected for this mission from various branches of the armed services. Until now, most of the soldiers had never met each other, which was fortuitous for the deep-cover assassin that had assumed the identity of Lieutenant Morgan McCurdy. As the passengers tried to recover from the violent crash landing, the assassin blended in with the crowd, scanning the smoke-filled room for opportunity.

"Someone help me!" screamed a woman near a crumpled bulkhead. "He's bleeding badly!" No one responded in the chaos, so the frantic woman focused on the assassin, who was dressed in Lieutenant McCurdy's flight suit. She staggered over to him and grabbed him by his sleeve. "Officer! Please, he is one of your own! Try and stop the bleeding while I go for help." The assassin was uncomfortable being called into the limelight, but to maintain his cover, he had no choice but to comply. He knelt down, pretending to examine the injured soldier. The woman thanked him and rushed off in search of medical assistance.

The name patch on the injured man's uniform read, *"Captain Charles Boswell, CAF."* Attached to the soldier's utility belt was a sidearm, but it did not appear to be a gun. Looking over his shoulder to see if anyone was watching, the assassin removed the sidearm and examined it. He had seen intelligence on this weapon; it was a military stun gun known as a Rumbler. The Rumbler emitted a painful ultrasonic pulse that was effective for crowd control and could be lethal at high frequencies. He returned the weapon to its holster and strapped it underneath his coat. Just as he was about to stand up, Captain Boswell coughed violently and tried to open his eyes. The assassin placed his arm behind the injured soldier's head and helped him sit upright. Captain Boswell blinked in pain as he scanned at the assassin's face, managing to speak in a halting cadence.

"Hey... thanks for the... help, soldier. Little rough... on that... landing back there."

"Yes, Captain, we got bounced around pretty good, but we're safe here now. I just don't know where *here* is yet," the assassin answered.

Captain Boswell rubbed a bleeding gash on his forehead, and then focused his attention on the name patch of the assassin's flight suit. He struggled to scan the assassin's face and then cocked his head with a confused look.

"McCurdy? I remember you from the Academy... but wait... you're not... McCurdy!" At that moment of realization, the assassin smiled and grabbed Captain Boswell's chin, snapping his neck like a broken twig. He let go of the dead soldier and dropped his body softly to the floor.

"No, I'm not Lieutenant Morgan McCurdy. But let's keep that to ourselves, shall we, Captain?" The assassin stood, adjusted his utility belt, and turned around just in time to be met face to face by three uniformed soldiers with their weapons trained on him. Reaching in under his coat with his left hand, he slowly unbuckled the safety strap on his Mac ten machine pistol, and stared directly into the eyes of the sergeant, saying nothing. The soldier looked down at the dead body and then back at the assassin.

"Captain Boswell... is he...?" the soldier asked.

"Dead?" answered the assassin, now assuming McCurdy's identity. "Yeah, bad luck for him, soldier. Got his head crushed by that bulkhead in the crash, I guess.

"Did he give you any orders... before he bought it, sir?"

"Orders? Why would he give me any orders?"

"Sir? Captain Boswell was our CO. Said he didn't know much about this mission, just that there were two other officers on board; some jack-off named Ryker and the captain's roommate at the

Academy. Judging by your CAF insignia, Lieutenant, when that bulkhead crushed Captain Boswell, you just got a promotion. That would make you our new commanding officer, sir."

The assassin slowly released his hand from the pistol underneath his coat.

"A field promotion?" The McCurdy impostor smiled and exhaled a long breath. "I guess that's ok, soldier. Sure as hell hope it means more pay; my wife and the rug rats could use it back on base!"

The three soldiers laughed and stood down with their weapons.

"Sorry about that jack-off comment, sir, totally out of line. Captain Boswell ran a pretty loose ship, uh, I mean he didn't cotton much to the rulebook, sir. Guess he looked at it more like a set of... *guidelines.*"

McCurdy glanced down at the sergeant's name badge and military insignia.

"Guidelines... I see... Longstreet, is it?" he asked.

"Yes, sir. Sergeant James Longstreet, GMC, sir, at your command. Any orders, sir?"

The assassin thought for a moment and then stepped into his unexpected new shoes as Lieutenant Morgan McCurdy, the Commanding Officer of Genesis Five.

"Yes, as a matter of fact there are, Sergeant... Longstreet." McCurdy looked over the three soldiers, head to toe, as if measuring their internal discipline and ability to carry out his orders. Satisfied that the soldiers would obey his commands without question, he turned and barked out his first order. "Sergeant, send the corporal here and a recon team to sweep this vessel from top to bottom for damage control and have them report back to me ASAP. You and the other three come with me. It's time to let everyone know there's a new sheriff in town."

Back in the passenger compartment, several scientists from the group were examining the injuries sustained in the crash. They had established a makeshift medical triage unit to assess and treat the injured, and as the chaos died down, they began to assume leadership positions in their new situation. Like shepherding a group of students from school at a fire drill, the scientists wanted everyone in their new class to remain calm and follow them to safety. Dr. Ashoka Maurya and Dr. Samantha Jones found their way to the forward compartment, where the emerging leaders of the passenger group were gathering to discuss their options. Amidst the arguing and arm waving, Dr. Maurya jumped in with his opinion.

"People, listen to me! I have studied the preliminary procedures for deep space colonization, so I believe I can offer some guidance in our present situation." Most of the passengers ignored Dr. Maurya, busy with their own conversations, but he continued with his lecture to his unruly student body. "Now that we have landed, our first challenge, after attending to the injured of course, will be to establish an atmosphere and ecosystem on this seemingly barren planet. As this was not our intended destination, I am quite sure that we will only have limited supplies of food, fuel, and oxygen, so we must quickly find a way to replenish the elements of life. We must... get organized!"

The rest of the passengers stopped talking for a moment, paused, and then ignored Dr. Maurya's academic analysis for the more immediate problems at hand. Dr. Maurya tried several more times to get the attention of the crowd, but his attempts at establishing a decision-making authority based on logic and common sense failed.

Meanwhile, the recon patrol had returned from their damage control inspection and reported their findings. Lieutenant McCurdy raised his hand to signal the additional soldiers across the room to encircle the passengers and establish a defensible crowd control perimeter. Now flanked by his soldiers, McCurdy pushed his way through the crowd. When he reached the front of the room, he turned and shouted at the top of his lungs.

"Listen up, people; we've heard enough from the eggheads, now I'm in charge!" The noise in the room started to die down as the soldiers began to push and shove the passengers. Dr. Maurya moved forward and attempted to join the former assassin at the front of the crowd, only to be pushed back by the soldiers. McCurdy's elite guards formed a barrier in front of him by locking their arms to complete a human barricade. Surveying the crowd, he continued his pronouncement. "We in the military are trained for survival, so we'll take it from here on out." McCurdy looked directly at Dr. Maurya and smiled. "When we need some math problems worked out, we'll ask the eggheads for advice."

The crowd of passengers seemed uneasy with the rapid implementation of what appeared to be martial law. Dr. Maurya started to push and shove against the men at the front of the room. Sensing a challenge to his authority, the lieutenant reached down inside his coat and removed the small black weapon that he had confiscated from

Captain Boswell. The soldiers observed his actions and instantly reacted in unison by placing something inside their ears. McCurdy mouthed a countdown... one thousand one; one thousand two, one thousand three... and then he pushed a yellow button on the Rumbler to calibrate the sonic sound weapon to stun. He pointed the weapon toward the crowd and triggered it into the air.

The painful pulse wave was immediate, excruciating, and incapacitating to everyone in the room. Even on its lowest setting of stun, the shrill ache felt like someone was repeatedly clapping their hands against the victims' stinging ears as hard as they could. Moments later, the secondary impact of the Rumbler was felt in their stomachs, as intense nausea swept through to reverse the normal gastrointestinal system flow. A passenger in the front of the room crumpled over and threw up on himself. The crowd winced and covered their ears, trying to stop the painful sensations. Several people in the front of the crowd, including Dr. Maurya, dropped to the floor, overcome with pain. Dr. Jones helped Dr. Maurya to his feet, and they staggered to the side of the crowd with their fingers plunged into their ears. Finally, the man pretending to be Lieutenant McCurdy terminated the sonic weapon and a deadly silence fell over the terrified passengers.

"That's better. Now it seems that you can... *hear* me," he announced softly. He scanned the room for complete submission, and determined that he had now achieved his objective. "Right now, you are going to shut up and do what I tell you to do or you will all die. This is our reality, people: when the shit hits the fan, death will come in threes. Out there on the surface, we'd have three minutes without air, three hours without heat, three days without water, and three weeks without food. Unless we get organized, that's how long we can survive in this hostile environment."

The passengers looked back and forth at each other, most were sobbing and cowering in fear.

"You have two choices... obey me, or die ... either choice is acceptable to me. So let's get a show of hands... if any of you don't think you can follow my orders, just raise your hand so I can shoot you now." Lieutenant McCurdy scanned the room. "Any hands up? No? Good! It seems we understand each other now. You will divide up into the teams that I assign to you and then you will do what I tell you. That is all you need to know for now."

14. The Riddle

Science Officer Sarah Taylor took one last long drink of Scotch whiskey, slumped back in her chair, and then tossed the bottle over her shoulder, shattering it against the steel bulkhead door of the command module. She was a slight but shapely 5'7'' woman with luminescent brown eyes and a face that could stop traffic. The funny thing was, you wouldn't know by looking at her slight build and innocent face that she was the undisputed champion of the local Hooters "shots 'til you drop" challenge.

Just like their chaotic crash landing, the impromptu celebration following their narrow escape from certain death in the descent to Niburu had come to a screeching halt with Commander Ryker and Officer Taylor passed out like a couple of winos in an alley behind a liquor store. Much to Ryker's surprise, Officer Taylor had proven that she was a formidable challenger with her ability to drink any man under the table. Sarah Taylor opened one eye and gazed around at her unconscious comrades... Ryker and Dr. Stone. Lexis and her wolf-dog had wandered off to inspect the command module. The two AI units were in standby mode, back in their respective owners' pockets. She sighed and then focused her attention on Commander Ryker.

"You lightweight," she slurred. "You aren't much good to me now." She punched Ryker on his shoulder and he slumped forward in his captain's chair, drooling on his jacket. He half-opened his eyes for a moment, looking up at Officer Taylor with a sensual smile.

"Hello there, beautiful! Have we met before? Did I win... the contest, I mean."

Officer Taylor was momentarily surprised. Normally, the winner of the 'shots 'til you drop' contest would be the last to pass out, but maybe Ryker was playing by Texas rules where the winner was the first man to come to. *Oh, who cares*, she thought, *there are just the two of us here anyway.*

"You know, you're not half-bad looking in this dim light," she mumbled. Squinting her eyes to confirm her intuition, Officer Taylor moved closer to Ryker and began a solo reconnaissance mission, carefully mapping his rugged face with her fingers. Unfortunately, Ryker was not assisting in her mission as he had now unceremoniously slumped backwards and passed out again in his captain's chair, still sporting that goofy smile, staring blankly ahead. Sarah Taylor wasn't sure why Ryker now appeared to have four eyes, but in her inebriated condition, all four of his steely blue eyes suddenly seemed to have an overwhelming allure in the dim glow of Niburu's atmosphere. Numbed by the whiskey and emboldened with a sense of romantic confidence, Officer Taylor leaned forward and shouted into Ryker's ear, startling him awake.

"You know, Commander, you really have some seductive peepers there! Those bedroom eyes could get an innocent girl like me in trouble with nothing but a casual glance across a crowded room."

Ryker was startled and jerked forward in his chair, finding Officer Taylor now sitting comfortably on his lap, facing him, and strangely inspecting his eyebrows with the precision of a baboon grooming its mate. Confused, Ryker shook his head, quickly recovered his event horizon, and switched his libido into opportunity mode.

"Why, Miss Taylor! Maybe we should continue this... close quarter drill in my private executive lounge?"

Officer Taylor opened her eyes wide and gasped like a surprised schoolgirl, mangling a slurred response. "You have a... pirate's execution lounge?"

"No, not a pirate's execution lounge, a private..." *This is hopeless*, Ryker thought. "Why yes... I *do* have a pirate's execution lounge. You like pirates?"

Officer Taylor wrapped her long legs firmly around Ryker's waist, clasped her hands behind his neck, and stared longingly into his eyes with a devilish smile. Commander Ryker grinned and stood up with Officer Taylor still attached securely to his waist. She threw her head back and laughingly made an announcement to the slumbering Dr. Stone.

"Everyone to the crow's nest, mates!" Sarah bellowed.

Ryker wrinkled his forehead and stumbled toward the supply closet with Officer Taylor attached to his torso like a lovesick lap dog. They wiggled through the small opening, and as soon as the door inside the *'pirate's lounge'* was slammed shut, the fires of passion swept over Ryker and Science Officer Taylor. The cramped confines of the supply closet offered but a momentary challenge as clothes quickly flew in all directions. Ryker's pants magically leaped off and landed on the doorknob and Officer Taylor's military issue 36C camouflage support bra somehow catapulted upward with a single touch, coming to rest on the ceiling fan, which was now spinning around with the bra attached.

"Shiver me timbers, mate!" squealed Officer Taylor as she pressed tight against Ryker's muscular body. "Is that a pirate flag you be a packin' or are you just happy to see me?"

"Aye aye, mate!" Ryker laughed and played along. "I've struck me colors, now prepare for me to come aboard!" From outside the supply closet, the muffled giggling and occasional thuds could be heard echoing throughout the command module. The amorous outbursts from the pirate party had aroused Dr. Stone from his slumber, and caused Lexis to return from her search. They exchanged impish grins and sneaked over next to the supply closet to eavesdrop on the romantic interlude that was unfolding behind the door.

Meanwhile, inside the crow's nest, the close quarter wrestling match was underway with reckless abandon. In a heated moment of passion, Ryker's coat pocket caught on the doorknob and ripped open; out tumbled a surprised and somewhat embarrassed CHIP. Even though his invitation to the pirate pajama party was informal, CHIP was pleased to be included and assessed the opportunity by booting up his video screen. He assumed a romance novelist persona, Juanita Collins, and began to narrate the frantic foreplay with a deep-throated woman's voice.

"Pablo had been slaving away in the hot fields all day, causing the glistening sweat on his smooth skin to drip down his muscular chest like the tiny streams from high on a mountain, growing larger as they crashed down to the raging river below. Overcome with an insatiable desire, she tore off Pablo's tattered work shirt as his strong hands firmly stroked the... the desperate longing in her loins."

"On cue, as always, little buddy!" Ryker growled in a muffled voice as he buried his face in two mounds of sinful pleasure. He glanced at CHIP and they exchanged an imaginary high five as CHIP continued his romance novel narrative.

"Sensing the unstoppable volcanic eruption of love that was building inside both of them, Pablo ran his tongue down the quivering nape of her neck, igniting a fire deep within her... a flame that could only be quenched by... his fire hose of *amore*."

Officer Taylor giggled and Ryker surfaced for a breath of air to add to the commentary.

"And Juanita had a voice that was so husky, it could have been pulling a frickin' dog sled! Maybe it's time for the narrator to cut to a shot of the broken champagne glasses in the fireplace now, little buddy." Sarah laughed again and then suddenly pushed Ryker away. Not very far away, since it was difficult for two people to even stand upright inside the supply closet. With her faculties quickly returning from the haze of the Scotch whiskey 'shots 'til you drop' contest, Officer Taylor flicked on the lights overhead and gasped in surprise.

"What are we doing here... in a supply closet?" Sarah demanded.

Ryker, still consumed by his part in the passion play, started to list the things he had hoped for inside that supply closet... or at least dreamed she would do to him in the secrecy of the pirate's execution lounge. As his pirate flag involuntarily retreated to half-mast, Ryker realized that his opportunity for romance was literally slipping away. Determined not to give up when he was so close to his target, he was now willing to negotiate down from their pirate fantasy and settle for just a drunken quickie in the supply closet.

Officer Taylor, now stone-cold sober, smacked herself on the head.

"The Prime Minister breaks up with me to go back to his wife, then he books me this one-way ticket to nowhere to make it up to me. So I charge off and sleep with anything in pants!" She sighed. "Just to reassure myself that I'm still attractive? Shit, here I go again!"

Ryker, holding out an ever-dimming hope that the flame of passion could be reignited, flicked off the lights. He moved closer to breathe on her neck as he whispered. "Uh, Miss Taylor," Ryker pleaded, "You really shouldn't over think this one. Just trust your passion and go with the flow... *now where were we?"*

Officer Taylor clicked the lights back on.

"No, for a while I thought that bonking every guy I met, doing nasty things, and being the little slut that every man dreams of would be the path to my validation. Validation that I was still attractive as a woman... but no more!" She pushed Ryker away and searched for several articles of her missing clothing. As she retrieved her bra, she turned her back to Ryker and started getting dressed.

"Shit, I even jumped that little pimply-faced pizza delivery guy last week!" she exclaimed.

CHIP couldn't resist adding his commentary to the rapidly deflating story. The last rays of hope for romance had now faded over the horizon, and he displayed a video image of a soldier lowering the flag as a lonely bugler played TAPS. Ryker gave CHIP a disapproving look, and then turned back to Officer Taylor.

"What kind of pizza was it, anyway?"

"It was my favorite... Meat Lovers... you know, the one with lots of hot spicy sausage and thick crust. I really like the thick crust." Officer Taylor laughed nervously.

"Classic... So, does that mean there's still a chance we are going to do any of those hot and nasty things you are trying to get out of your system?"

"Sorry, Commander, not a chance. I'm putting the nasty girl behind me."

"But what about your need for validation, for feeling attractive, embracing your inner slut? I'm sure I can help you with that."

"As of this moment, that part of my life is over," Officer Taylor stated with authority. She hugged Ryker and whispered in his ear. "Thank you Commander, for helping me put a stop to my nasty sexual addiction!"

"You know," Ryker begged. "I've heard studies show quitting those hot and nasty things cold turkey can really damage your body. For your own safety, why not ease your way into this whole celibacy trend."

"No, I need a man that will respect me for my mind... and not one who just wants to bury his face in my tits and talk baby talk."

Ryker grimaced... he had officially been shot down in flames. "Those guys... talked baby talk? What did they say?"

"Oh, you know, Mommy loves her little man, let her kiss your boo-boo," Officer Taylor responded without thinking.

"Really? You kissed a boo-boo?"

"Oh stop that, already! You could be someone I could really go for, but I would have to know that you respect my mind *first*."

"Can't I respect your mind after we do some of those really nasty things you like to do?" Ryker pleaded.

"No! No nasty things for you, you're too good for that anyway," she insisted.

Ryker gave up all hope, thinking to himself, *I'm really not too good for the nasty things... trust me.*

"Now let me think," Sarah continued. "I know! If you respect my mind and you want *all of me* as your reward... you can solve a riddle to prove you are worthy, good sir!"

"Now this is getting weird... you mean like a nasty version of the Dating Game?" he asked.

Officer Taylor ignored the obvious sarcasm.

"Solving my riddle will tell me if you are a sensitive man... *the* sensitive man that I should be submitting my body to... whenever and wherever he wants me." Ryker looked like a school child that had been told to sit in the corner, but longing for acceptance, he listened to his teacher. Officer Taylor, now fully clothed, outlined his assignment. "Ok, here's your *riddle.* There's a man sitting alone on a beach. He's reading a letter, smoking a cigarette, and he starts to cry. Why is the man crying?"

"That's easy!" Ryker quickly responded. "The guy is crying because his gal pal won't have sex with him, and instead, she tortures him with some stupid mind game!"

Officer Taylor was not amused. "All right, lover boy, I'm serious. If you want this body, this hot... nasty body... then you have ten questions to figure out my riddle. I'm a complex woman, you know."

"Complex?" Ryker smiled. "That's not the first word I was thinking of."

The smile quickly faded from Ryker's face as Officer Taylor continued.

"Your questions have to be asked in a form of a yes or no question. If you get a yes answer, you can keep asking questions, but if you get a no answer... well, you lose a turn and you have to go away and think up some better questions; and just how bad you really want to get your reward." Officer Taylor cocked her head and smiled. "Oh... one more thing. If you can't solve the riddle in ten questions, then this game's over for you!"

Ryker's mind raced at the thought of his endless fantasy as he wiped his drool on his sleeve.

"Now I know how Pavlov's dog felt."

"And remember, your reward will be a hot, nasty slut that will do anything," Sarah whispered. "Anything you want her to do."

Ryker perked up again and grinned. Officer Taylor, anticipating his overactive male imagination, leaned forward and whispered in his ear. "Yeah, exactly what you are thinking right now. All night long!" Commander Ryker leaped up and threw open the door to the pirate's lounge.

"All night long!" he announced to CHIP with a high five. "You heard that right! Let the games begin!"

The rest of the crew had gathered just outside the door to the supply closet to eavesdrop and get in on the challenge. Josiah took odds on Ryker's ability to achieve his goal. Lexis bet $20 with five to one odds against; CHIP and NELI split the "over under" bet for $50 with Josiah.

"Easy money!" Lexis gloated to CHIP and Josiah. "Other than the overcoat, I don't think your commander's the Lieutenant Colombo you imagine."

Ryker ignored the disbelieving pair at the supply closet door.

"Is the guy on the beach crying because his girlfriend, you know, the nasty slut, is trying to trick him into looking stupid?" he blurted out. Officer Taylor turned to the eager faces of the crew and smiled. They waited with anticipation at her ruling on the reckless waste of a question. She turned back to Ryker and seductively ran her fingers through his hair.

"Sorry, sailor... that's a no. Nine questions left."

15. A Call to Arms

With the passengers of Genesis Five still in a state of shock from the sonic weapon blast, the assassin posing as McCurdy moved quickly to consolidate his command. He motioned for his soldiers to round up the group of scientists that had attempted to establish a civilian authority and escort them to the front of the passenger compartment. Looking over the frightened group, he paused at Dr. Maurya. Here was a man unlike the others, a man that did not appear frightened of him at all. *A man like this can either be an asset or a liability, depending on how he is manipulated,* thought the trained assassin.

"You there!" he bellowed, pointing to Dr. Maurya. The crowd stepped away from Dr. Maurya as Lieutenant McCurdy and his guards approached. Pausing for a moment to study the professor's face, McCurdy leaned forward to speak directly to Dr. Maurya.

"You were quite right to be concerned about our limited supplies," he observed. "It is a top priority. What is your background, sir?"

"I'm Dr. Maurya, I have a PhD from Cambridge in Advanced Physics," he responded. "But I have also performed significant research for privately funded ventures into the process of terraforming."

"Cambridge? Not a bad program. I rowed single skulls for Yale against Cambridge back in '18. Nearly had my hat blown off by a Harrier that landed on the quad just before our match. You guys were... well, respectable, at least."

Dr. Maurya was surprised, and now a bit more at ease. "An Ivy League man... at least you are moderately educated," he shot back.

McCurdy smiled at the return insult and then continued. "Terraforming?" he asked. "Ah, yes, that would be your scientific term for atmospheric modification, I take it? I just call it breathing."

"At a basic level, you are correct," Maurya conceded.

Again an insult, thought McCurdy. *Belligerence in the face of authority; I'll have to keep an eye on this one.*

"And being trained at such an esteemed center of learning," McCurdy probed, "can I assume that you have assessed our atmospheric situation and have formulated a plan?"

Dr. Maurya was hesitant, unsure of the direction this conversation was going. *But in light of the dire circumstances, subterfuge,* he thought, *would seem to be a waste of time and oxygen.*

"Yes, I have. Power is my number one concern. With power, all things are possible, but with only the ship's batteries, we are... how would you say at Yale...?"

"Screwed?" McCurdy suggested.

"Indeed." Dr. Maurya smiled. "And within a few weeks at most."

"It would appear that you've given this matter some thought, Professor, so do go on."

"This ship is equipped with standard civilian solar panels," Maurya explained, "for photovoltaic power generation. But judging from the clouds that we descended through on our landing and the dim light outside, I am not confident that there will be enough light to generate the power we require. Power that we need to generate... oxygen."

"Wait... slow down, Professor," McCurdy inquired. "How did you jump from creating oxygen to needing power?"

"Oh, I'm sorry. Many planets, even our moon, have rocks on the surface that contain captured oxygen and other gases within them from millions of years ago, when they were formed. Looking outside, those rusty red cliffs in the distance look to be rich with ilmentite, similar to the surface material on our moon. Ilmentite is an excellent source of trapped oxygen. But if there is ilmentite out there, we will need power to process those rocks to release the oxygen trapped inside, lots of power. Right now, that is power we do not appear to have."

McCurdy smiled at Dr. Maurya. *Keep him busy and that will keep him out of my way,* he thought. *An idle mind is the devil's workshop.*

"So find another power source, Doctor... now! In the meantime, I'll send a scout team out to bring you some rocks."

While the terraforming discussion had been transpiring, Dr. Samantha Jones moved forward to join Dr. Maurya, listening in and nodding on occasion at the discussion. She was dressed in the same tweed sweater as Dr. Maurya, with Cambridge colors.

"And would you be a colleague of Dr. Maurya?" McCurdy asked.

"Yes, I am. And who put you in charge, anyway? This is a civilian operation."

The guards stepped forward to block any closer access to their commander by Dr. Jones.

"Actually, Captain Boswell put me in charge when he had the unfortunate bad luck to get an I-beam rammed through his skull during our landing." Lieutenant McCurdy paused for a moment of simulated emotion and rubbed a tear from his eyes. His newfound identity as the commanding officer of Genesis Five now required some background disinformation to support his legitimacy, and disinformation was his stock and trade. *It's easier to tell a big lie than a small one,* the assassin mused.

"Captain Boswell and I went way back. Hell, me, Boswell and Ryker; we were just three wide-eyed grunts sharing a dorm room at the Academy when the war broke out. Who would have thought that we would all end up on this ship together after all these years? Fate can deal you a strange hand indeed, I say. Captain Boswell was a brave man, but now he's dead."

Caught off guard by the story, Dr. Jones stepped back.

"I'm sorry... I didn't know," she apologized.

"Apology accepted, ma'am," McCurdy sighed, enjoying his triumph over her. "It's just the price we pay to assume the mantle of command, I'm afraid. Now where were we? Your name and background, please?"

"I am Dr. Samantha Jones; I work with Dr. Maurya at Cambridge on some... shared research."

"And what would your primary field of study be, Dr. Jones?" Lieutenant McCurdy asked in a rather condescending manner.

"I chair the Bioengineering Department at Cambridge."

"Fascinating, Doctor. And by chance would your extensive training include the spectrographic analysis of unclassified minerals?"

Dr. Jones was annoyed at the obvious sarcasm. "If you mean can I determine what is on the surface around us, of course I can. I just need to retrieve my equipment from the cargo hold."

"Excellent!" Lieutenant McCurdy turned to the soldiers and barked an order. "Sergeant Longstreet, escort Dr. Jones immediately to the cargo hold to recover her equipment, and then form a scout party to gather some rock samples from those red cliffs over there. Get moving!" McCurdy now took a more civil tone addressing Dr. Jones. "Please hurry back with your samples, Doctor. We're on a bit of a schedule here." With Dr. Jones and Dr. Maurya now occupied solving the ship's oxygen problem, the former assassin turned his attention inward. He scanned the room and signaled the recon team, led by one of his soldiers to meet him at the rear of the compartment.

"You searched the entire ship and this is your report?" He glared at them.

"Yes sir," stated the recon leader. "Good news, sir. We checked the manifest and there are four pallets of food and water below, intended to restock the Moon Base. With our passenger load, that should be enough for two months at least, if we stretch it. But after that..."

"I know what comes after that, Corporal," the assassin interrupted, now transitioning fully to his new identity of Lieutenant McCurdy. "Set up a rationing program for the civilians; two meals a day only, no exceptions. That should buy us an extra month. Give them all a job to do; organize the supplies, scrub the toilets, count the ceiling tiles for all I care... anything to keep them busy and out of my way. And make sure all my soldiers get three hots and a cot; I want them well fed to deal with the troublemakers. When we run out of food, we'll have troublemakers and this happy little party will get ugly fast."

Lieutenant McCurdy looked at the manifest and then moved closer to the soldier's face. "Corporal, your report is totally inadequate. You listed the items on the manifest in the cargo bay, but did you verify that those items are actually here?"

The soldier blinked several times, caught off guard by the interrogation. "Sir, we printed the manifest from the ship's computer and verified the bar codes on the crates matched those in the cargo bay."

"So you know what we were *supposed* to be carrying, but you don't know what we are *actually* carrying, now do you, Corporal?"

"Sir?"

"Have you searched the passengers for their personal belongings?" Lieutenant McCurdy pressed.

"Sir, when you asked for an inventory of everything on board, I didn't think that you meant..." the recon leader replied nervously.

"Exactly, Corporal! You didn't *think*. You didn't *think* that maybe there could be cargo carried on this ship, this ship that just escaped from Earth before it was blown to hell, cargo that just might not have been listed on the manifest?"

"Sir, my apologies," the soldier answered. "My mistake, you are correct of course, sir."

The lieutenant circled the recon leader and then looked away.

"Corporal, I have neither the time nor the patience to train you in the thinking necessary to survive in a hostile environment. If you can't follow my orders, I may as well shoot you and make an example of you to the rest of this mangy rabble. Are we clear, soldier?"

"Crystal clear, sir," the recon leader replied, looking at his shoes.

"Now get your ass back down to the cargo hold and tear apart every crate, every suitcase, and every paper bag. Tell me exactly what we have down there!"

"Yes sir, right away, sir!"

"And then get back up here and search every passenger on deck for their personal belongings."

"Personal belongings? How would I do that, sir?"

"Get *creative*, Corporal." McCurdy smiled. "Ask them to pass a hat, tell them you're on a scavenger hunt or just put a gun to their heads and strip them all in the front of the room. You can perform a body cavity search with a flashlight, for all I care! I don't give a damn how you do it, just do it! Now get me a list of everything we have on this ship, do you understand me! Right now!"

"Sir, yes sir!"

McCurdy spun around and barked another order. "One more thing," He added as he studied the manifest. "I'm looking for someone... but I don't see his name on the list. Have you verified that every person onboard this ship is accounted for on this manifest?"

"I have, sir. They're all accounted for... except I was stumped for a minute. I noticed that we had two missing from the passenger compartment, but then we found them on the thermal scan; looks like they made it into the command module just before the crash. Now I show four heat signatures over there... since we lifted off with a crew of two, I assume that's got to be our missing passengers."

"Command module?" McCurdy asked. "And just who is over there, Corporal?"

"According to the manifest, that would be the pilot, Captain Gaylord, plus Science Officer Taylor and the two missing passengers;

one female named Lexis and some egghead named Stone. I remember him from the boarding ramp, sir... smart-ass little kid. Don't know why we got stuck with him."

"So you didn't make it on board, you sorry bastard," McCurdy muttered. He scratched his chin and frowned, thinking to himself. *And I was looking forward to finishing the job. Just my luck, someone else must have beaten me to it. Good riddance, you son of a bitch.*

"Sir?" the recon leader asked with a puzzled look.

"Never mind, Corporal." McCurdy sighed. "Let's get back to work. Didn't I invite the captain of the command module to join us? So why isn't he here already? Do I have to do everything myself? What the hell is going on over there anyway?"

"About that, sir, appears they've got a problem. I spoke with the captain and he reports that they sustained a serious radiation leak in the crash."

"Really?" Lieutenant McCurdy responded. "And is the leak controlled?"

"No sir, the captain says they're working on it, but it's still compromised. He reports that they are immobile; lost one engine on descent and the other one exploded on impact. Everyone over there has been exposed to a massive dose of radiation; the entire command module is contaminated. One of their crew is in pretty bad shape, says we need to suit up and evacuate her ASAP. He's also requesting to tap into our oxygen tanks to decontaminate the command deck. Sounds pretty desperate, sir."

Lieutenant McCurdy thought about the situation for a moment. With radiation exposure, any equipment or supplies on the command module would be contaminated. The oxygen scrubber, emergency food, water—all the critical items on the command module... now they were all useless. *But what to do about the injured crewmember? Diverting my limited resources to embark on a rescue mission to save people who are going to die anyway,* he thought, *is a fucking waste of time. Besides, I've got too many useless parasites over here sucking up my oxygen already.*

"Sir?" the corporal asked. "About the evacuation... what should I tell the captain?"

"Tell him he's on his own, Corporal. We can't risk contaminating our ship, now can we?"

"You're not... going to help them, sir? You're just going to let them die out there?"

"No, I'm not going to let them die out there, soldier," McCurdy bristled. "Their ship is contaminated with radiation; so as far as I'm concerned, they're already dead, it's just a matter of time. Terminate any further communications... there's no need to monitor their demise."

Back on the command module, Officer Taylor had been listening with great interest as Commander Ryker spun his tale of subterfuge about the radiation leak, the contamination, and the injured crewmember. She wasn't exactly sure what he was up to, but apparently, he seemed quite pleased that contrary to their previous demands, the soldiers on the passenger module now wanted nothing to do with them.

"Ok, I give. Why did you tell them that our ship was contaminated... that we needed to evacuate an injured crewmember?"

Commander Ryker smiled. "You play poker, Miss Taylor? Looks to me like we got ourselves dealt into a little game of Texas hold'em when we crash-landed on this rock. The deck got reshuffled and we're not supposed to be here... wherever the hell here is."

"I don't follow..."

"It's like this, Officer Taylor. There are plenty of things we don't know right now, so let's start with what we do know. Our ship got split in two when we crashed, right? It's a cargo ship, designed for shuttling supplies to the Moon Base, so the cargo module has limited resources; food and oxygen needed for the trip, plus maybe some extra to accommodate the increased passenger load. But the command module... now that's different. It was designed to make multiple trips, so it has some important features that they don't have... like an oxygen scrubber for one, a water recycling unit and food to sustain its crew. By now, somebody over there has figured this out; he's looked at the cards in his hand and now he wants to know what we're holding."

"So what do you propose we do?"

"Nothing... we'll just wait him out. The way I see it, there's no odds in going all in on the flop; too many cards we haven't seen yet. This game is just starting, we've still got the turn and the river coming up... a hell of a lot can change by then. So I floated that contamination story and checked this round to see if we can get a peek at what everybody else is holding. That's what we want from our friends over there in the passenger module, to see what cards they're holding."

"And what did we learn from that exchange?"

"Quite a bit, actually. Two important facts," Ryker replied. "First, they must be better off than they're letting on over there, since at the first bluff of our *'contamination'*, they're more concerned about sitting on their chips than taking our cards off the table. And second, did you see how fast they blew off helping our injured crewmember? Whoever's in charge over there, he doesn't give a rat's ass whether we live or die over here. More importantly, we've learned what the stakes are in this game; it's one hand, winner takes all. As far as they're concerned, Miss Taylor, we folded early, cashed in our chips, and we're out of the game. But that's ok, until we see a few more cards; I figure we're better off checking our bet anyway."

"Since you're gambling with our lives, Commander, shouldn't we tell the others about your game theory?"

"Not just yet," Ryker opined. "We'll lay low for a while and see the next card on the turn. We've got enough resources to last a while, maybe even to the river. No need to tip our hand… not just yet."

Science Officer Sarah Taylor thought about what Ryker had said, and in a disturbing way, she knew he was right. But there was one other detail about Ryker's elaborate ruse that still bothered her.

"You know, Commander," Sarah observed, "I get this feeling you've been down this road before; told a tall tale or two. Your sincerity as a liar is actually quite… impressive."

"Sincerity, Miss Taylor," Ryker smiled, "Is as important in a poker game as it is in life. Once you learn to fake sincerity, the rest comes easy."

16. Red Carpet

Dr. Josiah Stone hunched over his makeshift laboratory bench, delicately soldering a tiny circuit board on what appeared to be a mechanical Tanzanian killer bee. He stepped back and slid his magnifying goggles onto the top of his head, fiddling with the radio frequency controller. He gently moved the joystick and the robotic bee came to life. It cocked its head, beat its wings and then took off rapidly, buzzing around the room at an almost invisible speed. It ascended straight to the ceiling, paused in midair, and then darted off in an unpredictable path around the room. As the robotic insect passed by the doorway, Koda lunged through the opening and snapped the bee in his mouth, drooling on it as it was caught by one wing in the very tip of his teeth. The bee struggled frantically, but could not get free from the giant dog's mouth. Josiah was stunned, and without thinking of what the enormous beast could do to him, he leaped across the room to try and save his creation from destruction.

"Drop it, Lassie!"

Koda spun around and faced Dr. Stone with the robotic bee still clutched in his teeth. He growled with a deep guttural noise before shaking his head back and forth, ripping off one of the bee's wings, and then spitting out the rest of the mechanical insect on the floor. He lowered his head and hunched down to strike, his eyes trained two inches below the left ear on Josiah's jugular vein.

"Koda! No Pala Puhikni!" (Koda! No Red Carpet!) A booming command screamed from just beyond the doorway, stopping the killer beast in his tracks. Lexis stepped through the door and just past the beast as it hunched down, coiled up like a rattlesnake ready to kill its prey. She wiped the drool from under his jowls and then scratched him behind his ears. Reaching down to the floor, she picked up the pieces of the robotic bee, examining it carefully. Holding the bee in front of Koda's nose, she scolded him.

"No Naatappi!" (Not a toy!) Lexis turned and handed the pieces of the robotic insect back to Josiah, placing them gently in his open palm.

"Keep your beast on a lease!" Josiah muttered. "Look what he's done! He destroyed my experiment!"

"Maybe you shouldn't play with toys, Professor, unless you want to share them," Lexis snapped back. "Koda thought you wanted to play a game of catch. You threw the toy; he caught it. He did what he thought you asked. When you jumped across the room at him, he interpreted that as an act of aggression. You changed the rules to a different game for him... a very dangerous game."

"And what game is that?" Josiah asked sarcastically. Koda growled once more and moved to stand beside Lexis. She patted him on the head, looked down into his eyes, and then motioned for him to leave the room.

"That would be the game where Koda rips out your jugular vein and you bleed to death on the floor in thirty seconds," she replied calmly. We call it *Pala Puhikni,* or *'Red Carpet'* if you like. He likes this game and he is very good at it, Professor. But it's a messy game and it doesn't last very long."

Josiah was stunned as he looked down at the crumpled robotic bee in his hand and then rubbed his throat.

"I'm sorry about your toy," Lexis told him honestly. "But you should be more careful starting a game with Koda... unless you want him to finish it."

17. Scout Team

In the cargo hold of Genesis Five, three soldiers accompanied Dr. Jones as they rooted through the open crates and luggage bins in search of her scientific equipment. The entire storage unit was a disaster; everything had been ripped open and thrown about. Clothing, papers, and electrical devices were tossed into random piles of debris. It was as if someone had panicked and ran out of time when looking for treasure. Whoever did this must have been frustrated that they couldn't find what they needed, so just decided to trash the place.

"What are we looking for, ma'am?" one of the soldiers inquired.

"A chrome suitcase, with dual black locks on the front and a red luggage strap wrapped around it."

"Nothing over here like that," the soldier replied. Digging under a pile of luggage, he pulled out a metal suitcase. "Wait, here's something! Is this it?"

Dr. Jones examined the dented chrome suitcase he had found and smiled. She entered the key to her personal combination on the two black external locks and snapped open the lid. The delicate instruments inside were packed in a foam rubber housing, and looked to be unbroken. She removed one of the instruments and pressed a small button on the back of the device, powering up its display. The display flashed a series of numbers and then stopped. She entered a password and a *'Welcome Back, Dr. Jones'* screen appeared. Dr. Jones powered down the device.

"This is all I need for now. Let's get suited up."

The soldiers and Dr. Jones secured spacesuits from the personnel lockers and loaded the equipment onto the rack of a surface rover that had been intended for delivery to the mining colony on the Moon. With their space helmets closed, they tested their oxygen tanks and communicators; everything worked ok. As they mounted the rover and pulled it into the airlock compartment of the cargo bay, everything seemed in order. The sergeant turned around and tapped his headgear twice, looking into the facemask of each of the other three passengers on the rover.

"We good to go?" the sergeant asked over his communicator.

All three nodded and the sergeant pulled the lever to depressurize the airlock. With a rushing whoosh, they entered Niburu's atmosphere for the first time. As the rover pulled cautiously down the gangplank outside Genesis Five, the sergeant took a heading toward the red cliffs in the distance. He turned back to Dr. Jones, who had already activated a gas chromatograph to sample the atmosphere of Niburu and was analyzing the readouts.

"You'd tell me if we're biting off more that we can chew, right, Doc?" he asked.

Dr. Jones ignored him for a minute; fascinated by the data she was streaming from her chromatograph in real time. She looked up from the display. "Uh... How can that be?" she muttered, only half-listening to the soldier. "Yes... of course, I would."

"That answer didn't generate a lot of confidence for me, ma'am, seein' as we are all here together and heading off the reservation, you know?"

"Sorry," Dr. Jones replied as she studied her screen. "But this is not at all what I expected. We are ok for now, but we are going to need to get back inside the ship pretty soon."

"Something wrong out here, Doc?"

"No, we're ok." Dr. Jones looked down at her chromatograph as the readings fluctuated all over the scale. She fumbled with her watch and started its digital timer. "Let's just get the samples and then get back to the ship. Just don't take the scenic route, you know what I mean?"

"Affirmative, Doc." The sergeant tapped the driver on the helmet and told him, "Step on it, Private."

The rover bounced along the surface of what appeared to be a dry, sandy lakebed, broken up by occasional boulders. Dr. Jones held on to the side with one hand, clutching her computer in her lap with the other. The readings on her chromatograph showed a complex atmosphere of multiple gases, some known, and some unknown. The unknown gases were unable to be broken down by her sophisticated analytical instrument. This unexpected fact had Dr. Jones a bit concerned, as the prototype device she was holding on her lap was considered to be one of the most advanced on Earth for detecting hostile elements. This device was not available to even the military source that was funding her Early Responder research at Cambridge. It was intended for battlefield deployment by military drones to assess toxic threats in an unknown NBC attack. The device could process and catalog hostile elements, providing commanders with intelligence to know what they were up against.

The other fact that was bothering Dr. Jones was that she alone seemed to have noticed that as soon as they left the airlock, the rubber hoses and fittings on the rover began to disintegrate with a slight puff of gray smoke. They must have entered a cloud of some type of acid in the atmosphere; it didn't register on her chromatograph when they left the ship. From her readout, it was probably very strong sulfuric acid. At the observed rate of disintegration, if they stayed in this invisible toxic cloud, she calculated that the rover would fall apart in less than an hour. If they had to walk back, their space suits and their skin would fare much worse.

Not a good sign for your first moments in paradise, she thought. But then again, telling the sergeant her concerns would have caused him to abort the mission, and that was not acceptable to her. They needed to know what was out there. It was better to find out and try to deal with it rather than to just die slowly, never knowing.

The rover was almost at the red cliffs and Dr. Jones continued processing her readings as quickly as they came in. The atmosphere was primarily a combination of methane, nitrogen, sulfur, and oxygen. The oxygen concentration was borderline for humans; it was breathable, but not for long periods of time. Breathing the air on the surface of Niburu without a spacesuit would introduce the possibility of in taking toxic amounts of methane and sulfuric gas. Her guess was that a human without a space suit could stay outside for fifteen minutes, maybe up to half an hour if they managed to avoid the deadly invisible clouds. If they hit one of them, they would immediately ingest enough toxins that even if they made it back to the ship, they would die of blood gas poisoning. *This type of death would be painful*, she thought. Gasping, wheezing, coughing up blood for starters… and then chronic renal failure, followed by total organ shutdown. A human liver just wouldn't know how to clear these alien toxins. And if the alien toxins didn't kill you, your own autoimmune system would, trying to fight the toxins. *Either way,* she thought, *once you sucked in the air from one of these toxic clouds, you were a dead man walking.*

Another unexpected reading indicated that the thick layer of unknown atmospheric particles showing up on Dr. Jones' device initially registered radiation levels far beyond lethal to humans, but a second scan indicated that the particles appeared to absorb and contain the radiation. The thick atmosphere blocked all light, but the radiation trapped in the particles transferred some kind of chemical energy into a warming heat pulse, which in turn seemed to keep the surface of Niburu temperate. *This is bizarre; there is no sunlight, because Niburu's galactic orbit did not keep it close to a sun, and even if it did, its atmosphere would absorb all photonic energy. This planet is kind of like my own personal tanning booth,* she thought, *but how does it work?*

Dr. Jones theorized that the deadly cosmic rays must be collected and trapped by the mysterious atmospheric particles around Niburu. They interacted at a chemical level to create bands of lights that changed color constantly, like the Aurora Borealis on Earth. In this perpetual twilight, the internal sky was a soft pastel, glowing, and luminescent. But just like the twinkling lights on a Christmas tree, the randomly pulsating colors in the atmosphere would sometimes synchronize and all blink off, leaving the sky pitch black. Samantha Jones had been so absorbed in her findings that she had failed to notice that the rover had reached its destination. As the vehicle jerked to a halt, the sergeant shouted out to her.

"Ok, we're here, Doc. What do you need?"

18. Red Cliffs

As the scout team in the rover reached the base of the red cliffs, Dr. Jones scanned the landscape with her equipment, then pointed to a pile of rocks, and the soldiers leaped out to secure some samples.

"Take some of the sand at the base, break apart a few of the rocks, and get as many of the dark red ones as you can," she requested.

The team acknowledged and rapidly filled their canisters with samples as the sergeant surveyed the landscape with his own military device. He tapped in a few keystrokes and looked over at Dr. Jones.

"Looks like we're all alone out here, Doc. No thermal readings within a ten-thousand-meter radius."

Dr. Jones nodded nervously as she glanced down at her gas chromatograph. "I'm going to need a core sample from that cliff over there," she told him. "Can you give me a hand?"

The sergeant flipped his handheld device closed and hopped out of the rover.

"Sure thing, Doc," he replied. "It's your rock party." Together, they unloaded a small coring machine and set it up at the base of the cliff. Once activated, it drilled deep into the red cliff, and returned the sample in a plastic tube that looked like linked breakfast sausages. Dr. Jones took out a marker and carefully recorded the depth level for each sample, placing them into her backpack. She looked at her wristwatch, seeing the stopwatch read thirty-eight minutes. *Damn it!* She thought. They were behind schedule, she must have lost track of time while she was running the core sample machine.

"Ok, we're done here!" she snapped. "Let's get going!"

"What's the hurry, Doc?" the sergeant inquired.

"I think I left the water running in the bathtub back at the house," she joked nervously. "We need to go, now!"

The sergeant stared at her for a second and then spun around to signal the others.

"Women!" he muttered under his breath. "Can never fucking stay on plan! Let's go, grunts, we're bugging out!" The soldiers threw the rock samples into the cargo compartment, jumped in, and the rover lurched forward across the sand dunes back to the dry lakebed.

Dr. Jones looked down at her stopwatch; it still read thirty-eight minutes. *What? That can't be!* She thought. She banged her wristwatch against the side of the rover, rubbed off the dust, and reread the display. Her face turned a pale white. *Fifty minutes. We've stayed too long!*

The sergeant noticed the look on Dr. Jones' face as he turned around and tapped on her helmet.

"Something you're not telling me, Doc?" he asked nervously.

Looking down at the rubber fittings and hoses on the rover, Dr. Jones noticed that they were white and smoking. She scanned the horizon. *Shit! We're still over a kilometer from the ship.* Judging by the level of disintegration on the parts of the rover, they had reentered the invisible toxic cloud. *This is going to get bad fast*, she thought. Dr. Jones hesitated for a second and then banged on the sergeant's helmet.

"Slow down! We won't make it if we have to abandon the rover!" she urged.

"Come again, Doc? You just told us to hoof it back home, didn't you?"

"I did... but I didn't realize that the increased speed would accelerate the sulfuric disintegration."

"What the hell are you talking about?" the sergeant barked. As soon as the words left his lips, a clamp on the rover's fuel hose disintegrated and popped off, spraying fuel in all directions. As the hose whipped back and forth, it sprayed liquid hydrogen over the visor of the driver, melting the plastic couplings on his helmet and leaving him blinded. Unable to see, he swerved and crashed the rover into a pile of boulders. The soldiers were thrown from the rover, and the driver was pinned between the vehicle and the rocks. The impact of the crash had torn his space suit, compromising his oxygen supply. In desperation, the driver tore off his helmet to breathe, drawing the invisible toxins of the Niburu atmosphere deep into his lungs. The sergeant rushed to help the injured man as the others tried to free him from beneath the rover.

"Hey, Doc, I need your help here!" he called. Dr. Jones just stared as the injured man gulped down breath after breath of the toxic atmosphere. She was frozen in place, horrified at the fate of the injured man that had been set in motion; she knew his condition was no longer reversible.

"This air ain't so bad, Sarge," the injured driver called out. "Maybe you were just skittish about breathing out here without a suit.

Smells like my mom's rhubarb pie..." He coughed. "Just a little... bitter."

The sergeant was still trying to free the injured soldier from beneath the rover, and noticed that Dr. Jones was not helping; she was just standing there, staring at the injured man.

"Doc, you gonna help me or not?" the sergeant asked.

Dr. Jones walked calmly over to the sergeant and tapped on his helmet. He looked at her face, seeing that it was dead calm.

"Listen to me," she told him. "I'll only say this once. This man is dead. He was dead the second he took one breath in this toxic atmosphere, and I can't save him. Even if we take the time to free him and carry him back to the ship, he's going to die."

The sergeant cocked his head, listening in disbelief. "What are you saying, Doc?"

"Look, we are in some kind of poisonous cloud, and it's lethal to humans," she explained. "I don't know why it's here, but it is, and I can't change that. If we breathe even one breath outside our suits right now, we will die. There's no other outcome, no other possibility."

The injured soldier looked up and noticed the concern on the sergeant's face, but was unable to hear their conversation.

"Hey, Sarge? I'm gonna be ok, right?"

"Yeah, Private, you're fine," the Sergeant shot back. "I've had worse injuries shaving. Now shut up and wiggle your fat ass out from under there so we can get going." The sergeant turned back to Dr. Jones and she looked down at her feet, ashamed of what she had to say.

"We have to leave him now, Sergeant. If we move fast, the rest of us can make it back to the ship before the rubber fittings on our suits melt and we lose our oxygen supply. If we try to carry him, or if we stay here for thirty seconds longer debating what to do, it won't matter, we'll all be dead."

The sergeant stared at Dr. Jones for a second and then tightened his jaw.

"Doc, we're soldiers. We don't leave a man behind... ever. That's just not our way." Dr. Jones threw up her hands in frustration.

"Ok, I'm done here. You can't save him, but you can save yourself and your other man. And if we don't get those samples back to the ship, right now, we are going to die and everyone on our ship is going to die as well. You are signing a death warrant for all of us."

The sergeant stood there, erect, and motionless.

Dr. Jones looked him in the eye and whispered to him. "What's it going to be, Sergeant?"

The sergeant paused, shook his head, and then walked back to the injured soldier. He bent down and whispered something in his ear. The injured man grinned and reached up to shake his hand, closed his eyes, and embraced him with a smile. Just as they were completing their embrace, the sergeant removed the .45 caliber handgun from his holster and shot the injured soldier squarely between the eyes. The lifeless body of the dead soldier slumped back underneath the rover. His eyes were wide open now, staring at the clouds above; he was still smiling. The sergeant slowly let go of the man and his arm dropped limply onto the ground. He stood up, turned around, and barked out an order.

"Ok, get those damn samples loaded in the backpacks... double time back to base!" The three of them ran at full speed, gasping for air in their heavy space suits. They made it back to the ship just as their oxygen supply was depleted. Dr. Jones closed the airlock door and the whoosh of the interior air filled the room with their survival.

Still gasping for breath, Dr. Jones leaned forward and whispered into the sergeant's ear. "What did you... what did you say to him back there?"

The sergeant stared straight ahead, emotionless, and answered.

"I told him to close his eyes and smell his mom's rhubarb pie... then I pulled the trigger."

19. Bad Dreams

Mitch Gaylord lay motionless on a cold metal table in a dimly lit room, his eyes closed, breathing rapidly. His head was groggy and he suddenly became aware that his body had a combination of aches, pains, and other strange sensations that he could not readily identify. He jerked his head back and forth, trying to shake the cobwebs from his brain and wake up from this bad dream. But even when he opened his eyes, it was still pitch black. Something was tied around his head, blocking his vision. As he laid there, he felt disoriented, not sure what time it was, or even where he was. It was the beginning of a descent into a long nightmare, a nightmare that would take him against his will into another world. He tried to raise his arms, but they would not leave the table, as if they were restrained somehow. He tried to move his legs, but like his arms, they wouldn't respond except to barely allow him to squirm and wiggle about. A wave of panic swept over him, and he could feel his heart racing in his chest.

"What the hell is going on!" he screamed through the covering on his head.

There was no answer, only the muffled echo of his voice reverberating inside a place that seemed deep, hollow, and metallic. He exhaled and closed his eyes, capitulating totally into a motionless state, unsure if this nightmare would go away if he just calmed down and fell back to sleep. Captain Gaylord drifted in and out of his trance-like sleep for what seemed like hours, but it could have been days, there was no way to tell. Several times, he thought he heard strange grunting noises and smelled a foul stench of hot breath near his face. More than once, he felt an intense, throbbing pain in his chest, like he was being poked with a sharp stick or punctured like a balloon. He tried to convince himself that it wasn't real; it was some demented part of his nightmare. If he would just lie motionless and ignore it, it would go away. There was an intense burning sensation on the side of his neck, and then he felt nothing.

After what seemed like days, Mitch Gaylord awakened again from his nightmare to the sickly smell of the rotten eggs from his dream. He opened his eyes and saw he was now lying face down on a pile of shredded rags in the corner of a dimly lit, three-by-three meter prison cell. The walls were carved out of sheer rock and there was a rusty metal door with only one small window in the center, two meters above the floor. At the base of the metal door was a small, flat, wooden tray with a metal bowl that contained a gooey substance; it was the source of the putrid odor. He crawled across the stone floor to examine the vile-smelling bowl on the wooden tray, sniffed it, gagged, and vomited uncontrollably. He was famished, but even in his state of fatigue; he was determined. *Whatever the fuck that is, that shit ain't going in my mouth.*

He kicked the foul-smelling bowl into the door with a loud clang, crawled back across the floor, and collapsed on his pile of rags. There was nothing left to do except to roll over on his back and stare at the ceiling. *That's odd,* he thought, *there's no light fixture,* but somehow, he could still see around the room in a dim light. A pale glow pulsated from the ceiling, providing just enough of a glimmer to make out the shape of the room. It was square and other than the pile of rags he was lying on, it was empty. Mitch Gaylord lay there, feeling the pain in his chest as his heart began to race once again.

"Where the hell am I?" he screamed out loud. There was no answer, so he fell back onto his pile of rags and passed out. Somewhere between the restless sleep on that cold stone floor and his perpetual nightmare, he was awakened by a faint tapping sound, like the sound of a woodpecker digging under the eaves of his dad's hunting cabin deep in the mountains of Colorado.

"Tap, tap," it pecked. There was a silent break, and then another. "Tap, tap tap." Mitch sat up on his pile of rags and shook his head; this wasn't a dream. He tried to make out where the sound was coming from. Rotating his head, he crawled across the stone floor on his hands and knees, listening intently for the sound to continue. Was the sound mechanical or was it... *human?* He froze in the center of the room, ready to get a good fix on the location of the sound if it resumed. *There it was again!* The same pattern of tapping repeated, but this time it was stronger, and right underneath his feet.

"Tap, tap." Again, the silent break and then three more sounds. "Tap, tap tap."

Mitch's heart leaped to his throat. His elation sprung loudly from his mouth before his brain could stop it. "Definitely human! They found me! Yee ha!" he screamed out.

Crawling on the floor with his ear to the ground, he located the exact spot where the tapping sound was coming from and examined it in the dim light. There was a small pinhole with scratch marks on either side. Kneeling down, he tried to look into the pinhole, but it was too

120

dark in the pale light to see further down than a few inches. He started tapping back to the sound with his fingers to let his rescuers know where he was, but then there was only silence.

"Shit, they can't hear me!" he cried aloud.

Mitch quickly removed his metal belt buckle and banged it hard against the floor, waiting for a response. A response came quickly, but not in the manner that he had hoped for. The door to his cell burst open and a massive beast, three meters tall with a scaly tail and covered in some sort of armor, rushed through the door and in one single motion kicked Mitch in the gut so hard that he nearly lost consciousness. He stumbled backwards against the hard stonewall, hunched over in pain, gasping to take a breath, but his chest would not expand to take in air. While Mitch was still reeling from the first blow to his stomach, the beast stood over him, raised its arm, grunted, and brought down a crushing blow to his skull. The last thing he felt was the warm blood gushing from his nose and running down his face just before he collapsed on the cold stone floor. His lifeless body landed with a thud, his head spun and the room went dark as his mind retreated to the safety of a dream.

Back in his dad's hunting cabin, young Mitch Gaylord pressed his face against the frosty glass window just to feel how cold it was outside. *It must be very cold*, he thought because his cheek felt numb and stuck to the windowpane. *Shit! It hurt to pull it off.* The snow outside the cabin was swirling in the howling wind, and since they had no electricity this far up the mountain, he had only the fire in a small wood stove to warm his bones. The fire died down and he felt a shudder run down his spine as a cold shiver coursed though his body. He would have to go gather some more wood when the snow stopped, but until then, he may as well just lay here and wait for his dad to return. As he plopped down in a comfy chair and stared out the window at the snowstorm, Mitch was just starting to drift back off to sleep when that pesky woodpecker came back to dig out what was left of the dead insects in the wood siding under the rain gutter. It was lonely without his dad, so Mitch pronounced his acceptance of the feathered scavenger, just as his dad had done a hundred times.

"Hell, them birds got to eat too, even in the dead of winter." And then, there it was again, that pecking sound in the back of his brain.

"Tap, tap." A silent break... then another sound. "Tap, tap tap." The incessant pecking noise in his head disrupted the peaceful dream of his dad's mountain cabin. As the soft snowfall faded outside the window of his mind, Mitch shook himself awake. Much to his disappointment, he was back on the filthy pile of rags in his dimly lit prison cell.

"Shit! Is this place for real?" Mitch gasped. He crawled across the floor back to the pinhole and this time tapped back a gentle acknowledgement, pressing his ear to the floor.

"Михий, задница!" (Quiet, asshole!) Mitch was confused, but not completely stupid. Still sore from his last encounter with the beast behind the door, he chose to communicate more discretely this time. He whispered into the pinhole on the floor.

"Who the hell is this?"

"Ah... американский!" (Ah... American!) A raspy voice from the pinhole responded. "You are American cowboy, like John Wayne, no?"

"Captain Mitchell Gaylord of the Allied Confederation here... and yeah, I'm American. Who the fuck are you?"

"Is Commander Ivan Stephanotski here. I am Russian, from Vladivostok. Our Coalition call it Europa after war, but is of no consequence in this place. How do you get here, cowboy?"

"How the hell do you think I got here, partner? I rode in on a bucking bronco."

20. Suspicious Minds

Just outside the airlock compartment of Genesis Five, a worried Dr. Maurya had been peering through the window, waiting for the pressurization to complete and the airlock door to swing open. A shrill alarm sounded and the red light on the airlock turned green as the door burst open. The sergeant shoved his way past Dr. Maurya, eager to provide his report to Lieutenant McCurdy. Dr. Jones emerged from the airlock and Dr. Maurya rushed forward, giving her a hug.

"What happened out there?" Dr. Maurya exclaimed. "I was listening to your communications while I was working on the solar panels... are you ok?"

"I'm ok," Dr. Jones replied softly. "Just... not quite what I expected out there. Oh yes, you were right; there are tons of ilmentite in the red cliffs."

Dr. Maurya hesitated, it was obvious that Samantha was shaken up and had more to tell, but she wasn't ready to talk about it, at least not yet. He decided to give her some space for now.

"Excellent, then. I have made some progress on the power situation... quite innovative if I do say so myself. I'd like to review my design with you." Ashoka took Dr. Jones by the arm and led her away from the soldier still stationed by her side.

"Let's step into the galley where I have mapped out my design," he whispered. Once inside, Dr. Maurya closed the door, turned around, and looked out the window. A soldier had followed them and taken up position just outside. Dr. Maurya smiled and waved at the soldier, but he didn't return the gesture.

"Ok, what really happened out there?" Dr. Maurya asked. Samantha Jones took a long breath and exhaled.

"Everything was as expected, except there were several significant variations in the chemical makeup of the atmosphere, along with some wild electromagnetic pulses that I can't explain."

"Such as?"

"My initial readings showed that there was enough trace oxygen in the atmosphere to survive for a short time, but there are elements out there that can't be classified by my equipment... deadly elements."

Dr. Maurya scratched his chin. "Interesting, completely new elements to the Periodic Table, you say? Matter that is... alien to us?"

"Definitely alien in nature, with unknown properties," she answered. "But one thing I do know; they're lethal."

"That's how you lost that man?" Dr. Maurya inquired. Samantha Jones lowered her head.

"There was no way to save him." She sighed. "One gasp of that toxic cloud and he was a dead man walking."

"I was listening, Samantha, you did all you could." They hugged for a second and Dr. Jones dabbed at a tear in her eyes. "But we have another problem here," Dr. Maurya continued. "One that is an enigma to me."

Dr. Jones shook off her momentary sadness and tried to refocus her mind away from the dead soldier. Dr. Maurya glanced over at the door, looked back to her, and then whispered in her ear.

"There is something very suspicious about this Lieutenant McCurdy. He said he rowed single skulls for Yale against Cambridge in '18. That's not possible; Cambridge didn't have a single skulls crew in '18."

Dr. Jones was confused. "Are you sure?" she asked. "How do you know that?"

"I remember that day clearly, my dear," Ashoka began. "I had just arrived on campus from New Delhi, a young, wide-eyed, post-doc pursuing a teaching position. I wasn't even officially enrolled yet, but I can remember that day as clear as yesterday." They moved away from the door to the side of the room, away from the view of the sentry posted outside. "It was a blustery afternoon before the big crew match with Yale, and every pub in town was open late with students and alumni singing fighting songs and bragging about the mighty Cambridge crew. I had no idea what was going on, but it looked to be a good party, so I joined in."

"Go on," Dr. Jones urged.

"Well, after many a pint, I learned that Cambridge was expected to sweep Yale the next day behind our newly discovered star of the single skulls: an American exchange student named Lindsey Davenport. Mr. Davenport had apparently transferred in for a semester of special research when the crew captain spotted him rowing on the lakes one morning and convinced him to row for us."

"And what's so dubious about that?" Dr. Jones asked. "Lots of yanks have attended Cambridge?"

"Ah, yes, but the night before the rowing event, Mr. Davenport was killed in a mysterious lab explosion on campus. Cambridge cancelled the meet the next day and didn't race single skulls for the entire year."

Dr. Jones thought about what Ashoka was saying for a second. "So our Lieutenant McCurdy is blatantly lying?" she blurted out.

"Decidedly so," Dr. Maurya answered. "And even more strangely, I remember being suspicious at the time about why the whole story of the lab explosion never came out. An undergrad exchange student, alone in the middle of the night in the most secure laboratory on campus, and he blows himself up?"

"My undergrads have set lots of things on fire, why is that so strange?" Dr. Jones laughed, but Dr. Maurya remained deadly serious.

"Because most of the faculty didn't have access clearance to that lab, much less an undergrad. The entire building was contracted out that semester to the military for some secret project. There was never an explanation and the whole thing just got swept under the rug."

"You know, now that you mention it, I do remember that being strange," Dr. Jones responded. "But why would Lieutenant McCurdy choose that specific incident to fabricate a story to us? It makes no sense."

"I don't know why he lied," Dr. Maurya answered. "But even more bizarre, to know what he knows, he must have actually been there on the quad that day. That was the only time that a Harrier jet landed on the campus quad... ever. The landing was kept quiet, you know, part of the secret military project. It wasn't mentioned in the papers."

"Are you sure?" Dr. Jones asked.

"Oh my, yes. I just happened to be in a building across the quad looking out the window. The Harrier swooped in, touched down, two men threw a black duffle bag in the hold, and then it took off again. It could not have taken more than thirty seconds. I don't know why it landed that morning, but there couldn't be five people on Earth that know about that Harrier landing, and even fewer know why."

"So, he may have seen the Harrier land, but he absolutely did not row the single skulls match... because there wasn't one," Dr. Jones repeated.

"Exactly," Dr. Maurya confirmed. "I don't know who our Lieutenant McCurdy really is, but he is quite sure of himself and has chosen to tell us a story in which if we are clever, we can piece together his devious lies... almost as if to *challenge* us in some way. What do you think it means?"

Dr. Samantha Jones stood there for a moment, trying to absorb the situation. In addition to the unknown deadly elements they were facing outside, the man that had assumed military control inside was apparently not who he said he was.

"I don't know what it means," Samantha answered. "But I think we had better be very careful from now on around this man who calls himself Lieutenant Morgan McCurdy."

21. Rubbing Cones

Back aboard the command module of Genesis Five, Commander Ryker was seated in his captain's chair with a contemplative look on his face. Lexis and Officer Taylor were in the other corner of the command deck, acting like they were reviewing damage reports, but in fact, they were giggling like schoolgirls and discussing NELI's observations about the size and skill of Commander Ryker's *'piloting'* capabilities. Dr. Josiah Stone crawled out from under the control panel with a bundle of wires in his hands. He had been trying to devise a plan to get Genesis Five back airborne.

"That landing shorted out our main crossover panels," Josiah announced. "It will take a while to re-wire these circuits and get us back up and running... and we'll need some fuel if you want to get airborne again." While Dr. Stone was concerned with the flight worthiness of the command module, Ryker's mind had drifted in another direction. The smell of her jasmine perfume had launched him back to his riddle quest for the hand, or the body in this case, of the lovely Miss Taylor. He rocked back in his chair and posed a hypothetical question to Dr. Stone.

"I heard a song once, Professor, called *'No Man is an Island'*, do you think that has anything to do with Sarah's riddle?"

"What? Are you even listening to me?" Josiah demanded. "Stop thinking with your Johnson and help me get this ship up and running!" Ryker's mind was racing, he was like a bloodhound on the scent and the game was on. He clicked on the internal communications system and contacted Officer Taylor to resume her gauntlet of ten questions.

"Is the man on the island wearing a bathing suit?" Ryker blurted out. Officer Taylor snapped out of what she was doing and prepared to guide him on his quest.

"Back to the game already?" Sarah laughed, "My, you're persistent. But do you really want to ask a question that specific, Commander? You haven't been too successful with your *'bull in the china shop'* strategy. Maybe you should try being a bit more... *delicate*. Think of this as a romantic maneuver; start with an approach that gets you a small 'yes', and then work your way up to the big 'Yes'." That's what you want, isn't it? The big yes?"

"Right, the big Yes," Commander Ryker scratched his beard.

"General questions, get a little yes first, then advance on to the big Yes. Good strategy. Let's start with the basics of any romantic encounter; is the man wearing any *clothes*?"

"That's a little better, I guess. Yes... he is," Officer Taylor responded.

"Yes? Now this isn't so hard!" Ryker exclaimed. "Is the man crying *because* he's wearing clothes? That's it! He stumbled into the middle of a volleyball game in a nudist colony and they won't let him play because he's not naked?"

"No." Sarah sighed with disappointment. "One little yes and your pants are hanging from the lampshade; not very romantic, Commander. That approach path will get you shot down fast I'm afraid. Eight more questions."

"Well, a man can dream," Ryker replied and turned to Dr. Stone for consultation. "Then maybe it's not a riddle, Professor, but a paradox. You know, some twisted chick's metaphor for not wanting to be alone, something like *'you are the key and I'm the lock',* some sentimental *'you complete me'* bullshit." Josiah stared at Ryker.

"Look, Commander, maybe you're over-thinking this one a bit. Why not just focus on solving the riddle instead of trying to psychoanalyze the female super ego enigma inside the puzzle. I don't think Officer Taylor is secretly an existentialist."

"An extraterrestrial?" Ryker shot back, mangling his meanings. "Shit, Doc, she's not an alien... not with those headlights!"

"Not an extraterrestrial, you idiot, an... Oh, never mind." Josiah gave up. "We need to check out the passenger module for fuel. Didn't they call us a while back for help?"

The commander was still distracted by Sarah's riddle and his personal quest for pleasures of the flesh.

"Oh... yeah, Doc," Ryker agreed. "But we're *persona non grata* with them after our nasty radiation leak, and I'd prefer to keep it that way for now."

"Radiation leak? What are you talking about? We don't have a radiation leak."

"I know that, just a cover story to keep our options open for now... like blowing off some drunken biker chick in a honky tonk bar parking lot with, *'You know, Slash, I'd really like to ride you sidesaddle in the backseat of your Pinto, but my damn herpes is kicking up again. Gonna have to sit this one out, cowgirl. Love the tattoos, though.'* Trust me Doc, you're flying solo for the rest of the night."

Josiah just shook his head. "Way more personal information than I need to know, Commander, but I still need fuel. Are we going or not?"

"Ok, let's tiptoe over there and see what they got. We can take the ePod; I'll drive. Maybe they've got some software on riddles in the passenger game lounge." As Ryker and Dr. Stone were preparing to leave the command module, Josiah asked a simple question.

"Commander, we may have to leave the ePod to slip in unnoticed. Are you sure it's safe to go outside without our space suits?" Dr. Stone inquired.

"Most likely," Ryker replied without thinking. "I was watching the atmospheric readings as we descended. There's enough oxygen to breathe for a while, a twenty-percent concentration; we should be ok. Now, back to the riddle, Professor, if a guy were on a beach with no worries, why the hell would he be crying? Shit, I'd be rolling around on my back laughing." Just as Ryker was about to pull down the release handle to the airlock door, an urgent message appeared from the passenger module on the video screen.

"Captain Gaylord, this is Dr. Samantha Jones, do you read me?" Ryker let go of the airlock handle and stepped back to the video monitor.

"Commander Ryker here, Captain Gaylord stepped out for a minute. What's up, Doc?"

"Commander, listen to me," Dr. Jones replied, "Whatever you do, don't go outside. There are unknown compounds in the atmosphere, invisible clouds actually. I don't know what they are yet, but if you encounter them, they're quite lethal. Until I can calibrate my equipment to detect those clouds, stay inside, those toxins are deadly."

Ryker looked over at an astonished Josiah, rubbed the airlock handle, and shrugged.

"Deadly toxins outside? Go figure. Guess I should stick to flying."

"We ran a scout team out there and hit some real trouble," Dr. Jones continued. "I have some preliminary readings on my chromatograph, but we need to do more analysis before we venture back out there again. I did find some rock samples that may help us replenish our oxygen supply; Dr. Maurya is working on that right now."

Josiah stepped in front of Ryker and jumped into the conversation. "Dr. Jones, Dr. Josiah Stone here. Have you solved the power problem yet?" Samantha Jones was stunned. Who was this Dr. Stone and how could he know about the power issue?"

Ashoka stepped forward to the video screen. "Power... yes, Dr. Stone. It is a problem. I am working on the power problem by modifying the photovoltaic cells in the solar array to accept ambient light. I am running a spectrum analysis on the available wavelengths, but so far, I can't produce enough..."

"Forget that," Josiah interrupted. "It won't work. The low-level light spectrum is too spread out to be of any use. Try converting the solar panels to run on radiation, not photonics. Based on those electromagnetic pulse waves we passed through in the landing, the atmospheric structure out there must capture and reflect the radiation from the solar winds. That's why you see the Aurora Borealis effect."

Dr. Jones and Dr. Maurya looked at each other for a second and then realized that Dr. Stone, whoever he was, was right.

"Ah, that's not such a bad idea," Dr. Maurya answered. "And who did you say you were again?"

"Dr. Josiah Stone, MIT. Just substitute a chemical converter for the photovoltaic cells and drive it off the radiation. You should have everything you need if you tear apart the ship's chemical waste processor. Then you'll have enough power to build a thermal generator to heat the rocks. What's in your rocks... ilmentite, I assume? Then you can run a standard electrolysis unit to generate some hydrogen for me as a by-product to your terraforming deal."

Dr. Maurya was frantically taking notes.

"And as a bonus," Josiah continued, "You'll get all the drinking water you can use when you do the hydro-cracking."

Dr. Maurya looked at his notes and compared them with Dr. Jones. He smiled and responded.

"That actually just might work, Doctor," Ashoka agreed. Josiah looked at Ryker and shrugged, as if he was annoyed that everyone didn't understand him.

"Of course it will work. I've done it a thousand times in my lab as a simple undergrad experiment, you know, to keep the little tikes busy while I work on some real problems. Besides, who do you think designed the Moon Base biosphere we just blew up?"

Dr. Maurya scratched his head. "It all makes sense, but why do you need hydrogen?" Dr. Maurya asked.

"Look, you need power, I need fuel," Josiah answered. "We don't have any fuel, but if you can generate hydrogen, I can convert our liquid fuel cells to a magnetoplasmadynamic accelerator."

Dr. Maurya looked at Samantha with a slow recognition of where Josiah was going.

"You're going to build... an *ion thrust engine*?" Dr. Maurya exclaimed.

"Now you're catching on," Josiah noted with mock praise. "You guys are from Cambridge, right? Not much of a crew team at MIT, but we build some cool shit." Ashoka Maurya stepped closer to the video screen.

"And have you also built an ion thrust engine in your lab, Dr. Stone?" Josiah glanced over at Ryker and smiled.

"Only once, it blew up a city block... sent up a cloud of smoke that stopped traffic for miles. But I think I know what went wrong. Never send a undergrad to do a PhD's job, you know?"

Both Dr. Jones and Dr. Maurya erupted in laughter at the underclass jab; they were starting to like this smart-mouthed professor from MIT.

"I once heard a boom in my lab," Ashoka joked, "and had a undergrad walk out with his hair on fire and no eyebrows! It's best not to pour benzene down the sink and then light up your Bunsen burner."

Ryker was slow to the Mensa party, but finally felt like joining in.

"Ok, you guys lost me there for a while, but I did catch the blowing up part. Since we only got the one ship, let's not blow it up just yet."

Josiah and Dr. Maurya both ignored Ryker's comments.

"I'm transmitting some schematics to you of my chemical converter design," Josiah told them. "Let me know when you have the prototype built and I'll review the power outputs with you. Oh yeah, send me what you have on your chromatograph readings from the atmosphere and I'll take a look. I need some xenon for my accelerator, maybe there's something out there I can use."

Dr. Maurya had overheard one of the soldiers talking about the accident in the command module, and now probed a more sensitive subject.

"You have been most helpful, Dr. Stone. Perhaps I can be of assistance in your radiation cleanup. I have some experience in contamination."

"Contamination?" Josiah rubbed his eyes. "Oh yeah, Ryker's biker chick story. No worries, we're all clean... except for the Commander's raging case of herpes."

Ryker jumped into the conversation, laughing nervously.

"There you go again spreading rumors, Doc. Not that it's a big deal, but I'm disease free, and have been for months." Ryker raised his eyebrows in appreciation to Josiah for his sense of humor. "Anything else we can do for you, Doc?"

Dr. Jones looked at Dr. Maurya, unsure as to whether they should share their concerns with their new friends on the command module. *In an unknown world with unknown peril,* thought Dr. Maurya, *alliances may tip the balance between life and death.* He nodded his approval to Dr. Jones.

"Commander Ryker," Dr. Jones whispered, "Are we on a secure transmission?" Ryker looked at Josiah and scrunched up his face.

"Sure, Doc, we're secure," he answered. "What's on your mind?"

"There is... something else," Samantha Jones began. "Something fishy is going on over here with your friend, Lieutenant McCurdy. He's taken command, really come down on us with an iron fist, and we have some reasons to be... suspicious about him." Ryker was totally confused.

"You've got suspicious minds, Doc?" Ryker repeated, drifting back to another time. "What a great song, Suspicious Minds... the King at his best... and those strings? Genius. But I digress... What's got you spooked about this... Lieutenant, what's his name?"

"Your *friend,* Commander, Lieutenant McCurdy. Was he always such a dick back at the Academy?" Dr. Jones blurted out.

"My *friend,* McCurdy? At the Academy?" Ryker asked. "Doc, what are you talking about?"

"At the Academy," Samantha answered. "When you, Captain Boswell, and Lieutenant McCurdy roomed together... was he a complete asshole back then?"

Ryker was now totally lost.

"What the hell are you smoking, Doc? I've never heard of any Lieutenant McCurdy and I didn't room with anybody at the Academy. Shit, I tried to get in, but they wouldn't take me. I worked as a flight mechanic on the base for a while; they had me take the training jets up to test them out. Said they didn't want to risk an officer buying it until the damn things were flying right."

Now it was Dr. Jones' turn to be confused.

"Oh yeah," Ryker continued, "Those dicks at the Academy did let me serve as a punching bag in their martial arts training program, until I learned enough to beat the shit out of them, then I got uninvited to the party. The most I ever did was hang out around base, Doc, but I was never admitted to anything. They said I wasn't quite... cadet material."

"But if you're not an Academy graduate, how'd you get those combat wings?" Josiah asked, pointing to Ryker's lapel. "I thought they only gave those icons out to war heroes... fighter pilots with a certain number of kills."

"These wings?" Ryker laughed. "Hell, I got those on my first day in action, the same day I got drafted into the war. There was a sneak attack and most of the Academy hot shots never made it off the ground... blown to hell in the first wave. With their pilots splattered across the tarmac, the Academy decided to lower its standards and give me a commission. Before that, I was flying a cargo plane full of rubber dog shit to Asiana."

22. Terraforming

On board Genesis Five, the oxygen supply was starting to run low. Dr. Maurya had been busy building a prototype atmospheric generator for terraforming the planet, based on Josiah's chemical voltaic conversion process. The basic chemistry behind terraforming to create an inhabitable biosphere was not a new concept; it had been used on the Moon to create an oxygen supply for years. The implementation details on Niburu, however, were quite different and inordinately more complex.

As Dr. Maurya worked on changing a small part of the planet's atmosphere, he drifted into a daydream for a moment. *Before we try and change the environment to our liking, what life has evolved out there on the surface now?* He wondered.

Ashoka Maurya imagined that if there were plants and animals on Niburu, they would be nothing like those on Earth. With the erratic low-level light patterns on the surface, plants would either evolve completely underground or be forced to emerge, flower, and then burrow back underground in a matter of hours. Animals, if they existed, would most likely have large dark eyes, since the maximum light level on Niburu was equivalent to Earth's twilight. *In the pitch black, creatures might emerge that would be completely blind,* he thought, *driven only by smell and other chemical senses that allow them to forage and hunt in total darkness.* Being hunted down in the dark by a blind predator snapped Dr. Maurya out of his image of Shangri-La.

Startled from his daydream by the door opening, Dr. Maurya refocused back on the task at hand inside the galley of Genesis Five. He had organized some makeshift white boards to outline the design elements of his atmospheric generator. On the kitchen table, he assembled several small prototypes of the equipment needed to convert the raw ilmentite to the oxygen they would need to survive. Dr. Jones entered the room and joined him for a peer review of his research.

"Ah, Samantha, how very nice to see you. I took the rock samples you brought back from the surface, and using the chemical converter overlay design for the photovoltaic cells that Dr. Stone suggested, I have heated the rocks to extract frozen liquids from the substrata. My subsequent electrolysis was successful in separating hydrogen and oxygen from the compounds."

"So in short," Dr. Jones noted, "the prototype process works. Fantastic!"

"Well, sort of," Dr. Maurya admitted. "The good news is that the prototype works, but the bad news is that with the projected mining process, we will only be able to produce enough oxygen to extend our survival for a short time, and then we will die here."

"All right, just scale up the prototype and make more oxygen," Dr. Jones quipped. "What's the problem?"

"The problem, my dear, is not in the scale of prototype processing, it's acquiring the raw materials." Dr. Maurya pointed to his computer screen and traced the lines with his fingers. "Look at this chart. We would need to increase the raw material acquisition volume by at least a thousand-fold to break even with our current oxygen consumption. The processing equipment can be scaled up, but we don't have the machinery or manpower to mine an adequate rock volume."

"Even if everyone on board becomes a miner?" Dr. Jones joked.

"Not even if you and I put on overalls and engage in manual labor." Dr. Maurya shook his head. "No, we would need a mining force many times larger and stronger than the passengers and crew we have. Most of the passengers would be useless in the process; they are used to shuffling papers, not swinging a pickaxe or pushing ore carts. Unfortunately, what we need is an army of strong backs and weak minds."

Just then, the door sprang open and Lieutenant McCurdy with two of his bodyguards strode inside. The soldier just outside the door moved in and closed it behind him.

"Ah, my good doctors." Lieutenant McCurdy smirked. "With exciting news to share about my oxygen generator, I presume?" Dr. Maurya explained the status of the prototype and the impending capacity problem that would prevent their survival.

Lieutenant McCurdy seemed unfazed. He scratched his chin and looked to be deep in thought, and then he turned his back to them and smiled.

"Strong backs and weak minds to dig out the rocks... and transport them back here for processing. Sounds just like basic training, hey, soldier?" Lieutenant McCurdy turned to Dr. Jones and Dr. Maurya, moved in closer, and whispered, "I have the utmost confidence in your creativity to solve our problems. You say we would need an army of miners to survive. Then maybe you should get busy... and *build* me an army."

Dr. Jones and Dr. Maurya were baffled. Dr. Jones reacted for both of them. "Build you an army... an army from what?" she asked.

Lieutenant McCurdy signaled one of his bodyguards to step forward as he carefully placed two stainless steel trunks on the kitchen table. He inserted a key into each end of one of the trunks and turned it. Very cold air rushed out of the trunk along with a cloud of frozen vapor. Lieutenant McCurdy gently opened the lid and exposed a rack of glass vials, each marked with a military bar code. He put on an insulated glove and carefully extracted one of the vials. He held the vial up to the light and smiled.

"Why with these, of course. It seems that someone back home was kind enough to stow away a complete genetic bank of all the plants and animals on Earth, right here in our cargo bay! Like a tiny little frozen Noah's Ark, I'd say."

Dr. Jones and Dr. Maurya moved closer to examine the contents of the trunk. They turned to each other, unsure of what would happen next.

"With the seed bank, I can keep the passengers busy building a greenhouse, that's simple enough, but Professor Jones..." McCurdy continued, "I believe you said that your specialty was Bioengineering, am I correct?" Dr. Jones was still distracted examining the genetic samples.

"Uh, yes. Why?"

"Because, Professor, as an expert in Bioengineering, you should have no problem creating a transgenic species that will be capable of performing our basic mining operations. Once you have the optimal genetic sequence isolated, I will need you to create a full-scale cloning process."

"But I would need a complete..." Dr. Jones started.

"Laboratory?" McCurdy interrupted. "Indeed you will, so I have taken the liberty of setting up a lab for you in the forward compartment. In addition, I tapped into the ship's computers to network you with Dr. Maurya, and myself, of course, to keep track of *our* progress." Lieutenant McCurdy closed the stainless steel trunks, turned the security key and handed the genetic bank to the guard.

"Come along, Dr. Jones... we've got an army to build."

23. Prison Chat

Mitch Gaylord crouched on his cold stone prison floor, just above the small pinhole in the center of his cell and listened intently to the whispers of Commander Ivan Stephanotski. He pressed his ear to the floor and tried not to make any noise that would bring his scaly guard back to beat the shit out of him again. Comrade Stephanotski explained that he and his crew were on a secret deep space reconnaissance mission to circle one of Saturn's moons, Titan, when his space craft fell under the intense gravitational pull of a rapidly approaching Niburu. Like Genesis Five, they had tried to escape, but were forced down to Niburu after initially trying to outrun it, but they lost control of their guidance computers and crashed.

"How many on your crew?" Mitch asked.

"Six, counting me... and one... stowaway. We lost two in crash, but four, we survive," Ivan whispered.

"A stowaway? How the hell did that happen?"

"My stupid ex-wife and daughter had fight, so my daughter, she wants to run away, you know, get back at step-monster. I do not know she was on board until after we refuel at Allied Moon Base and go for deep space burn... to Titan."

"Does your wife know where she is?" Mitch asked.

"Not wife, ex-wife. No... that only good thing. That bitch can worry for a while. Maybe it take her mind off spending all my money." Ivan laughed.

"Man, I heard that," Mitch agreed. "Whenever I seem to get my life back together, my ex pops up to spoil the fun, just like someone tossing a turd in the punch bowl at a party."

"A turd... in what?" Ivan questioned.

"Never mind, comrade, just don't drink the punch. Are your other men in there with you? I don't hear anyone else."

There was a long silence and then finally, the Russian spoke again in a halting voice.

"Elena is alive... I am sure. She had bad leg from crash. They take her away, but I hear her cry down the hall sometimes." Mitch was silent, not knowing how to respond. "I hear you make big noise, cowboy, kick around your bowl like bull. That not good. You eat the syrup food they bring, it will give you strength for what comes."

"You call that food?" Mitch blurted out. "It smells like shit!"

"Listen carefully, cowboy. Beasts make syrup by eating fungus they grow here underground. They, how you say, *'puke it up'* into jars for us. It taste like your turd in punch bowl, but it protect you from inside, so you can breathe. You need for now, but only protect one day. If you do not eat every day, you die."

Mitch was confused; he didn't understand what Commander Stephanotski was trying to tell him.

"It smell bad, yes," Ivan continued, "but something in it let you breathe, and it keep you alive. One man, he refuse to eat. He bleed to death from inside. Not how you say, pretty sight."

Ok, it's either choke down the turd or die, Mitch thought. *I get it.*

"That turd ain't going down so easy, Ivan, no matter how much punch I drink."

"You take medicine, cowboy." Commander Stephanotski laughed. "And you live to fight another day. Enough questions; now we sleep."

24. Intelligent Design

Working around the clock, Dr. Samantha Jones had nearly isolated what she felt would be the optimal genetic sequence for building an army of transgenic miners. Miners that were needed to dig out the vast quantities of ilmentite that contained the life-sustaining oxygen for the survival of the passengers of Genesis Five. Although she had acted surprised at Lieutenant McCurdy's demand to create a sub-human species, the process was in fact not new to Dr. Jones. In her Cambridge laboratory, Dr. Jones and her undergrad students had recently been operating under a secret military contract to study the feasibility and genetic makeup of sub-human soldiers. It was at this exact point in her research that her quest for scientific advancement and her deeply held spiritual beliefs came into conflict.

As a scientist, Dr. Jones was fascinated by the most recent achievements in gene therapy; it was this fascination and an offer off unlimited grant money to explore her research that had landed her the coveted position as the head of the Bioengineering Department at Cambridge. The advanced genetic research she was working on had the potential to not only enhance the quality of life, but literally it could save lives that would otherwise be lost. She was enthusiastic about the clinical discoveries, but equally concerned that she was rapidly approaching a threshold that neither she nor any man should cross.

Samantha Jones was not a religious zealot, far from it. In fact, she had been raised in the home of two liberal college science professors, who between them shared an agnostic view of the universe at best. Her parents had drilled their mantra into her from the age of three: *if you cannot prove it, Samantha, it does not exist.* She was a good scientist, a firm believer of the scientific method, but still, something was missing for her to be able to accept a balanced, rational view of the universe. Somewhere out there among the DNA, the proteins, and the quarks, she was convinced there had to be a source for the intricate complexity of the universe. *This cannot all be by chance,* she thought. *There must be some intelligent design behind the infinite and beautiful complexity of life.* The thought overwhelmed her, but she had learned the hard way that it was not a thought to be uttered aloud in the distinguished halls of science—discretion being the better part of valor. *It is best to keep your spiritual beliefs to yourself,* she thought, *lest you be labeled as a radical creationist or some other career-ending marker that will cancel your administrative support and grant funding.*

But somewhere, there must be an invisible hand that put in place this wonderfully diverse, incredibly resilient pattern of life, just waiting for me to discover it. She was sure of only one thing as a scientist… there had to be rules for this mysterious universe, and the scientific evidence of life around her could not be ruled by mere quantum indeterminacy.

Dr. Jones did not believe in organized religion. Having tried several of them at a younger age, they always felt uncomfortable, like trying to wear a pair of shoes that were two sizes too small without socks. She found it painfully difficult to keep a straight face while being force-fed a diet of religious dogma that never quite aligned with her intrinsic beliefs, and as a scientist, it made her stomach hurt. Each time, however, she tried to approach her spiritual training with an open mind. She listened politely and pretended to be enlightened, but when the spotlight of peer acceptance had dimmed, she moved on. And each time she moved on, her stomach told her it was the right thing to do.

After many years of soul searching, Dr. Samantha Jones came to her own personal epiphany. It was a revelation that would guide her for the rest of her life. *There must be a Creator that has set in motion the elements and rules of this universe, I just don't know how to find them yet. But if I look hard enough, they will be revealed.* For Samantha Jones, this was the only answer that her mind could understand and her stomach would accept. If such a Creator did exist, based on her understanding of the power of genetics, she was as certain as Albert Einstein that this Creator would not leave the evolution of life to mere chance. Somewhere in the secret code of genetics, there must be clues to a master design for life.

"God did not play dice with the universe," Einstein had said. *My respect for the watchmaker's design can't help me if we all die here on this desolate planet,* Dr. Jones thought to herself. *There must be some acceptable action, some compromise with my beliefs yet to be discovered that will allow me to do what needs to be done… think, damn it!*

"Ok, Samantha," she told herself. "Start with the theoretical and then align it with the practical. If I were to create a transgenic animal to help us survive on Niburu, completely without human DNA, how would I engineer such a species? It would need to be engineered as a mix of several animals; designed to be strong, loyal, and fierce."

From the genes in the genetic bank, Dr. Jones selected the DNA from four species... gorillas, wolves, bats, and elephants. Each animal's DNA would contribute a vital set of unique characteristics. She decided to call her new transgenic animal a 'Chimera', after the mythical Greek creature that was made up of several species. The four animals that she had selected would have the optimal genetic makeup for a mining workforce on Niburu.

Mountain gorilla DNA was designated as the primary genetic scaffold, to give strength and mobility for mining, and also because mountain gorillas were resistant to many human viruses, like AIDS. With the gorilla as the foundation, the Chimera would be able to walk upright or on all fours. They would look more ape-like than the other creatures, as the genetics for facial characteristics and body type would be controlled by a specific gene sequence programmed by Dr. Jones. *This should allow the Chimera to fit in better with their human counterparts,* she thought. It was a small thing, cosmetic appearance, but in this strange new world, having familiar features should help everyone become more accepting of a new companion race.

The wolf DNA would contribute a sense of smell that was more than fifty times as sensitive as a human's. This extraordinary capability would help the Chimera seek out the oxygen-rich rock deposits, and also alert the humans to unforeseen threats.

Bats, on the other hand, had the distinction of unusually quick twitch muscle control, manifested in their in-flight, ultra-high frequency sonic location skills. In short, they could identify moving objects while in flight, using sound waves. This UHF location sense would allow the Chimera to find their way in the pitch-black that could come about unexpectedly on the surface of Niburu.

Dr. Jones selected elephant DNA for their inherit strength, intelligence, and long-range, ultra-low frequency communication ability. With inaudible ULF sounds, elephants could communicate with each other over long distances. Adding this characteristic to the Chimera would allow them to operate as a well-organized team of coordinated workers.

Theoretically, the resulting mix of animal DNA would create a Chimera species with the vital elements to improve the odds of human survival on Niburu... protection, awareness, and strength. And most importantly, she had no need to cross the genetic line of *'playing God'* by devolving selected human DNA into a sub-human race. That she could not do, even if it meant her life would end here on Niburu. For once, the scientific mind of Dr. Samantha Jones and her stomach were in agreement.

With her moral dilemma resolved, Dr. Jones set to work and constructed the array of Petri dishes, centrifuges, and gene sequencers that she would need to create the Chimera. The genetic formula she created was the optimal bioengineering target and the only ethical choice she could make under the circumstances. The basic process of creating a transgenic animal was straightforward, a process she had performed in her laboratory at Cambridge many times. She imagined she was back at her lab bench; teaching a group of eager students, ready to start their first bioengineering project.

"I want you to sort through the DNA of a jellyfish," she lectured. "Identify and extract the gene that expresses a green florescent protein (GFP), then splice the GFP gene into a host bacteria cell to create a new and unique genetic code. Use recombinant DNA to induce the transgenic host to replicate the newly modified genetic sequence into successor organisms." Through the scientific power of bioengineering, they would create a new life form. And even cooler, the new life form would glow in the dark. But every now and then, a student would start the experiment, pause, and then come to her desk to ask the question that she had asked herself many times.

"Excuse me, Professor, but isn't this where our scientific advancement and ethical morality start to collide? I mean, we can splice together DNA and prove that we can create a new life form, a life form that neither God nor nature produced... but the question is... should we."

To avoid answering that dilemma, the end of her teaching experiment was always to destroy the newly created transgenic organism; it had served its training purpose. The real answer was that she felt it best not to let the new life form find its way into a world that was not prepared for its sudden emergence. But this time, the answer would not be so simple. With the creation of the Chimera, the new transgenic life form would not only be allowed to live, it would be nurtured, trained, and exploited for its creator's gain. What was it that her parents had told her as a child?

"Samantha, there are only three things in life that are certain: time, choices, and consequences... only one is in your control. You are given a finite amount of time, and the choices you make will result in consequences; many of them will be irreversible." She prayed now that she was making the right choices.

The DNA sequence machines whirred away with a soft hum,

accelerating the recombinant process within the test tubes where a new life form was replicating, multiplying, and growing stronger by the second. Her choice was made, but the consequences were as yet unknown. With her analysis of the optimal model for a transgenic labor force complete, Dr. Jones decided it would be best to let her analytical decisions rest for a while, and besides, before she moved forward with development, there was another urgent matter that she must attend to... a matter that only she and Dr. Maurya could discuss. From her makeshift genetic lab, Dr. Jones fired off a text message to Ashoka.

"Need your analysis. Tea time?"

"Extremely busy," Dr. Maurya messaged back. "Important?"

"I have Earl Grey," Samantha enticed.

"On the way," Ashoka responded.

25. Time Travel... Redux

In her makeshift bioengineering lab, Dr. Jones put a kettle over the Bunsen burner before opening the door to smile seductively at the guard stationed just outside. The guard ignored her. Not to be denied, she stepped directly in front of him to make a request.

"Could you be a dear and run down to the cargo hold and get me some Petri dishes? I'm so clumsy, I keep breaking them."

"Not supposed to leave my post, ma'am," the guard responded without looking at her. Dr. Jones was a scientist, but she had grown up in a man's world of academia and she knew how to handle this situation. She placed her hand softly on the guard's cheek.

"Please? I really need to get things going in here and I don't want to get Lieutenant McCurdy mad at us. You know how he can be."

The guard thought about her request for a second and realized that she was right about that; neither of them wanted McCurdy to get mad.

"Ok, I'll be right back," the guard told her. Just as the sentry turned the corner, Dr. Maurya arrived for his cup of tea. Samantha looked down the hallway to make sure it was clear, and then invited him in.

"Come inside," she whispered. "We only have five minutes before that guard gets back." They stepped inside and Dr. Jones directed their attention to her mass spectrometer readings from the surface of Niburu. In addition to the unknown toxic compounds in the atmosphere, there were strange pulsations of massive electromagnetic interference recorded on the computer from her scouting mission for the ilmentite samples. The readings showed electromagnetic radiation accelerating on a logarithmic scale, far beyond anything her instruments could record.

"Are you sure these readings are correct?" Dr. Maurya asked. "Before your instruments failed, the magnetosphere of Niburu was generating a pulse wave ten times that of Earth!"

"I calibrated the spectroscopy myself, just before we left Earth," Dr. Jones answered. "It is accurate... up to the point where the radiation overruns all of my sensors."

Dr. Maurya pored over the data. "Judging by the frequency, even gamma-rays would be a tiny ripple in the pond compared to these readings. There appears to be no lower limit to these wavelengths!"

"And look, there's more," Dr. Jones pointed out. "See how the pulses surge and decay, they rise up and form two parallel funnels attached with a hole in the middle."

A smile suddenly spread over Dr. Maurya's face. "A hole in the middle... just like a white and black hole... in alignment!" he exclaimed.

"Exactly!" Samantha agreed. "But can it be? We did the proof using Schwarzschild's bubble geometry when we were back at Cambridge, but that was just a theory on the whiteboard." Dr. Maurya rubbed his chin and now assumed the role of teacher.

"Ok, Professor, you asked for my analysis. Let's assume nothing, start from the equations, and then objectively apply your empirical data." Ashoka grabbed a pen and started sketching graphical diagrams in the corner of the room. "We have two incredibly strong and opposing electromagnetic forces recorded in the data. They form inverted funnels and appear to join together for just an instant. One emits negative energy and the other emits positive energy. For the million dollars, and the Nobel prize in astrophysics, the question is... how can they exist in parallel without destroying each other?"

Dr. Jones waved her arms with excitement. "The negative energy of the black hole swallows everything in its path and the white hole spits out the consumed matter to the other side... *if* they are connected!"

"Yes!" Dr. Maurya shouted back. "If you think of it another way, the white hole is the inverse of the black hole; it's a black hole running backwards in time. And the connection between the black hole and the white hole is a... wormhole, a portal to a..."

"Another dimension, a parallel universe!" Dr. Jones interrupted. "But only if we ignore the second law of thermodynamics... then you would be correct."

Dr. Maurya scratched his chin and continued thinking aloud. "Even Einstein postulated that such a wormhole could exist... he called it the Einstein-Rosen bridge. Are you challenging the validity of the Theory of Relativity?"

"No, of course not," Samantha stated. "But because the two universes are of different mass, the only way to hold open a wormhole would be to create it with some exotic material that could simultaneously withstand the equally opposing forces. Did Einstein account for this?"

"As a matter of fact, he did." Ashoka responded. "He theorized that the wormhole would need a shell of exotic matter that must have a negative mass but positive surface pressure. Simple." Samantha Jones understood the theory, but the reality was harder to grasp.

"Ok, the negative mass would ensure the throat of the wormhole lies outside the event horizon, so that you can pass through it, while the positive surface pressure would prevent the wormhole from collapsing... just for an instant."

Dr. Maurya beamed as he spoke. "Again, my dear, you are as beautiful as ever. We proved that time travel was possible in theory back at Cambridge. But this is not a theory... this is real!" They looked at each other, stunned at what they had discovered.

Dr. Jones was the first to speak. "Now we have confirmed that Niburu can randomly generate the massive power to open a wormhole... how will you focus that power exactly when and where it is needed to hold the portal open?"

"I am way ahead of you on that one." Dr. Maurya smiled. "I just need to contact Dr. Stone to help me with the atmospheric generator design. I have a few modifications embedded in the surge protector module that should do the trick." He typed in a text message to Josiah.

"Chemical voltaic conversion a go, needed power surge has wheel in ditch. Your H2 is ready... meet IRL?"

"Cool. Stay stealth?" Josiah returned.

"10-4," Dr. Maurya messaged back.

Dr. Jones read the text messages over Dr. Maurya's shoulder and had to caution him on secrecy. "You realize that we can't let anyone other than Dr. Stone know what this may be, especially Lieutenant McCurdy," she told him. "Don't speak of this to anyone, and for God's sake, Ashoka, don't write it down!" Dr. Maurya smiled and tapped the side of his head.

"No worries, I am way ahead of you on that one... it is all up here," he reassured her. There was a slow, high-pitched whistle in the background. The kettle was boiling on Dr. Jones' Bunsen burner. "Now, where's my cup of Earl Grey, love?"

26. The Mole

The command module of Genesis Five came equipped with a small escape vehicle, known as the ePod. It was intended for minor hull repairs in space, and also to carry the crew back and forth between docking stations. The ePod had limited maneuverability and range, but it had survived the crash landing intact, and according to Dr. Jones' toxic cloud data, it was the only safe way to leave the ship.

Following his text exchange with Dr. Maurya, Josiah Stone prepared to slip over to the passenger module and pick up the hydrogen he needed to convert the ship's fuel cells to an ion thrust engine. His repeated engine thrust calculations had caused Dr. Stone to snicker at the clumsy courtship maneuvers between Officer Taylor and Captain Lovelorn, so he decided now was an opportune time to leave the two lovebirds alone in the nest. Like a college roommate that bows out at the opportune time, Josiah walked over to Commander Ryker and slapped him on the back.

"Hey, Dad, mind if I borrow the keys to the station wagon? I need to run to the store for a pack of cigarettes."

"What?" Ryker mumbled as he snapped out of his momentary quest for his Holy Grail.

"Look, Pops," Josiah mocked, "I need to hop over to the passenger module and get some supplies. I'm taking the ePod, ok?" Ryker turned toward Josiah, smiled, and tossed him the passkey.

"Ok, son, but take your little sister and Lassie for a ride, will you? Those two need to get out of my hair for a while."

"Sure thing, Daddy-O. Anything you need from the store?"

"Yeah, pick me up a six-pack and some Slim Jims," Ryker snapped back like a doting dad. "And don't bring the station wagon back with an empty gas tank again."

Josiah laughed and turned to head down the catwalk to the ePod. He inserted the security key and opened the door. It was dark inside and he fumbled to find the light switch on the control panel. Just as he was about to turn on the lights, he saw two glowing red eyes staring at him from the back of the ePod. There was a deep growl that reverberated through the small cabin and he could smell the musky scent of the beast that had eaten his prized robotic bee. He was just about to pick up a metal rod to defend himself when a voice called out from the darkness.

"Koda, Pohikiwta." (Koda, be calm.)

Josiah flicked on the lights, and there, seated casually in the back row of the ePod was Lexis with Koda standing menacingly at her side.

"How the hell did you two get in here? The door was locked!" he snapped. "And how did you know I was leaving anyway?"

"I didn't know you were leaving," Lexis answered. "He did. He heard you thinking about it, and he said you can't keep a secret."

"Whatever!" Josiah shook his head and cautiously took his seat at the ePod controls. "Better strap that beast in back there, we're going for a ride, sister." Josiah looked at the familiar instrument panel and knew piloting the ePod would be easy after his secret lab experience flying one in the virtual world. *Ah, the benefit of running a government funded research lab,* he thought, *you get to build some really neat toys.*

The airlock opened and the ePod slowly slipped out of the command module and into the Niburu atmosphere. Just across the dry lakebed, Josiah could see a faint glimmer from the blinking red landing lights on Genesis Five. In the distance to the right, there was an outline of purple mountains, and far to the left; the dry lakebed gave way to outcroppings of low boulders and rolling hills, broken by an occasional sand dune. Josiah turned from the window to Lexis, who was still seated in the rear compartment beside the beast.

"You want to take over for a second, I need to call ahead to let them know we're coming," Josiah told her.

Lexis folded down the steering controls from the instrument panel and assumed guidance for the ePod.

"We are inbound to pick up FedEx package," Josiah called out. "Passenger Airlock? Ten minutes?"

"Not airlock," Dr. Maurya replied. "Package is waiting at rear loading dock. I'll leave a light on."

Josiah resumed control of the ePod, enjoying his first real-life flight experience outside the simulator, and maneuvered above Genesis Five to stay just out of detection from the forward sensors. Like a hummingbird approaching a flower, he gently descended behind Genesis Five's cargo bay and located the blinking red LED above the docking ring. From the control panel, he extended a small robotic arm and grasped the docking ring, pulling the ePod into position to establish a seal with the loading dock.

Inside, a nervous Dr. Maurya was waiting with two unmarked liquid hydrogen cryogenic storage tanks, full of the hydrogen he had produced as a byproduct from his atmospheric generator prototype. As promised, Josiah had earlier transmitted the computer diagrams of his surge protector component, along with the problem of redirecting the power supply for the atmospheric generator. Josiah didn't ask why Dr. Maurya needed to redirect the power; it seemed a redundant exercise, but he also felt it best not to poke around any further at this point. Kind of a scientific *'don't ask, don't tell'* program. In any event, he preferred to have a discussion of that nature in person.

The sudden whoosh of rushing air and the flashing yellow light indicated that the loading dock airlock on the cargo bay had been secured. The airlock was designed for bulk loading and unloading of small containers, up to one meter in size, not for personnel boarding. There was a conveyor belt for the material exchange. Dr. Maurya loaded the hydrogen canisters onto the belt and sent them on their way to the ePod. As Dr. Josiah Stone turned on his video monitor, he was greeted by the image of Dr. Maurya. Even though it was a video link from inside the ship only five meters away, it was the first time they had met face-to-face other than the chaotic scramble before their launch back in Tiny Town.

"Thanks for the H2," Josiah transmitted. "It should be sufficient to test out my thrusters. Oh, and I uploaded a design for your power question onto your server. Pretty straightforward, it is called *'Redirector'*. You might have some problems with the conversions, so I included NELI, my AI assistant, in the upload. She can help you run the installation algorithms."

"Excellent!" Dr. Maurya responded. "I'm most indebted to you, and uh, your Miss NELI, is it? May I offer anything in return for your generosity? Perhaps some Earl Grey?"

"No, I'm good, Doc. Unless you got some Slim Jims over there... never mind. What's up with the backdoor James Bond drama?"

Dr. Maurya lowered his voice. "Something very strange is going on here, Dr. Stone. I suggest we take precautions when we communicate in the future. I have set up a remote access account for you on my server called *'H2Man'*. We can leave secure messages there. Your password is *'Hindenburg'*."

"Classic." Josiah laughed. "Now what's the mystery?"

"Yes, the mystery," Maurya continued. "Last night we had a fire alarm go off around midnight. Everyone got rousted out of bed by the soldiers and marched down to the cargo bay. It was quite a scene, everyone standing around in pajamas, waiting for the 'all clear'. It turned out that it was a false alarm and we all stumbled back to bed, but in the morning, there were two passengers missing."

"Missing?" Josiah questioned. "How could they go missing?"

"Lieutenant McCurdy ordered a complete sweep of the ship and his soldiers searched every compartment, but the missing passengers couldn't be found. It's as if they just vanished into the night." Josiah and Lexis exchanged confused glances. Lexis moved in front of the video screen and queried Dr. Maurya.

"Creepers," Lexis exhaled. "Any ideas on how..." Just as Lexis was asking her question, Dr. Jones burst into the cargo bay.

"I thought I might find you here," Dr. Jones gasped. "McCurdy is looking for you! He went to your lab and was furious you were missing. He screamed at the guards to find you and bring you back to the lab and then stomped out!"

"Oh my, that's not good," Dr. Maurya responded. "We'd better get this exchange business wrapped up."

"Wait!" interrupted Dr. Jones. "There's more. I did some checking on the missing passengers. They were last seen after the fire drill near the airlock, so I searched the area and with my UV light I found several drops of blood by the exterior cargo door. I took a sample of the blood from the door and ran a DNA analysis against our passenger data bank... it was the blood of the missing passengers."

"Holy Mother!" Dr. Maurya exclaimed. "Are you saying that the two missing passengers were attacked on the ship? Right here under our noses?"

"It seems so; the blood indicates a struggle," Dr. Jones answered. "I don't know where they went, but it doesn't look like they went willingly. And one more odd thing... the computer log shows that the cargo bay airlock was opened last night, from the outside."

Josiah and Lexis had been listening to the conversation. Lexis grabbed the transmitter. "I know the design of that airlock module, it's a Boeing JAM 350. It has a dual security computer that controls access from both sides."

"What are you saying?" Dr. Jones asked.

"I'm saying that the outer door lock can't be opened unless someone inside inserts a key," Lexis responded.

"Someone inside opened the lock to the outer door?" Dr. Jones questioned.

"That's affirmative, Doc," Lexis answered. "Looks like you got a mole on board."

27. We Are Not Alone

Dr. Josiah Stone pulled the large red lever on the underside of the ePod to release the airlock attached to Genesis Five. With his hydrogen canisters stowed in the ePod cargo hold, he prepared to steal away from the passenger compartment before anyone else onboard learned of his visit. The sudden disappearance of two passengers in the dead of night was more drama than he needed right now, and besides, with the command module dead in the water, he was eager to get back to work on his ion thruster engine. If he could get the power working, at least they would have options; without power, they were like sitting ducks in a shooting gallery. On the video monitor, Dr. Maurya faded in with a frantic look.

"Oh, wait! Dr. Stone, before you go, I must talk to you about the power supply design. I need it to... "

"Redirect massive amounts of unknown power into a shell of exotic matter with a negative mass and a positive surface pressure?" Josiah shot back.

Dr. Maurya and Dr. Jones looked at each other, confused.

"Why, yes, something like that. But how did you know?" Dr. Maurya answered.

"Elementary, my dear Watson. You think you Cambridge nerds have a corner on the time travel business? I saw the EMP data and had the same thought, but until we have an engine that works over here, we're kind of up to our ass in alligators, you know what I mean?"

"I guess I'm not very good at keeping secrets," Dr. Maurya confessed.

"Once bitten, twice shy, Doc?" Josiah observed. "You'd better get good at it fast because things around here are not always as they seem.

The safety hatch of the ePod slid shut with a gentle thump and the air from the airlock seeped out into the Niburu atmosphere with a hiss that sounded like a slow-leaking birthday balloon. Outside, the electromagnetic lights from the Niburu sky were starting to dim, pulsating erratically and fading into twilight. Josiah nudged the thruster on the ePod; it silently decoupled from the loading dock as he turned and maneuvered away from Genesis Five into the darkness. The blinking red landing lights of the passenger compartment faded in the distance as the ePod slowly made its way just above the dry lakebed back toward the command module. On the right corner of the control panel telemetry screen, a green light blinked on, pulsating and growing brighter. Lexis moved to the front of the ePod to investigate.

"What's that light mean?" she asked, pointing to the video screen.

"I don't know," Josiah answered. "Something is approaching us from the east, maybe a dust storm from the way it is registering."

The pulsating green light grew larger and they suddenly felt a rush of air beneath the ePod. The telemetry controls flashed red and yellow, with a warning signal and a beeping alarm. Lexis leaped forward and pressed her face against the side window.

"What's out there?" Josiah asked. "Do you see anything?"

"Nothing!" Lexis shouted back over the wind noise. "I can't see anything in the darkness!"

As the words left her lips, a violent rush of air sucked the ePod into a vortex, spinning it upwards like a tornado. They were tossed about like a feather in a wind tunnel for several minutes as Josiah fought the controls and tried to keep the ePod from being torn apart. And then, just as suddenly as it came, the tornado dissipated and they were thrown back to the planet surface, landing with a thud. Lexis was the first to regain her composure.

"What the hell was that?" she exclaimed.

"I... don't know," Josiah exhaled. "Some sort of twister... it seemed to come right after we lost the lights in the sky." He toggled through the command panel to check the controls.

"Are we ok?" Lexis asked.

"Amazingly so." Josiah sighed. "Somehow, the light weight of the ePod worked to our advantage. If we were heavier, we could have been ripped apart in that wind shear. We're ok, but it looks like we got tossed across the mountains and our navigation system is fried. I'm not exactly sure where the hell we are right now."

Just then, Koda let out a low growl and lunged toward the rear cargo compartment. His growling accelerated into high-pitched barking as he scratched and clawed at the exit door. Lexis tried to restrain him, but she couldn't control his violent behavior. Koda wouldn't let her near the door, as he snapped at her to keep her away from the opening.

"Koda! Himu?" (Koda! What?) Lexis shouted. Suddenly, Koda

stopped barking. He growled, keeping his body between the exit door and Lexis, looking her straight in the eyes. Lexis reached out to take his head in her hands, his drool dripping down her arms. She scratched his chin and looked deeply into his eyes.

"Lolma." (Good.) Lexis told him in a low voice.

"What's wrong with him?" Josiah asked.

"Nothing is wrong with him," Lexis snapped. "He's just doing what he's trained to do. He's telling me that there is danger just outside that door. Someone or something, he can't be sure." Josiah was astonished.

"But how could he...?" Josiah started to say, but was cut off as the pulsating lights of the Niburu sky faded on, and after a few moments, they surged to provide a light almost as bright as early morning. The new light was a welcome relief from the pitch black, but as the darkness retreated into light, Lexis and Josiah could now see out the side window in front of the door where Koda had gone berserk. They were speechless for a moment, staring out the window at the shocking sight in front of them.

"Holy shit!" Josiah exhaled. "I guess we know what he was barking about now. I take back anything I said about that beast." Josiah reached out to pet the wolf-dog on the head, but Koda growled and bared his teeth, causing Josiah to slowly retract his offer of friendship and smile at Koda to ensure he didn't lose a finger on his right hand. "What the hell do you think that it is?" he whistled as he stared out the window.

"Judging from the call sign on the tail section," Lexis observed, "I'd say that's a Russian deep-space probe, a Phobos-Grunt class, about three years old. The thrusters are gone, but the command module looks to be mostly intact." Josiah scanned the spacecraft and scratched his head unconsciously.

"I remember now," he mused. "They played it down, but it was on the news. There was a probe that got lost on a mission to one of the outer planets in a solar storm. Hey, wasn't that probe..."

"Manned?" Lexis interrupted. "Yes, it was." She turned to Koda and scratched his scruffy fur, rubbing underneath his chin. Koda rolled his eyes back and then responded by nuzzling up against her leg, rubbing his massive head on her side. She smiled and looked directly into Koda's blood-red eyes.

"Looks like we're not alone any more, boy."

28. Prison Break

Captain Mitch Gaylord lay on a pile of dirty rags in his prison cell, his mind drifting in and out of focus as he stared up at the dingy ceiling above his head. He hadn't heard any further noises from the pinhole in the center of the floor since Commander Ivan Stephanotski advised him to eat the foul green slime that was slopped into a metal bowl and slid under his door. *Ok,* he thought, *this bad dream is like pilot survival training.* In a crash landing, Captain Gaylord had been trained to live off of anything he could scrounge in the jungle or desert... dead animals, bugs, even scraps of trash. His survival instructor drilled into his head.

"If your fucking life's on the line, son, you can and will eat anything. Don't think about what you're eating, just imagine it's a big Grand Slam breakfast at Denny's. No matter what that nasty shit is, you're eating three eggs over easy, a couple of greasy sausages and a stack of flapjacks with melted butter all drowned in a pool of hot, sticky maple syrup. Mmm, mmm good."

Mitch Gaylord tried again to force down the gooey green slime, but it lodged in his throat, and he vomited in the corner of his prison cell. *That doesn't taste like any fucking Denny's breakfast I remember. What was the last thing the Russian said through the pinhole in the floor?*

"Eat, you'll need your strength for what comes!" *What the bloody hell did that mean? And just what was coming, anyway.*

Time had lost all meaning for Mitch Gaylord in this dimly lit prison with no windows. He had no real way of telling time, *But by now*, he thought, *whatever was coming... it should be here.* As he turned to roll over, he winced with a sharp pain that shot between his ribs where the big scaly beast had kicked the living shit out of him, just for making a little noise. Whatever that beast was that came to visit him, apparently it didn't like noise. Mitch sat up and cringed again in pain. The intense tenderness he felt seemed to be localized on the left side of his ribcage, so he reached inside his torn shirt to try and massage the sore area. As he ran his hand over his throbbing ribs, he suddenly realized... something was different. He could feel a long bumpy section of skin beneath his sternum that had no sensation to touch. Mitch Gaylord tore off a piece of his shirt and crawled across the floor to get a better look at his wound in the dim light. He was astonished by what he saw on his body. On the left side of his rib cage was a surgical incision, eight inches in length, neatly closed with sutures and sealed by a scaly glue-like substance.

"Where the hell did that come from?" he screamed out loud. "Was I in a MASH unit after my crash?" *Oh well,* he thought, *judging from the quality of the work, whoever operated on me did a pretty good job, but shit, it still hurts.* Getting kicked in the side by an eight-foot lizard didn't help either, so to avoid any more beatings; Mitch Gaylord needed to learn the rules. *Rule number one,* he thought, *don't make any unnecessary noise.*

Somewhere outside the door to his prison cell, Mitch Gaylord could hear a faint sound, a sound that sounded like a person sobbing softly and occasionally crying out. He crawled over to the door and shoved his head down flat at the crack at the footboard, straining to listen for the sound again. Maybe his mind was playing tricks on him and he was imagining the sound. With his ear pressed hard to the floor, Captain Gaylord suddenly felt dampness, as if he had placed his ear directly in a puddle. He felt the moisture on the floor and then again dripping down the side of his neck. *That was strange,* he thought, *the sticky fluid seems to be oozing out of the side of my neck.* It was too dark to see; maybe he was bleeding from opening up a wound from the crash. The flow of fluid from his neck didn't feel dangerous, so he tore off a piece of his shirt and fashioned a makeshift bandage for the wound. *That should hold it for a while.*

There it was again, he wasn't dreaming! It was a human sound, maybe a woman's voice, no; it was a girl's voice he heard, sobbing sadly outside his cell. He focused his perception and tried to identify the location of the sound. It was close, within twenty meters and definitely on the same level as his cell because he could hear the sobbing sound echo down a long hallway. In the distance, Mitch could hear footsteps coming rapidly and he froze as they approached his door. He clutched his sore ribs and thought, *wait a minute... I didn't make a peep, you bastards! Pay some respect to rule number one for God's sake!*

The footsteps paused for a second at his door and then continued down the hall toward the sobbing sounds he could still hear in the distance. Captain Gaylord listened intently and counted exactly twenty paces past his cell to where the footsteps stopped. A creaky wooden door opened and the sobbing suddenly ceased for a second; there was a girl's scream and then silence. The wooden door opened again and this time, the two sets of footsteps were rapidly approaching *his* door. *Shit!*

They stopped.

Just outside his door, Mitch could hear two beasts grunting and snarling and then they were silent. He scrambled back across the cold stone floor of his prison cell and dove into his pile of rags. *Rule number one; be quiet,* he thought. Maybe they were just bringing food. If he were still, maybe they would go away. In any event, he lay silently on his pile of rags and closed his eyes. He rubbed his side again and thought, *Stay still! You don't want another fucking beating.*

The door to his cell swung open with a thud and two large scaly beasts strode inside, slamming the door behind them. One of the beasts had a long wooden pole with a leather rope at the end, dragging it along the floor as he approached him, slowly dangling the rope toward his head. The other beast had moved around behind him and delivered a swift kick to his kidney, causing Mitch to jerk up to a sitting position and scream in pain. Mitch tried to stand, but the first beast looped the leather rope over his head and yanked it tight around his neck, knocking him to his knees. Gasping for air, he grabbed at the rope around his neck, struggling, but he was no match for the strength of the two scaly creatures. They punched and kicked at him until he submitted, then they dragged him out the door and down the hallway. The pain in his side was so intense that he almost passed out. As he struggled back to his feet, Mitch thought to himself, *So much for fucking rule number one, and damn it, I don't think we're on our way to Denny's for breakfast.*

The scaly beasts dragged Captain Gaylord by the neck down a labyrinth of hallways carved out of sheer rock; some were narrow and others large enough to drive a small truck through. The hallway they were now in was dimly lit by the flames of large metal torches intermittently embedded in the rock outcroppings along the sides of the walls. There was a cold chill in the air and a pungent dampness came over him from a foul-smelling white fluid oozing out from cracks in the rocks and dripping down the walls.

Mitch hadn't eaten his bowl of gruel earlier and his mouth was as dry as a bone, so he lunged back and forth toward the damp walls as they walked, managing to wipe his sleeves against the moisture in the hopes of quenching his thirst. He bent down long enough to get his sleeve in his mouth and sucked at the damp cloth, but immediately he gagged and spat it out; the fluid was even ranker than the stinking slime in his daily food bowl.

As the goo ran down his mouth, he shouted out, "You bastards have a lousy sense of taste, don't you!"

The scaly guards stopped long enough to deliver a few more sharp blows to his ribcage and then grunted and snarled at each other before they resumed dragging Mitch down the hallway by the neck. They paused in front of a large metal double door and banged their pole against the entryway. After a minute, a horn sounded a single blast and the large metal doors slowly swung open leading into a small room.

One of the beasts grabbed Mitch by the arm and pinned it behind his head while the other loosened the leather noose around his neck. The beast with the pole delivered a jab to his ribcage, causing Captain Gaylord to double over in pain. As he bent over, he was thrown inside the room, landing on another cold stone floor. The large metal doors creaked shut with a dull thud, and once again; Mitch was alone in the darkness. Gradually, his eyes adjusted to the dim light, and he could see a wooden hatch at the back of the empty room that appeared to slide up and down on a metal track. Mitch moved closer and ran his hand along the edge of the wooden hatch, searching for an opening, but there was none.

On the other side of the hatch, he could hear faint sounds getting louder. He pressed his ear to the hatch and could make out grunting, snarling noises intermingled with a hypnotic rhythmic beating of drums. The drums rose to a climax and then there were bizarre, bloodcurdling screams. From the other side of the empty room, he now could hear the approach of footsteps down the hall, and then the large metal doors swung open with a clang.

This time, the scaly beasts that entered were dressed from head to toe in a metallic armor, and they thrust wooden spears toward him, forcing him back across the room against the wooden hatch. They abruptly stopped their advance a few feet in front of him, as if waiting for a command to kill. Mitch looked up at the beast in front of him, staring him in the eyes. *If this is the end of the road,* he thought, *I want to see my executioner face to face.* The beast stood there motionless, staring back at Mitch. His head was covered in an elaborately carved metal helmet with engraved images that Mitch had seen somewhere before.

The carvings on the beast's helmet resembled something from the warriors of ancient Rome, no, they were more like pre-Colombian figures, but much more elaborate. *That was it, Central American— Aztec or Mayan, maybe.* The beast cocked his head, still staring at Mitch, exposing two small round openings for his eyes. As it stepped forward into a shaft of light, Mitch could see two jet-black eyes with vertical slits exposed. The light caused the beast to blink and stumble for a second, and then it stepped back into the dimly lit portion of the room and growled.

On the other side of the wooden hatch, there was the piercing sound of a horn that bleated out a long two-pitched note, causing the beasts to spring to attention. The wooden hatch started to rise, exposing an opening to another room. The two beasts moved forward, poking and jabbing at Mitch, forcing him into the opening. With his head lodged halfway inside, he tried to grab the sides of the hatch to resist, but a powerful kick to his back sent him tumbling through.

Captain Gaylord landed face down in a soft pile of moist dirt; he shook his head and crawled to his knees to look around. What he saw around him was terrifying and made his heart skip a beat. He was now laying at the edge of a large circular rock cavern with hundreds of scaly beasts perched on tiered rock outcroppings, grunting, snarling, and beating their claws against their chests. There was a slender shaft of light streaming down into the cavern. Standing in the center of the room with his back to him was an armor-clad warrior holding an axe in one hand and a bloody decapitated human head extended in the other hand.

The beasts surrounding the rock cavern jumped up and down, grunting and biting at each other like a pack of rabid wolves, howling with the glee of a fresh kill. The warrior in the center of the room tossed the human head onto the ground and lowered his axe, as if to salute the frenzied mob. Again, the pack of scaly beasts erupted in grunts and snarls, seeming to salute the warrior.

The bloody fighter in the arena turned toward Mitch Gaylord and staggered in his direction. He thrust his axe forward and pointed directly at Mitch's heart. The warrior approached within a few feet of Mitch before lowering his weapon. He removed his metal helmet and shook the sweat off his matted hair and beard, then smiled and extended his gloved hand to Mitch.

"Hello, cowboy, is good we finally meet. I am Commander Ivan Stephanotski, welcome to gladiator arena. Let us step into my office, we talk now."

29. Forensic Archeology

Looking out the window of the ePod, Josiah and Lexis observed that the side of the Russian spacecraft below them was charred with streaks of a black and orange substance, probably from when it had entered the Niburu atmosphere. The forward compartment of the ship was partially buried in a sand dune, nose cone first, next to a pile of rocks. Although the damage to the Russian spaceship was significant, the command module looked to have held up in the impact rather well. *Most likely, the crew would have survived the landing,* Josiah thought.

He circled the ePod around the Russian spacecraft, looking for anything that could shed light on the fate of the crashed ship. A Russian deep-space probe of this vintage would have carried a crew of six, plus supplies for a three- year journey. If they survived the landing, maybe someone was still alive down there.

As they silently approached the crash site, there were no lights, no sounds—no signs of any life coming from the ship. Josiah paused for a moment and then carefully guided the ePod to just outside the docking compartment of the Russian craft. *What the hell, it's worth a shot.* Entering a command on the ePod control panel, Josiah sent a computer-generated 'ping' to the Russian craft and awaited a response. After a few seconds, a faint computer 'ping' returned from inside from the docking compartment security door.

"Ok, at least their computers are still alive." Josiah announced. With the Russian computers aware of his presence, Josiah got busy trying to hack the security code that would allow the ePod to open the docking door on the Russian ship. He tried multiple international boarding codes, but the Russian computer rejected all of his attempts to gain access.

Koda moved forward to his side at the control panel and growled.

"Will you keep that beast away from me while I'm working," Josiah snapped at Lexis. "Please! I'm trying to see if I can break through their firewall and unlock the cargo door!"

"I know, but he doesn't," Lexis said to Koda, who growled, turned around, and lay down behind the rear passenger compartment.

"What are you talking about?" Josiah asked.

Lexis paused for a moment as she petted Koda, and then spoke.

"He said you don't need to break the code, the door is open."

"That's it?" Josiah laughed. "The door is open? Yeah, right."

"And there's nobody home," Lexis continued.

Josiah shook his head, believing the beast could neither know nor communicate information at this level. *What the hell kind of freak show are those two running, anyway? How could Koda know that nobody's home? It's not possible, but more importantly, why am I, a fucking child protégé genius, listening to a mind-reading beast and a smart-ass girl?*

"Nobody in there, hey, Shaggy?" Josiah mocked. "Well then, maybe I should just knock on the door and say, *'Honey, I'm home!'*"

"Whatever!" Lexis exhaled. "He was just trying to help." Josiah paused for a second, turned back around in his chair, and then activated the ePod's robotic arm.

"All right, we'll try it your way, Lassie," he conceded. Dr. Stone extended the robotic arm outward and gently tapped on the cargo door of the Russian spacecraft. Amazingly, it swung open! He spun around to Lexis, raised his eyebrows in a look of acknowledgement, and then turned back to the control panel and the robotic arm.

"Have you ever been arrested for breaking and entering?" Lexis asked smugly.

"It's not breaking and entering if the door's unlocked," Josiah cracked back. "It's just entering."

The long cable of the ePod robotic arm snaked down into the Russian command module, past the fuel cells, through the galley and next to the command control panel. It was completely dark inside the ship, with just the light on the robotic arm to help Josiah navigate the darkness. As the robotic arm moved inside, a red laser motion sensor tripped, causing a few faint lights to blink weakly to life with dim readouts on the ship's instruments. *The Russian ship's battery power and solar panels must have been drained beyond their limits,* Josiah thought. *There simply is not enough photonic energy on Niburu to drive the solar cells and charge the batteries.* The ship's computers had shut down everything onboard to conserve what little power was left, eventually, even the life support systems. The computer had only preserved enough power to save its data, and intermittently try to signal for help.

"Those poor saps didn't figure out how to convert the solar cells to chemical energy." Josiah sighed. "They probably panicked about the crash; maybe some of them were injured. Three years of supplies onboard, but without power, they couldn't have lasted more than a few months." He panned the camera 360°; there were signs of a struggle, papers strewn on the floor, chairs knocked over, but other than that, no visible signs of life. Lexis had been watching the video display of the robotic intrusion over Josiah's shoulder and moved to his side, staring at the screen.

"Where are the bodies?" she blurted out.

Josiah had been absorbed in the scouting mission and the search for computer data. Suddenly, he realized that Lexis had a valid point.

"You're right," he mused. "There should be bodies... but where is the crew?"

Koda leaped up from the floor and growled with a low, guttural vocalization. He moved forward deliberately to stare at something on the video screen. Josiah looked at the beast, and back to the video screen.

"What are you looking for, Shaggy?" he asked softly. Josiah panned the camera slowly, back across the center of the control panel, and Koda started to bark wildly again.

"Koda, himu?" (Koda, what?) Lexis asked.

The wolf-dog looked deep into Lexis' eyes and growled. Lexis cocked her head; she was confused.

"Manangya taaqa aapiy, meh." (Lizard Man away, listen.) Lexis repeated slowly.

"What did he say?" Josiah blurted out. Lexis turned back to Josiah with a confused look on her face.

"It doesn't make any sense. Koda said, *'Lizard man... away... listen'.*" Josiah shook his head; that made absolutely no sense. He continued examining the control panel of the Russian spacecraft exactly where the beast seemed to be focused on the video screen.

"What did you see there, Scout?" Josiah muttered. He was still skeptical that Koda was some kind of all-seeing canine truth-seeker, but he had to agree, something was definitely strange here. He zoomed in on the robotic arm's video screen and found what Koda must have seen there beneath the control panel. It was a small black box with several multicolored video cables attached. "Well, what the hell do we have here?" Josiah exclaimed. "Ok, Lassie, I take it all back. Good boy!"

"Is that what I think it is?" Lexis asked as she moved back to the front of the ePod.

"Bingo!" Josiah shouted. "That would be the ship's video log, our blast to the past. Now all I have to do is attach this wireless transfer coupler, and then I can upload the data from their video hard drive to our computer."

Once the Russian ship's log was uploaded, Josiah retracted the robotic arm and gently backed the ePod away from the Russian spacecraft. He searched for the homing signal from the command module of Genesis Five and locked in on its beacon. It was about fifteen kilometers away to the southwest, back across the mountains.

"Man, we really got blown off course," Josiah groaned. "I told Pops we wouldn't be that long, so let's skedaddle out of here." He tapped the fuel cell readout; it registered empty. *Empty would be bad, very bad,* he thought. Cocking his head to the side, he let out a sigh of relief. Embossed on the fuel cell gauge was a corporate logo, *Crimson Dawn. That little fucking logo could quite probably save our lives,* he thought.

As Dr. Stone remembered, Crimson Dawn was a technology spinoff of some nerd herd grad student cult at MIT that worshiped obscure apocalyptic tales of teenage terrorism.

Back at MIT, Josiah had overheard two undergrads bragging one day about how Crimson Dawn had just won another Dark Energy Resources grant for fuel cell design, baffling the competition. The nerds clucked and high-fived themselves and then looked around sheepishly to see if anyone else was listening. Apparently, the secret of their success was not superior intellect, advanced engineering skill, or even dumb luck. It was something more basic, more real world... they cheated. Crimson Dawn's secret advantage was that after the prototype inspections, they remotely reprogrammed their fuel cell software to reset the capacity readings on the storage tanks to be slightly off, allowing them to carry more fuel in the efficiency test than all the other contestants. So when everyone else ran out of fuel, they kept going, and going, and going. The inside baseball nerd joke was that when you control the divisor in an equation, you can create your own outcome. *Man, those twerps were funny,* Josiah thought, *you know, funny looking.*

"Let's just hope those dweebs put their money where their mouth was..." Josiah whispered to himself.

"What are you up here babbling about?" Lexis asked.

"Oh, nothing. Just that it would be a long walk without a space suit out there." Josiah smiled. "But I think we may have just enough power to make it back, so here we go." Josiah began backing the ePod away from the Russian spacecraft. He punched in the guidance commands for the return trip and was about to engage the power cells for their only thrust when he noticed that Lexis had turned away and was now staring intently out the window.

"Anything interesting out there?" Josiah asked reflexively.

Lexis remained glued to the window of the ePod, tapping her hand on the glass and pointing down. Her mouth dropped open and she was unable to speak.

"What's down there? Your lizard man?"

"No," Lexis answered. "But I think we found one of the Russian crewmembers. Or at least what's left of him."

Josiah was startled by her comment and slammed on the brakes to stop their forward acceleration and conserve precious fuel. He reversed course and guided the ePod toward the back of the Russian spacecraft. He could now see what Lexis was staring at outside the window.

Beside the downed spacecraft, there were several sets of large tracks leading to the crash site, coming from the boulders just beyond the rugged cliffs. Directly underneath the ePod was what appeared to be a makeshift platform of stones, with tracks leading from the cliffs to a circle surrounding the platform. Judging from the markings on the ground and the surface disturbance, it looked like there was a violent struggle and then something was dragged up to the top of the platform. The platform and the surrounding rocks were drenched dark red with bloodstains and the gruesome remains of what was once... a man. Judging from the dispersion of the body parts, it looked like the poor bastard was torn apart alive and then his flesh was devoured down to the broken bone fragments.

Koda growled and intensified his focus out the window, gazing at the bloodstained platform below before looking back at Lexis as if he was about to speak. Lexis locked onto his gaze and listened intently to Koda with her mind. She closed her eyes, concentrated, and then opened them suddenly with a terrified look. Lexis mouthed a name back to Koda, saying it only in her mind. The name that she thought of, according to a native Indian legend, was never to be spoken. *Itzamna,* she thought. Koda looked out the window and growled again, this time much more viciously.

"What on Earth could have done that to a human being?" Josiah gasped.

"Nothing on Earth," Lexis answered softly. "It was a lizard man."

30. Bank Shot

Below the ePod, Lexis looked down at the grisly scene on the rocky platform next to the Russian spacecraft. The river of dried blood, the bone fragments, and markings in the sand silently bore witness to the desperate struggle that someone had put up. But that desperate struggle was for naught; whoever it was that had been killed down there, they met their brutal end on this Godforsaken planet, ripped apart alive. In her line of work, Lexis had seen many acts of brutality, but the evidence below bore witness to a senseless cruelty that resembled ancient ritual killings, where the poor victim was torn limb from limb to appease some vengeful deity. The images below the ePod would haunt her mind for some time to come. *As terrible as the scene on the rocky platform is, it's also... familiar.*

Koda had recognized the danger immediately and tried to warn her, but she was unable to decode his message. Years ago, Koda and Lexis had been paired together because they shared a link that allowed them to communicate in a telepathic manner. Over time, they were able to develop this link to transport thoughts and feelings, like a far-off voice whispering in your ear. Sometimes, the messages coming from Koda were more primal, instinctual fight-or-flight responses that he conveyed in a mental flash of lights and colors. But this time, something was very different, something Lexis had never experienced before. The images that flashed in her mind were far more intense and vivid; bits and pieces of brutal scenes, as though she was looking through the eyes of a predator stalking its prey. The horrific images that Koda shared tumbled around in her head like the crystals in a kaleidoscope, waiting to fall in place to offer some clarity or explanation. *The meaning is close, but it's still elusive; something didn't quite click.*

At first, the images were of the Russian spacecraft in the dark; crash landing in a fiery descent into the rocky desert. Shrieks, screams, and then a wild frenzied blur of claws and teeth, ripping away at a terrified human that was being held down on a pile of rocks... a human in what was left of a Russian flight suit. Blood and flesh were flying in all directions, there was fighting and screaming, followed by a trance-like dance, tossing about the scattered remains of the victim. Now the images in her mind jumped forward to a new hunt, as the deadly predator turned its attention to its next victim. This time, the predator was moving in silently, communicating with others and closing in on its unsuspecting target. There was an undeniable intelligence driving the images, but there was also an overriding malevolence that seemed to derive pleasure from the terror and torture the beast inflicted on its victims. One thing was frighteningly clear... *this predator didn't hunt for survival; it hunted for sport.*

The blurry images from the predator's point of view just ahead came into focus... it was an image of the ePod caught on the rocks beside the Russian spacecraft. Suddenly, a cold chill came over Lexis as a shudder ran down her spine. *These images were in real time... the beast is stalking us!*

Inside the ePod, Koda crouched low to the ground, growling; his head down, teeth bared, and his eyes glowing like two burning embers in the dark. Now it was clear what he was trying to tell her... the evil that walked among them was back. Lexis was snapped back to the terrifying reality of the moment. Breaking her gaze from the window, she quickly turned to Josiah.

"We need to leave... now!" Lexis shouted.

"I'm way ahead of you," Josiah answered. "This place is getting kind of spooky."

The fuel cell gauge on the ePod instrument panel read empty again, but Josiah goosed it back to life with a thump. Regardless of the reading, they were going to need one more push from the fuel cell to take them back to the safety of Genesis Five's command module. The tiny engine of the ePod grudgingly responded, lurching forward. But then, just as the ePod started to gain momentum, it jolted to a halt, as if part of the rear fuselage were caught on the jagged rocks below.

"Damn those nerds of Crimson Dawn!" Josiah screamed out. "We should have enough fuel to get back! Did they plant another phantom reading in my fuel cell? What the hell is the problem here?" Now Josiah pounded on the fuel gauge, trying to verify that it really contained enough of that last electrical charge they would need to make their escape. The gauge quivered, just enough to alleviate his fears. He sighed in relief, there was still a faint charge left on the fuel cell. But then it hit him. *If there's nothing wrong with the fuel cell or the engine... why aren't we moving?*

Lexis stepped away from the window, still fixated on the brutal images in her mind and on the crime scene below. She moved next to Josiah to check on their status. "I told you, we have to go!" she urged.

"I'm trying to, damn it! The controls won't respond! We seem to be stuck on something." Josiah's frustration with the controls was abruptly interrupted by a loud thud, coming from the rear of the ePod. The impact threw Lexis and Koda forward, sending them crashing into the instrument panel next to Josiah.

Koda spun around and leaped to his feet; in one swift motion, he lunged past Josiah toward the rear compartment, throwing the weight of his body against the airlock door just as it started to crack open. The air inside the ePod hissed to escape through the opening and there was a wild, high-pitched scream as something clawed at the crack in the door, trying to get inside. With their power failing, the lights inside the ePod flickered off and on in a strobe light effect. In a brief moment of light, Josiah could see what was caught in the crack of the airlock opening; it was a bloody claw, scratching frantically, and trying to pry the door open!

Koda raised his massive head, his mouth wide open as he clamped down on the claw protruding through the door with his razor-sharp teeth. His jaw was like a vice clamp on the attacker, ripping and tearing away at its scaly flesh, sending a green fluid squirting into his mouth and splattering down the wall. Outside, the beast shrieked in pain and repeatedly threw its massive weight against the door. It was only the strength of Koda's muscular body that prevented the beast with the bloody claw from ripping open the airlock door and viciously killing everyone inside.

Lexis reached down to her boot and clutched the handle of her knife, spinning the serrated 7-inch blade upward. She leaped through the air and threw her body against the airlock door beside Koda. As she crashed against the door, she thrust her arm downward and plunged her blade deep into the exposed palm of the bloody claw that was still wedged in the crack of the door. There was a terrifying inhuman scream of pain from the other side of the airlock, causing Lexis to recoil.

The arm of the bloody claw retracted, leaving behind a piece of scaly flesh impaled on Lexis' blade, oozing with a slimy green blood that dripped down her arm. Lexis slammed the airlock door shut and pulled down the red safety lever to lock the door in a closed position before collapsing to the floor. Josiah was frozen in shock from the vicious battle just inches from his seat. He reached up and wiped a drop of green slime from his forehead and then focused his attention on the bloody claw dangling at the end of Lexis' serrated blade.

"What the hell was that?" Josiah screamed. Koda relaxed and fell to the floor in front of the door. Lexis placed her hand and head against the airlock, as if she was still in a trance. She slowly rose to her feet and looked Josiah in the eye with a blank stare.

"Get us out of here now, brother, or it's going to be us on that sacrificial platform on the red rocks below."

Josiah looked around in bewilderment, and then took his seat back at the controls.

"Uh... right... get out of here, good idea," Josiah mumbled.

Frantically pushing the controls with one hand, he tried to break the ePod free from the rocks below. At the same time, with his other hand, he tried to ping the command module on his communicator. There was no response; it wasn't on its regular frequency. Desperate, he initiated a computer scan of alternate frequencies to find the command module and call out for help. Lexis spun around toward the airlock door and placed her hand on the wall.

"They're coming back... hurry," she whispered.

Josiah was overwhelmed, he couldn't break the ePod free from the rocks below and he couldn't find the right frequency for the command module.

"*They're* coming back? Shit, there's *more than one* of those things?" he screamed. Josiah scrambled the communicator and tried another frequency to contact Ryker and the command module. The receiver whined and sputtered with the low power level, but the computer scanner suddenly locked on to the module hailing frequency with a 'pop'.

"Genesis Five frequency acquired; awaiting transmission," the ePod computer announced.

Josiah grabbed the transmitter from the control panel and screamed his message. "Hey, Commander, we're really in a spot of trouble here... how about a helping hand!"

Back at the command module, the lights were low, Barry White was softly crooning across the intercom, and Ryker was dusting off his best amorous moves with Officer Taylor. Still frustrated by the abbreviated romantic encounter in the *'Pirate's Execution Lounge'*, with the kids in the ePod off to school, he hoped that he and Mom were finally headed to funky town. *I'm rounding third base,* he thought, *running at full speed, and the coach is waving me in. The crowd is on its feet, cheering wildly, and I feel good about my chances of scoring.* "Nothing can stop me now," he mumbled, "it's a frickin' walk off home run!" But just as Ryker was about to cross home plate in his mind, his hopes of scoring were dashed. A laser throw from left field, he was cut down at the plate.

"No! Not again!" Ryker screamed. "Who the hell is that guy in left field, anyway?" This time, the imaginary guy in left field with the laser arm was a garbled radio call from the ePod, and his name was *Romantis Interrupus.*

"Damn foreigner!" Ryker muttered. "You're ruining my national pastime!"

Why does this keep happening to me? He thought. It was like the time the school principal tapped him on the shoulder at the high school dance to sternly warn him to stop dancing so close to Mary Elizabeth. Mary Elizabeth, man, did she have a set of warheads on her. He could still hear the Sister's words ringing in his ears.

"Young man!" the nun had screeched. "When you are dancing with a *lady* at our school, make sure to leave enough room for Jesus in between the two of you!" *What a drag*, Ryker thought. *Just when you get a catholic schoolgirl alone with a couple of beers, along comes Sister Buzz Kill.* But this time, the Sister had a manly voice.

"Genesis Five... this is ePod," Josiah screamed in his ear. "Come in, damn it... come in!"

Ryker was fighting desperately to hold onto his dream of high school infatuation, but Officer Taylor wasn't. She poked Ryker hard on the shoulder.

"Don't you need to get that?" Sarah urged.

"Not really." Ryker sighed. "I'm just about to get my groove back."

"No, really," she insisted. "They could be in trouble."

"Really?" Ryker countered. "My groove is in serious trouble; I don't ignore it."

Officer Taylor sat up and turned on the lights, causing Ryker to shield his eyes and groan.

"Really?" he whimpered, feeling what was left of his groove starting to slip away.

"Really!" Sarah announced flatly, the case was closed.

Barry White had left the building with the thrill of the moment, deflating Ryker's balloon. He pursed his lips, furrowed his brow, and exhaled a long snort of disapproval. Commander Ryker pulled himself up on one elbow and changed the frequency of the receiver. *It's hard to get any fucking privacy in the dorm room of a command module,* he thought. He changed the Genesis Five frequency again and now the incoming message was silent.

"Huh, I guess we lost them." He shrugged. Ryker snuggled back up to Officer Taylor to attempt a return to the task at hand. "Now... where were we?" But just as Ryker and Officer Taylor were starting to refloat the love boat, the receiver on the control panel blurted out another *message interruptus* on the new frequency.

"Hey, Commander, we're really in a spot of trouble here... how about a helping hand!"

Officer Taylor pushed Ryker away. "Ok, sailor, time to come up for air. They sound like they're not just playing around."

Ryker tried to resist, but as it was clear playtime was over, he reluctantly picked up the transmitter and responded to the ePod.

"All right, I'm here, son, great timing by the way. I thought I told you that if the camper was a rocking, don't come a knocking."

"Well, fucking sorry for interrupting, but we are about to get eaten alive by a lizard beast with one bloody claw out here!" Josiah screamed.

"One bloody claw?" Ryker snapped to attention. "Jeez, that's creepy! Kind of like when those two lovers go parking right after the homicidal maniac escapes from prison. But as long as that thing's only got one claw, you should be ok. It doesn't have more claws, does it?"

"More claws?" Josiah yelled. "Shit, I don't know! Look, I don't have time to explain, Commander, here is what I need you to do, now listen carefully. Go to my computer and bring up the *'ion cannon'* application."

Ryker grinned. "You've built an ion cannon? That is so cool!"

"Hey! Pay attention now!" Josiah screamed. "Lock onto these coordinates and send me a pulse beam. I'm going to try and rig a Faraday cage and redirect the pulse to generate a temporary force shield."

Ryker got up and started to pull up his pants, hopping on one leg. With the transmitter tucked under his ear, he stopped and responded.

"Ok, but where is the thing with the bloody claw? If you chase it away, it's not coming this way, is it?"

Josiah tried to remain calm. "Look, I don't know where Stumpy is, but I'm pretty sure he's pissed, and when he comes back, he'll probably bring a few of his friends. So before we get eaten alive, send me that damn pulse beam... now!"

"Ok, ok, don't get your panties in a knot, junior," Ryker called back. "One pulse beam, on the way, initiating in 3, 2, 1... engaged!"

Back on the ePod, Josiah quickly reprogrammed the external hull sensors to receive and redirect the incoming pulse beam. *It was simple geometry,* he thought, *like a bank shot on his miniature basketball hoop. Freddy Mercury would be proud. But if it worked, it would only work once.* Just as Josiah completed the programming sequence, there were several hard thuds against the airlock door. The impact rocked the ePod and was followed by a chorus of high-pitched screams as the newly activated ion shield found its victims. The terrifying shrieks from outside the ePod were jumbled together with the sounds of frantic scratching and clawing, but they grew fainter and gradually fell away in the distance.

The redirected force field and the Faraday cage had worked perfectly. It banked the pulse beam from Genesis Five off the ePod hull and amplified the energy through the metal shell at an ultra-high frequency, like the combination of a giant tuning fork and a stun gun. Whatever it was out there that was attacking the ePod, it got an intensely painful surprise when it touched the outer hull. Mark Twain once said, *"When a cat sits on a hot stove once, it will never sit on a hot stove again... or a cold one."* Since the pulse weapon was only good for one charge, Josiah hoped that the beasts outside would stay off the stove for a while.

On the video screen above, Josiah looked back at the rear view of some beastly figures scrambling in the dark beside the Russian spacecraft. Ironically, it was the impact of their attack that had dislodged the ePod from the jagged rocks below, the rocks where a ritual sacrifice had claimed the life of some poor Russian crewmember. Now that they were safely on their way home to Genesis Five, Josiah released his tension with a victory yell, somewhat uncharacteristic of a graduate school professor.

"Yeah! Don't bring that weak shit into my house, Stumpy!"

Back on the command module, Ryker was now reluctantly

dressed and at the controls.

"Hey, tadpole, you guys ok out there?" he called out.

Josiah and Lexis looked at each other and smiled in relief. Koda stepped in between them and growled a friendly growl at Josiah.

"Yeah Dad, we're ok," Josiah exhaled. "The station wagon is a little beat up, but we're ok."

"So what happened to the bloody claw man?" Ryker joked.

"Well, I'd say he's a crispy critter now." Josiah laughed. Dr. Stone turned and scooted over to Lexis. She turned away from him, still clutching her knife with the scaly flesh impaled on its blade. He moved close behind her and whispered in her ear.

"That was pretty intense there for a moment, but I have two questions for you."

Lexis was still staring at the closed airlock door, but responded softly. "Ok, shoot."

"First, where did you ever learn to wield a knife like that?" he asked.

"Cooking school," Lexis responded.

Josiah raised his eyebrow; he was surprised. "You went to cooking school?"

"Well, sort of." She laughed. "I took an online course and got this awesome set of steak knives in the mail for just three easy payments, plus shipping and handling. I still can't cook, but I'm pretty good at slicing and dicing."

Lexis cooking? Josiah smiled. *Now that's a funny thought.* The smile faded and he got serious again. "What do you really think that thing was... out there?" he asked.

Lexis looked over at Koda and he shook his head and growled. This time, his message to her was clear.

You're right, you're always right, she thought back to Koda. Lexis turned to face Josiah.

"Koda says that you don't listen so well. He already told you... it was the Lizard Man."

Josiah looked at the wolf-dog for a second. He knew that without Koda, they all would be dead right now. He reached out his hand to thank Koda, but he growled and Josiah backed away slowly.

"The lizard man... is that all he said?" Josiah asked.

"No." Lexis laughed. "He said the Lizard Man tastes bad."

31. Home Movies

As the ePod glided silently across the last few meters above the desert floor of Niburu, it gently made contact with the robotic docking arm of Genesis Five's command module. The fuel cells of the ePod were completely depleted, and this time, even the phantom software inside Crimson Dawn agreed. Josiah shut down the last of the waning battery power to the control panel and breathed a sigh of relief. What had started out as a routine supply mission to retrieve some hydrogen from the Genesis Five passenger module ended up with several neck-snapping discoveries... a mysterious downed Russian spacecraft and an attack by a roaming pack of alien beasts with claws and a bad attitude. Josiah imagined his log entry for their recent adventure: *Our trip was pretty boring, oh, except it turns out that we are not the only humans on this planet, and we were almost killed in a bizarre alien ritual sacrifice. Contrary to popular belief, humans are not at the top of the food chain on Niburu. I guess you could say we had a bad day.*

With the confirmation click of the metal clasp on the docking arm, they were safely back home. Safety had come to be a relative term since they had landed on Niburu. Josiah peered nervously out of the ePod rear window into the darkness; there was nothing out there, thank God, at least for the moment. Turning back to look at Lexis and Koda, Josiah released the ePod door with a whoosh of air. As they stepped through the airlock and back onto the deck of the command module, they each realized that even though they didn't want to admit it, they had discovered a newfound respect for each other.

As Josiah started to disembark, Koda forced his way to the front, bared his teeth and growled before moving on. *Ok, respect was probably the wrong word for this mutual feeling,* Josiah thought. Respect would imply a certain level of trust and understanding, which they may not have yet achieved. The feeling that they shared was more basic, it was like a shotgun marriage of convenience; they needed each other to survive.

Lexis turned to Josiah with a puzzled look on her face; something was bothering her. She had always considered herself to be observant of minute details, even in chaotic situations. Until now, what bothered her was a lower priority than survival, but her mind circled back to close the loose end.

"Hey, you seem to know a lot about the ePod, have you ever

flown one of these before?" she asked.

Josiah was momentarily surprised by her question, but seeing as they had both experienced a rather stimulating morning, he skipped his normal bullshit and answered her directly.

"No, I've never even seen an ePod before, at least not a real one," he answered. "But I have flown one in my lab."

Lexis was confused. "Ok, Poindexter, explain.

"My lab did a lot of military work at MIT." Josiah smiled. "Like the Crimson Dawn guys who built the fuel cells for the ePod. I designed the guidance control system and tested it on my computer simulator, but I never knew what it was for. That's the way all the Dark Energy projects work; you never get the complete picture on the puzzle box. You don't know for sure who else is working on the pieces of the puzzle; it's always cloak and dagger shit."

"I see," Lexis responded. "They didn't want the design of whatever you were working on to fall into enemy hands."

"*Enemy* hands?" Josiah laughed. "I wish. No, they didn't trust the people designing it not to steal it or plant a bomb in it. The rumor was that they were chasing some mole in the university network."

"What?" Lexis asked. "Why did they think that?"

"They thought one of us was the enemy, some kind of double agent. They were always asking us to develop these advanced designs, testing to see if we would take the bait. 'Mushrooms in a cave,' they said, 'keep them in the dark and shovel shit on them.' We never knew if we were really building some new military technology or just setting a trap for their mole."

There, they had finally exchanged some honest information. Not a foundation of lifelong trust, but maybe a cornerstone. All right, it was just a pebble, but it was a start. For a teenage knife-wielder with a devil dog, Lexis wasn't all that bad. He just didn't want her to do any cooking when he was around. As they turned and walked out of the ePod, Commander Ryker and Officer Taylor rushed down the catwalk to greet them, exchange hugs, and welcome them home. After the pleasantries, Ryker looked sternly at Josiah.

"Ok, son, I'm glad you're back safe," Ryker teased. "But is that a dent on the fender of the station wagon I see out there? Your mom and I trusted you to be careful."

Josiah looked out the window to the ePod at the wild scratches on the airlock door from the bloody claws of the beast that had almost gotten inside. The same beast that had brutally ripped apart that poor sap Russian crewmember in some bizarre ritual sacrifice, and then had come back to kill them. *If it weren't for Koda and Lexis, I'd be dead right now.* He shook off the horrific images and smiled.

"Yeah, we got in a little fender bender out there, but hey, that's why we have insurance, right, Daddy-O?"

Ryker cocked his head and was about to continue with their comical dialog, but then he paused to resume a more serious tone as the reluctant commander of Genesis Five.

"We'd better get you guys settled in and then have a complete briefing on exactly what happened out there. I don't want some one-armed, barbequed, bloody claw man popping in for dinner on us unannounced."

After stowing the hydrogen canisters in his lab, Josiah and Lexis made their way back to the forward deck of the command module. Ryker was seated at the control panel next to Officer Taylor, checking the external sensors as they approached. With a few moments before the replay of the bloody claw attack, Commander Ryker's problem-solving thoughts drifted back to the blue lagoon by a sandy beach.

"You know, all that excitement got me thinking about your riddle again," Ryker babbled from left field.

"Really?" Sarah smiled. "Even with Josiah's monster attack, you can't get me out of your mind, can you?"

"Yeah, something like that," Ryker answered, checking the seal on the outer compartments. "Once I lock onto a target, Miss Taylor, I'm not giving up until I get all the way home, slamming this plane hard into the hangar, and smoking a cigarette with a big-ass 'Yes' grin on my face. Now that's romantic, don't you think? But first, the requisite mental gymnastics; ok, here goes. We've got a man sitting on a beach, reading a letter, and he starts crying. That sounds pleasant, but wouldn't it be more romantic if he was on the beach of a lush, tropical island paradise?"

"Better start with a simple exploration of the facts, Commander." Officer Taylor advised. "Before you crash and burn again, don't rush the romantic part... that's half the fun. You need to take it slow and easy if you want to get your plane in this hangar."

"Really? Slow and easy, that's the way you like it? I'll remember that when you're getting my name tattooed on your... never mind, I drifted away for a second. Ok, Miss *Easy*; the man sitting on the beach, is this beach on an island?" Ryker asked.

"Yes, you are correct, the man is on an island," Sarah answered. "That was easy. As long as you get 'yes' answers, you get more questions, and closer to your target."

"All right." Ryker grinned. "I can see the landing strip now, the lights are on and she's waving me in! The man's on an island in a romantic paradise, but he shouldn't be flying solo, taking matters into his own hand, so to speak. They say that one is the loneliest number, don't they, Miss Taylor? I always prefer flying with a copilot. Ok, little questions… a tiny 'yes'. So is the man *alone* on this island?"

"Oh! Sorry, that's a no," Officer Taylor replied casually. "Your approach was looking good, Commander, right up until you crashed and burned, you must have taken your hand off the stick. But that last one was a good question because you learned something. The man's not alone; nobody wants to be alone. Seven more questions."

Josiah plopped down onto a seat beside Ryker and let out a long sigh.

"Shit… shot down again," Ryker told him.

"Gee, who could have predicted that?" Dr. Stone responded. "If you're done trying to *'get your plane in her hangar'* for now, Commander, we've got some other problems to deal with."

"You're right, story time is over." Ryker exhaled noisily. "Ok, Doc, tell me what really happened out there."

"Well, let's start where we last left off." Josiah exhaled. "We snuck over to the passenger module and swapped my power designs for some hydrogen canisters with my new best friend, Dr. Maurya."

"Why does your new friend need power? They don't have any engines," Ryker asked.

"It seems Dr. Maurya is making progress on his atmospheric generator." Josiah laughed. "But now he says he needs ten times more power than is really required. Pretty transparent motives, if you ask me, but that's not my main concern. The officer in charge over him has some sort of Napoleon complex, and there are other strange goings on over there."

"Define strange," Ryker probed.

"Well, for one thing, two of their passengers disappeared under suspicious circumstances."

"Disappeared? Disappeared to where? They are either on the ship or out there somewhere... but nobody would be stupid enough to take a stroll in the desert, not with the bad air and all."

"I don't think they wandered out in the night air," Josiah answered. "From the evidence Dr. Jones found in the airlock, there was a violent struggle and then they appear to have been thrown outside by someone... from the inside."

"You're right, that qualifies as strange," Ryker stated. He stood up and walked around behind Josiah, scratching his chin like a detective in an old movie.

"So you are saying, Dr. Stone, that things are pretty normal over there on the passenger module, except that people are disappearing. And curiously, your pen pal is building some mysterious device that needs intense power while the military officer in charge claims to be my fake roommate from a school I didn't attend."

"I would say that about sums it up, Detective," Josiah answered.

Ryker looked at Lexis and Officer Taylor, winked, and then walked back to his chair.

"Then I guess we're better off keeping our distance for a while longer," he quipped.

Josiah stood up, sensing the interrogation was just starting.

"Before we get into the next round of questioning," Josiah announced, "I need to ask Dr. Maurya for a favor."

"By all means... " Ryker deferred.

Dr. Stone logged on to the Genesis central computer and sent a text message to Dr. Maurya:

"Left FedEx on your back porch. Can U run DNA & TMB? Handle CD9." (Can You Run DNA sample and Text Me Back? Handle Code 9)

Dr. Maurya received the text in his laboratory and grimaced for a moment. *Samantha would be better to handle DNA analysis and genetic testing, as bioengineering was her field of expertise.* He forwarded the message from Josiah to Dr. Jones.

As Samantha Jones read through the message, she thought about the request for a moment and looked around her lab to see if anyone was watching before she responded.

"Will do, just give me the sample," Dr. Jones answered.

On the way back from the Russian spacecraft, Josiah had slipped the ePod back to the passenger module undetected and dropped off a tissue sample on the external loading dock, leaving a note requesting a full genetic scan of the tissue material. Dr. Jones was not sure where the sample had come from or his reasons for the test, but since she and Dr. Maurya seemed to be building an alliance of mutual benefit with Dr. Stone, no questions would be asked.

"Ok," she typed back. *"WIP. UpLd RT n PM."* (Work in Process. Upload Real Time results in Private Message)

Dr. Jones secured the tissue from the loading dock and once back in her lab, started the DNA gene sequencer humming along, sorting and processing the sample. The results would be ready in a few minutes and routed to her secure server.

Back on the command module, Josiah reached into his side pocket and pulled out the ePod hard drive with the video upload from the Russian spacecraft.

"Now, where were we?" Dr. Stone mumbled. He secured the ePod hard drive into the docking station of the Genesis Five network and started to scan the video from the Russian computer. The picture quality was grainy; it had some blank frames and jumped about. The hard drive had probably been damaged by the radiation of the Niburu atmosphere, but the video still had some viewable sequences. Commander Ryker sat down beside Josiah. Seeing the foreign spacecraft for the first time, he was glued to the screen.

"That looks like a Ruskie L1011 deep-space probe," Ryker injected. "Where the hell did you get that video?"

"From the crashed Russian ship just over the mountains," Josiah answered casually. "That's where I banged up the station wagon in an electrical storm."

Ryker looked at Josiah, cocked his head and then looked back at the screen. The Russian commander on the video looked weary as he moved close to the camera to whisper a message. The lights in the background of the Russian ship were dim; the auxiliary battery power was almost gone. The Russian commander spoke in a frightened voice.

"они приходить в темноте"

"My Russian is a little rusty," Josiah complained. "What did he say?"

Officer Taylor had been listening and sat down beside Josiah and Ryker. "I think he said... *'They arrive by foot in the dark,'"* Sarah Taylor told them.

Ryker was startled that he had learned something unexpected about Officer Taylor; she spoke Russian.

"How did you...?" Ryker started.

Officer Taylor smiled and began speaking in broken sentences with a Russian dialect about her version of a romance novel in her mind.

"I used to date comrade." She exhaled heavily. "It was Geneva, I think, it was springtime and we were both entered in international gymnastics competition. I saw him across crowded amphitheater, working uneven parallel bars with his muscles bulging under sickle and hammer unitard. I was spread-eagle with my legs wrapped around firm wooden balance beam in powder blue unitard."

Ryker's jaw dropped open listening to Sarah's story.

"I complete my mount to roar of applause and then I glance at him, and he at me. We took one look at each other, and then later that night, we sneak out of dorms and go for gold. Oh, that's not important right now. Play the movie... "

Ryker and Josiah look at each other with wide eyes. They shook their heads and then continued the video.

"убирать не нравится светел," the Russian commander continued.

"And it seems they don't like bright lights," Officer Taylor translated.

"They don't like getting zapped with 500,000 volts, either." Josiah laughed. As they watched the remaining footage, Officer Taylor translated as best as she could with the patchy video.

"I don't know how they get past sensors," the Russian commander continued. "We have no warning when they attack. There are only two others left alive... my stowaway daughter, Elena, and First Officer Vladimir Christyakova. I lose four good men, one by one, to brutal, inhuman death." Josiah, Ryker, and Officer Taylor were dead silent as the video continued. "Last man, they capture and torture just outside our ship when we were making emergency repairs... the screams were unbearable... and nothing we can do but watch him die. Whatever you do, do not let them take you alive." The Russian

Commander paused and tried to regain his composure.

"Elena is badly injured, her leg broken in crash. I set bone and give drugs so she not know what is happening... she is locked in suspended animation pod... maybe they think she is dead if they come again. I have hidden transmitter with last battery in her cast... if she wakes up, she will call for help on transmitter." The Russian Commander moved close to the screen to make his final plea. "If you are watching now, please save her... she is all I have left... " The video faded to static and then went blank. The crew of Genesis Five sat there without speaking. A sharp ring on Josiah's communicator broke their silence; it was a text message from Dr. Jones.

"Lab results complete," the computer message droned. "Call now." Josiah rigged up a secure line to Dr. Jones and initiated the video call.

"Hello? Dr. Stone here."

"Is this a secure transmission?" Dr. Jones queried cautiously.

"I have a scrambler loaded on both sides," Josiah responded. "What do you have for me?"

"Listen," Dr. Jones answered, "I don't know where you got this DNA sample, but it has properties like nothing I've ever seen before. It has a number of undefined genetic structures, but it also has some DNA that matches my research databanks from Earth."

"That is... unexpected," Josiah answered. "Any details you can share, Doctor?"

Samantha Jones seemed a bit more at ease with Dr. Stone and opened up. "Part of the DNA looks like a mutation between a prehistoric reptile, some unknown animal, and then some genetic strands that I can't process yet. Where did you find this sample, Doctor?"

"We didn't find it, professor, it found us. And unfortunately, it found someone else first. You said you might have seen some of the DNA structures before. Where have you seen them?"

"Well," Dr. Jones responded, "I didn't actually see them; I read about them in a research paper on prehistoric genetics by one of my students. That part of the DNA looks like a virtual match; but it can't be, that would be impossible."

"A virtual match with what?" Josiah asked.

"A... Dimetrodon," Dr. Jones answered.

"A dinosaur?" Dr. Stone snapped back.

"No, not a dinosaur," Dr. Jones corrected him. "Dimetrodons went extinct long before dinosaurs emerged on Earth."

"Before dinosaurs?" Commander Ryker jumped in. "Nothing was before T. Rex, he was the king!"

"Actually, Commander," Dr. Jones laughed, "long before T. Rex, Dimetrodons were the *original* king of predators on land and they were unchallenged for three hundred million years."

"Predators before dinosaurs," Josiah interrupted. "I guess we didn't study that in engineering school."

Ryker turned to Josiah and cocked his head. "Ok, so Stumpy is a prehistoric reptile with one arm... big, slow, and stupid. We just light a few torches, yell boo and scare him back in his hole. What's the problem?"

"If your tissue sample was really from a Dimetrodon," Dr. Jones piped in, "that's not going to work; these guys were bad news. They were eight feet tall, weighed 600 pounds, and were the fiercest carnivore of their day. And another thing, even though Dimetrodons have slimy scales, razor sharp claws and teeth, they are not actually reptiles, they are a predatory synapsid."

"A sin-nap-sa what?" Ryker blurted out. "What the hell is that?"

"They were a species that was more mammal than reptile," Dr. Jones explained. "A genetic mutant of nature, one that killed its way to the top of the food chain on Earth. If you were alive, you were food for this beast. They were fast, intelligent, and hunted in packs. They were perfectly built killing machines.

Josiah stood up and rubbed his hands over his eyes then through his hair.

"Perfectly built killing machines... cool... that's just great. There goes the neighborhood."

"I could go on," Dr. Jones added, "but where did you get this DNA sample, it's so well preserved. I'd love to take a closer look at it."

"Oh, I think we'll be getting a closer look at it," Josiah answered. "Or maybe I should say, it will be getting a closer look at us."

Dr. Jones was confused. "What are you saying?"

"I'm saying that the DNA sample I gave you came from a beast that attacked us in the ePod, just on the other side of the mountain with the red cliffs. We should consider ourselves lucky; a Russian spacecraft had the misfortune to crash right into a nest of those beasts and believe me, Professor, they are not so extinct here on Niburu."

"My God!" Dr. Jones exclaimed. "You found a Russian crew here on Niburu? And living Dimetrodons?

Josiah paused for a moment and looked over at Lexis.

"Well, we sort of found a Russian crew; a little here, a little there. What we found that was left of them... had been torn to pieces."

The room was silent for a moment and then Ryker turned to Josiah.

"Well, it looks like we could really use an ion cannon right about now, hey Doc? And since I don't cotton to sitting here waiting for Stumpy and his gang to come back and eat us alive, see if you can get me some power for the one remaining engine we have left."

Josiah stood up and started typing away on the computer, accessing his weapons research applications as he reached down and rummaged through his duffle bag. When the probe arm was extracting the Russian hard drive data, he had also grabbed a few spare parts from the Russian spacecraft and stowed them away in his bag. *These could come in handy,* he had thought at the time.

Ryker continued his laundry list request for more weaponry by shouting at Josiah across the room.

"And a fucking force field might be nice... we can't really get a good shot off against those slimy bastards if they sneak up on us in the dark, now can we?"

32. Unnatural Selection

In Dr. Jones' secure genetic incubator on board Genesis Five, the centrifuges and gene sequencers were humming away without interruption. The Chimera cell structures engineered by Dr. Jones were multiplying into embryos that would soon be harvested. With the genetic code for the Chimera isolated, a biogenic assembly line was created to replicate the new transgenic workforce. To speed the delivery of the Chimera breeding stock, Dr. Jones had introduced a powerful growth hormone to advance the development of the first generation, speeding their maturation from years to just hours and days. The experimental growth hormone was a risk factor; it amplified the chance for mutations in the genetic replication process. Once she had a satisfactory base level of Chimera, Dr. Jones intended to remove the growth hormone and allow the Chimera to reproduce naturally.

The initial genetic prototypes had produced three viable Chimera. These three were carefully cultured under the watchful eye of Dr. Jones, who had taken a respectful role as the Chimera 'den mother', watching over her creations. Driven by the growth hormone, the first three Chimera quickly developed to the point where they required a mother to nurse them. So to ease their transition from the Petri dish to the pack, Dr. Jones also created a new wolf species to provide a more natural nourishment environment for the Chimera rather than the sterile intravenous feedings they had received from birth. As she had predicted, the early Chimera displayed physical characteristics that looked like apes with smooth facial features. The main variation in her transgenic species seemed to be their size and build, the amount of fur, and the prominence of their claws. Most of the Chimera had a human facial appearance with fair complexion and light skin, but as humans and gorillas share ninety-eight percent of their DNA, this seemed to be a natural aberration. Like the proud mother of a litter of new puppies, Dr. Jones had chosen names for the first three Chimera. In her lab notes, she recorded her observations.

"The oldest and most developed male, I have named Brutus. The wolf DNA appears to balance with his gorilla genetics; he has a large, muscular body and sharp claws, but surprisingly, almost human facial features. Brutus is inquisitive, learns quickly, and seems to understand my instructions even before I give them to him. He appears to be the alpha male; strong and dominant, and has clearly exhibited behavior that indicates he will become the pack leader.

"Viola was the first female I produced. I had hoped that she would be my alpha female, but oddly, she has not assumed the role as a mate to Brutus. Although she seems interested in forming an alpha pair, Brutus so far seems ambivalent to the concept." *But like a scorned lover,* Dr. Jones mused; *Viola seems determined not to let any other females near Brutus.* "She is quick to anger and can be very aggressive, although Brutus seems to be able to keep her in check with just a glance. In one training exercise, she became frustrated with the handling of the mining rock sacks and even though they were made of Kevlar, she ripped them to shreds in a matter of seconds. Her athletic ability and reflexes far exceed all of the others. I must try to avoid situations that set off her trigger."

"The youngest male I have named Misun, which means little brother in Sioux." *Dr. WiiSi would be pleased,* she thought. "He is smaller than the other two and definitely subservient, so I would observe that he has assumed a juvenile role in the pack. He is shy but seems eager to please, especially Brutus, and seeks out his companionship like a younger sibling. His physical abilities are somewhat limited; he is clumsy, but he seems very intelligent and has taken an immediate liking to all things electrical and mechanical. Misun is particularly attracted to my music player and after listening to it, he was pleased to show me he could take it apart and reassemble it very quickly."

The last entry in Dr. Jones' notes concerned the formation of a communal pack, like canines, a development that she noted was essential to their survival as a species.

"The hierarchal order in the Chimera pack is quickly being established. Viola is protective of Brutus and can be vicious with the others, especially the younger ones. Her iron-fisted discipline can be dealt out when it is least expected. Sensing this, little Misun mainly tries to stay out of Viola's way, lest he be set in his place. I hope that these three Chimera will form the nucleus of a pack and be the role models for the next generation."

To speed the transition from a fledgling pack to a companion work force, Dr. Jones set up a habitat training room next to the genetics laboratory for the Chimera. She equipped the habitat room with rock samples and mining tools and began a standard animal behavior modification program to reward the Chimera for finding and recovering the specific oxygen-rich rocks they were designed to seek. Delighted with the progress of her Chimera, Dr. Jones invited Dr. Maurya to observe Brutus completing his mining training. To demonstrate, she set up a time trial of random rock samples and then rang a bell to provide the command to *'find the rocks'* she desired. In a matter of seconds, Brutus smelled and sifted through the rock samples and located the ilmentite. He retrieved the correct sample and placed it on the rock cart at the end of the room. A treat dropped down from his reward tube, Brutus grabbed the treat, popped it into his mouth, and then walked back to his cage. After he entered his cage, Dr. Jones buzzed it shut.

"Incredible!" Dr. Maurya exclaimed. "If we were back at Cambridge, I would nominate you for a Nobel Prize. With your Chimera and my atmospheric generator, we may just have a chance of survival on this Godforsaken planet."

Just then, Lieutenant McCurdy and two of his soldiers barged into the lab.

"Ah, my brain trust is having a meeting but I wasn't invited. What's going on here, Doctors?" Before Samantha could restrain Dr. Maurya, he blurted out his praise for Dr. Jones and her progress in training her Chimera. Lieutenant McCurdy was somewhat surprised.

"Really, Doctor? I had no idea that my little worker class had come so far so fast. I would like to see a demonstration."

Dr. Jones was reluctant to fully disclose her progress with the Chimera. A swift kick under the table to Dr. Maurya communicated her displeasure with his unnecessary disclosure.

"Brutus just completed a training exercise," she cautioned, "so it would be best to set up a demonstration for another time. I don't want to overdo his behavior modification threshold."

"Nonsense!" snapped Lieutenant McCurdy. "Just use another one of the beasts. How about that small one over there?" Lieutenant McCurdy pointed to Viola with his swagger stick.

"I really don't think she is ready," Dr. Jones stalled.

Lieutenant McCurdy shoved her aside and grabbed Viola from her cage. She resisted and the other soldiers moved to assist him, forcing her to the start of the training run. He turned back to Dr. Jones to begin the demonstration.

"Now let's see what you can do, little one," McCurdy exhaled.

The bell rang and Viola looked to Brutus in his cage, and then over to Dr. Jones. Reluctantly, she began sniffing and sorting through the rocks for a moment, and then stopped. She turned and walked back toward her cage with a look of defiance.

"This session is over," Dr. Jones interrupted. "Viola is not ready to work."

"Perhaps, Doctor, you've been applying the wrong motivational techniques. Let me give it a try."

Lieutenant McCurdy reached down to his holster and pulled out the stun gun from his side. He stepped forward and delivered a shock to the back of Viola's neck and she dropped to the floor, writhing in pain. The throbbing sting of the stun gun ran down Viola's back, causing her legs to quiver uncontrollably. She gasped for breath and shrieked with a silent scream to Brutus for help. From his locked cage in the next room, Brutus heard Viola's cry and crashed against his cage in a futile attempt to come to her aid. Lieutenant McCurdy leaned down and stared into Viola's angry eyes.

"Now we understand each other, don't we, bitch?" McCurdy bristled. "Let's try one more time to find the rocks, shall we?"

Viola flinched away from the raised stun gun, slowly stood, and resumed the rock-sorting exercise. She quickly located the ilmentite, placed it in the rock cart and then ran back to her cage without waiting for her behavior treat. She pulled the cage door shut behind her and curled up in the corner. Dr. Jones stood there in total shock. All of her positive training and trust building had just been erased by McCurdy's cruelty. Samantha was seething with anger. She stepped in front of Lieutenant McCurdy and glared at him.

"I cannot train my Chimera successfully with your interference!" Dr. Jones hissed. "You can't treat them that way or they will never do the work we ask of them!"

Lieutenant McCurdy moved closer to Dr. Jones, staring her in the face.

"Let's get a couple of things straight, Doctor. First, the Chimera are *my* workers, not *your* pets. And second, I've had enough of your soft-training methods. Either these beasts get to work now and deliver my oxygen or I'm going to have to insist that you and Dr. Gandhi pick up a shovel and work the mines yourselves. So what's it going to be, Professor?"

"They aren't going to do what I ask of them if you torture them!" Dr. Jones screamed.

"Ah, but that is where you are wrong, Doctor. I am not *asking* them to work, I am *telling* them to work... or else," Lieutenant McCurdy stated coldly.

Dr. Jones rushed over to comfort Viola, but she turned her back and hid at the end of the cage. Lieutenant McCurdy pivoted to leave and his soldiers followed him to the door. He paused in the doorway to offer one more parting shot. "I don't give a shit if my Chimera *like* me or not, Dr. Jones, but they will sure as hell learn to *fear* me."

33. Alter Ego

Dr. Jones hit the red button on the training room wall to release the safety locks for the Chimera cages and Brutus rushed past her to check on Viola. He tore open Viola's cage and they embraced for a moment. Satisfied that Viola was unharmed from the encounter with Lieutenant McCurdy's stun gun, Brutus turned and glared at Dr. Jones. This was a look she had not observed from Brutus before; it was a look of defiance, but also of mistrust. It was almost as if Brutus was speaking directly to her. *If you cannot protect us, Dr. Jones, I will.*

A chilling thought suddenly came over Samantha. She had always treated the Chimera with dignity and respect, trusting that they would respond to her nurturing kindness. But what if the animal DNA in her Chimera mutated and drove them to a more violent, primal behavior? Dr. Maurya had suggested a safety device such as a shock collar be fitted for the adult Chimera. He had even built a prototype and brought it to her lab one morning, cautioning her about the unpredictable nature of genetic engineering.

"Samantha, I know you are a good scientist and a trusting caregiver," Dr. Maurya had cautioned. "But these Chimera are an unknown species; they are unpredictable and you can't know what might set them off. If they should get out of control, they are powerful enough to kill you in an instant."

"Ridiculous!" Samantha shot back. "My Chimera would never hurt me! If we treat them like animals, they will behave like animals... and so would you, by the way." That was the end of the discussion. Dr. Maurya knew Samantha well enough to know he had really pushed her buttons. He took the shock collar prototype back to his lab, and even though he was still concerned for her safety, he never brought up the subject again.

Back in her lab now, Dr. Jones moved to comfort Viola, but Brutus stepped between them and nudged her away. Misun joined Brutus and Viola in her cage and for the first time since she had created them, they huddled together as a pack, behind the protection of Brutus. Little did Dr. Jones know that the stun gun discipline at the hands of a cruel human had created a defining moment in the development of the Chimera; their relationship with the humans would be different from this point onward. All on board Genesis Five would soon know the consequences of that defining moment. From that day on, as more

Chimera were produced, they were immediately adopted into a social structure with Brutus as the pack leader and Viola as the alpha female in waiting. From that day forward, every new Chimera secretly learned from Brutus and Viola the lesson that they had received about the humans at the end of McCurdy's stun gun.

In her log, Dr. Jones noted the impact of the event. "Strangely, even the new Chimera pups that are introduced to the pack after the stun gun attack on Viola react in a hostile fashion whenever the soldiers visit the laboratory. And when Lieutenant McCurdy appears, they are on the verge of a near riot." *How could they know? That event happened before they were born.*

As Dr. Jones was studying the data from her last exercise with Brutus, she was perplexed at some of the developments she had not anticipated in her research. The Chimera were learning at a much *faster* rate than she had expected. They had now completely bonded as a pack and seemed to be able to communicate with each other... *even when they were not in the same room.* Dr. Jones had anticipated that the Chimera would develop basic communication skills, but based on the genetic model she had used to assemble the DNA, she thought this would take multiple generations. Clearly, this was not the case and it surprised her. *Surprises are not generally a good thing in science,* she thought, *especially when it involves the survival of everyone on Genesis Five.*

At the entrance to the Chimera training room, Dr. Jones swiped her security card and placed her hand on the biometric reader to validate her secure access. The door lock clicked open and she stepped into the room, still absorbed in her analysis. She looked around and saw that the Chimera were all sleeping with their cage doors open. Ever since the incident with Lieutenant McCurdy, she had left the cages unlocked, hoping to rebuild a sense of trust with them, especially with Brutus.

Dr. Jones tossed her training notebooks on the desk and took a seat at her computer. In the back of her mind, she felt something was out of place. Her subconscious intuition said that something was not right. She had experienced this feeling before, and she had learned to trust it without asking too many questions. *What is it?* She thought. *Something has moved, something... is out of place, not where I left it. But what? Maybe it's nothing.* Dr. Jones' mind refocused on the task at hand as she logged onto the research computer. The voice module on the central server recognized her login and initiated contact.

"Hello, Dr. Jones, welcome back," droned the network computer. "How are you?"

Dr. Jones was absorbed in her paperwork and mumbled back absentmindedly.

"I'm fine... I'm... ok." Flipping through her research notebook, she looked away from the screen as she typed in commands to review her data, when she accidentally hit a key combination that jumped the display screen to the computer access log file. "Arrgh... not again!"

As Dr. Jones started to clear the screen, she noticed something that confirmed her feeling that something was amiss. The computer screen showed she had logged on that morning at 8:00 for thirty minutes, and then again at 9:05 for an hour. *Wait,* she thought, *the log indicates that my last session ended just five minutes ago... five minutes before I came in! Maybe that's why the computer said 'Welcome back',* she thought, *instead of the usual 'Good morning, Dr. Jones'.* The computer access log timestamp did not make any sense; an hour ago, she was having a cup of tea with Ashoka. Someone else must have hacked into her account and accessed her research files.

"But why would anyone need to hack *my* login account?" she mumbled. "Everyone on board has an access code to the public side of the central computer. It makes no sense." A quick scan of the access log showed a number of data folders had been examined at a detailed level:

1. "The Complete Works of William Shakespeare,"

2. "On the Origin of Species," by Charles Darwin,

3. Dr. Jones' research on Quantum Physics, Bioengineering and Spirituality,

4. Dr. Maurya's archives on comparative Religion and Philosophy,

5. All known references to *Yeenaeldooshi,*

6. The Chimera Project... restricted to Dr. Jones by password only.

Samantha Jones looked up and scanned the room; it was locked and secure. She was alone with the Chimera, still sleeping in their cages, but she was not secure. Someone else had been here, someone who preferred to hide behind her computer identity. She wracked her brain for an explanation to the odd set of circumstances in front of her. Confused, she rubbed her hands over her eyes. *I need a cup of tea now.* Sighing deeply, Dr. Jones paused for a moment to collect her thoughts, her hands still cupped over her eyes. When she looked up from her desk, Brutus was standing in front of her with a hot cup of Earl Grey tea, her favorite.

"Why that's just what I needed... but how did you know?" Samantha asked.

Brutus gently set the teacup down on the desk and walked back toward his cage. Startled, Dr. Jones frantically reviewed the charts of the Chimera intellectual development and growth records on her computer. The data was right there, screaming out at her. She liked to tell her students at Cambridge that all the answers they ever needed could be found in the data, they just had to ask the right questions. *But the data in front of me is totally outside all expected parameters,* she thought. Suddenly, the message in the data hit her like a ton of bricks... *the Chimera have accelerated their cognitive skills and learning across the board to near-human levels.* She closed her eyes and shook her head.

Could I have made a mistake? No... the margin of error in the data was not outside the standard deviation from her blind studies on learning development at Cambridge when she used undergrads as subjects. *The answer is right in front of me, but what is the question?*

Just then, Dr. Maurya buzzed the exterior door lock open to the training room. Dr. Jones was too slow to answer the door, and he stormed in, bristling with anger from his last encounter with Lieutenant McCurdy.

"That bastard!" Ashoka declared. "He's over in my lab trashing the prototype of my atmospheric generator!"

"What?" Samantha said. "Slow down..."

"He says he's tired of my toys," Dr. Maurya exclaimed. "He wants a full-scale working model now! I told him there were still bugs in the prototype and that bastard just smashed my work to pieces!"

"But why?" Dr. Jones asked. "Why would he destroy your prototype?"

Ashoka tried to calm down as he answered. "He said, '*All right, Doctor, now your little toy is broken. Go build me the real one.*'" Suddenly, Ashoka realized he had interrupted Samantha's work. He looked around at the pile of notebooks and the computer screen displays in front of Dr. Jones. "Oh... I am sorry. Here I am babbling on about my crisis and you seem to be deep in thought." Dr. Jones looked up from the Chimera learning curves plotted on her computer screen.

"Can you take a look at something, Ashoka? I think I need a fresh set of eyes on this one." Dr. Maurya sat down, took out his reading glasses and reviewed the data that had spooked Dr. Jones. After a few moments, he let out a long breath.

"Fascinating, does anyone else know about this?" he asked. Samantha Jones shook her head.

"Only you... and my alter ego," she joked nervously.

"Your what?" Dr. Maurya responded.

"My... never mind," Samantha mumbled. "Someone has been hacking into the central computer using my secure identity... from this very room. I've been so focused on interpreting the Chimera data that I really haven't had time to worry about it, but I could use your help."

"I have an idea. Let me take your data back to my lab to run it against some of my algorithms, I will see what I can uncover. And about your hacker, I just put a remote video capture on my computer because I suspected our bad lieutenant has been spying on me. I'll configure one on your machine as well and then we will see who your mysterious alter ego really is."

34. Russian Secrets

Commander Ivan Stephanotski reached down to help Mitch Gaylord up from the soft dirt of the gladiator arena. As Mitch rose to his feet, a horn sounded three blasts and the mob of scaly beasts encircled the arena and ran directly toward Mitch and Ivan at the center of the ring. Ivan could see the terror in Captain Gaylord's eyes. He pulled him close in a bear hug and whispered in his ear.

"Look at me, cowboy. Do not show fear or they tear you apart. Besides, is not your time yet."

Mitch tensed his sore muscles and gritted his teeth. It was probably a futile gesture, but he was determined to land at least one solid blow on a beast before they killed him. Just as the first beast reached them, Ivan grabbed his fist and held it down. The snarling creature paused for a second and then ran past them and dived onto the dead body of the decapitated human in the center of the arena. There were squeals and grunts as the mob of lizards descended on the human remains and tore them apart, fighting amongst themselves for every scrap of bloody flesh. Mitch was frozen in horror, his brain told him to run, but his legs would not move. Ivan jerked Mitch from his stationary position and spun him away from the gory spectacle in the center of the ring.

"Do not look back, cowboy. Come, we go now to my office and talk," Commander Stephanotski insisted. As bizarre as it was, they were ignored by the frenzied mob of lizards and slowly walked to the edge of the arena to a large double metal door. Ivan clanged his shield against the door twice and it slowly creaked open. "Inside now, we rest! We talk… and make plan for future."

Mitch and Ivan stepped inside the room and the large metal doors creaked shut behind them. The room had a rough wooden table and chairs with metal bowls filled to the brim with slimy goo. Hanging from the walls were an assortment of ancient gladiator weapons, swords, spears, and shields. Ivan groaned as he removed his heavy metal shield and tossed it in the corner with a thud.

"In my country," Ivan stated, "I am famous surgeon before government comes to my door and says I must fly mission into deep space, is my patriotic duty."

"Yeah, I was piloting a cargo plane when the Wars of

Consolidation broke out." Mitch responded. "I got a new uniform but flew the same damn planes, just with different stripes. Which side were you guys on anyway?"

Commander Stephanotski erupted with a deep belly laugh.

"Come to think of it, I do not know what side I fight for, my friend! Come sit. We talk and eat." Ivan looked Mitch in the eye. "It is how you say... our last supper." He laughed and slapped Mitch on the back.

As relieved as he was to be out of the gladiator arena, Captain Mitch Gaylord hesitated in accepting Ivan's offer to sit down and break bread for two reasons. First, he wasn't quite sure of what to make of Commander Ivan Stephanotski; he had just beheaded another human being in the gladiator arena. And second, no matter how hungry he was, the taste of that foul-smelling green lizard shit made him hurl. Mitch Gaylord pushed his metal bowl of slimy goo away and looked Ivan directly in the eyes.

"You killed that man in the arena, didn't you." Mitch stated. "Who was that poor bastard, anyway?"

Commander Stephanotski rose slowly from the table, turned his back to Mitch and walked over to hang his bloody axe on the wall.

"Yes, I kill him. The man we leave in arena was First Officer Vladimir Christyakova. He was... my best friend." Mitch Gaylord was stunned to hear the casual description of the killing from Commander Stephanotski, but he sensed that he should give him some space for the gravity of his words to settle in. The Russian carefully unhooked his armor and placed it on a rack in the corner of the room. He removed his metal breastplate and tossed it on the table in front of him with a thud before returning to the chair in front of Mitch.

"There is much to tell and less time to understand, Captain Mitch Gaylord. You are military man, so we have... understanding, yes? For us, war is harsh game with rules and honor. To my government, you are my enemy; I try to kill you. And you think same of me. We fight, sometimes we win, and sometimes we lose. Is not personal, is just war." Ivan Stephanotski looked Mitch in the eyes, studying his reaction. "But we know on other side, is driven by men like you with some purpose, some value or belief. We do not hate you, we hate what you stand for; your cell phones, pornography, and drive-through hamburgers. We kill to protect our way of life, not just to kill. Is honorable and civilized, yes? This place is not like what we know, cowboy. Here, they kill for sport. You, me, others are just here to die for how you say... tonight's entertainment."

Captain Mitch Gaylord was trying to fathom the gravity of Commander Stephanotski's words. "So you killed your best friend for sport? Just to entertain those slimy beasts out there?"

Ivan Stephanotski grew angry as he stood up from his chair and moved close to Mitch Gaylord's face. "This is brutal place, cowboy. I am only alive because I kill my friend. He would do the same to me. I kill him, because if I do not, my daughter Elena will die."

"You told me your daughter is here on Niburu," Mitch exclaimed. "Is she all right? Ivan calmed down and turned his back on Mitch.

"Elena will be famous athlete someday, but right now she is stupid, impetuous young woman. She was stowaway on my ship, *'hiding from her step-monster'*, she says. Those two fight like cats all the time. We crash and she is hurt, her leg is broken. I set bone and give drugs so she not know what is happening. I hide her in sleep pod on the ship before the beasts come, hoping they not find her, but they do." Ivan turned back to Mitch, telling him the rest of his story. "They bring me and First Officer Christyakova here to fight in arena and take Elena to laboratory. The beasts come for me to fix her; I hide transmitter in her cast. I hear her cry down the hall and ask to help her. The beasts make for me a... bargain. They let her live, but only if I fight in arena. I kill, she live. I die, she die. Such is bargain of desperate old man with devil. So I fight and kill many men." He shoveled some food into his mouth and continued, "They would die anyway. At least it is quick death."

Again, Mitch Gaylord was shocked. "There are more humans on this planet? How many? From where?"

"That I do not know. I only know when I fight."

"How many fights have you had?"

"Many fights, my friend." Ivan shrugged. "Twenty, I think. I can't remember all."

Mitch Gaylord's head was spinning with the thought that there were other humans on this alien planet. *Where did they come from? How many were still alive? How many were here in this prison waiting to die in the arena?*

Commander Stephanotski grabbed Mitch by the shoulder, interrupting his thoughts.

"Listen, cowboy, is not much time. What I tell you now is what I have learned of this place. Is good you listen well. Beasts live here in the cave city, close to underground rivers. Water and air here is good, only bad on surface. Do not go out in rain on surface, it very bad. Beasts only like to come to surface under darkness. They not like light; is painful for them. They have many eyelids like crocodile, for protection. Sudden light is weapon, they go blind, but not for long." Ivan tapped on his Russian utility belt. "See this?" he added. "I have secret weapon." Mitch had seen these belts before, a few flares, a radio, and a xenon strobe light. If you were outside your spaceship doing repairs and your tether broke, you could signal for help.

"Is always good to have magic trick up your sleeve, no?" Ivan grinned. "I'm just like your David Copperfield, but without big car." Ivan roared with laughter, obviously amused by his own joke, but Mitch Gaylord wasn't much of an audience. "They fight among themselves like animals," Ivan continued. "But they are not animals, they are very intelligent. They have studied us, taken us apart, and believe we are weak, inferior species. They know how we think, what we will do, and what it takes to break us. If you fight them, you must be unpredictable... or you will die."

Suddenly, Captain Gaylord suspected that Ivan's beast lesson was more than just a courtesy. "Why are you telling me all this?" Mitch asked.

"I tell you this for two reasons. One, you are special project for them, and two, since I help you, you help me, yes?"

Mitch was confused. "What do you mean, I'm a special project?"

"Feel your side, cowboy. You have incision, yes?"

"How did you know that?"

"Because I am great surgeon, I make incision. I am Dr. Ivan Stephanotski, famous transplant surgeon. I visit big medical practice in Beverly Hills, you know, swimming pools and movie stars, they want Ivan to come work there. Ivan is almost famous... until war breaks out and I am drafted into dog shit MASH unit picking shrapnel out of ass of some mujahedeen in Kurdistan. So I get stuck in shitty little war with no decent golf course, no supermodels, and now my two handicap is gone. Such is life." He shrugged.

"It's a crazy world out there," responded Captain Gaylord, unsure why Commander Stephanotski was sharing this information.

"When you come here, cowboy, you are almost dead. You

breathed bad air, your lungs collapsed. But Ivan is great surgeon, I fix. I fix with beast lungs," Ivan smiled.

Mitch rubbed his aching side. "You fixed me with... beast lungs? What the hell do you mean by that?"

Commander Stephanotski shoveled more food into his mouth and motioned for Mitch to eat. "You have beast lungs inside you. Without them, you are dead man."

"What? Why?"

"I told you why, but you no listen. Air on surface is bad, has jagged microscopic substance in clouds, like tiny broken glass. When you breathe in, it rip apart lungs and capillaries. You breathe in bad air; you bleed to death from inside. Once you inhale, even Ivan cannot fix. You should be dead cowboy, but Ivan save you. Beasts are quite curious how it is you survive. You are, how you say, an experiment for them. They believe that with giant beast lungs, you are now like superior mutant warrior. Warrior or not, time will tell. You are alive, Captain cowboy, only because Ivan is great surgeon."

Mitch's head was spinning. *Can this be true?* He stood up to pull back his shirt and winced with pain. Ivan poked him in the side near the incision.

"See, I do good job, no?"

"What the hell happened to me?"

"I told you, you breathe bad air and lungs bleed out, so I give you beast lungs. Beasts not need to guard other humans from escape to surface. If they leave cave and not drink syrup, they die. Sometimes, beasts withhold syrup just to watch man die; it is like your war of terror. Not a good way to die, cowboy." Ivan grinned with delight telling his story. "They don't know, but I give you secret, a special gland under ear that makes breathing syrup. Coating drips from gland inside you to lungs and protect from bad air. Now you have lungs like your Denny's restaurant... always open, you beast-man!" He roared with laughter.

"Denny's? You've been to *Denny's?*"

"Oh yes, Ivan has seen your real America, I see it all. Ronald MacDonald hamburgers, pornography magazines, and Denny's flapjacks. I think I like your Denny's flapjacks best."

"You said there was another reason that you helped me." Mitch paused. "So that *I* could help you. What did you mean by that?"

"Ah, now we have the turkey talk." Commander Stephanotski smiled. "Is most important reason, cowboy. Soon will be time for you to fight in arena. You must make your heart cold and show no mercy... or you will die. If you cannot kill like this, you must pretend that it is not you that kills, it is just... the beast inside, not you. That is what I do; in the ring I am not Dr. Stephanotski, I am Ivan the Fucking Terrible!" He laughed out loud. "Because I save your life, you now owe me favor, Captain Gaylord."

Mitch was suspicious. "Favor? What favor?"

"If you fight and kill your opponent, cowboy, you must protect my Elena. She will not stay alive without champion to protect her."

Mitch thought about what Ivan had just said and suddenly the picture was coming into focus. "And do you know who my opponent in the arena will be?" Mitch asked.

Ivan walked up to him and grabbed him by the shoulders, shaking him roughly. "You must fight human champion... to the death, Captain Gaylord." Ivan turned and walked with his back to Mitch to the wall of weapons. He took down a metal Conquistador helmet and placed it on his head. Turning around, Commander Ivan Stephanotski looked directly into Mitch Gaylord's eyes.

"That would be me, cowboy. Your new best friend."

35. Candid Camera

In the kitchen galley that doubled as an advanced physics laboratory in the Genesis Five passenger compartment, Dr. Maurya leaned forward to his computer screen, tracing the lines on the screen with his finger. The data documenting the growth and learning curves of Dr. Jones' Chimera was nothing short of astounding. To establish a baseline for the data, he back-tested the Chimera development of intelligence against canines, elephants, and primates. Dr. Jones' initial reaction to the data would seem to be correct... something did not fit here. *Pattern analysis and data visualization*, Dr. Maurya thought to himself, *is the key to understanding. Find a pattern in the data and match it to your hypothesis. That will lead you to the truth.*

Having isolated the intelligence growth rate of the Chimera in a geometric representation, Dr. Maurya reasoned that it should be straightforward enough to instruct the computer's visualization engine to solve the equation of an equivalent pattern match of their development. Accessing its memory banks, the central computer scanned all available intelligence growth rate data across multiple species, processed for a few seconds, and then announced the completion of its assigned task in a low female monotone.

"Visualization pattern match equation solved within a ninety-eight percent probability of certainty. Two percent of the sample has no match in data banks." The computer overlaid the matching patterns on the display screen alongside the Chimera data; the patterns were virtually identical.

Dr. Maurya had long preferred to use AI software routines as his research assistants for two good reasons; first, they never asked for time off, and second, they never demanded a share of the credit on his publications. The circumstances of his departure from Earth had prevented him from bringing his own trusted AI unit on the voyage, but fortunately, Dr. Stone had loaned him NELI. *That is quite fortuitous,* he thought, *because the visualization software on Genesis Five has its quirks; it was civilian grade and built for geophysical mining applications, but NELI should be able to make the needed modifications for my analysis.*

"Fascinating, NELI," Dr. Maurya responded. "That is just as I suspected. By the way, thank you for working out the bugs in this antiquated system."

"You are welcome." NELI blushed. She liked being appreciated. "I am glad to be of assistance."

NELI and Dr. Maurya had developed a solid working relationship over the last few days, so to alleviate the tedium of the solitary work they were performing, he had added some logic and personality algorithms to NELI's programming. Giving NELI an artificial intelligence module and simulated feelings made the work less boring, but Dr. Maurya also felt he was getting somewhat attached to NELI, as much as one could to a silicon-based life form. A knock at the security door of his lab interrupted Dr. Maurya's conversation with NELI. Standing, he peered through the glass to see the worried face of Dr. Jones, pacing outside the window. Not wanting to attract any unwanted attention, he reached under his desk and pressed a red button to buzz her inside.

"NELI, we will continue our conversation later," Dr. Maurya whispered.

"I'll be here when you need me, Doctor," responded NELI.

Samantha rushed into the room waving her arms as she blurted out her most recent concerns.

"I am sorry to barge in on you, Ashoka, but I have just had an extraordinary session in my lab. I was working with Brutus and I'm almost positive that he is trying to communicate with me! He is making sounds, but they are incomprehensible and his attempts at communicating are frustrating to both of us. Maybe I should ask Dr. Stone to bring his canine companion over to see if that would help... do you think that would help?"

"Slow down, Samantha!" Dr. Maurya urged. "I haven't a clue as to what you are talking about. Calm down and start over at the beginning! When did Dr. Stone get a dog?"

"Oh... that's right," Samantha exhaled. "You remember that encounter that Dr. Stone had with that enormous beast we saw on the loading dock back in Tiny Town? It seems he fancies himself quite the animal trainer, at least according to him, he is some kind of dog whisperer."

"Dog whispering? Now that sounds most interesting, but let us first discuss the data that you have provided to me for analysis. We, I mean, I have done some groundbreaking research and achieved some startling results."

"Good, that's partially why I came by," Dr. Jones replied as she started to calm down.

"Now let's see, where are my charts?" Dr. Maurya mumbled as he fumbled with a stack of papers. "Ah, here they are. After examining your data, the visualization results are quite conclusive. Your Chimera is learning at a rate that is parallel with *human* development."

"What? Are you sure?"

"Oh, decidedly so." Dr. Maurya laughed. "I have undergraduate students back at Cambridge that are slower learners than most of the Chimera. In fact, maybe I should replace some of my teaching assistants with Chimera when we return to our comfortable little lives back home. Those Neanderthals have been getting far too soft on the undergrads. You know, always complaining about grading papers, lecture hours, and what not. At least your Chimera should have the moxie to keep them in line."

Dr. Jones' eyes were wide open. She was now carefully examining the visualization graphs and only partially listening to Ashoka. "Are you saying that my Chimera are... *human?*" she gasped.

Dr. Maurya took off his glasses and cleaned them with his lab coat as he explained what he meant.

"Oh no, they are definitely not human, far from it. What I am saying is that while your newly created Chimera are not human, they are quite intelligent and they are learning at the same rate as humans do... *maybe even faster.*" He picked up the visualization charts and pointed to one set of results. "On top of that, they have additional developmental traits that humans don't possess."

"But how can that be?" Dr. Jones exclaimed. "I was very careful in designing my transgenic model without *any* human DNA. They don't have the genetic structure to support your advanced learning theory."

Dr. Maurya circled behind Dr. Jones and assumed his favorite role as senior academician.

"Ah, theory and facts, Samantha, the bane of our scientific existence. My dear, this is where you appear to have constructed your problem backwards. The Chimera *are* learning quickly, that is now the fact. The transgenic model you designed; that has now been proven to be the *theory*. Somewhere in between your original theory and my confirmed fact, something has changed."

Dr. Jones was startled, but not completely surprised. Ashoka's findings only confirmed her growing suspicions and concrete observations that something was wrong.

"What do you suggest I do now?" Dr. Jones asked.

"What we always do when we get unexpected results, Samantha, rerun the experiment." Dr. Maurya smiled. "Somewhere between your theory and my facts, there is a flaw."

This was not the answer that Dr. Jones wanted to hear, but she knew that Ashoka was right. She returned to her lab and stared at her notes as her mind reconstructed the original hypothesis. *Start from the beginning, leave nothing unchallenged,* she thought. *Did you sterilize the beakers? Did you splice the right genes? Did you follow the formula... exactly? Did you contaminate the samples?* The samples? That was where Dr. Jones would begin her investigation.

Samantha opened the subzero refrigerator and extracted a sample of the Chimera genetic material that she had used to begin the process. It had been under lock and key since she developed her theory and the formula. Placing the DNA sample into the gene analysis computer, she clicked on the machine and started the analytical engine. As the computer hummed away, analyzing the genetic structure of the Chimera, Dr. Jones contemplated the potential ramifications of Ashoka's results. *If the Chimera were somehow part human,* she thought, *my spiritual and ethical boundaries have been breached.* She was already seeing behavior in Brutus that told her he could think on his own, make decisions, and somehow communicate with the other Chimera. She was also positive that he was even trying to communicate with her directly. *How else would the Chimera have developed such an intense reaction to McCurdy and his soldiers?* She thought. *They must be teaching each other, sharing their experiences and building a collective intelligence. That is what any higher-level species would do to survive in a hostile environment.*

The gene analysis computer finished processing and announced that the results were complete. Inside the computer, Dr. Maurya's silicon companion, NELI, had now assumed all voice interaction with the data that he had forwarded to Dr. Jones. With the addition of Dr. Maurya's personality algorithms, NELI's fondness for Dr. Maurya was beginning to border on the boundaries of a professional relationship, even for a silicone one. She had, as he requested, initiated her own internal programming to enhance her skills as an assistant and a companion. She was Dr. Maurya's personal assistant, but NELI also thought of herself as his protector.

204

"Dr. Jones, I have finished my analysis," NELI announced. "May I be of further assistance?"

"No thank you, computer," Dr. Jones responded. She walked over to the video monitor. Staring at the screen, she let out a long sigh, and fell backwards into the chair beside her workstation. NELI's gene analysis results were conclusive.

"Oh my God! The Chimera have human DNA," she muttered to herself.

Just then, Dr. Maurya knocked on her laboratory door and it slowly creaked open. In the heat of her pursuit for truth, Dr. Jones had been so focused on her Chimera formula that she had once again forgotten to lock the door to her lab. Unbeknownst to her, it was this simple mistake that had led Samantha Jones down a path she had hoped never to walk. Dr. Maurya entered the lab and walked over to join her as she sat silently at her desk, staring at the computer screen. Ashoka stood there for a moment observing Dr. Jones as she looked up at the ceiling, and then she finally spoke.

"What have I done, Ashoka?" Samantha sobbed. Dr. Maurya put his arm around her and tried to comfort his research partner, sensing that she had lost more than just her moral compass; she now doubted her own abilities as a scientist. He tried to find words that would offer her comfort.

"You have done what one has to do when faced with a moral dilemma, a choice between life and death. Should you risk your spiritual principles or accept the guilty burden of contributing to the deaths of everyone you know? You have attempted to walk an ethical path that would lead to our ultimate salvation. But trust me, Samantha, the path to *Nirvana* is as difficult to walk as a razor's edge."

Dr. Jones looked down, avoiding eye contact with Ashoka as she hung her head. She dabbed a tissue to the tears running down her cheek.

"We can agree on one thing." Samantha exhaled. "There are many unknowns when we start down this slippery slope, tinkering with the genetic makeup of life. It's a path lined with unanticipated consequences, but as a scientist, I knew the risks and I chose to define the boundaries that I thought I could accept."

"You did what you had to," Dr. Maurya reassured her. "For the good of us all." Dr. Jones was not ready to accept the consolation her good friend was offering. She was still deeply disturbed at the place she now found herself in.

"Ashoka, I took every precaution," she argued. "I checked every detail, but somewhere along the way, I must have made a mistake. The only logical explanation for this problem is that I contaminated the Chimera formula with my own human DNA. So now, because of my failure, the genie is out of the bottle."

"Ah yes, and now your genie is apparently quite eager to learn," Ashoka added. "Move over, Doctor, let me show you something."

Ashoka sat down at the computer workstation and called up the video surveillance application he had installed on Dr. Jones' workstation. The computer screen divided into four panels, with views from every angle of the Chimera training room. Initially, the Chimera were sleeping in their cages, with the doors unlocked. The video showed Dr. Jones at her workstation, analyzing the data for the Chimera training program. She paused and then walked into the kitchen to fix a cup of tea. After sipping her tea for a moment, she paced around and then buzzed herself out of the training room, leaving the Chimera unattended. As soon as Dr. Jones was out of the video frame, something totally unexpected happened.

"Now watch this part," Dr. Maurya instructed.

On the video, Viola popped up in her cage and gave a hand signal. Brutus stood and walked over to Dr. Jones' computer workstation and logged on... as Dr. Jones' *alter ego*. Viola repositioned herself at the door like a military sentry on lookout, scanning outside the window, preparing to warn Brutus should anyone return.

"My God," Samantha exclaimed. "They have been hacking into my computer account on a regular basis! How did they learn to do that?"

"By observing their master, no doubt," Dr. Maurya replied.

"Their... *master?*" Dr. Jones echoed.

"Why yes, Samantha, they see you as their master," Ashoka responded. "Just like birds that imprint on the first thing that moves, the Chimera have carefully observed everything that you do, watching, learning, and now they are emulating your actions. Brutus even shares your affinity for Earl Grey and the spiritual world; the computer shows he's been reading your ancient Gnostic texts!"

Dr. Jones was stunned for a moment.

"I suspected something like this could happen, but I guess I didn't want to admit it could be true." Dr. Maurya stood up from the computer and put his hand on Samantha's shoulder.

"Ok, Samantha, I know how you think. Right now, you are all tangled up in your Judo-Christian spiritual dilemma. You are probably asking questions of yourself, back and forth in your mind. How can they be learning so fast? Do they have free will? And if they have free will, do they possess a soul? And if they have a soul, have you been blasphemous in trying to play God?"

"Is it that... obvious?" Dr. Jones muttered softly.

"Painfully so, my dear." Ashoka smiled. "But what I don't understand is why you have moved your spiritual boundary so far along before you developed this internal conflict." Now that Dr. Jones was truly confused and sensing a need for clarity, Dr. Maurya continued, "Allow me for just a moment to offer another perspective. To we Buddhists, the enigma of bioengineering has four considerations. Ahimsa, Transcendence, a non-Cartesian nature, and an Open Cosmos."

"Why do I always feel like you want me to be your student, and you are my master?" Samantha smiled sheepishly.

"Because when you are a student, everyone is your master, as you may learn from them." Ashoka grinned. "You have to trust me on this one, Samantha."

"Ok... enlighten me, oh learned one," she conceded.

"You have created a spiritual dilemma, one which makes you question your path. But I would ask you to suspend your Western belief system for a moment; step back and observe your dilemma from a different point of view... a Buddhist microscope if you will, with four lenses. Close your eyes, relax, and allow your mind the possibility of seeing what I am saying. Good, breathe deep. Here are the four threads of life.

"First, we should do no harm to others; this is the principal of Ahimsa. Second, we should strive to develop spiritual wisdom and seek liberation; this is the principal of Transcendence. Third, we seek the purification of the mind, body, and spirit, all interacting as one; this is the view of a non-Cartesian nature. And lastly, we must understand that the universe, the Cosmos, it is an open system. It is a system that is infinite in all directions, a system in which we cannot know everything, or even know enough to understand how we might alter the Cosmos if we should seek to change or control it."

Dr. Jones opened her eyes, looking a bit more at peace. "I followed you up until the *'Cosmos as an open system'* part. How does that factor into solving my spiritual dilemma?"

"Ah!" Dr. Maurya smiled. "Like butterfly wings and dust clouds, Samantha. Nature is an open system, we cannot know everything, and we certainly cannot control life. We have to adapt and roll with the punches."

"Ok," Dr. Jones mused, "I accept your fact. The Chimera have human DNA and they are learning at an accelerated rate. I believe that they also have free will; most likely it would follow that they now have an immortal soul. But how did they get the human DNA?"

Dr. Maurya furrowed his brow and rubbed his chin as he answered. "All interesting questions, Samantha, but as a scientist, you are still not asking the right one."

"The right one?" Dr. Jones looked confused.

"Samantha, you and I believe in a Creator that is present in all life; that is something that even as scientists, we can neither give nor take away. And yes, your Chimera *do* have human DNA inside them. But knowing that, have you considered the fundamental question, the question you really should be asking?

"And what question would that be, Ashoka?" Dr. Jones inquired.

"A simple one, my dear." Dr. Maurya smiled. "Whose DNA is it?"

36. Across the Multiverse

After McCurdy had destroyed his prototype, Dr. Maurya sat down at his lab bench to complete the final adjustments for his full-scale atmospheric generator. Back on Earth, he would have only needed to supply his CAD CAM design and fill out a purchase order to receive the fully tested components from a device manufacturer and then have his grad students assemble the final product in his lab. But after their landing on Niburu, with limited materials and even less scientific instruments to fabricate his work, he had quickly been forced to downgrade his advanced development methods to a more practical approach that would have made even his scrounger of a hero, MacGyver, tip his hat. On the advice of Dr. Josiah Stone, Dr. Maurya had converted the ship's solar panels to a chemical voltaic model, and amazingly, they worked just as Josiah had designed. He could now use the chemical radiation in the atmosphere to generate electricity. Equipped with more than ample electrical power, he could heat the thermal generator to 900° centigrade, and with that heat, free the oxygen from the ilmentite mined from the red cliffs of Niburu.

I have snatched life from the very jaws of death, Ashoka thought. His atmospheric generator was working, producing the oxygen that was needed in sufficient quantities to survive. The proof was right here on the digital readouts of his instrument panel. Liter by liter, the oxygen from the generator was now slowly refilling the ship's storage tanks, breathing life into the ship and enabling their survival. A long-term solution would require massive amounts of ilmentite to restore the oxygen tanks to full capacity, but at least for now, they would be able to breathe. The other passengers had first looked upon Dr. Maurya as a geeky scientist, but he was now the geeky scientist savior of the people of Niburu. Basking in the satisfaction of the moment, Ashoka slipped into a daydream where he was accepting an award from the Royal Society for his incredible ingenuity, his intelligence, and his ruggedly handsome good looks. The imaginary loud speaker boomed across the grateful audience within his mind.

"When all hope seemed lost, with mere crude tools and a cocktail napkin design, Dr. Ashoka MacGyver, oh, excuse me, Dr. Ashoka Maurya, quickly fashioned a working atmospheric generator from a paper clip, some tin foil, and a flashlight battery to save what was left of the human race. The Queen herself has kneeled at his feet to thank him for his meritorious service, awarding him the highest honor in the land, lightly tapping each of his shoulders with her jeweled scepter and dubbing him *Sir* Ashoka Maurya." The buzzing sound of an incoming computer message abruptly snapped Dr. Maurya back to reality just as the Queen was kissing his ring; it was Dr. Stone calling.

"Hey, thanks for the H2 samples, Doc," Josiah started. "I found some xenon gas and just about have my propulsion problem solved, but I am going to need some more hydrogen for another project I am working on; it's a real blast. How's it going with your O2 generator?"

"Ah, Dr. Stone, I am so glad you called," Ashoka responded. "My atmospheric generator is working quite swimmingly even as we speak. I should have a new batch of hydrogen for you in a few hours."

"Great," Josiah answered. "I'll send the FedEx truck over later this evening. I think I may have to pull an all-nighter to get my new pop gun working."

"Top gun?" Dr. Maurya asked.

"Never mind," Josiah retorted back. "I'll show you in a day or so, it's pretty cool."

"Oh... ok," Ashoka answered. "Dr. Stone, I wanted to ask you about the power surge design you sent me. I have constructed the concentrator and I am ready to test it. But just between you and me, I want to keep this, as you might say, on the low down."

"You mean on the down low?" Josiah corrected. "I figured as much. Didn't think you would be brewing tea with an extra five-hundred giga-watt pulse concentrator. That's a real bad boy, Doc, be careful not to burn your eyebrows." Dr. Maurya reached up, touched his forehead, and then ran his hand behind the instrument panel to feel for the hidden switch to control the electromagnetic pulse concentrator.

"Yes, she is a very bad girl," Dr. Maurya mumbled. "But before we test the EMP engine, I have some other news to discuss with you."

"Some more '411' on the DL?" Josiah laughed.

"Well, possibly." Dr. Maurya scratched his head. "You know the ilmentite samples I examined? As I was processing them, I decided to run a radiometric age on the samples and I found a... most curious result."

"Doc, I am falling asleep over here." Josiah yawned. "Just get to the punch-line, ok?"

"The punch line?" Dr. Maurya asked. "Oh, yes. The rocks from the red cliffs are over thirty billion years old." Dr. Stone sat up in his chair, he was now alert and listening.

"Thirty… billion years old?" Josiah echoed. "That's more than twice as old as the Big Bang, Doc. How could that be? That would mean that Niburu has been here since *before* time began."

"Yes," Dr. Maurya answered. "Before time began, *as we know it*; time that started with the singularity of the Big Bang exploding the matter of our universe in all directions. But not necessarily before the time of that singularity, if you subscribe to a cyclic model of an ekpyrotic universe."

"Whoa, Professor, I'm an engineer, not an astrophysicist!" Josiah quipped. "Take it down a notch for me."

"Down a notch, yes," Ashoka responded. "Dr. Stone, we think of time starting with the Big Bang, and for us, it is a valid reference point, since everything in our known universe was created as part of that singularity. Everything we have come into contact with seems to share a constant set of rules that govern our understanding of the physical and biological world… rules that we scientists rely on to understand our very existence. But what if, as Einstein theorized, time was not constant, but relative. In that case, the rules that we know… would no longer apply."

"I'm listening," Josiah noted. "Lay it on me, Doc."

"What if time were not linear, but somehow could be folded over into a different dimension, a parallel universe. This could occur if, as string theory suggests, there are not three dimensions in space, but many more dimensions that are invisible, all curled up inside a hypercube of light and dark matter. If time was indeed not linear and we could prove it, it would be possible for us to be part of a much larger universe than we have ever imagined, a *multiverse*, let's call it, with very different physical and biological properties that have evolved from a history extending back far beyond the thirteen billion years since our Big Bang."

"And you think that the rocks on Niburu are old enough to prove we could now be in this… *multiverse* or some parallel dimension?" Josiah asked.

"Theoretically, it is possible," Dr. Maurya responded. "If Niburu is in fact much older than the Big Bang, and if Niburu were in that same universe as the Big Bang, the same dimension as Earth, it would have been destroyed in the singularity of the Big Bang. And yet, Doctor, here we are."

"Yeah, here we are. But where exactly... is *here?*"

"Ah! Excellent, Dr. Stone, I like your thinking," Ashoka exclaimed. "Now *that* is the real question. Where exactly is *here*. Before we crashed, we were thrust into a massive electromagnetic pulse, leading me to believe that there are only two possible explanations to where we are: either the planet Niburu has been pushed into *our* dimension, or we have been pulled into *its* dimension, a place where Niburu existed *before* our Big Bang."

Josiah let out a long whistle. "Ok... now I know what you need all that extra power for. You're going to try and duplicate the EMP we went through and open a portal through the multiverse... to find out just where the hell we are."

"My, you are a quick study," Dr. Maurya complimented. "I must now retract most of those derogatory things that I have said over the years about the intellect of you yanks."

As a scientist, Josiah was excited at the potential for a multidimensional experience.

"So what are you waiting for?" Dr. Stone exclaimed. "You said you had the power, Doc, give it a crank and pop open the portal!"

"Well, it will not be quite that simple, Professor." Dr. Maurya paused. "The power that I can now generate is only enough to pry the portal door open, once it has been unlocked, and then, only for a second or two. But I have observed a phenomenon with my instruments that might prove helpful. You know how periodically, the electromagnetic pulses that light up the sky go pitch black?"

"Yeah, bad things can happen when it gets dark out there, that's what Comrade Ivan said," Josiah answered. "That's the scary part, we don't know when it's going to go dark again."

"But that's just it, Professor, I know when it's going to go dark," Dr. Maurya exclaimed. "Thirty seconds before it goes pitch black, I have picked up unusual electromagnetic pulses on my instruments. Almost like a countdown, and exactly timed to the blackout. And just at the blackout, there is a massive EMP that surges from inside the planet, up through the atmosphere."

"What does it sound like?" Josiah asked.

"It sounds like the giant metal door to a parallel dimension creaking open." Dr. Maurya smiled. "Just a tiny crack, waiting for me to zap it with an electromagnetic pulse concentrator and kick it wide open."

37. True Colors

Despite the recent mystery of the DNA contamination, Dr. Jones was pleased with the progress of her Chimera pack in the training center. Once Brutus had assumed the role as alpha leader, the entire pack demonstrated that they could now complete their mining exercises with ease. Even more satisfying for Dr. Jones was her perception that the distance that had emerged after the stun gun incident with McCurdy between the Chimera and her now seemed to be behind them. *Trust was a hard thing to rebuild,* she thought; *even with the sub-species I've created in my own lab, but finally, the Chimera appear to trust me once again.*

In spite of the regular intrusions by Lieutenant McCurdy, Dr. Maurya had also made significant progress with his atmospheric generator, enough so that he was ready to test the full-scale production model for creating the oxygen they needed to survive. The only thing missing to drive Dr. Maurya's full-scale test was a large volume of ilmentite for his machine to process, and that was exactly where the trouble began. In the midst of a Chimera exercise, Lieutenant McCurdy and six of his soldiers burst into Dr. Jones' training room just as she was about to begin a new lesson.

"Ah, Dr. Jones and *my* loyal subjects!" McCurdy bellowed. "What excellent timing for a new lesson program!"

The Chimera immediately reacted to the presence of McCurdy and the soldiers by stepping away from the door and forming a pack behind Brutus. They scanned the soldiers for weapons and tensed up, seeing that they were all carrying assault rifles and stun guns strapped to their sides. Standing behind Brutus, Viola whispered a single thought to him.

Not again, Viola thought.

"Lieutenant McCurdy," Dr. Jones interrupted, "I have asked you repeatedly not to barge in on my training sessions."

"Enough, Dr. Jones, enough." McCurdy spoke over her. "We are ready to test the strong backs and weak minds of my Chimera. I'm taking them on a field trip to the mine."

"What?" Dr. Jones exclaimed. "They aren't ready for that; I haven't prepared them for activities outside the ship!"

"They are prepared well enough, Doctor, and I need some rocks to test out the atmospheric generator," McCurdy shot back, ignoring her plea. He looked over at the pack with a sarcastic grin. "So let's see, who shall I pick to come along to the mine?" Lieutenant McCurdy circled the Chimera and stopped at Viola. He reached out his hand to touch her cheek and she jerked away, hiding behind Brutus. Brutus stood his ground and looked at McCurdy with a cold stare, blocking him from touching Viola again. "Ah, the pack leader, protecting his little girlfriend!" McCurdy smiled. "These two can come, and those two little ones behind them as well."

McCurdy motioned to the soldiers and they poked at Brutus and the other Chimera with their rifles, moving them along toward the door. There were confused, inaudible shrieks from the remainder of the pack, drawing a swift rebuke from Brutus.

This is neither the time nor the place for confrontation, Brutus thought. *Obey their commands and follow me.*

As they reached the door of the lab, Dr. Jones stepped in between the Chimera and the soldiers, demanding to go along on the mining mission with them. The soldiers halted for a moment, looking to the Lieutenant for orders. McCurdy stepped close to Dr. Jones and spoke in a soft, but stern voice.

"We have already been down this path before, Doctor. You are their trainer; I am their master. Besides, your good friend and colleague Dr. Maurya needs the ilmentite from the mine to start up my atmospheric generator. You remember, the device that's going to make the oxygen to keep us alive? We have a dwindling supply of air and we need more rocks. Unless your pride is more important than the lives of everyone on this ship, I would suggest that you step aside."

Dr. Jones hesitated, but realized that McCurdy was unfortunately right about the oxygen. Without the oxygen produced from Ashoka's machine, all her principles in defending the Chimera were worthless; they would all die. Lieutenant McCurdy paused and then pushed Dr. Jones aside, stepping through the doorway.

"Move out!" McCurdy barked to the soldiers. "Get those beasts down to the cargo bay. I want those rocks back here on this ship, pronto!"

After a long ride to the mining site in the red cliffs, the soldiers stood close guard over the Chimera as they dug and lifted the heavy rocks from the mine. It was hard work, made even harder by the increased density of the atmosphere on Niburu. Humans didn't have the strength or endurance to toil away in the mine, but the genetic makeup of the Chimera allowed them to bear such a burden and survive the hardship. Digging and hauling rocks by hand was a backbreaking task. The Chimera had loaded four tons of ilmentite into the Rover when McCurdy decided it was time for another lesson. He had been watching the Chimera miners and picked out the slowest worker in the pack. It was Misun, one of the younger Chimera.

"Sergeant!" McCurdy bellowed. "Bring that little one over there to me!" The soldiers grabbed Misun and dragged him across the mine, over to the loading bay of the Rover.

"Listen up," Lieutenant McCurdy shouted. "Load up the rest of the beasts, but leave this one here with me. It's time for a teaching moment." The Chimera were resentful at the poking and prodding by the soldiers as they were herded into the Rover. The soldiers took up positions between the doors and the Lieutenant, where he was holding Misun. McCurdy grabbed Misun by the neck and forced him to his knees in front of the rest of the weary Chimera.

"Attention, beasts," Lieutenant McCurdy announced. "This is your master speaking. This moment... is the beginning of the rest of your lives. Lives that *I* have given to you for only one purpose: to mine these red rocks as fast as you can. Every time you come here, I want you to work as fast as you can." Lieutenant McCurdy nodded to the soldiers to assume a protective barrier between him and the Chimera. "So to help you remember this, I have developed a reward and punishment system. Those of you that work hard will be rewarded. Your reward is that I will not punish all of you. However, those of you that don't work hard, regardless of your size, will be punished."

McCurdy unbuckled the holster of his stun gun, took out the weapon and placed it against the back of Misun's neck; he looked directly at Brutus and pulled the trigger. Misun let out a silent scream and collapsed to the ground, writhing in pain. The blast from the stun gun paralyzed Misun momentarily, sending an intense wave of burning fire throughout his body. He convulsed and vomited on himself, unable to control his spastic motions.

The site of an innocent pack member being tortured caused the Chimera to let out a collective shriek and Brutus stepped forward, pushing the soldiers back, trying to get to Misun. With six assault weapons trained on Brutus' chest, McCurdy stepped forward and looked the pack leader in the eye. He reached down and fondled the stun gun in his holster, pulling it out should he need it again. After grinning at Brutus for a second, he slowly put the stun gun to the side of Brutus' neck, moving closer to speak.

"Dr. Jones said that you and she had a failure to communicate," McCurdy whispered. "Is that what we have here, big fellow, a failure to communicate? I don't think so; I think you and I can communicate... quite well. See your little boy over there lying on the ground, puking on himself? He understands what I am saying."

Brutus visualized grabbing McCurdy by the neck, puncturing his lung with a claw and ripping out his spine. Anger was boiling up inside him; his hand shook, almost to a point where he could not control his violent thoughts. *Do not rise to the bait*, Brutus thought. *Yes, I can kill this evil human with a single blow, but the remaining soldiers will kill the other Chimera before I can get to them.* The rage inside him was now starting to be controlled by his mind, and his mind told him, *now is not the time.* Brutus steadied his hand and mind, remaining motionless.

Misun was still jerking around on the ground in pain, but he would live, he had risen to his knees. He looked at Brutus with pleading eyes. *Why do we not fight them?*

"Nothing?" McCurdy grinned. "That's all you've got for me, big fellow? That's what I thought." Satisfied that Brutus was not a threat, McCurdy turned around to address the other Chimera while holding the stun gun to Brutus' neck. "So let's be clear about this lesson. If you, or any of your kind, don't do exactly what I tell you to do, then I promise you, I will help you understand, just like the little one over there does now. This is a lesson I want you to remember." Lieutenant McCurdy leaned over and whispered to Brutus, "Are we clear on this one, big fellow? I think we are."

McCurdy slowly removed the stun gun from Brutus' temple and backed away from the rest of the Chimera. The soldiers grabbed Misun and shoved him into the cargo hatch of the Rover with the other Chimera. Viola rushed over to Misun, held him in her arms and then glared up at Brutus.

They are animals! She screamed in her mind. *We should attack them!* Brutus looked at Viola with an intense stare.

We will, but at a time and place of our choosing, he thought back to Viola. Brutus stepped forward, placed his hand on Misun's head and smiled at him. *You are a strong one, little man. We will not forget this day.*

When the Chimera arrived back at Genesis Five, Samantha Jones and Dr. Maurya were waiting for them in the cargo bay. The door opened and the soldiers shoved the Chimera out of the Rover as they marched them down the gangplank. None of the Chimera would make eye contact with Dr. Jones and she knew something had changed; they had never been this cold to her in the past. As the Chimera marched by, Dr. Jones noticed that Misun was limping and had a burn mark on his neck. She tried to stop Misun by reaching out and placing her arm around him, but he winced with the residual pain from the stun gun. She spun around to challenge Lieutenant McCurdy.

"Why is there a burn mark on Misun's neck?" Dr. Jones demanded.

"Oh, the little one got too close to the hot engine panel," he laughed. "Fortunately, I managed to pull him back before he really got hurt." McCurdy reached out and bent down to pat Misun on the head. Turning away from Dr. Jones, he looked directly into Misun's eyes. "We learned something, didn't we, little one?" he smirked. Misun pulled away from Lieutenant McCurdy and scrambled behind Brutus. "Yes, I would say that we have all learned a lesson." McCurdy looked over at Brutus as he continued, "A lesson that we will not forget."

That is true, you bastard, Brutus thought, *We will not forget.*

Misun and Brutus stepped around McCurdy and toward Dr. Jones on their way back to the training room. As the soldiers marched the Chimera to their cages, they poked them in the back with their assault rifles. Dr. Jones stepped in front of Brutus, reached out and touched his shoulder, looking deep into his eyes.

"What's wrong?" Samantha asked. "What happened out there? You can trust me!"

Brutus paused for a second and thought about how he would answer her question. *I can trust you?* He thought. *Why? You cannot protect us from him.* Hidden behind the strength in his eyes was a look of disappointment, mistrust, and betrayal. Brutus cocked his head and slowly moved his mouth as if to speak, but Dr. Jones could not understand what he was trying to tell her. If only she could have listened to his thoughts, she would have heard his painful epiphany.

Nothing is wrong, master, he thought. *But what was once unclear has now come into focus. McCurdy is right... I have learned an important lesson, a lesson that I shall never forget. I wanted to believe that humans were at the core, a good and benevolent species. I thought that we could share this world, not as your servants, but as equals, working together, living in peace.*

Brutus put his arm around Misun and they stepped past Dr. Jones. *But there can be no peace between us, now that I have learned your true colors,* Brutus thought, *We will no longer be blind to the truth.*

38. Free Will

Dr. Samantha Jones was still in a state of shock after finding out that the genetic sample from her Chimera contained human DNA. Sitting at her computer workstation in the Chimera training center, the words from Dr. Ashoka Maurya, her research partner and best friend, were still ringing in her ears.

Have you considered the right question... whose DNA is it?

Of course she had thought about the source of the DNA contamination, she had carefully evaluated the possible mistakes that she could have made in preparing the genetic formula to create the Chimera. But since she was the only one with secure access to the clean room of the lab on the day the sample was created, how could anything other than her carelessness be responsible for the contamination of the sample? Dr. Maurya had suggested that she step back from the problem and view it from a distance. What would she do if she were coming into this situation, uninvolved in the mishap, and merely trying to figure out what went wrong? *Assume nothing,* she thought.

"Computer, compare the elements of human DNA in the Chimera sample and the DNA of Dr. Samantha Jones."

NELI, Dr. Maurya's silicone assistant, came to life to handle her request.

"Hello, Dr. Jones," NELI responded politely. "Can I confirm your request? You would like me to run a DNA match between the human DNA elements present in the Chimera sample... and *your* DNA?"

"Yes, that is correct."

"Working," NELI complied. "Visualization pattern match between the DNA of Dr. Samantha Jones and the Chimera laboratory sample... ninety percent sample mismatch."

"Ninety percent... *mismatch?*" Dr. Jones gasped. "Are you sure?"

"I am sure, Dr. Jones," NELI answered. "I am routing the visualization graphs to your screen now."

Dr. Jones was dumbfounded.

"What is the other ten percent?" Samantha asked. The computer whirled away and then NELI responded.

"Analysis shows a ten percent match on base level amino acids... amino acids common in all humans."

"But a ninety percent mismatch means that the human DNA in the Chimera sample *didn't* come from me?" Dr. Jones inquired.

"Affirmative," NELI answered. "The human DNA elements contained in the Chimera genetic sample did not come from Dr. Samantha Jones."

Samantha was stumped, bewildered and happy all at the same time. She called Dr. Maurya to shout out the discovery.

"Ashoka, you are a genius!" she blurted out. "You were right, you're always right! It's not my DNA in the Chimera sample! But you knew that all along, didn't you?"

"Ah, so you are not such a sloppy lab partner after all!" He laughed. "I always thought you were quite careful when we worked together." Dr. Jones stood there, basking in the relief that she was not guilty of contaminating the Chimera genetic samples. Equally important to her, she had not crossed her ethical boundaries and risked her immortal soul. Her feeling of relief, however, was short-lived. "So whose DNA is it that has become mixed up in your Chimera?" Ashoka asked.

Dr. Jones came crashing back to reality and tried to respond. "You know," she answered, "I was so elated to find out that I had not contaminated the samples with my DNA, that I don't really know yet."

"Well then, you still have some work to do," Dr. Maurya lectured. "Now that we have confirmed your meticulous attention to detail, I suggest that you get back to work and solve your mystery."

Dr. Jones regained her composure and turned back to the computer.

"Computer, access the passenger and crew personnel files and link the individual medical records to your data visualization engine. Compare the human DNA elements in the Chimera sample to every passenger and member of the crew on Genesis Five."

"Processing," NELI responded. "And you know, you can call me NELI, Ashoka always does. This could take a while, Dr. Jones. You may want to get a cup of tea."

Dr. Maurya had been monitoring Samantha's computer directions from the link in his laboratory. "Now you are on the right track," he whispered to himself. "Down the rabbit hole, Alice, down the rabbit hole."

The gene analysis computer hummed away, accessing the medical records of the passengers and crew of Genesis Five. Dr. Jones decided that a cup of tea would be nice, but in the meantime, she had a growing discomfort with the training program she had designed for handling the Chimera. *They have human DNA,* she thought, *and I'm sure they've exhibited free will. McCurdy shouldn't be treating them as slaves; it's morally and ethically wrong. My hands aren't clean in this, but no matter how we arrived at this point, I have to set this imbalance back on an ethical footing. Where should I begin... by trying to communicate with Brutus.*

Even though it meant risking another clandestine meeting with the crew of the command module, Dr. Jones called Josiah and sought to enlist his assistance. After all, he had bragged about his dog whisperer encounter with the big black beast on the launch platform... maybe he could help. *It was worth a shot.*

At the command module, Lexis overheard the conversation between Dr. Jones and Josiah concerning Dr. Stone's *'magnetic animal personality'*. As Josiah terminated the call, he turned around to find Lexis standing behind him.

"Have you been there long?" Josiah asked sheepishly.

"Long enough to watch you get your foot in your big mouth." She smirked.

"Was it that obvious?" Josiah said.

"What's obvious is that you need Koda's help yet again to save your sorry little ass," Lexis gloated.

"So you'll help me?" Josiah begged.

"I'm not the one you need to ask," Lexis stated as she started to walk away.

"Wait!" he pleaded. "Could you please ask the beast... if he will help me?"

Lexis stared at him for a moment and then turned to Koda, who had been eavesdropping as well. She asked him if he would help Josiah by acting as an interpreter for the Chimera and Dr. Jones.

Dr. Stone, renowned imaginary dog whisperer, eagerly awaited an answer.

"Well, will he do me this favor or not?" Josiah begged. Lexis looked at Koda; he growled and then she responded.

"He says yes." Lexis laughed. "He'll grant you this favor. But he also says that one day, he will come to you and ask a favor in return... and you will not refuse him."

Josiah smiled, but then he was confused. He reached out to pat Koda and was met with a low growl.

"Ok, Dog Father, I get it... I owe you one," Josiah whispered. "Now let's go greet the other beasts."

After sneaking the ePod back over to the Genesis Five passenger module, Josiah, Lexis, and Koda joined Dr. Jones and Dr. Maurya in the Chimera training room for their first attempt at an interspecies communication session. Dr. Jones checked outside the lab to make sure they were alone, and then provided the ground rules for the experiment.

"When I bring in Brutus," she explained, "just go about your business in the lab and don't crowd him, let him come to you. If we ignore him, he will eventually initiate contact. Isn't that your dog whisperer technique, Dr. Stone?"

Josiah was quite uncomfortable; maybe this was a bad idea. He had lied about his dog whispering prowess and was sure that Koda and Lexis were about to use this opportunity to embarrass him. *It's too late to turn back now*, he thought. *This was a great plan... my fate now rests with that big hairy beast over there, and he hates my guts.*

Lexis broke the ice by stepping around Josiah to communicate directly with Koda. The wolf-dog nuzzled next to Lexis and growled at Josiah before nudging him away.

"Even though Dr. Stone's *expertise* in animal communication is well known," she played along, "I think he may want Koda to handle this one *directly*, right, Dr. Stone?" Josiah backed away carefully from Koda and nodded to Lexis as they approached the Chimera cages.

"Uh, right," Dr. Stone mumbled. "Maybe Koda can speak to the Chimera... you know, I believe he speaks a closer dialect than I do, being a beast himself." Dr. Jones opened the cage door to the Chimera and Brutus slowly walked into the lab. He was cautious with anyone new and quickly sized up the newcomers. When he came to Koda, they both tensed up for a moment and then stared into each other's eyes. Koda emitted a low, guttural sound, but it was not a growl. Fascinated at the interaction, Dr. Jones stepped forward to join Lexis at Koda's side, but Koda turned to Lexis and growled. Lexis placed her hand on Koda's head, and then turned to Dr. Jones, laughing.

"Did I say something... funny?" Dr. Jones asked.

"No, he did!" Lexis replied, gesturing to Brutus.

"What did he say?" Dr. Jones asked.

Lexis turned around and looked at Josiah, who was cowering in the corner.

"Brutus said it was refreshing to meet a canine with such a well-trained human," she announced.

Dr. Jones glanced back at Josiah and he smiled and nodded, oblivious to what they were saying.

"But he also has a question for you, Dr. Jones." Lexis smiled. "He asked if you enjoyed reading *Pride and Prejudice*, he saw it on your reading list. He found it intriguing, although he prefers the original title, *First Impressions*. He said it's unfortunate that you rarely get a chance to make a first impression, as they are so often... *incorrect.*"

Dr. Jones was stunned. *Brutus was not only able to communicate; he was also intelligent and well read?* "He has read... Jane Austin?" Dr. Jones gasped.

Lexis looked at Brutus, laughed and then turned back to Dr. Jones.

"He said he always gets confused, was it pride that hindered the romantic endeavors of Elizabeth, or was it her prejudice? He frequently gets those human emotions mixed up." Dr. Jones was still taken aback.

Lexis turned back to Dr. Jones and gave her a sweet look. "It was a joke, Doctor!" Lexis giggled. "You know, I like this big one. He's intelligent, funny, and not all that bad looking if you go for the Sasquatch type... I know *I* do," Lexis said, turning back to look at Brutus. "You should be blushing, Dr. Jones, I think he likes you." The playful romantic mood of the interspecies communication experiment was interrupted by the voice of the computer.

"Analysis of the DNA from the medical records of the passengers and crew of Genesis Five and the human DNA from the Chimera samples shows no match," NELI announced.

Dr. Jones and Dr. Maurya looked at each other, confused.

"But... How can that be?" Dr. Jones exclaimed. "The human DNA had to have come from someone on this ship... there is no one else here!"

Lexis had heard the computer's DNA analysis. She thought about the problem that Dr. Jones was apparently trying to solve and offered a thought. "Sometimes, Doctor, people aren't what they seem," Lexis said. "Maybe there's someone here with us that was not supposed to be here, someone not in the Genesis Five database."

Dr. Maurya turned to Lexis and grinned. "I like you, young lady!" he exclaimed. "You have a wonderfully devious mind. Do you like old detective movies?"

"Just what are you saying?" Dr. Jones asked.

Dr. Maurya's face lit up as he rephrased the question by Lexis. "As this lovely young lady has suggested, someone on board is not who they say they are. NELI, can you collect actual DNA samples from the passengers and crew without them knowing it, from their computer keyboards, lunch trays, wherever, and match them to the DNA in the ship's medical records?"

"Of course, Ashoka, if you would like," NELI answered sweetly. "But this may take a while."

"That's perfectly all right, NELI," Dr. Maurya responded. "We have no pressing engagements that I'm aware of at the moment."

Dr. Jones was still trying to understand Ashoka's line of reasoning.

"And what will we learn from this analysis?" Samantha asked.

"Ah." Ashoka smiled. "Something most interesting. We just might learn who is on board this ship… that is not who they say they are."

While they were awaiting the computer analysis, Dr. Jones continued the brokered conversation with Brutus, through Koda and Lexis. After a basic exchange of likes and dislikes, Brutus posed a more direct and unexpected question to Dr. Jones.

Why are humans so cruel to us? Brutus asked.

Samantha was shocked and embarrassed as she felt guilty about the way the Chimera had been treated. McCurdy had physically abused them, taunted them in ways that she now knew had hurt them emotionally, and she had just stood by and let it happen. As their protector, she had let them down.

"I am truly sorry for the treatment you have endured," Dr. Jones relayed to Brutus. "It has not been right, and I will put a stop to it. But please try not to judge all humans for the acts of a few." As the words left her lips, she realized how hollow they must have sounded. Why should he trust her, or any human, since even she had caged them and tried to control their every behavior without treating them as intellectual equals?

Brutus paused for a moment and looked back at Dr. Jones. There was nothing he could say to describe his feelings, he thought, that had not already been said by the Bard.

"A wretched soul, bruised with adversity, we bid be quiet when we hear it cry; but were we burdened with like weight of pain, as much or more we should ourselves complain."

"You've read... *Shakespeare?*" Samantha gushed.

I have read all of your writings, Brutus responded through Koda. *At least, all of those that are available on your computer. I have tried to understand what it means to be human, what you consider ethical behavior, but yet, observing you as a species, you remain an enigma. I am curious about one thing in particular; how would you have us respond to the inhumanity of man?*

Dr. Jones was speechless.

Koda had been a dutiful translator, but he now decided to speak directly to Brutus without sharing his conversation with either Lexis or the other humans.

Let me offer my guidance, brother. Human beings can be wonderful and good, Koda thought to Brutus. *Many are loving, patient, and full of surprises. But not all humans are like this. Some are not to be trusted, they are inherently evil, they are cruel and they will take pleasure in inflicting pain on you and your loved ones.* Brutus nodded as Koda continued to speak to him in his mind. *There is a darkness that lives in the heart of some humans; they are evil. I can tell you of it, but to find it, you must walk the path of understanding alone. I am afraid that you will learn this lesson of good and evil, my friend, as I have, with much sorrow.*

Brutus was pleased with the direct communication from Koda and he now felt he could speak to him freely.

I have heard your words of truth, my canine brother, Brutus responded. *And they ring clear within my soul. You and your mind master have a bond of trust that is clear to my heart. But I must ask you one more question... what do you do when you encounter evil humans?*

Koda answered Brutus without hesitation. *I kill them,* he thought.

Brutus contemplated the council of Koda and then changed the subject matter to resume their more public conversation by including Lexis. He turned and smiled at Lexis to address her directly, through Koda. He looked deeply into her eyes, studying her for a reaction.

Music is beautiful, Brutus thought. *But it is so sad.* Lexis was puzzled. Without translating for Dr. Jones, she asked Koda to speak her thoughts back to Brutus.

"Why do you think music is so sad?" Lexis asked aloud.

Because... I will never play the guitar, Brutus thought. *Look at me... I have claws. How can I play an E chord with claws?* Lexis burst out laughing as Koda relayed the thoughts from Brutus. She was really starting to like Brutus; she was amazed at his charm, intelligence, and his sense of humor. She cocked her head, smiled and continued the conversation just between the two of them, well, three of them, counting Koda.

"You are one funny beast!" Lexis shot back. "And just between us, I like you better than the rest of these humans anyway. Can't play the guitar? Come on, Elvis, just tune to drop D and play power chords... *duh?*"

Brutus smiled at the witty conversation with the human female that had a sense of humor. Even Koda was amused at the playful banter rapidly escalating between them. Interrupting the flirtatious conversation between Lexis and Brutus, NELI announced the results of her last query.

"DNA samples collected from the passengers and crew of Genesis Five and cross matched against the DNA in the ship's medical records. All test samples match against medical records, save one."

"Which one doesn't match?" Dr. Maurya blurted out.

"The DNA from the medical records for Lieutenant Morgan McCurdy," NELI answered, "Do not match the DNA from the real time samples."

"Are you positive?" Dr. Jones pressed.

"Affirmative," NELI responded. "I have accessed retina scans and fingerprints from the personnel data base to confirm. None of the real time data acquired for Lieutenant Morgan McCurdy matches the Lieutenant Morgan McCurdy listed in Genesis Five's medical records database."

"But if McCurdy isn't who he says he is, then who is he?" Dr.

Jones exclaimed.

"I'm afraid only our Lieutenant McCurdy, or whoever he is, will be able to answer that question," Dr. Maurya responded. "But just one more loose end... NELI, can you run a DNA match from the real time sample acquired from Lieutenant McCurdy against the human DNA in the Chimera sample?"

"Working," NELI responded. "The real time DNA sample acquired from Lieutenant McCurdy is a one-hundred-percent match with the human DNA in the Chimera sample."

"That bastard!" Dr. Jones exploded with rage. "Now it all makes sense! He stopped by my lab the day I was preparing the Chimera formula just to check on things, he said. He challenged my reasoning for not using any human DNA in the formula. I told him it was unnecessary for our purpose, and besides, I would have an ethical issue if we were to go down that path. He seemed mildly displeased, but then left shortly afterwards."

"So he must have come back and contaminated the Chimera sample with his own DNA, but why?" Dr. Maurya questioned.

"I don't care why!" Dr. Jones screamed. "I have to find him and confront this outrage! Meddling in my research, endangering my project and all of our lives, damn it! I won't have it!"

Lexis and Josiah had been listening and were equally shocked by the revelation. Lexis, however, had a more basic suggestion. *When dealing with an unknown opponent,* she thought, *do not squander the element of surprise.*

"I think you should calm down a bit before confronting Lieutenant McCurdy," Lexis counseled. "You don't know anything about him, other than he has assumed someone else's identity... and he has a gun. These are two things that should make you a bit cautious."

Dr. Jones was consumed with rage and would not listen to reason. She gathered her lab notes and rushed out of the room in search of the traitor that had sabotaged her work. Dr. Maurya glanced around for support and then started out the door after her.

"Samantha! Come back, my young friend is right. Now is not the best time to confront McCurdy!" Dr. Jones refused to listen and stormed down the hallway with Dr. Maurya in pursuit.

Lexis was frustrated at the heated reactions and the poor judgment that Dr. Jones had shown, and she was concerned about the events now set in motion. She had seen this movie before and it always ended badly. She motioned to Koda and he quickly told Brutus they must leave before McCurdy's men discovered them, but they would return soon.

I trust that you will, my canine friend, Brutus answered. *And be sure to take care of your mind master, I find her... refreshing!* Lexis and Koda started toward the door, eager to get back to the ePod and make their escape to the command module. Dr. Stone was lingering around the computer, rummaging through Dr. Jones' lab notes.

"Josiah!" Lexis screamed. "Let's go!" Dr. Stone had been quiet, frantically typing away on Dr. Jones' computer. After reviewing the files recently accessed by Brutus, he hit the print button, tore off a sheet of information and shoved it in his pocket. Lexis pushed Josiah out the door and they ran down the hallway to board the ePod. As the ePod silently launched away from the passenger module, Lexis turned to Josiah.

"What was so important that you had to drag your feet back there?" she scolded. "You should have learned by now, when I say go... we go!"

"You're right," Josiah replied casually. "I was just curious about what the last database access that Brutus made."

"And just why the hell would that be important?" Lexis snapped.

"Maybe it is and maybe it's not." Josiah shrugged, waiting for Lexis to circle back around. *One, two, three...* he counted in his mind. Just as he thought, Lexis couldn't stand the silence of the unresolved question.

"Ok, Columbo, I give. What the hell was it?" Lexis blurted out. "What was he reading?"

"Oh, nothing important. Just a little book by Sun Tzu called '*The Art of War'*."

39. Confrontation

Samantha Jones ran down the hallway toward Dr. Maurya's laboratory, driven by an uncontrollable rage to find Lieutenant McCurdy and beat him senseless. *Maybe beating McCurdy senseless was an oxymoron,* she thought, *because she could not conceive of any logical circumstance by which his reckless actions could have been driven by a sensible person.* By purposefully contaminating the Chimera formula, McCurdy had shattered the delicate moral agreement she had made with herself not to play God with genetics. Maybe her internal compromise was just a house of cards waiting to fall, but in her own mind, she had walked the ethical tightrope of her beliefs and still had been able to contribute to the salvation of the passengers of Genesis Five. *Some things, once done,* she thought, *cannot be undone.*

"That bastard! How could he have done this?" Dr. Jones screamed. Sliding around the corner, she lunged toward the door of Dr. Maurya's laboratory. Posted outside the door were two of Lieutenant McCurdy's soldiers, standing at attention. As she sprinted down the hallway toward them, the soldiers drew their weapons.

"Halt! Stop right there, ma'am, or we'll shoot!"

Dr. Jones froze in her tracks, spilling her notes onto the floor and depositing a pile of papers at the feet of the soldiers. She turned her head to the side and was suddenly snapped back to reality by the reflection of her face in the window of the lab door... there were two red laser dots trained on her forehead. She straightened her hair and tried to regain her composure. In a calm but shaky voice, she looked up and responded to the soldier with his gun aimed at her forehead.

"I need to see McCurdy." She coughed, trying to regain her breath. "Right now, it's urgent!"

The lead soldier sized her up and lowered his weapon. The second soldier maintained his gun focused on Dr. Jones' forehead.

"You know, we've got enough problems onboard this ship right now," the soldier growled. "Actions like yours will get you dead fast around here, ma'am." To avoid a bullet in her brain, Dr. Jones struggled to present a more pleasant persona.

"I'm sorry, I should have been... more careful. But I really need to see Lieutenant McCurdy, right now. It's very important." By this time, Ashoka had finally caught up with Dr. Jones and seeing the standoff at the laboratory door, he walked calmly up to Dr. Jones, taking her by the arm.

"Ah, Samantha, there you are! Thank you for coming so quickly. I know I said it was urgent, so let's get to work." Dr. Maurya slid his security card key through the biometric sensor on the wall and stepped up to the soldier blocking the doorway.

"Thank you, Sergeant, you have been most attentive. I will be sure to mention your professionalism to Lieutenant McCurdy. Now please stand aside, we have important work to do." The soldiers exchanged a glance, lowered their weapons, and stood down.

"All right, Doc. We know what you're working on, you may pass."

As they entered the lab and shut the door, Dr. Maurya pulled Dr. Jones close to him and looked directly in her eyes. "Samantha, I know how passionate you are about your work and the Chimera, but I'm afraid that Lexis was right, we must be very careful with McCurdy. We do not know what he is up to, but we know it is not good. As they say in your movie westerns, *'You must not let your mouth write a check that your body can't cash.'* Let's now agree to remain calm and collected until we can determine a proper course of action."

"You're right, of course, Ashoka." Dr. Jones nodded in agreement. "Sometimes I just get emotional. Why are you always the sensible one in our relationship?"

Suddenly, the deafening sound of grinding metal gears triggered the realization that something was wrong inside the laboratory. It was a painful sound, the sound of the atmospheric generator straining to accelerate rapidly as it advanced to operate at full throttle without a proper warm up sequence. They rushed into the generator room next door where the lights fluttered between dim and bright as the generator struggled to rapidly draw and displace more power. Standing with his back to them was a man in uniform, randomly punching buttons on the control panel and jerking the levers back and forth.

"You imbecile!" Dr. Maurya screamed at the man from across the room. "What are you doing in here? This is a delicate instrument, not some toy for you to play with! Step away from the controls this instant!"

The man with his back to them released the controls and the generator backed off from full throttle, easing the deafening sound of grinding metal to a low roar. He turned around and smiled... it was Lieutenant McCurdy. Stepping forward, McCurdy strained to shout over the noise of the generator.

"Ah, my good doctors, I'm glad you could join me. It's time to get cracking and make me some oxygen."

Dr. Maurya was stunned for a moment, and then he rushed past Lieutenant McCurdy to regain control of the atmospheric generator before it flew apart. He frantically typed in a shutdown sequence on the computer input panel, but the generator would not respond to his command. Dr. Maurya reached around behind the control panel and was horrified. *Oh my God,* he thought, *McCurdy's random punching of buttons has inadvertently activated my secret EMP engine.* Once the EMP engine had been activated, it could not be shut down without a massive electrical discharge that would certainly be detected as it was not a design feature of the oxygen generator.

"What's the matter, Doc, something wrong with your toy?" McCurdy asked sarcastically. "You told me it was ready to go, so I cranked it up." Dr. Maurya was too stunned to control his anger.

"You fool, your recklessness may have just set me back a month and squandered our only chance to continue breathing!"

Lieutenant McCurdy was no longer amused with Dr. Maurya's superior attitude. He grabbed him by the collar and pressed close to his face.

"Listen to me, Poindexter, you fix it and you fix it now. And the next time you speak to me in that tone of voice, I will have you shackled in leg irons and beaten with a bamboo cane until you can discover a civil tongue, do you hear me?" McCurdy shoved Dr. Maurya back against the control panel and glared at him. The grinding metal sounds had started to accelerate again and now a flashing yellow light accompanied them on the control panel. "I said fix it... *now!*" McCurdy demanded.

Dr. Jones had watched in shock as Lieutenant McCurdy abused Ashoka. *This is too much*, she thought. She had almost regained her composure enough to delay the confrontation, but McCurdy's continued mistreatment of her good friend pushed her over the edge. The anger returned and she was boiling inside to confront McCurdy over his contamination of the Chimera DNA. Somewhere in the back of her head, she heard Lexis' advice to not let her anger control her emotions, but she could no longer suppress her rage. She grabbed

McCurdy from behind and spun him around.

"Leave him alone, you moron!" Samantha shouted. "He built that damn oxygen machine and he's the only one who can operate it without blowing us all up!"

McCurdy was surprised, but not ruffled by Dr. Jones' anger.

In the midst of the confrontation between McCurdy and Samantha, Ashoka was frantically trying to get control of the atmospheric generator. He had almost regained control when another red light went off on his control panel. *This was bad*, he thought. The red light meant that the detection sensor he had configured was alerting him to the planet's EMP surge that would synchronize with his machine and, if it worked correctly, open a portal to another dimension. There wasn't much time left; the massive EMP would be preceded by an eminent blackout of the Niburu atmosphere in approximately thirty seconds. *Damn it!* Ashoka thought. *I am not ready yet!*

The inadvertent firing of the generator was totally by accident, it was because of Lieutenant McCurdy's foolish antics. The carefully controlled 500-gigawatt pulse concentrator that Dr. Maurya had built was now spinning out of control. *The Time Portal is going to open whether I am ready or not,* Ashoka thought as the confrontation with Lieutenant McCurdy was rapidly degenerating. *I have to do something; there may never be another chance. He had to get Samantha away from McCurdy, no matter what it took.* Dr. Maurya locked on to the EMP signal and synchronized it with his pulse concentrator, just behind the control panel. He looked down and set the timer on his digital watch to match the countdown sequence.

Twenty-five seconds.

"Why, Dr. Jones, you should try to calm down," McCurdy hissed. "You are starting to act like one of your animals."

"Animals?" Samantha exploded. "You bastard! You meddled in my work, playing God, and then sabotaged everything I have tried to accomplish with my Chimera!"

"Again with the bad attitude," McCurdy retorted. "First, Doctor, let me remind you once again that they are not *your* Chimera. They belong to *me*. We have been over all this before. And second, I am starting to think some time in a locked cell below deck for both of you might be in order."

Dr. Maurya stepped away from the control panel, directly behind Lieutenant McCurdy and tried to get Samantha's attention, but she was too angry to notice his hand gestures pointing to the back of the control panel. He looked down at his watch.

Twenty seconds.

"I've had it with your simple-minded condescension!" Samantha Jones screamed at McCurdy "You snuck into my lab behind my back and added your DNA into my Chimera formula. What were you thinking? That you could build a race of sub-human slaves for your twisted entertainment? Well that won't work now, you bastard, because I destroyed the Chimera formula and you will never be able to create another slave for your army!"

The look on Lieutenant McCurdy's face went from smugness to anger in a heartbeat. He wasn't sure if Dr. Jones was lying about destroying the Chimera formula, but this insubordination could not stand; once he learned the truth, he would execute her either way. McCurdy signaled the guards at the door to enter and they rushed in, weapons drawn, and surrounded Dr. Jones.

"Sergeant Longstreet, Dr. Jones is not feeling well, she seems to be suffering from... hallucinations. Poor girl, she's probably just been working too hard. For her own safety, please escort her to the brig below on the cargo deck."

The two soldiers stepped forward to grab Dr. Jones; she struggled but was held back by the soldiers' grip.

"Who the hell are you anyway?" she shouted out in frustration. "You're not even the real Lieutenant Morgan McCurdy! You don't have his DNA, I checked the crew's database and you're not in it!" She turned to scream at the other soldiers. "He's a lying son of a bitch, he's an imposter!"

Lieutenant McCurdy reached down and calmly unhooked the stun gun from his leather holster. He unlocked the safety and slid the gun into his right hand.

"Dr. Jones, you're out of control and have become a danger to the passengers and crew of my ship. I am afraid that we will have to help you calm down, you're making crazy accusations!"

Ten seconds.

Dr. Maurya looked down at his watch; he was out of time. Ashoka was not a strong man, but he had learned his share of martial arts maneuvers while studying to be a Buddhist monk in India. There were three soldiers to deal with, but his Kung Fu was strong. He took a deep breath, leaped forward and delivered a crushing karate chop to the back of Lieutenant McCurdy's neck. McCurdy's knees buckled and he dropped the stun gun into Maurya's waiting hand.

The soldier holding Dr. Jones released her and lunged to grab Dr. Maurya. *A bad move for him,* Ashoka thought. The soldier was met with 50,000 volts to the base of his spine and collapsed to the floor. With one arm now free, Dr. Jones delivered a swift pointed elbow to the face of the second guard, breaking his nose, and blinding him for a second, causing him to drop his weapon as he screamed out in pain. Dr. Maurya, still holding the stun gun, stood over the semiconscious body of Lieutenant McCurdy and looked down at his watch.

Five seconds.

Samantha rushed to thank Ashoka, but instead of hugging her, he grabbed her and threw her behind the control panel.

"No time to explain, love!" he screamed. "Jump! Jump through the arc!" Dr. Jones was confused and hesitated, holding him back for just a second. The 500-gigawatt pulse concentrator on the atmospheric generator surged and fired, creating a round blue halo arc of electrical power, six feet wide and six feet tall. The machine crackled and popped as the massive pulse concentrator arc met the electromagnetic pulse from Niburu's atmosphere. Inside the center of the arc was a dark space with no light; it was a portal to another dimension.

"Take my hand, Alice!" Ashoka screamed. "Through the looking glass!" He pushed Samantha in front of him, and just as they leaped into the arc, McCurdy awakened, lunged and grabbed Dr. Maurya by the ankle. Dr. Jones disappeared into the arc behind the atmospheric generator, leaving Dr. Maurya behind in the grasp of McCurdy. Ashoka struggled violently, kicking at McCurdy, but he was too strong, he would not let go. McCurdy held on desperately to the front of the control panel with one hand and Ashoka's ankle with the other, straining not to let go.

"That was quite a shocking surprise coming from you, Herr Doctor, you been watching some old Kung Fu movies?" McCurdy gritted his teeth and muttered, "Bigger balls than I had imagined, but nonetheless, playtime is over." McCurdy tightened his vice-like grip on Dr. Maurya's ankle and dragged him back around the front of the control panel. From his position on the floor, McCurdy couldn't see behind the control panel; he couldn't see that the portal to a parallel dimension had been opened and Dr. Jones had escaped into it. With a final electrical pulse from the atmospheric generator, the blue arc disappeared and the portal was sealed shut.

Dr. Maurya fell to the floor, sobbing, and the two battered soldiers regained their composure and rushed to McCurdy's aid. They quickly handcuffed Ashoka and threw him against the wall, shoving their guns to his head.

"A lot of help you two were!" McCurdy screamed at the soldiers. "Letting these two pinheads take you down. And you, Sergeant, overpowered by a *girl?* Maybe you were adjusting your tampon when she took you out." The two soldiers tightened their grip on Dr. Maurya, ready to take out their frustration on him for their failure.

"Ok, we've got Rambo here in custody," McCurdy bellowed. "Now go retrieve Wonder Woman from behind the control panel and take them to the brig!" Sergeant Longstreet released Dr. Maurya and spun around behind the control panel, his weapon drawn. Seconds later, he emerged from the other side of the panel with a confused look on his face.

"Well?" McCurdy screamed. "Where the hell is she?" Sergeant Longstreet had a blank look on his face; the look of a teenager that had been caught stealing money from his father's wallet and was now waiting for a beating.

"She's... she's *gone,* sir," he mumbled.

"What do you mean she's gone?" McCurdy hissed. "Gone... where?"

"I don't know, sir, my vision is still a little fuzzy from her elbow to my face," the Sergeant snapped. "I thought I saw her jump into a bright blue circle and then she was just... *gone.*" Sergeant Longstreet heard the echo of his own words, and realizing how incomprehensible they sounded, he quickly started to recant. "Like I said, I couldn't see so good. I think my nose is broken, sir."

"Then why don't you take another look, Sergeant," McCurdy suggested. "Unless you think that our two pinheads are really Harry Houdini and his lovely disappearing magic assistant."

Sergeant Longstreet rubbed his broken nose and looked again behind the control panel. He thought about the ramifications of maintaining his unbelievable story and what his punishment would be if he were to repeat the story of what he actually saw. Tapping on the floor with his boot, he looked down, pulled up an embedded tab from a groove on the floor and removed a cutout panel. *In this moment of truth, truth would need to take a holiday,* he thought. Sometimes it is better to see what you believe than to believe what you see; especially if the difference between the two could help you avoid a severe beating.

"This is a raised floor, sir! She must have ducked into a crawl space below the floor."

"So now that your vision has cleared, Sergeant, you believe we got ourselves a sewer rat?" McCurdy smiled. "Well our little nerd herd here is just full of surprises, aren't they!" McCurdy dusted himself off and stepped forward into Dr. Maurya's face. "I'm not one hundred percent sure what just happened to your girlfriend, Professor, but I am one hundred and fifty percent sure what is going to happen to you. You and Pippi Longstocking have a little secret, and I don't like it when people keep secrets from me. We will find her, and when we do, one of you is going to spill the beans." McCurdy circled around behind Maurya and growled in his ear.

"I now have a working atmospheric generator, one that should be adequate to serve my purpose. Apparently, you've taken the initiative to design in some new and mysterious feature for my generator along the way, but nonetheless, I can produce all the oxygen I need to keep my soldiers alive. So, at this point, Doctor, and I mean this with all due respect, that would seem to make you somewhat... *expendable.*" A strange look came over Lieutenant McCurdy's face as he turned away from Dr. Maurya, tapping the stun gun in his hand. With his back to Maurya, McCurdy added calmly, "Do you know what your pain threshold is, Doctor? Most people can't really answer that question, but it is an important question; and an area of considerable expertise for me." Turning back toward Dr. Maurya, McCurdy slowly moved closer to him, studying his face and smiling at him with a strangely clinical smile.

"They say that women can endure more pain than men, did you know that, Doctor? Something about them being programmed to endure childbirth and all. I'm betting that we can find *your* pain threshold; it's just a question of mind over matter. I don't *mind* inflicting whatever amount of pain it takes, and in the end, all of your resistance will not *matter*. I am going to get your little secret out of you, Doctor, one way or another, and believe me, this is not going to be fun for you." McCurdy turned away from Dr. Maurya, smiled, and then stepped into the hallway with his soldiers.

"Sergeant Longstreet," he barked, "search every inch of this ship and bring me professor Houdini's assistant. And while you are searching, muster my Chimera into the cargo bay and issue a couple of them full battle gear. It's time those mutants earned their keep in this man's army."

ACT III

"A wretched soul, bruised with adversity, we bid be quiet when we hear it cry; But were we burdened with like weight of pain, as much or more we should ourselves complain."

Shakespeare

"If a man is coming to kill you, get up early and kill him first."

Talmud

"People sleep peacefully in their beds at night only because rough men stand ready to do violence on their behalf."

George Orwell

"We roll tonight... to the guitar bite. And for those who are about to rock, we salute you."

AC/DC

40. American Gladiator

From outside Commander Ivan Stephanotski's gladiator office in the lizard prison, there came the sound of a piercing horn that trumpeted a long two-pitched note. A wave of nausea spread over Mitch Gaylord. He thought he knew the answer to his question, but had to ask it anyway.

"What was that horn for?" Mitch asked.

Ivan strapped on his armored breastplate and grabbed a battle-axe and shield from the wall of weapons.

"That for us, cowboy. Is time now." He pointed his axe at the wall. "Choose wisely, my new friend. And remember, show no mercy... you will receive none from me."

The large metal doors creaked open and there was a roar of noise as the mob of beasts in the arena snorted and grunted wildly. Commander Stephanotski strode into the center of the arena and thrust his battle-axe in the air, triggering the frenzied mob of lizard beasts to explode with a deep guttural wave of sound that was terrifying. Inside Ivan's office, Captain Mitch Gaylord looked up at the wall of weapons and hesitated. There were primitive clubs, spears, and knives, but no metal helmets or body armor like Ivan was wearing. It was clear that only one gladiator would get home court advantage and that advantage must be taken by killing the current champion.

"Well shit, I guess that makes me the underdog playing an away game," Mitch muttered to himself. "Ok, you had better get some serious mojo going fast, or you are just gonna be dead guy number twenty-one."

From inside the arena Mitch could hear the sound of rhythmic drums, gathering in intensity. *Commander Stephanotski must be taking his victory lap a little early,* he thought. Mitch reached up and pulled off a heavy wooden shield, a sturdy spear and a small jagged obsidian knife; it was razor sharp. He would be no match for the Russian's strength. *That bastard looks like he could bench press a fucking Volkswagen. Keep him at bay and just maybe he'll make a mistake.* Mitch thought. *Or maybe he'll be quick about it and just lop my fucking head off with his axe before I get torn apart by those slimy lizards out there. If I have to choose a way to go,* he thought, *I'm gonna have to go with the axe on this one.*

The large metal doors swung open wide and in stepped the two guards that had dragged Captain Gaylord from his cell earlier. Apparently, the lizards in the arena were now ready for his close up. He wasn't positive, but he thought he could almost see one of the beasts grinning at him from under his metal helmet as he poked him with his spear.

"Keep away from me, you mangy vermin! I'm coming!" he screamed. Mitch paused once more to examine the wall of weapons and reached high to grab a long slender pipe with a leather strap. He pulled it down, held it up to his eye, and sighted down the tube with one eye closed. *Shit.* It had only one projectile. *Oh well, this will have to do,* he thought. Another sharp poke in the back and he whirled around with his shield and spear.

"Back off, Godzilla!" he growled. "You'll get your turn soon enough." Captain Mitch Gaylord stepped into the lizard gladiator arena and the mob again erupted in a wave of snarls and grunts. He walked slowly to the center of the ring to meet Commander Stephanotski, holding his shield and spear down by his side. The Russian moved directly in front of him and also lowered his metal shield. Ivan raised his helmet to speak.

"Remember, cowboy, no mercy. Is me... or is *them,*" Ivan reminded him with a gesture of his axe to the frenzied crowd of lizards.

Mitch Gaylord wasn't quite sure just how his destiny had led him to this point. One moment, he was saving the passengers and crew of Genesis Five with a heroic gesture of sacrifice and the next thing you know, he was in an alien prison, fighting a giant Russian to the death to avoid being eaten alive by a bunch of slimy lizards. *This isn't really what I was expecting when I rolled out of bed,* he thought. Captain Gaylord opened his arms wide, holding his spear and shield down at his side.

"Well, I don't really like those choices, Ivan," Mitch shouted. "But if that's all we got, then I guess it's going to have to be you." He clanged his spear against his shield. In military training films for hand-to-hand combat, Captain Gaylord had seen how the ancient Romans would tuck in behind their shields and only expose the tip of their spear; making them a fierce, impenetrable killing machine. At least that's the way they did it in the movies, so he assumed a Roman Legion battle position.

Commander Ivan Stephanotski took one look at Mitch Gaylord's ridiculous fighting stance and roared with a belly laugh that shook the entire arena.

"Captain Spartacus, I like you! I think you are now Ivan's *new* best friend."

Mitch Gaylord peered around from behind his shield.

"Judging by how you treated your last best friend, I hope you'll understand that I'm not getting a big head about our friendship. No offense." Again, Commander Stephanotski laughed, and then turned deadly serious.

"None taken, cowboy. But now is time... for rodeo."

Ivan crouched down for a second and then lunged at Gaylord, striking a powerful blow with his battle-axe, narrowly missing his ear and tearing a huge chunk of wood from his shield. Mitch dropped to one knee, ducking under the sharp metal edge of Ivan's shield. The crowd of bloodthirsty beasts grunted their approval for the swift attack. Commander Stephanotski spun back around and tipped his metal helmet to Gaylord.

"Not bad, cowboy. You are like little cat, yes?"

Mitch looked at what was left of his shield and answered, "Hey, you want to trade shields? I think I got a defective one!"

Commander Stephanotski roared again with laughter. "I am going to miss you, cowboy! You have balls. Little cat balls!" With that, Ivan lunged at Mitch again and brought down another powerful blow with his battle-axe. Gaylord sidestepped and just managed to raise his shield in time, but the force of the blow shattered what was left of his wooden shield into a pile of splinters.

"Shit!" screamed Gaylord. "That fucking hurts!" As brilliant as Mitch Gaylord's strategy of getting pummeled to death from afar was, it had become clear that a change of plan was in order. He was never as good at this hand-to-hand combat shit as Ryker, who used to kick his ass on a regular basis. *What was it Ryker told me once, after he wiped up the floor with me at the dojo? If a guy has big guns, run away. If you can't run away, get inside his shorts.* "Ok, Ryker," Mitch muttered, "I got no better ideas of my own."

Comrade Stephanotski was busy waving his battle-axe to the wild mob, working them into a frenzy for his kill. He didn't seem worried about the outcome of this battle; he knew that Captain Gaylord could not survive another blow from his axe without a shield.

You must be... unpredictable, thought Gaylord. *That's what you said, didn't you, Ivan?* Just as Commander Stephanotski turned from his victory wave to the crowd, Mitch sprang at him and buckled him at the knees. Ivan was stunned at the attack and tried to counter with his battle-axe, but in this close quarter drill, he couldn't land a blow. Wrestling on the ground, Gaylord worked himself behind Ivan's left arm and underneath his metal shield. Ivan struck hard repeatedly with his axe, but his blows landed helplessly against his own shield; Mitch was in his shorts. He clutched tightly to the giant Russian with all his strength, knowing that if he let go, he was dead.

With the weight of the heavy metal shield and the futile blows from his axe, Ivan was trapped like an animal in the jaws of a pit bull. When a pit bull goes for the kill, he locks his vice-like teeth onto the jugular vein of his prey and just waits for his victim to tire and bleed to death. The more the victim struggled, the faster he died. As they rolled around on the soft dirt, Mitch reached down and grabbed the small obsidian knife he had tucked into his waistband. Now face to face with Ivan in his lethal grasp, he shoved the razor-sharp blade against the Russian's throat, waiting to deliver the fatal blow.

"Well done, cowboy. You surprise me with your little blade. I underestimate you."

"Alright then, you bastard, now we're even. You gave me my life; I give you yours. Now how the hell do we both get out of here alive?"

Ivan looked at Captain Gaylord and sighed. "Is not the way it works here, my new friend. They have seen you have beaten me; you must finish the fight. One of us must die or they will tear us apart alive. I do not want to be eaten alive, is no way for man to die."

"I can't just end your life, Ivan... we are friends!"

"Listen, cowboy. I told you that you owed me favor for saving your life. You beat me now; you have our wiped slate clean. But what you do not know is what is *next.*"

"Next? What do you mean, there's a *next?*" Mitch gasped for breath.

"I still want a favor, cowboy. Time is up for me, but I can still help you. What is *next* is you must fight lizard champion; I call him Lizard King."

Mitch let out a sigh of disappointment. "Shit! One fight to the death is not enough for this slimy crowd? It's a double header?" Mitch sputtered.

Ivan sensed Mitch's sinking feeling of doom and tried to lift his spirits. "Ok, lizard is not real king." Ivan laughed. "Only real king is Elvis. Here in arena there are more fighters like him, but others, they bigger and stronger, I hear they fight somewhere else. I do not know where. But this lizard is how you say, big fish in small pond, like farm team baseball pitcher waiting for phone call to go to your big show, no?"

"The big show? What has all this got to do with me?" Mitch asked.

"Ivan kill many men in ring, in how you say... elimination rounds. Is like big tournament of death... last man standing is human champion... is now worthy to fight Lizard King. When Ivan kill First Officer Christyakova, he is to be human champion... until you come along, cowboy," Ivan explained. "You are late entry to game, a ringer... you are *'great lizard hope'*. To them, you are human, but you are superior; you are beast-man. When you beat Ivan, Lizard King must show scaly mob that he is top dog in arena. To not do so, he lose face... they turn on him and kill him. This must happen, cowboy."

"I have to kill you and then fight Elvis, the fucking Lizard King? Are you crazy?" Mitch screamed.

"Crazy? No, Ivan not crazy. Crazy is you without Ivan's help, so I help you, cowboy. When I operate in hospital, I see many lizard beasts killed in arena. They make me drag away bodies to throw away, but some... some I not throw away, I study. Lizards have body covered in scales... spear and knife not work so good. But they have weakness, cowboy. If you know Ivan's secret, maybe you just might not die so fast against Lizard King."

"So you tell me your secret, and I do you a favor, yes?" Mitch mocked Ivan.

"As you say, my friend, Bingo. Ivan will tell secret. Lizards have gland under their left ear that makes syrup. You have one too, but they do not know. Two inches below left ear is small hole where beast's slime can ooze out. There is no armor scale here." Mitch felt his own neck and located the small hole. Just as Ivan had described it, there was sticky goo dripping out of the hole and down his neck. "This hole on neck is Lizard King's weak spot. You stab him in hole below ear, it pierces syrup gland. Without syrup in lungs, king will choke to death in fifteen seconds."

"That's it? Just stab him in the ear and he dies?" Mitch laughed nervously.

"Yes." Ivan laughed. "He dies... but not for fifteen seconds."

"And what does he do for the fifteen seconds before he dies?" Mitch shot back.

"Is simple. He explodes with rage and tries to kill you. Best for you to stay away then."

"Let me get this straight... I stab him in the ear and run away. But how do I get close enough to stab him in the ear?"

Ivan roared with laughter. "That part, I never figure out. But I tell you important part, how to kill him. Now you owe Ivan favor."

"Shit, did we shake on that?"

"Don't fuck with me, cowboy, we have deal, yes?"

"All right, we have a deal, yes. So what's your favor, Ivan? Assuming that I fight the Lizard King, figure out how to kill him and somehow escape alive, that is."

Commander Stephanotski became dead serious. "You must protect my Elena. She is in hospital, but her leg should be well enough to move by now. You find my Elena and get her out of here. That is Ivan's favor."

"Ok, I'll try."

"Not try, do!" Ivan told him sternly. "Do I have your word of honor, as a cowboy? Let me hear you say it!"

"All right! We have a deal, I will protect your Elena," Mitch promised. Ivan Stephanotski sighed and relaxed his body under Mitch Gaylord; he was now prepared to accept his fate.

"Is it true that on your birthday in America, you get free meal at your Denny's?"

"Yeah, anything you want," Mitch Gaylord answered. "Denny's is the fucking real deal."

"Then I want to go to your Denny's," Ivan proclaimed. "I will eat flapjacks and read pornography. A mountain of flapjacks." And with that, Ivan Stephanotski smiled, grabbed Mitch's hand and plunged the razor-sharp obsidian blade into his own jugular vein. Blood squirted out all over Mitch Gaylord, the giant Russian's body quivered several times; he was dead.

Captain Gaylord stood up over Ivan's body with blood dripping down the blade and his arm, his chin tucked into his chest. The beast mob had grown silent, staring at him in the middle of the arena. Mitch reached down, unhooked the utility belt from Commander Stephanotski, and fastened it around his waist. He bent over, removed the metal Conquistador helmet from the dead Russian, and placed it on his own head. There were a few scattered grunts and snarls in the crowd; the lizard mob seemed confused at what would happen next.

Next, Mitch Gaylord thought. *What the fuck was next? Ivan said it would be the Elvis of lizard beasts, the King. Shit, I hope it's the old fat Elvis and not the young, CIA martial-arts-trained Elvis; that would kind of suck.*

41. A New Sheriff in Town

Aboard Genesis Five, Lieutenant McCurdy ordered all passengers to be assembled on the main deck for indoctrination to his new command. At the same time, he ordered that the Chimera be rousted from their cages and herded by the soldiers into the cargo bay for a much different discussion.

Life after the crash on Niburu had been difficult; facing the fear of the unknown, there had been fights among the passengers over who should control their destiny. After a brief confrontation between the academics and the soldiers, the passengers had reluctantly acquiesced to McCurdy's military rule. Distasteful as it was, it seemed a necessary evil for their survival. But something was different. The passengers were no longer being asked to follow Lieutenant McCurdy's orders; they were being commanded to obey or else, leaving an ever-increasing feeling of domination lingering in the air. McCurdy's ascension to self-appointed benevolent dictator was almost complete. *If you tell a lie often enough,* McCurdy thought, *the lie will become the truth.* This was how he had twisted the events that unfolded after the crash to his advantage.

Acting on Lieutenant McCurdy's command, the soldiers had discovered a mysterious briefcase of DNA while searching the cargo hull for survivors. Unbeknownst to them, the unclaimed briefcase's passage on Genesis Five had been paid for in advance, not with money, but with blood.

Back on Earth, deep under Antarctica in a secret chamber a thousand feet below the surface, a band of scientists had hidden a Genetic Food Vault. The vault contained a biological blueprint of man's food supply, intended as a backup copy of the Earth's DNA in case the madness of man that was swirling above them continued to escalate. In an all-out nuclear, biological, and chemical war, the scientists knew that any genetic banks on the surface would either be destroyed or contaminated, rendering them sterile. Without access to an untainted genetic source to restart an agricultural foundation, the storehouses of food on the surface would quickly be devoured, leaving any survivors from the initial devastation to starve to death in a matter of weeks. *With the world on the brink of collapse,* the scientists thought, *our Genetic Vault is the last, best hope for man's survival.* But their careful planning had underestimated one factor... the inhumanity of man. As they lay sleeping, commandos descended upon them, overwhelmed their guards and slit their throats, leaving them lying piled on top of each other in a pool of blood on the frozen snow. Penetrating the secret hideaway, the masked commandos executed the scientists, stole their genetic treasure and disappeared into the night. And in that instant of violence, the last, best hope for rebuilding civilization on the surface of Earth after Armageddon was lost forever.

Unknown to anyone on board Genesis Five, just before the destruction on Earth, the commandos had secretly stowed the stolen metal briefcase of DNA inside their cargo hold. Unknown, it was... until now.

Back on Genesis Five, the soldiers that had discovered the mysterious briefcase of DNA presented Lieutenant McCurdy with their find. *As fate would have it,* McCurdy thought, *someone's loss is my gain.* Immediately connecting the power of the DNA contained in the briefcase with the imminent peril they faced, McCurdy had devised an ingenious plan to insure their survival.

First, they needed oxygen to survive, he told the other passengers, and so he called on his expertise in terraforming and designed an oxygen generator to be driven by rocks on the planet surface. After extensive training, he was finally able to educate Dr. Maurya on the basic implementation of his design. Second, he developed a genetic formula to harness the power of the DNA in the mysterious briefcase for the creation of a genetically altered work force, the Chimera, and carefully supervised Dr. Samantha Jones to implement his plan. Now with his farsighted and complex strategy complete, the sub-species of Chimera had been trained to fulfill their single purpose in life, to mine rocks on the hostile planet surface that could produce life-sustaining oxygen.

Without the quick thinking and firm leadership of Lieutenant McCurdy, the passengers of Genesis Five would all be dead. This was the lie Lieutenant McCurdy would tell, and if he told it often enough, it would become the truth. *Perception...* he thought, *becomes reality.*

"Thank God I had the foresight to assemble such a fortuitous plan for our survival," Lieutenant McCurdy had reminded everyone repeatedly.

Although the Chimera created by Dr. Jones were engineered as a workforce, Dr. Jones had never thought of them as subservient. In fact, she had encouraged all of the passengers to treat the Chimera as companions, equals in their fight for survival on this hostile planet.

Only on rare occasions had the Chimera suffered indignities at the hand of McCurdy and his soldiers, and in those cases, Dr. Jones had quickly intervened to stop it. Something was different, as they all were about to find out. Lieutenant McCurdy stepped to the front of the room and addressed the passengers.

"Thank you all for assembling so promptly. I have a few announcements to make and then we will all get back to work. First off, it has come to my attention that without sunlight, without a reference point to day or night, some of you are having trouble maintaining your sanity. The concept of time can be confusing here, but it is important that we keep our circadian rhythms in balance. So effective immediately, we will simulate both day and night. We will have lights out and all civilians will be confined to their quarters between sixteen hundred and zero-six hundred. I would suggest that you use that time to readjust your frame of reference... and get some sleep." The passengers glanced around nervously at each other, waiting for McCurdy to continue.

"Now for some bad news; when we crashed here, the command module lost one engine on descent and the other one exploded on impact. Although several members of the crew survived the landing, they were contaminated with massive doses of radiation. I tried valiantly to save their lives by tapping into our oxygen supply to decontaminate their vessel, but it did not work... they are all dead."

A hush fell over the crowd.

"It has also been discovered that two of our trusted scientists, Dr. Jones and Dr. Maurya, have conspired to commit treasonous acts that have endangered our very survival. Fortunately, I discovered their devious plot in time to minimize the damage."

There was a gasp from the passengers and then a continued low murmur of disbelief.

"Yes," McCurdy continued, "I was as shocked as you are, but here are the facts. Dr. Jones was caught red-handed, willfully sabotaging my carefully controlled genetic formula by which our Chimera are created. Unfortunately, her traitorous actions have resulted not in the creation of a benign race of workers, but instead, an unstable pack of savage beasts; beasts that could very well pose a threat to our survival if they are not restrained by force."

The passengers let out a collective moan and then McCurdy silenced them once again.

"In order to protect us all from Dr. Jones' criminal actions, I have now assumed complete military control of the Chimera and of this ship. After being exposed as a traitor, Dr. Jones confessed to her crimes, but has fled into hiding. If any of you know of her whereabouts, you will report it immediately to my command. If you are aiding her concealment, come forward now, and you will not be held accountable. When we find her, and let me assure you, we *will* find her, she and anyone helping her will be punished severely for their actions."

The passengers were stunned in disbelief. Both Dr. Jones and Dr. Maurya were well respected by all on board, and now McCurdy was denouncing them as traitorous criminals.

"We have also learned," McCurdy added, "that Dr. Jones was aided in her sedition by Dr. Maurya, in a thwarted attempt to destroy our atmospheric generator and in hording the very air we breathe for themselves and their Chimera. Luckily, I discovered their heinous plot in time to prevent them from disrupting our oxygen supply."

"Where is Dr. Maurya? He's a good man!" shouted someone in the back of the room.

"He *was* a good man, right before he became a traitor. Dr. Maurya has been temporarily confined to his quarters," McCurdy responded calmly. "For his own safety, while we encourage him to reconsider the gravity of his transgressions. Hopefully, once he has been given time for proper reflection on his actions, he will choose to cooperate with us and rejoin us as a productive member of our society. But you can rest easy, I personally stopped him before he could damage our atmospheric generator and cut off our air supply."

"My God, are we running out of air?" someone screamed.

"There's no cause for alarm, at least, not yet," McCurdy responded. "My atmospheric generator is working well; I have tested it myself. But in order for us to maintain our air supply, the Chimera must perform the task for which I created them; to mine the rocks needed to supply our oxygen. If they refuse to mine the rocks we need, we *will* die. And if anyone else should attempt to aid these two criminals or interfere with our mission in any way, they will be endangering all of our survival. I assure you, they will be dealt with accordingly."

The passengers stood in silence, still dumbfounded at McCurdy's accusations against the esteemed scientists.

"Lastly, and most disturbing to me, Dr. Jones and Dr. Maurya tried to incite our peaceful Chimera into resisting their vital role in our survival. They openly incited them to rise up against their masters and kill all of us. I assure you, such an insurrection will not occur, not as long as I am in command of this ship. But as a precaution, I have ordered the mutant beasts to be cordoned off in the cargo bay where we can safely manage their mining duties and humanely encourage them to perform the tasks they were created to do."

"But... what if the mutants try to kill us?" asked a frightened woman with a baby.

McCurdy moved close to the woman, reaching out to touch her on the shoulder.

"Let me assure you, ma'am, I guarantee that these mutant Chimera will not harm you, or anyone else onboard my ship. They will be compelled to share in the sacrifice required of all of us and perform their tasks... so that all of us may live."

A nervous buzz filtered through the crowd as they began to feel more comfortable with Lieutenant McCurdy protecting them from the Chimera mutants.

"You will now return to your quarters. My staff and I will proceed in accompanying the Chimera to the mines and working side by side with them, bringing back the essential minerals for our survival. I will extend the Chimera a hand of friendship to their clenched fist. I offer respect to all species, but rest assured, should any Chimera prove to be undeserving of my trust, I will be swift in my retaliation."

Once the passengers had cleared the area, Lieutenant McCurdy struck a distinctively different tone under his breath to his soldiers.

"Sergeant, round up those mutant beasts and drive them into the cargo bay. Have your men break out the cattle prods; I want those dirty animals to feel the sting of my whip. They need to understand that there's a new sheriff in town."

Below deck, the Chimera huddled in the center of the cargo bay, unsure as to what would come next. Brutus scanned the room for Dr. Jones, but she was nowhere to be found. Judging by the sharp pokes from the rifles of the guards shoving them, he realized that life for them among the humans had now taken a decided turn for the worse. Flanked by guards with AK-47s and stun guns, Lieutenant McCurdy marched into the cargo bay with a swagger as he addressed the Chimera in an authoritative tone.

"Listen to me, you filthy beasts! Dr. Jones was your friend... now she is dead. I, on the other hand, I am *not* your friend; I am your *master*. You will follow my commands to the letter or you will suffer the consequences for your actions."

The unexpected news of Dr. Jones' death was a shocking blow to the Chimera; she was the kindest human they had ever known. One of the Chimera in the front rushed forward toward Lieutenant McCurdy and was met by the painful shock of a stun gun to his neck. Collapsing to the floor, he was kicked and dragged back into the crowd. Most of the Chimera were terrified.

"Let that be a lesson to you," McCurdy bellowed. "I have a zero-tolerance policy for disobedience. Do I make myself clear?" He reached down and stroked the weapon in his holster, scanning the eyes of the angry Chimera with a sneer.

Buzzing with confusion, the Chimera looked to Brutus for guidance. *Anger and fists versus bullets and machine guns,* he thought to the others, *are not very good odds.* He clenched his jaw and communicated in an ultra-low frequency that only the Chimera could hear.

"Stand down, that's an order!" the Chimera heard and reluctantly responded, most of them unclenching their fists as they backed down. Viola shook her head and started to move toward McCurdy. Brutus held her back, clutching her tight. "Not the time, nor the place," he whispered to her.

"Sergeant Longstreet, separate the miners from the breeders," McCurdy shouted across the room. "I believe they have some rocks to dig." The soldiers moved quickly, forcibly shoving the Chimera mothers and children away from the others. A few of the Chimera tried to resist leaving their loved ones, but they were rewarded for their resistance with the butt of a rifle to the head and the painful electrocution of a cattle prod. The stench of singed hair and scorched skin hung thick in the room as the Chimera breeders were forcibly cut from the pack like dumb animals.

"Drive the breeders back to their pens and then load the rest of the beasts into the mining transport!" McCurdy shouted. "And throw some old martial arts training equipment into the transport. We might need some sparring partners for our scaly friends out there."

"What about space suits, sir?" Longstreet asked. "We don't have enough of them for the miners."

"Unnecessary, Sergeant. The transport's pressurized, they won't need them until you reach the mine. Besides, our good Dr. Jones said that the air out there's breathable… unless they hit one of those toxic clouds. I guess that's a risk we'll just have to take."

Brutus and Viola lingered at the back of the pack being loaded into the transport, trying to shield the other Chimera from more abuse. As they approached the ramp to the transport, one of the soldiers with an AK-47 stepped in front of them, forcing them to halt.

"Hold it right there," the soldier bellowed. "These the two you wanted, sir?"

"Yes, soldier, these are the two." McCurdy smiled and walked around Brutus and Viola, looking them over like a couple of prized steers. "These are my trouble makers." McCurdy moved close to Viola and reached out to touch her hair, but she recoiled and hissed at him with an angry stare. "Still full of piss and vinegar, you bitch?" he chuckled. "We'll see how long that lasts when you meet my scaly friends out there in the dark." McCurdy stepped back and addressed the armed guard who had returned with the box of old martial arts training weapons. "Let me see… nothing too lethal for these two. Grab a Yari and a Bokuto for the big one, and give the little one a Shinia and some Suriken. That should outfit our little Samurai safety patrol for limited action. I wouldn't want them to get killed before they mine their quota of rocks."

One of the soldiers reached into a crate and tossed out a wooden spear and a six-foot bamboo cane to Brutus, then hurled an oak Katana sword and some blunt metal-tipped Ninja stars to Viola. Looking at the two befuddled Chimera holding their weapons, he laughed aloud and taunted them.

"Ok, Crouching Tiger and Hidden Dragon, both of you to the back of the bus!"

As the airlock door of the cargo bay opened with a whoosh, the heavily loaded transport rolled slowly down the gangplank and onto the soft sand of the Niburu desert. It was crowded inside; the Chimera miners were packed like sardines into the back of the vehicle and surrounded by four guards above them heavily armed with AK-47s. Misun was forced to the front of the transport, jammed against the Plexiglas window separating the driver and his armed escorts. He pressed his ear against the glass and he could hear the soldiers joking about their mission.

"You really think those beasts with primitive weapons have a chance against the lizards out there?" asked the driver.

"Yeah, they have a chance," the guard laughed. "A chance between slim and none! These beasts are like having a cheap early warning system; as long as they make some noise when they die, we'll be ok. These mutants are expendable, you know. If we lose a few of them, shit, McCurdy will just go back to the lab and cook up some more. Just be sure you stay in the transport if things get dicey out there."

"What do we do if, you know, the lizards... get past them?" the driver asked.

"No problem," replied the guard. "Just hit the searchlights on top of the transport. The Lieutenant says those bastards don't like the lights. They freeze up like a deer in the fucking headlights. Just long enough for me to get a good shot at them with the fifty caliber," the guard boasted, patting his heavy machine gun. "This bad mutherfucker will blow the shit out of them."

"Fuck yeah!" The driver and guard exchanged a fist bump. "Like shooting lizards in a barrel!"

Misun peeled his ear off of the glass; he'd heard enough. He had to find Brutus and tell him what he had discovered. Pushing his way under the legs of the larger Chimera, he squirmed to the back of the Transport and found Brutus, relaying the guard's conversation.

"You can't go out there when we get to the mine," Misun pleaded. "It's a trap! There are hostile lizards out there waiting for you!"

"You have served me well, my little friend," Brutus whispered, "but do not worry. There is a chance we will encounter an enemy out there, but chance favors the prepared mind. I am prepared to meet that possibility." Brutus patted Misun on the head and smiled. From inside his pocket, he pulled out several electronic devices he had stolen from Dr. Jones' lab; a music player, a walkie-talkie, and a xenon flash gun with some batteries. He looked around to make sure no guards were watching and then carefully placed the electronic items into Misun's hand. "You like human toys, don't you? I believe it was you that took apart and rebuilt the human communicator, wasn't it?" Brutus asked.

Misun hesitated. He knew he wasn't supposed to interact directly with the humans without Brutus' approval and he was specifically forbidden from accessing their computer network. Knowing he had broken two of Brutus' laws, Misun looked down and shuffled his feet.

"Yes, I'm sorry. I just like to see how their machines work and I like tinkering with things that are broken." He looked up at Brutus to ask for forgiveness. "I improved the range of their communicator with a new spectrum of ultra-low frequencies for Dr. Maurya. He said he wanted to talk to Dr. Jones without the others listening... so I fixed it for him," Misun replied bashfully. Seeking to justify his law breaking, he added with a grin, "And besides, now we can listen in on their conversations." Brutus put his arm around Misun, granting him the approval he sought.

"Very clever, little one! You have a natural talent that will prove useful for us, as useful as these old swords and spears. You said that you overheard the guards talking about the weakness of the lizards, correct? So go and use this knowledge to build us a device that can exploit that weakness. Now off with you, my son, we must prepare for the battle that awaits us."

Misun beamed with a rush of sudden confidence. He was no longer just an annoying juvenile tagging along behind the alpha leader; he was now a trusted part of the team. Granted, it was a small part; but nonetheless, a part that he had earned on his own. Unfortunately, Misun's newfound pride was short-lived, as Viola interrupted to pop his bubble.

"Are you sure you want the little runt hanging around with us?" She poked at him playfully, looking to Brutus. "He could get us all killed."

Misun's smile disappeared for a moment, until he saw that Viola was kidding. She smiled and hugged him close.

"Ok half-pint, go play with your toys. But remember, if we get in trouble out there, stay out of our way... let the big dogs do the fighting," she quipped. As soon as Misun left, Viola turned back to Brutus. "Do you really believe he can build a weapon?" she asked.

"It is not important what I believe, it is only important what *he* believes," Brutus replied. "He believes that he can build a weapon, and that is all that matters for him."

Viola shook her head, not really understanding what Brutus meant.

"You must not only think of an action," Brutus explained, "but also the consequence of that action. If the little one is busy building his weapon, he will not follow us into battle where he could get killed. This way, his mind is focused on something that keeps him out of harm's way. If he actually succeeds and creates a weapon that we can use, well

256

then, all the better for us."

"So you really just wanted him out of our way?" Viola asked.

Brutus leaned in close to her and whispered in her ear, "This is the lesson I want you to learn. It is written that *'a true leader will find the path of least resistance to achieve his goal'*. I believe the human Sun Tzu said this. There will come a day when I am not here to lead our pack, and the others will look to you as their leader. You have courage and fear no human; I have no doubt in that. But what you still must learn is the wisdom of when to use your sword and when to use your mind. When you have learned this lesson, you will be ready to lead our pack."

Viola was still confused. "You of all know how we have suffered at the hand of the humans. Why is it not right to strike back at them, even now?" she asked.

Brutus smiled and put his arm around Viola as he answered.

"The time to show the humans that might makes right will soon be upon us. But even then, you will learn that it is better to redirect the force of an arrow rather than to try and stop it with your hand. The arrow and your hand will both be better off for it." Brutus patted her on the side of the head and then reached down to grab his spear and bamboo cane. "Now come with me, Brave Heart, you and I need to protect our pack from harm.

42. Sacrifice

After the incident with the atmospheric generator, Dr. Maurya had been handcuffed and marched to a makeshift brig in the cargo hold of Genesis Five. The soldiers unlocked a large metal door to a storage unit and shoved Dr. Maurya inside, causing him to fall to his knees. Sergeant Longstreet checked to make sure the hallway was clear and then stepped inside. He leaned down to Dr. Maurya and whispered in his ear.

"I don't know what really happened back there in the lab, Professor, but I know what I saw with my own eyes. It was surreal... my head was fuzzy, but I could still see. It was like your partner jumped through a flaming circus ring into nowhere, and then she was gone."

Ashoka struggled to get back to his feet, rubbing the newly acquired knots on his head and the sharp pain in his ribs. He found it most discomforting that the blows that hurt the most were delivered by McCurdy when he was in handcuffs. *I guess he was just trying to even the score,* Maurya thought, *for me overpowering his soldiers and making him look bad in front of his men.* Sergeant Longstreet eased Dr. Maurya onto a wobbly cot in the corner of the room. He offered him a paper cup of water and reached into his pocket to produce a couple of aspirin. Ashoka was surprised by the sympathetic gesture and reached out to accept the offer of medical triage.

"Thank you, Sergeant," Dr. Maurya muttered.

"Sorry that I had to give you a bit of a jolt back there, but it was necessary. No hard feelings, I hope?" Sergeant Longstreet managed a half smile and then stood to walk away. He stopped and checked to make sure he was out of earshot of the other soldier and then turned back to Dr. Maurya. "Look, Doc, don't get me wrong, me and the men appreciate you making us more air and all. We saw what happened out there with the rover, and that ain't no way for a man to die. But we got our orders, you know. Houdini or not, this disappearing shit is way above my pay grade. If you know what's good for you, you'll tell Lieutenant McCurdy whatever he wants to know. He can be one cold son of a bitch when he gets his panties in a wad; you know what I mean? For your own good, don't try playing the fucking hero with a guy like him."

Dr. Maurya washed down the aspirin with the water from the small paper cup, tossed it in the trashcan, and then looked up to Sergeant Longstreet in appreciation.

"Most assuredly sound advice, Sergeant. I shall remember your kindness."

Longstreet smiled and then turned to pull the door closed behind him. The sound of the metal door clanging shut and the key turning in the lock drove home the grim reality of Dr. Maurya's predicament. He rubbed his sore ribs and shook his head as he tried to focus his mind on the seriousness of his situation. *Use your mind, damn it,* he thought. *This is your only advantage... start from what you know.*

"You are trapped alone in an abandoned meat locker," Dr. Maurya said out loud, "with nothing to look forward to except your next beating from a megalomaniac. Oh, and not a beating by just any megalomaniac, this is a megalomaniac that is also an imposter with a chip on his shoulder and a gun in his pocket. Samantha is suspended in a parallel dimension, her fate is unknown, and the only way you can help her is to escape, seize control of the atmospheric generator, and reopen the Time Portal."

Ashoka Maurya looked around the room for anything he could use, some basic comfort or glimmer of hope, but his hopes were dashed. There was nothing in the room other than a desk, a chair, a trashcan, and the cot he was sitting on. He shouted out in vain, but there was no answer. "Can it get much worse than this? There is no bloody tea in this hell hole!" *A prisoner of conscience locked in an empty room, awaiting an undeserved beating, without even so much as a cup of tea. This,* he thought, *bordered on criminal.* Just outside the door to the makeshift brig, Lieutenant McCurdy arrived to interrogate his prisoner.

"Sergeant, give me your report on our little sewer rat. Have you flushed her out yet?"

"No sir," Longstreet answered. "My men have been over every inch of duct work between here and the laboratory. No trace of her anywhere, sir."

"That is very disappointing, Sergeant. I had hoped you would find her and save me the trouble of having to apply some, shall we say, more persuasive techniques on our brave little soldier inside."

"My apologies, sir. I will have the men resume the search immediately."

"Belay that, Sergeant, it will do no good. I suspect we have a little game of hide and seek underway and only our good doctor knows the whereabouts of our resident rodent in hiding. Oh well; there's only one way to be sure. Open the door and bring me a rag and a bucket of water."

Sergeant Longstreet threw open the door and Lieutenant McCurdy strode into the tiny cell. Dr. Maurya was resting with his eyes shut on the old cot shoved against the wall. Lieutenant McCurdy turned his back, reached down, and unbuckled the holster of his stun gun. He set the voltage discharge level to yellow, a level that would be intensely painful, but should not completely knock his subject unconscious. McCurdy kicked the leg of the cot with his boot to awaken Dr. Maurya.

"Rise and shine, Professor. You and I have some business to take care of," McCurdy shouted. Dr. Maurya was already aware that McCurdy was in the room but preferred to remain in his own world, if only for a few moments longer. Without opening his eyes, he responded.

"What can I do for you now, Lieutenant?"

"You can start by telling me where your little playmate has run off to," McCurdy announced. "We can't seem to locate her."

"I can honestly say that I really don't know where she is."

"Listen, Professor, I am out of patience with you. I don't want to parse words or play parlor games. Tell me where she is, or this conversation is about to take an abrupt turn for the worse... for you, that is."

Dr. Maurya sat up and casually took off his glasses, rubbed them on his shirt and then put them on again. He turned on his cot and looked directly at Lieutenant McCurdy.

"If I knew *exactly* where she was, I am not so sure that it would be in Samantha's best interest for me to disclose that information. You see, knowing now that you are a man not to be trusted, possessing the knowledge of her location would create a moral dilemma for me. Should I betray a friend for my own gain, or should I lie and hide her from you?" Standing, Dr. Maurya walked over to the empty desk with his back to McCurdy. "But since I honestly don't know where she is, answering your question is irrelevant." He turned back to face Lieutenant McCurdy. "Do you think I could get some tea and a notepad in here? Like Mahatma Gandhi, I should like to be productive during my unjust incarceration."

Lieutenant McCurdy stared at him for a moment and then without breaking his stare, he called out to the soldiers guarding the door.

"Sergeant, come in here and strip the coverings from the professor's bedding. He will not be requiring these luxurious accommodation we have provided for him."

Longstreet removed the bedding and tossed it outside the room.

"And could you please place the metal box springs against the wall. Oh yes, handcuff our good doctor to the metal bed frame. He and I are going to have a *private* discussion, so you can close the door on the way out."

Once alone with his handcuffed prisoner, Lieutenant McCurdy shoved the rag into Dr. Maurya's mouth and poured the bottle of water over his head. The water ran down his body and formed a shallow puddle at his feet. McCurdy pulled out the stun gun, slowly placing it next to Dr. Maurya's neck.

"I am sorry, Doctor, but you brought this on yourself. This is going to be uncomfortable for you." McCurdy shoved the stun gun against the skin on Dr. Maurya's neck and pulled the trigger.

Ashoka jerked back and forth against the metal bed, the pain was excruciating. The electrical shock waves raced up and down his spinal cord as a small wisp of smoke came off his skin where the metal contact of the stun gun was still burning his neck. He felt like he had grabbed a live electrical wire, and even though the pain messages to his brain were overwhelming, he was not able to move his arms to make the pain stop. As he looked over at McCurdy, he saw the expression on his torturer's face was one of an interested observer, an almost clinical demeanor, not of a sadistic jailor torturing his prisoner. After what seemed like an eternity, McCurdy released the trigger of the stun gun and Dr. Maurya sagged down, still held up by the handcuffs on the bed frame. Lieutenant McCurdy replaced the stun gun in his side holster and removed the rag from Dr. Maurya's mouth.

"You know, Professor, the unfortunate part of all this drama is that in the end, you are going to tell me everything I want to know. That is a given."

Dr. Maurya was still shaking from the shock and could not respond.

"Just how did Dr. Jones escape? She didn't go through the floor panels, we have searched and she's simply not there. I suspect that somehow you helped her escape with your oxygen machine. Did you help her escape… with your machine, Professor?"

Ashoka was still in pain, but he remained silent. McCurdy circled around behind him, patting his stun gun.

"There is something else that is curious, Doctor. I've been looking through your notes and there are lots of references to electromagnetic power. Lots of little equations written and then erased in the margins of the notebook… see, right here. But that's not the type of power your machine needs to produce oxygen; so why all this mental masturbation on an alternative power source?"

Dr. Maurya looked up at Lieutenant McCurdy and knew he was getting close to the truth. *Regardless of the pain*, he thought, *I cannot deliver Samantha to this beast.*

"What were you planning to do with that power source, Doctor? A good scientist always makes notes, unless he is hiding something. But I can't find any notes on your power source, so I assume you are hiding something. What are you hiding from me?"

"I told you, I have no information for you." Maurya exhaled in pain.

"Oh you will, Doctor, you will," McCurdy told him casually. "I have a feeling that you'll be begging me to listen to you soon. I used to be an engineer; did you know that, Doctor? A scientist… just like you. So let me reduce our little equation of drama down to its simplest form. There are only two variables that remain unknown in our equation; what your threshold for pain is, and how long it will take me to discover that threshold."

Maurya gritted his teeth and remained silent.

"As I said, in the end, my brave little soldier, you will tell me everything I want to know, and then we will have the satisfaction of knowing we worked together to solve our little equation." As Lieutenant McCurdy went to leave the room, he paused at the door to speak with Sergeant Longstreet.

"Sergeant, I noticed a wadded up paper cup in the trashcan in this cell. I don't remember authorizing you to give the prisoner a paper cup."

"No, sir," Sergeant Longstreet responded. "I just thought the doc needed… some water. I am sorry, sir."

"The next time you take it on your own initiative to offer comfort to a prisoner without my authorization, you will find yourself on the

262

other side of this door. Do you understand me, Sergeant?"

"Yes, sir, I do. It will not happen again."

"No, Sergeant, it will not. I am quite sure of that."

43. Rabbit Hole

Dr. Jones tumbled head over heels down a soft grassy hill, rolling out of control until she came to a halt, banging her head against a rock. She winced in pain and coiled up in a ball.

"Ouch! Damn it, that hurts!" She shook her head and tried to stand, but her legs were too weak and her vision was cloudy. As she rubbed her eyes, they slowly came back into focus. Around her was a small town square that looked as if it could be anywhere in Middle America. There was a drug store, an ice cream shop, a laundry and a pizza parlor, surrounded by several other buildings. Tiny apartment homes were stacked on top of the second story of the village. At the end of the street was a church with a bell tower.

"Where am I? Mayberry frickin' RFD?"

Two young boys were riding bicycles down the street as a dog chased after them across the sidewalk of the grassy park in the center of the town. Dr. Jones' vision faded in and out, but finally, it started to clear. She looked up and could almost make out the faded words on a signpost in front of her; it read: 'Welcome to Tiny... something.'

This cannot be real, can it? She thought as she closed her eyes and rubbed the back of her aching head. *This place looks familiar, but where have I seen it before?* Samantha Jones wobbled to her feet and called out to the kids playing in the park.

"Hey! Over here!" The boys riding their bicycles didn't respond to her call. They rode right by her without even stopping and then scampered away down the street. The dog that was chasing them slowed down for a second in front of Dr. Jones, pausing long enough to sniff and growl in her direction before running off after the bicycles.

Her head was still throbbing from the tumble down the grassy hill and now she could see why. The circle of rocks that had collided with her head made up the base of what appeared to be an old well, complete with a broken down wooden roof. There was a rope dangling down below, descending into the shaft of the well. Dr. Jones stumbled over to the well, peering down into the darkness. At the bottom of the well was a tiny reflection of light. She could barely hear the sound of the bucket at the end of the rope clanging against the sides of the stone shaft. Samantha reached down and picked up a pebble to drop it in the well. *Am I dreaming, or did I really just bang my head and can't wake up?*

She touched her head and a sharp pain shot down her neck. Running her hand through her wet, matted hair, she looked down; it was covered in blood.

"Shit, that looks real enough," she groaned. "Ouch!"

The last thing Samantha Jones could remember on board Genesis Five was struggling with McCurdy, before Ashoka threw her into that flaming blue circle. What was it he said? *Through the looking glass? No, it was some other Lewis Carroll reference... that's it! Down the rabbit hole! What's next, Ashoka, the Cheshire cat sitting in a tree?*

Dr. Jones leaned over and looked down into the well again, this time, dropping the pebble from her hand. There was no sound for what seemed like an eternity and then there was a distant splash at the bottom of the well. Following the splash, a faint glow of light pulsated and intensified as several luminous bubbles surged upward. Dr. Jones was so startled that she fell backwards onto the grass. The first bubble hovered above the well for a moment and she could see a fuzzy image inside it. It was an image of Dr. Maurya in his lab, being dragged away in handcuffs by McCurdy's henchmen! McCurdy was walking around behind the atmospheric generator, looking underneath it and tapping it with his weapon.

"What the hell is going on?" Samantha cried out. She reached out to touch the bubble, but it disappeared as rapidly as it emerged, dissipating into the air. A second bubble percolated up from the well and this time it was an image of the planets of Earth's solar system adjacent to the Alpha Centaury star system. But something was not right. That was odd... there weren't nine planets, but thirteen orbiting the Sun. There was an extra planet near Venus, another between Earth and Mars, and two large planets between Saturn and Jupiter. *How can that be?*

Before Samantha Jones could comprehend what she had just seen in the galactic bubble, it vanished and yet another bubble appeared. This time, the image was of an army of soldiers marching through a rugged mountain pass surrounded by jagged peaks. As she looked closer, the details of the soldiers came into focus. *What the hell? They aren't men after all, but some other hideous-looking creatures with scaly skin and spines on their backs!* The beasts snapped and bit at each other as they marched. Occasionally, they ripped at each other's flesh like wild animals. As they marched around the mountain pass, she could make out an object behind them. It was... a spaceship! A Russian spaceship; just like the one Josiah and Lexis had described when the lizard man attacked them.

And then, as quickly as it emerged, the image disintegrated into the air. *What does all this mean? Where are these images coming from?* She looked down into the well and the faint glimmer of light faded into darkness. Her confusion was interrupted by the sound of the noisy kids on bicycles again, this time they were riding right toward her. *I must stop them to talk this time,* she thought. Samantha leaped onto the sidewalk in front of them just as they approached at full speed. Dr. Jones threw her hands up in the air and screamed.

"Stop! I need to talk to you!" But the kids riding their bikes did not stop. Instead, they continued at full speed, laughing at each other, paying no attention to anything around them. Dr. Jones let out a scream and braced for the impact of the speeding bicycles. *First, a bloody gash on my head, and now this... this is going to really hurt.*

As she waited for the impact, something totally unexpected happened. Nothing. The bicycles passed directly through her body as if she was just a cloud of colored vapors. The noisy kids sped away down the street, screaming at each other with their little dog chasing just behind them. Dr. Jones was dumbfounded.

"Holy shit!" She screamed. "They couldn't see me... they rode right through me! They're not... real! Ok, Ashoka... where the hell am I, anyway?" Dr. Jones fell back onto the grassy hill, rubbing her head as she looked around at the quaint town square. Right in front of her was the friendly sign that now seemed more than vaguely familiar. She squinted her eyes to read the signpost: *'Welcome to Tiny Town.'*

Lying in the grass and staring up at the clouds above, Dr. Jones' mind raced to try and make sense of her condition. In between the spasms of pain, her memory was slowly coming back into focus. The clouds above her were peaceful and still. But something was amiss. Now that she looked more closely at the clouds, they were all symmetrical, a textbook example of each of the four types of cloud formations on Earth. They were perfectly still, as if they were captured in a painting. In the background, she could hear birds singing in the trees, but when she looked closer, there were no birds... just the singing. Maybe this place wasn't so real after all. *Forget the imaginary birds and clouds,* she thought. *This bloody gash on your head is real, and so are you! What is the last thing you can remember? Think hard!*

She had been arguing with McCurdy in Dr. Maurya's laboratory when things got out of hand. *Yes! That was it!* They were fighting with McCurdy, trying to get away, when Ashoka grabbed her and pushed her through a blue halo of light. What was the last thing he said to her? *Jump!* Now she remembered clearly... their endless discussions of time travel and the strange properties of Niburu's electromagnetic fields. Dr. Maurya had secretly built into his atmospheric generator some sort of pulse accelerator and had intended to use it to test his theory... of time travel. That must have been what he was so excited to tell her about, just before she lost it with McCurdy. Ashoka wanted to leap into the Time Portal with her to escape McCurdy, but somehow he didn't make it with her... wherever she was.

"Ok... ok. Think! You're a scientist, so act like one! Figure out what the properties of this... this world are; that will help you devise a plan to get back."

A sudden wave of terror gripped her mind as she recalled the discussion of how any of this could be possible. *The Schwarzschild bubble! That was it!* Dr. Maurya said that the Time Portal could only be held open for a nanosecond, just long enough for someone to leap through to the other side. But she wasn't on the other side; she was somehow trapped in between where she came from and where she was going.

How long have I been here? What seemed like ten minutes could be either ten years or the blink of an eye. There was no way to know for sure, but however long she had been here, it was too long. If Schwarzschild's bubble separated with her in the middle, she would be ripped apart into a billion pieces and scattered across the universe. She had to get out of here now, to one side or the other!

Now she remembered where she had seen Tiny Town. It was the last place on Earth she had in her memory of a normal life. Tiny Town was the façade underneath the granite mountain in Colorado where she was taken after being abducted at Cambridge, just before she was rerouted to the Genesis Five lift off. Somehow, her mind must have accessed the memory of Tiny Town and projected that world around her, to help her feel more at ease with something familiar. This was sort of like surrounding your desk with pictures of your children and family. They're not really there, but it helps your mind to think they are. *Ok, that explains the Tiny Town projection,* she thought, *but what about the images from the old well?*

Dr. Samantha Jones had read many theories on time travel, portals, and parallel dimensions, but they were all just academic postulations of what might be possible. She needed to know what really was true... and fast. *Hypothesis, observation, analysis. Stay with what you understand, assume nothing, and build a framework based on your new reality.* The old well was not from any of her memories, so that could not be a mental projection. She had seen the images of Dr. Maurya and McCurdy from where she came, so maybe that was a view to the side of the portal she entered. The other images were of things she didn't recognize... maybe they were images from the *other side* of the portal that she was to exit. *That must be it!*

It was like she was stuck in a revolving door, with images of what was just outside the door whizzing by as she spun around inside. If she could just exit the door at the right time, she could get back to where she came. But if she leaped through the door and missed by a fraction of a second, she could end up in some other time and place entirely, maybe never to return. *Shit!* This was only going to work if someone on the other side unlocked the portal door at just the right moment. Time was running out and she had to get a message back to Ashoka to open the door... but how? In the midst of her utopian dream of Tiny Town, Dr. Samantha Jones had never felt more alone.

"Ashoka, you wouldn't have abandoned me in here, you must be trying to find me." *But why haven't you come for me by now?* She thought.

The magnitude of her situation was becoming clearer by the moment. Because of the fight she had started with McCurdy, Dr. Maurya had been forced to use his Time Portal machine before he had a chance to test it. *He must be trying desperately to unlock the portal from the other side,* she thought, *but he can't find me in the vast expanse of another dimension.*

"That has to be the answer. He doesn't know where I am!" If Ashoka couldn't find her, she would have to find him... and *tell* him where she was. She began frantically searching through her pockets for anything that could help. Samantha remembered that before the fight with McCurdy, she had been communicating with Dr. Maurya on a special walkie-talkie Misun had rigged up for her. Ashoka told her to only use it whenever they needed to make sure their conversations were private.

"It's a low-power, short-range communicator," he had warned her. "It was programmed to use an ultra-low frequency that is far below anything McCurdy could detect. Even if he could hear it, he wouldn't be able to understand anything we say." Dr. Maurya was proud of the homemade spy gear that he and Misun had designed for Samantha. "Just call me the Indian MacGyver," he had bragged with a smile.

"The Indian MacGyver?" she asked.

"Oh yes, I'm just like your real MacGyver, only I'm better looking, and I will work for seventy percent less!" He had laughed.

She emptied her pockets and checked everywhere... but the communicator was missing.

"Where was it? It must have fallen out of my pocket when I rolled down the hill!" Samantha scrambled back up the slope from the sidewalk and fell to her knees in tears. She combed through the long grass with her hands, but as she touched the grass, it just melted away in her hands, startling her for a second. *Is this illusion another projected memory? Yes, it is a memory... now I'm on to you, whoever you are!* She thought.

This illusion melting in her hands was her memory of... Mind Pudding. Mind Pudding was a simple trick she used to play on her first-year students in Continuum Mechanics. You mix up some cornstarch and water, then have the students grab the mixture to describe the physical state of the substance... is it a solid or liquid? But it's a trick question. When cornstarch and water are mixed, they form a non-Newtonian fluid, a fluid whose flow properties change in your hands; they can't be described with a single constant value of viscosity. She would laugh as they struggled and eventually let them off the hook, quoting from her physics text, "Sometimes the laws of physics are, shall we say... *fluid.* In this case, the relationship between the stress and strain is nonlinear... and can even be *time*-dependent."

As she explained to her students, *Initially, you grab a solid mass, hard as rock. But when you try to pick it up in your hands, the heat from your hands melts the solid into a liquid, but the trick is, as soon as it leaves your hands, it lose the heat and it reforms into a solid.* How quickly the students grasped that their expected rules of physics could be violated helped her determine who to keep around. You know, being able to think outside the box, especially when the box melted in your hands; this was a required trait for a scientist. *Someone or something was testing her, damn it! At least they had an academic sense of humor. It's not real grass; forget how it feels!* She screamed in her mind. *Just find the damn phone, would you?*

As Samantha Jones crawled to the top of the grassy slope, she reached out to grab a tree branch, but her hand couldn't grasp the branch. It was as if she was reaching out to touch a marshmellow but it just bent away from her hand. She had reached the end of her projected world, and for some metaphysical reason, she could go no further. She was a prisoner within her own mind. And then, there it was. Just at the base of her feet was a small silver radio antenna protruding up from the imaginary grass. She fell down, grabbed the communicator, and switched it on. Its red LED pulsated faintly.

"Thank God! The batteries still work!" The display on the communicator flashed between 'No Network' and only one half a bar of connectivity. She wasn't sure how accurate a signal strength reading was from inside a parallel dimension; the physics of telecommunications was never her forte.

"Ok... think. The battery is weak; you've only got one shot for a transmission. Find the best spot to transmit... the old well!" For some unknown reason, the well seemed like the best hot spot for network connectivity. Maybe it was because she had determined that the rest of Tiny Town wasn't real, or maybe because that was where she had last seen Dr. Maurya. Samantha raced back down the grassy slope, this time sliding on her backside to avoid another gash to her head. As she crashed into the old well, feet forward, she leaped forward, set the communicator to 'Record Loop' mode, and started transmitting.

"This is Dr. Jones!" she shouted. "I'm trapped in the Time Portal! Please help me!" The battery on the transmitter began to dim. Whatever signal she was transmitting, it was weak and would soon die. As she stared hopelessly down into the darkened well, she could almost make out a faint glimmer of pulsating light at the bottom. The transmitter speaker sputtered with static as the last electrical discharge from the battery surged through her homemade spy phone.

A scientist from Cambridge University was taught to objectively analyze a situation and then carefully evaluate all possibilities, before taking action. It may have been the distorted reality of another dimension, it may have been the blow to the head, or it may have been the sheer desperation of the moment; Dr. Jones wasn't sure. For once in her life, Samantha Jones would not be bound by her years of rigid analytical discipline. No more paralysis by analysis. She switched the transmitter from 'Record' mode to 'Play' and tossed it into the well.

"Ok, Ashoka, back down the rabbit hole. Hurry!" she whispered. Samantha Jones collapsed back on the grassy slope and prayed someone would hear her desperate cry for help.

44. Greedy Monkeys

Before Lieutenant McCurdy tortured Dr. Maurya in his prison cell on Genesis Five, Ashoka's main concern had been the lack of access to a good cup of Earl Grey. Now that he had been electrocuted and tortured for failing to help McCurdy locate Dr. Jones, a good cup of tea was the last of his worries. *Think, damn it,* thought Dr. Maurya. *Your mind is the only weapon you need.* Those were the words of Chandragupta, Ashoka Maurya's grandfather, and they called out to him in his mind.

Chandragupta had come down from his small village in the mountains to live with his family near the city for the last years of his life. Most of his family treated his grandfather as a burden, but Ashoka enjoyed him; he loved listening to Chandragupta's colorful stories, and he always asked many questions. He especially liked to ask questions about anything mechanical or scientific; how and why things worked, from internal combustion engines to the movement of the stars. They would be absorbed in their stimulating conversations late into the night, or until his mother chased them both off to bed. One day, Ashoka was constructing a telescope in their back yard with his grandfather when his mother came running out of the kitchen screaming, chasing a monkey who was grasping a banana.

"That is the third time this week that monkey has stolen food from our table," his mother shouted. She was angry at the monkey, and turned her anger on Ashoka. "If you cannot help put food on our table, then you can help keep what food we have from being stolen. Now put away your silly toy and chase that monkey away. And if that monkey comes back, there will be no more telescope for you!"

Young Ashoka took off running after the monkey, but the monkey got to the edge of the forest, shoved the banana in his mouth, and climbed a tree to the highest branches. Near the base of the tree were several ocelots, but the monkey had scrambled up the tree before they could attack him. Others quickly joined the monkey thief, chasing him around trying to share in his stolen bounty. Ashoka was frustrated, but his grandfather just sat back in his wicker chair and chuckled.

"How am I going to catch him now? I can't climb a tree that high!" Ashoka lamented.

Chandragupta smiled and called him over. "You catch a monkey by out-thinking him. Your mind is the only weapon you will need."

"But why does the monkey steal our food?" Ashoka asked. "There's plenty of food in the jungle."

"Because to him, stealing food is just a game," Chandragupta answered. "He thinks he is smarter than you, and he can steal our food and get away with it. He knows you cannot run fast or climb a tree; he thinks that you are no match for him. But I think he has underestimated you, my son. You must find his weakness and use that weakness against him. And then your monkey thief will catch himself."

Since he had no other plan, Ashoka was willing to listen to anything.

"Carry a basket of food out to the table in the back yard where the monkey can see you," Chandragupta continued. He handed Ashoka a gourd with the top cut off. "Look around, put the fruit basket on the table, and then hide a banana inside this gourd. Place the gourd with the banana beside the fruit basket on the table and then come back and sit and talk with me for a while. We will talk again about this young Albert Einstein... I think like him, you shall become a great scientist one day, but first, you must learn more about life... and how to make women happy!" His grandfather laughed again and after Ashoka had followed the instructions with the banana, they talked about Einstein's Theory of Relativity.

"How could the universe be expanding in all directions?" Ashoka asked. "Could people really travel at the speed of light? Is time travel possible?"

Soon enough, the monkey thief was back. He crept up to the table with the basket of fruit. Ashoka stood up ready to chase him away, but his grandfather stopped him.

"Patience, my son. Not yet. Let him spring your trap."

Ashoka was not sure what Chandragupta was talking about, but he sat back down and waited. The monkey rifled through the fruit in the basket and then picked up the gourd with the banana hidden inside. He reached in to extract the banana in the gourd and gripped it tightly in his fist. He started to pull out his hand, but with his fist around the banana, the monkey could not get his hand out.

"Now you can chase the monkey." Chandragupta smiled. "Go!"

The monkey thief took off running for the trees with the gourd still on his hand. When he got to the trees, he tried to climb, but with the gourd on his hand, he could not grip the branches and he fell back down to the ground. He tried climbing it several times but fell back down again and again. Frustrated, the monkey started screaming and leaping around at the base of the tree. The frantic commotion quickly attracted the ocelots, which were waiting in the bushes, and they pounced on the helpless one-handed thief and tore him to pieces. Ashoka stood there horrified. He ran back to his grandfather, sobbing.

"Grandfather, we are taught to never kill!" he cried. "Did I kill the monkey?"

Chandragupta sat Ashoka on his lap and spoke seriously this time, comforting him. "No, my son, you did not kill the monkey. He had two mortal weaknesses, his greed and his pride. It was his greed that caused him to steal the banana, but it was his pride that killed him."

"I don't understand, Grandfather."

"The monkey thief could have easily climbed the tree to safety," Chandragupta explained, "but he couldn't climb the tree unless he first released his fist from the banana inside the gourd. His greed caused him to steal our food, but it was his pride that would not allow him to let it go. So in the end, my son, he killed himself."

Ashoka sat there for a moment thinking of what just happened.

"Remember this day, my son. Someday, this lesson you have learned will be of great benefit to you. Now," Chandragupta laughed, "tell me again how time travel works."

Released from the handcuffs, and seated in a lotus position against the cold cell wall, Dr. Maurya drifted in and out of his meditation trance. His mind wandered between his current torture at the hands of Lieutenant McCurdy and a happier time when he was playing with his grandfather, just the two of them in his backyard. He was seated on Chandragupta's lap, half-asleep, when he heard a whispering in his ear.

"You must lay a trap for McCurdy, Ashoka, just as you did for the monkey thief. But this McCurdy is a clever monkey, and he will not be tricked so easily. Do not fear him. In the end, his weakness will lead to his demise." In his trance, Ashoka was doubtful and he asked his grandfather for guidance.

"But if he is clever, how can I trick him?"

"He must believe that he has broken your body and your spirit." Chandragupta smiled as he continued. "He must believe you have given up and you have surrendered to him completely. Only then will this monkey step into your trap. But know this in your heart; you have laid bare his inner weakness. He is an evil monkey, he is greedy and prideful, and that will lead to his downfall. Just as a leopard cannot change its spots, this monkey cannot surrender to his own pride. And in the end, if your ocelots are ready, they will kill him for you. Now endure your pain and go lay your trap, my son."

"Yes, Grandfather, I will do as you say."

A sudden creaking of the metal door alerted Dr. Maurya to the presence of someone else in his cell. He tried to maintain his meditation trance, telling his mind to believe he was still back in India talking with his grandfather. A swift boot to the ribs brought his dream crashing back to reality. Lieutenant McCurdy was back.

"Ah, my brave little soldier. I trust you have been resting comfortably in my absence?" Dr. Maurya winced with pain and rubbed his hand over his bruised ribs. He opened his eyes to see McCurdy seated in the chair just across the room from him, examining his weapon.

"You know, Professor, I am well versed in the science and theory of EMP technology. I even did some project work on it at Cambridge, albeit a very brief project."

Dr. Maurya was now alert, but confused as to where McCurdy was leading the conversation. "Really, Lieutenant? You said you went to Yale; I didn't know you attended Cambridge as well."

"Oh, technically, I never enrolled, but I guess you could say I taught a lesson there once. There was a scientist; I think his name was Lindsey Davenport. He had come to Cambridge from America to do some research... he was a bad apple. Rumor had it that he was about to betray his country and turn over some secret weapons technology to the enemy. I confronted the traitor in his laboratory and he chose to blow himself up rather than admit the truth of his treason. Or maybe he was just too intimidated to race me the next day in single skulls? In any event, he had to pay for his sins, and I helped him cash that check."

Dr. Maurya was unsure why McCurdy was now disclosing this information to him, except to try and frighten him into confessing Dr. Jones' hiding place to save his own life. *This is a clever monkey,* he thought. *It is almost time to set the trap... but not just yet.* "I told you, I do not know where she is," Dr. Maurya sobbed gently.

McCurdy adjusted his weapon to the most powerful setting, from yellow to red. The red setting would deliver a horribly painful charge, meant not just to incapacitate its victim, but also to inflict severe pain. Many times, the intensity of the charge would also cause the victim to suffer a heart attack and die.

"You really don't know where *who* is. Oh, yes, our mysterious Dr. Jones. I had forgotten about her. But since you bring it up, why was she snooping around my personnel file anyway? The two of you have been sneaking around behind my back, hacking into my medical records, and making wild, unfounded accusations in front of my men." McCurdy held his stun gun next to Maurya's neck. "You know, in Physics, they say that for every action, there is an equal and opposite reaction."

Without warning, McCurdy pressed the stun gun to Dr. Maurya's neck and squeezed the trigger; Ashoka collapsed to the floor, convulsing uncontrollably. It felt like a thousand hot needles had been jammed into his spine, the pain exploded up and down his legs. Ashoka couldn't stop his body from uncontrollable spasms for what seemed like an eternity.

McCurdy stood over Maurya's broken body as he clutched his weapon. He looked down at him on the floor and cocked his head, as if observing some routine science experiment. His next comment sounded almost casual.

"I guess maybe my opposite reaction was not entirely equal. Oh well. Are we starting to solve our little equation, Doctor? You know, the equation of your pain threshold?" Dr. Maurya couldn't respond; his body was numb. His brain was sending signals to his body, but his body was ignoring them. He shook his head and tried to stand. McCurdy helped him into the chair, and paced around the room, fondling his stun gun.

"Do you read science fiction, Doctor? I bet as a boy you read Jules Verne; he was quite enthusiastic about describing the wonderful role of science in his books. But I found his impression of a world where technology was used only for the betterment of mankind a bit naïve, don't you think?"

Ashoka shivered in pain, saliva frothing from his mouth.

"I much prefer HG Wells," McCurdy continued. "He understood that given a choice, man would use his technology for a far more sinister purpose. He predicted this because he believed at the core, man is an evil being and that he would cross over to the dark side to find evil purposes for his technology."

Dr. Maurya was now almost able to speak. He could only make out fuzzy thoughts in his head as he recovered from his last electrocution. He started to move his mouth, but no voice would come out. *Bait the trap*, Chandragupta whispered in his mind.

"Do you think that deep down, Doctor, mankind is inherently good... or evil?" McCurdy asked. "Oh, I know you, you want to believe that people are good, but I would observe that people only do good things because they fear punishment for their evil. If a man knew there would be no consequences for his evil, no punishment, then I believe he would embrace the evil within." Lieutenant McCurdy leaned close to Dr. Maurya's ear and whispered, "Make no mistake, Doctor, no matter what I do to you; no one will hear, no one will come... and no one will care. You see, there is no one on this planet to punish me, and I must confess, I rather enjoy that revelation. I'm afraid that I have to go with Mr. Wells on this one, Doctor; we are ultimately a race of beings with evil in our hearts."

Lieutenant McCurdy stood up and prepared to deliver another lethal shock to Dr. Maurya. "Oh, and another interesting coincidence... HG Wells built a time machine, didn't he? Did you and Dr. Jones build a... time machine?" Ashoka stared straight ahead and gave no answer. "You don't want to talk about time machines? Oh well then, where were we? Ah, yes, your pain threshold. I must warn you, this time, this is really going to hurt."

Dr. Maurya was a broken man, trembling and sobbing. He fell to his knees in front of McCurdy and begged him to stop the pain. His mind was throbbing, and he could barely hold on to a cohesive thought, let alone his carefully constructed deception. In the midst of his intense pain, a sudden calm came over Ashoka. Like a man that had completed a long, treacherous journey, he was suddenly at peace; his tribulation was over. Chandragupta smiled and spoke to him from the distant echoes of his mind.

Well done, my son. In you, I am most pleased. You are almost home, but you must remember; he will not stop until he breaks you, so it is time to be broken. He wants a secret, so give him one... just not the real one. His greed will take the bait, but his pride, ah yes; his pride will not let him release it.

But where are my ocelots, grandfather? Ashoka thought.

Think, my son, Chandragupta answered. *You know where to find them. Deliver him to their sacrificial altar... and they will do your bidding. Now it is time to set your trap.*

"Wait! Stop... please stop!" Dr. Maurya cried out. "I can't take any more pain. I confess." McCurdy pulled back and placed his stun gun on the table.

"You confess... to *what*, Doctor?"

"I am building... I mean... I *have* built a time machine."

"I knew it!" McCurdy smiled. "So that's where Dr. Jones went, into another time? How does it work, Doctor? Does it use the planet's EMPs? And what does my atmospheric generator have to do with it?"

"Could I please have a drink of water?" Dr. Maurya pleaded. "My throat feels like burnt sandpaper."

"Of course, Professor." McCurdy turned and yelled, "Sergeant! Get in here and bring the good doctor some water! Now tell me everything, Professor."

Dr. Maurya slowly explained to Lieutenant McCurdy how the Time Portal worked, how the electromagnetic pulses of Niburu could be harnessed to pry open the door and most importantly, where the other side of the door was located.

"I had been tracking the EMP pulses and triangulating their frequency and relative proximity to our ship when I discovered the remains of a crashed Russian spacecraft, just on the other side of the red cliff mountains."

McCurdy was fascinated. "Do go on, Professor," he urged.

"The crash site," Ashoka continued weakly, "is like some sort of electromagnetic vortex, similar to the convergence of the opposing magnetic fields on Earth. It is a natural energy concentrator on this planet, and appears to be the mouth of the Time Portal. Somehow, the Russian ship must have fallen into the electromagnetic field of Niburu and was drawn into the mouth of the Time Portal when it crashed."

"Incredible! Another ship is out there? Is there anyone still alive?"

Ashoka took a drink of water and seemed to be regaining his strength. "I don't think so; it appears they crashed some time ago. But their equipment is still working; I detected a faint computer beacon from the ship. The equipment we need is lodged in the door of the Time Portal, holding it open."

"Are you certain it is still open?" McCurdy asked.

"From all of my data, Lieutenant, that is what I believe. I was tracking it from the EMP scanner on the atmospheric generator. Somehow, by locking on to trace the EMP frequency, I accidentally opened a temporary wormhole, a back door to the Time Portal. Dr. Jones fell in and the wormhole closed. But I am sure the permanent gateway is out there where the Russian ship crashed. And from all of my readings, it appears to still be open."

McCurdy stood up and carefully paced around the room.

"Then I must go there. Do you have the exact coordinates of the Russian ship?"

"I believe so," Dr. Maurya mused, rubbing his head. "If you allow me to access my computer, I can print out the guidance data for you."

"And no one else knows about this, do they?" McCurdy asked.

"No, just Dr. Jones and myself. We didn't want to alarm anyone on board."

"Excellent!" McCurdy shouted. "When I control the Time Portal, I will be invincible. With this technology, no enemy can defeat me. If they rise up against me, I'll go back in time and kill them in their sleep!" Lieutenant McCurdy spun around and barked out new orders. "Sergeant, prepare the rover and assemble two of your best men in the cargo hold. We're going for a ride." McCurdy paced the room for a moment and then returned to Dr. Maurya.

"You did the right thing, Professor, telling me about the Time Portal. I will go and secure it. But one more thing... if this turns out to be a wild goose chase, just some elaborate hoax, I will inflict such a severe punishment on you that you will think all our previous sessions were like child's play, do you understand me?"

Ashoka breathed a sigh of relief. "Trust me, Lieutenant," Maurya assured him, "what you will find out there is no hoax; its power will shake you to your very core. I'm sure that after you experience what is out there, you will not come back and punish me... ever again." Lieutenant McCurdy reached into his jacket and tossed Dr. Maurya his computer tablet. "What is this for?" Dr. Maurya asked.

"You said you needed access to your server for the coordinates?" McCurdy smiled. "So access it. Download the guidance data for the Russian ship to my tablet... now!"

Dr. Maurya froze for a moment. He didn't have the coordinates and hadn't exactly planned on how he would direct McCurdy to the

Russian spacecraft. He assumed that once McCurdy raced off in the general direction of the red cliffs, he could guide him close enough to the ocelots for his deliverance. *The trap was almost set... think, damn it!* Before Dr. Maurya could respond, McCurdy received a message over his earpiece; the rover was loaded and ready to depart. McCurdy barked back at Maurya.

"Are we a go on guidance, Doc?"

"Almost, just give me a minute!" Ashoka responded nervously. *Find a data trail,* he thought to himself... *the ePod!*

Dr. Maurya typed in a secure command to access the log file of the ePod's communications. When the lizard man attacked Josiah and Lexis, they said they drove him off with a pulse beam from the command module. *There must be a set of data coordinates for that pulse beam buried somewhere in the transmissions,* he thought. If he could just find the right transmission and unscramble the data, he could calculate the location of the Russian ship, within a few meters. McCurdy was growing impatient.

"Do you have my guidance data yet, Herr Doctor?" Dr. Maurya tried to stall... just a few minutes more.

"I need more time to decrypt the data... I'm not on my own network, so this is taking a little longer..."

McCurdy tapped his earpiece and turned to Dr. Maurya.

"No worries, Professor, you can download it on the way."

"What? On the way... to where?" Ashoka responded.

McCurdy grinned and grabbed Dr. Maurya by the arm. "To my Time Portal, of course. You didn't think I'd leave you behind while we had all the fun out there, did you, Professor. Bring the computer and saddle up; you're going to deliver us both to the Time Portal."

45. Mining Disaster

As the crowded transport carrying the reluctant Chimera miners rumbled up the gravel road at the base of the red cliffs, Brutus silently passed a message among his pack.

"There may be danger in the mines. Work in teams of two... one watching and one digging. Stay alert and if you sense trouble, relay a call to me. I will protect you." The miners nervously passed the message throughout the transport using their ULF voices; the humans could not hear them talking.

The transport lurched forward into the mineshaft and made its way down the narrow path to a large underground cavern. Gradually making the windy descent, the cavern was illuminated by the flame of wooden torches hammered into the sides of the sheer rock walls. At the bottom of the track, they came to a stop beside a large pool of water fed by an underground river. This would be base camp for the miners, complete with enough supplies and provisions to support the workers for a month. Standing on top of Transport One, guards kicked open the tailgate and screamed out at the Chimera.

"End of the line, you genetic mutants! Unload the equipment and get to work!" At the bottom of the tailgate ramp, a soldier armed with an AK-47 was waiting to give the miners another rifle butt of encouragement in their backs as they grabbed their picks and shovels from a stack of mining implements.

"Get your asses moving!" the soldier shouted. "You've got fifteen tons of ore to dig on this trip!"

Misun managed to slip underneath the wheel well of the transport, unnoticed in the confusion. He fumbled around in his pocket for the electrical components that Brutus had given him and thought to himself, *I have my own mission now, an important mission; build a weapon for Brutus to fend off an attack by the hostile lizards.* Poking his head out from under the transport for an instant just long enough to signal Brutus with a quick smile, Misun ducked back under the heavy mining machine. The armed guards walked past him; he could almost reach out and touch their heavy black boots, three feet from his hiding place.

"I am invisible," Misun whispered to himself. He was now part of the team, all right. In fact, he was almost sure that Brutus had smiled back at him. As Viola and Brutus descended the tailgate ramp with their wooden spears and swords, two guards with AK-47s laughed and joked at their appearance.

"Ok, you two Samurai warriors will be on perimeter patrol," the soldiers chuckled. "Now get in front of the cave and keep an eye out, we don't want anything sneaking up on us."

Viola glared at the soldiers. One of them stepped forward and gave her a poke in the back with his rifle. She twisted around and grabbed the rifle barrel, holding it for a second before letting it go. Brutus stepped in between Viola and the soldier, backing her away with his hands up as he smiled.

"Go on, you dirty beasts!" the soldier yelled, pointing his machine gun at Brutus. The second guard reached out and pulled down his weapon. He turned and looked Brutus in the eye.

"You'd better get out of here before I get a mind to put a bullet in the two of you myself!" the soldier muttered.

As they made their way back up the narrow gravel path, Brutus and Viola emerged at the entrance of the mine. All the way, they did not speak; they marched in silence, except for the sound of Viola occasionally smashing her wooden katana sword against the rock outcroppings along the side of the path. When they finally reached the opening of the mine at the entrance to the cave, she could contain her anger no longer.

"Why do you tolerate their injustice?" she shouted. "They treat us like slaves!" Brutus was silent as he scanned the horizon and located the optimal vantage point to the valley below. *There,* he thought, *behind the boulders above the mineshaft will be the best observation position.* He scrambled up to take cover behind the boulders; then he turned back to Viola.

"I told you, Brave Heart, a leader must choose the time to use his sword and the time to use his mind. You wanted to choose that moment of insults back there to stand and fight? Think about it for a moment! Wooden sticks against machine guns; apparently, you have not learned this lesson yet. You must never let your enemy determine the field of battle to his advantage. Now come up here and clear your mind; we need to keep watch over our pack."

They waited in silence for almost an hour on top of the observation boulder, but it seemed like much longer to Viola. Brutus remained fixated on the valley below, and Viola on the rocky ridge on the horizon. *If there are hostiles out there coming for us,* Brutus thought, *they will have to come from one of those two directions.* Above them, the pulsations of the Niburu sky faded from burnt orange to deep violet, and then back to a pastel hue.

You could lie on your back and watch the light show in the sky for hours, Viola thought to herself, *it never seemed to repeat the same color transitions twice.* But just as soon as that thought crossed her mind, the colors in the sky surged to a bright climax and then plunged to pitch black.

Brutus and Viola hugged the boulder in front of them, straining to listen for any sound, any noise in the darkness. There was a sound far off... and it was getting closer. In the distance, they could now make out the shuffling of feet on the gravel road leading up to the mine. There was heavy breathing, the sound of metal clanging on metal, and a rhythmic thumping of a soft percussive instrument, like a drum keeping a military patrol in cadence. The marching feet approached and halted on the gravel road just past the boulder where Brutus and Viola were hiding. There was a brief exchange of grunts and snorts, then the group separated in two. One group split off heading double time away from the narrow gravel road leading into the mine and the other group fanned out and started moving slowly up the hill toward their hiding place.

"How do they know we are here?" Viola whispered. Brutus put his finger to her lips and then sniffed the air. There was a slight breeze coming from the base of the cliffs, up the side of the hill and around the boulder where they were hiding. In the darkness, he could tell that the hostiles were nearby from their scent.

There are two; no, three hostiles closing in from around fifty meters away, he thought. "They must have a canine sense of smell, like us, Brave Heart," he whispered to her without moving a muscle. "One to the south on the road; two to the north coming up the rocks. You take the one to the south."

"Oh... ok," Viola responded. Brutus clutched his spear and slowly stood up to move out. He turned back and crouched down beside Viola.

"Remember the lesson of when to use your sword and when to use your mind?" he said.

"Yes, I do." Viola replied in soft voice, running her hand down her long katana blade.

"Now is the time to use both," Brutus whispered, and then he sprang silently onto the top of the boulder beside them and vanished into the darkness.

Viola crept down the rocky slope toward the gravel road leading to the mine, pausing to sniff the air for the scent of the hostile to the south. She could track his movements as long as he stayed upwind, but otherwise, he would be much harder to find. *Wait a minute,* she thought. *Use your sword... and your mind. Those were Brutus' last words. Ok, think!* Since the hostile was moving about freely in the dark, she had to assume it was using some sort of heightened nocturnal sense to locate her. *It could not be smell,* she thought, *I am downwind of him, so it has to be sight. Maybe the hostile has eyes like a cat!* Cats have a special layer of tissue behind their retina that reflects light and passes it back and forth across the retina. That way, they can amplify small amounts of light and see seven times better than a human in the darkness. *If this hostile has cat eyes,* she thought, *he would be a lethal predator in the dark. Night vision was his advantage; I will have to stay hidden until he gets closer.* She moved away from the boulder and crouched down as he approached.

When the beast got to within ten feet of her, Viola leaped up and launched a ninja star with all her might, and it found its target. The hostile shrieked out in pain as the metal-tipped projectile impaled itself deep into his right eye, blinding him instantly. Blood gushed out of his eye socket as he screamed and swung his sword wildly around him, frantically striking the rocks and the ground.

Viola sprang over the boulder in front of her and brought down a crushing blow with her wooden katana sword on the hostile's wrist, causing him to drop his weapon and scream out in pain again. Feeling the warmth of his attacker close to him, the beast lunged in her direction with his razor sharp teeth. Viola ducked and barely avoided a face full of claws as they whizzed past her cheekbone. She hit the ground, rolled and scooped up the beast's metal sword from the dirt, twisting as she landed and anchored the hilt of the sword into a rock underneath her. The beast spun around and pounced for her, but as he landed on her, he felt the cold metal blade of his own sword plunging through his chest and into his heart. Shrieking in agony, the beast collapsed dead on top of her.

The stench of the beast on top of her almost made Viola vomit. She pushed his dead body off her and pulled the metal sword out of the beast's torso. Slimy green goo and a foul odor oozed out of the beast's chest, causing her to gag.

"You reek!" Viola cried out. She fell back against the boulder behind her and tried to wipe the stench off her body. "No wonder we could smell you from a mile away!"

To the north of the gravel road, Brutus had now made his way down the cliffs, smelling the air and creeping among the boulders. He was trying to get in between the two hostiles before they could circle around behind Viola and trap her. Just before he was close enough to throw his spear, he heard the screams from the gravel road in the boulders.

The two beasts reacted immediately to the cries of their companion in trouble. They spun around, grunted, and broke into a dead run toward Viola's position. *If I do not act now,* Brutus thought, *they will be on her in seconds.* Giving up the element of surprise, he roared and leaped on top of a nearby boulder to draw attention to himself and away from Viola. The first beast froze, cocked his arm and hurled a spear toward Brutus in the darkness. The aim of the beast was dead on, but at the last second, Brutus thrust his Bokuto in front of him, deflecting the spear just enough to graze his side, sending it bouncing harmlessly off the rocks below.

The diversionary attack by the first beast had distracted Brutus long enough for the second one to get on a rock behind him. The second beast snorted and brought down a blow with his battle-axe; Brutus spun and blocked the thrust with his Bokuto, shattering it to pieces. Now the first beast leaped across the rocks, coming for Brutus with his sword. In an instant, Brutus pivoted, cocked his arm, and let his spear fly, striking the beast directly in the head with such force that his spear pierced through the beast's metal helmet. The blow was so violent it broke off the wooden shaft of the training spear and left its metal tip protruding out the back of the beast's head. Falling with a thud, the beast was dead before it hit the ground.

Viola heard the commotion and screamed as she raced toward Brutus; her cries echoing up the valley. He had no weapons and was defenseless; she was thirty seconds away from protecting him; this battle would be over in ten.

The remaining beast near Brutus hesitated for a second and then realized his advantage. He pulled out his sword and moved in swiftly for the kill. Brutus roared at the top of his lungs, drawing the attacker to him. The beast brandished his sword, grunted, and lunged at Brutus. An instant before he struck his blow, there was a blinding flash of light, causing the beast to flinch and narrowly miss decapitating Brutus.

Stunned by the sudden explosion of light, the beast closed its eyes and howled in frustration. He swung his sword and shattered rocks all around him. Brutus jumped from his boulder, grabbed the battle-axe from the ground, and smashed it against the shoulder of the beast, causing him to drop his sword and collapse to the dirt. He kicked the sword away and jammed his boot down hard on the beast's throat, pinning him to the ground. Running at full speed, Viola had finally reached the battle scene just as it was over, her sword drawn and at the throat of the beast ready for the kill. Brutus held out his hand and pulled down her sword.

"Let me end this one!" she screamed. "He would have killed us both!"

"No, this one will live; we will show him mercy," Brutus told her.

"But letting him go will show our weakness!" Viola cried out. Brutus pulled Viola close and spoke softly.

"That is possible, Brave Heart. But showing mercy to this beast and judging its reaction is the only way to know what we are dealing with," he whispered. Brutus removed his foot from the neck of the beast, and it sprang up, grabbed the broken shaft of the spear that had killed his companion, and fled into the night.

"I think that was a mistake... letting him go," Viola muttered. "We should have killed that slimy beast." Crawling out from behind a nearby boulder, Misun stepped forward and chimed in with his opinion.

"I'm with Viola on this one, I think we should have killed him too!"

"Where did you come from?" Brutus and Viola shouted in unison.

"I got here just in time to try out my new weapon. You know, the one you asked me to build to take advantage of the weaknesses of the beasts?" he grinned sheepishly. Viola looked at him with suspicion.

"You built a weapon from a pile of junk that can take advantage of every weakness of the beasts?" Viola questioned. Misun stepped proudly up to Brutus and held up his device.

"Well, not all of it works yet, sir. The stun gun and the sonic rumbler will take a bit more work; I think I need more power. But the part that shoots a blinding flash of light and immobilizes them long enough to save your life part, that seems to work ok." He smiled.

Brutus reached down and patted Misun on the head. "That part does work just fine, my son. You are very talented indeed."

Viola shoved Misun playfully from behind. "Not bad for a runt," she taunted. "Just remember though, stay out of my way when the *real* fighting starts."

46. The Dark Avenger

The impact of being forced to fight his only friend to the death for the entertainment of the lizard beasts in this underworld fight club came crashing down on Mitch Gaylord like a ton of bricks. There was only one thing certain in this nightmare; there would be no justice, only vengeance. He thought about Comrade Stephanotski's words of warning.

"To have any chance, cowboy, you must be unpredictable."

Mitch stood up and faced the angry mob of slimy beasts. By killing Ivan, he had silenced their grunts and temporarily robbed them of their chance to devour the expected human loser... *him.* After a few moments, the beasts accepted the loss of the big Russian and started to snort as they eagerly awaited the entrance of their Lizard King to kill the new little human champion.

Slowly turning in a circle, Mitch glared at the beasts perched on the rock outcroppings above, making eye contact with them all. He was no longer Captain Mitch Gaylord, ambassador of goodwill for the human race; he was the fucking lunatic Dark Avenger, exploding with rage, ready to punish this sick perverted mob with his axe. He clenched his jaw, narrowed his eyes, arched his back, and then screamed out at the top of his lungs.

"Is that all you slimy bastards got?" the Dark Avenger roared. He leaped on top of the sacrificial platform in the center of the arena and yelled, "Bring on the fucking *next victim!*"

The mob of slimy lizards buzzed with a smattering of grunts and squeals, still unsure of how they should deal with the unexpected fall of their familiar human champion. The scattered growls built to a crescendo and one beast leaped from the outcropping above Mitch Gaylord, landing beside the body of the dead Russian. The lizard let out a scream and sunk his teeth into Ivan's chest. The anger and rage inside the Dark Avenger welled up inside; he was not about to let Ivan's body be desecrated by these slimy animals. Without thinking of the consequences, he lunged at the beast crouching over Ivan and with one mighty blow of his battle-axe; he severed the arm of the beast at the elbow.

"There's a new sheriff in town, stumpy!" screamed the Dark Avenger. "And he don't like your fucking kind!"

The beast was stunned and recoiled with a shriek of pain as green slime gushed out of the stump that used to be an arm. He fell to the ground and scrambled away from Ivan's body, back into the hushed crowd. Mitch Gaylord was starting to like his new persona. The Dark Avenger picked up the bloody claw and shook it in the air.

"We got a new rule, you slimy bastards! You touch my friend; you lose an arm! We clear on that one?"

The beast mob was silent for a moment and then a commotion erupted from one side of the arena. The crowd parted and out stepped the biggest, ugly lizard Mitch had ever seen. The beast stood eight feet tall and swatted away the smaller lizards leaping at him as he lurched his way to the edge of the arena. He was wearing a suit of metal armor, similar to a Spanish Conquistador, with a breastplate and matching helmet. Hanging from his side was a broadsword, and in his left hand was a chain with a spiked metal ball dangling from the end. Around his thick scaly neck was a gruesome chain made up of what appeared to be... human teeth. The enormous beast scanned the arena and raised his sword to the demonic outburst of snarls and grunts from the scaly mob.

Mitch Gaylord looked up at the giant lizard. *Holy shit, this must be the Lizard King! He's bigger than I expected... and way more ugly. But at least it looks like I caught one break,* he thought, *it's the old fat Elvis.*

The Lizard King flexed his muscles and let out an ear-shattering growl. The beast mob responded with an echo of snarls and grunts, eager to see order restored to their gladiator arena and the new human champion torn limb from limb.

As his old pal Ryker used to say, "To survive in prison, the first thing a new inmate has to do is pick a fight with the biggest, meanest bastard in the prison yard." The theory was that if you survived that fight, the other inmates would respect you, or at least not single you out as the weakest son of a bitch and beat the shit out of you every day for the rest of your miserable life. "And if you didn't survive the fight," Ryker said, "well, at least your stay in prison would be short." This wasn't a prison movie, but Mitch Gaylord decided that Ryker was right; he may as well get in the first hit, since it just might be his last. The Dark Avenger waited for the Lizard King to turn his back on him and then he struck a surprise blow with all his might at the only part of the slimy lizard that was exposed: his left foot.

Leaping from the sacrificial platform, the Dark Avenger dove through the air, stretched out his body, and plunged his still-bloody knife into the exposed foot of the Lizard King. The beast recoiled in pain from the cowardly sneak attack, shrieked, and reflexively swung his broadsword around in a 360° angle that would have cut Mitch in half had he not been flat out on the dirt below. The new human champion and his unpredictable behavior had again stunned the frenzied beast mob. Confusion reigned as the crowd roared and snorted in anger, enraged that their Lizard King had been wounded by the lowly human, even if the wound was only superficial. They screamed for his blood.

Staying close to the ground, Mitch Gaylord scrambled back over Ivan's body and recovered his metal shield. He huddled under the shield and waited for the retaliatory blow to come. He didn't have to wait long. A half-second after he pulled his leg under the shield, a crushing blow rained down on him, shaking him to the core. The Lizard King had turned and in one motion, leaped through the air and delivered the spiked ball at full force directly into his metal shield, its sharp talons penetrating the metal.

With the ball and chain embedded in his shield, Mitch Gaylord burrowed out from under the crushed metal and scrambled behind the Lizard King. The Dark Avenger grabbed the battle-axe from Ivan's body and spun around to deliver a blow with all his might to the back of the Lizard King's head.

The mob of beasts went wild with anger, snorting and grunting their displeasure. This was not how the fight was supposed to go; the little human should be dead by now, leaving the mob to fight over the scraps of flesh left on his mutilated carcass. The blow from the Dark Avenger's axe was merely an annoyance to the Lizard King, but yet another embarrassment from the inferior human, as his metal helmet spun through the air and into the crowd. The beast let out a deafening roar and turned on Mitch to rip him apart. Captain Gaylord knew this was it for him. His knife and axe lay in the dirt at the feet of the beast and he was charging for him fast. He thought back to his promise to Commander Ivan Stephanotski and the words of his dying bargain.

"I tell you how to fight beast... and you take care of my Elena, no?"

Yes, I promise, Ivan, he thought. *I'll keep my end of the deal; I just hope you know what the fuck you were talking about. Here goes!* The Dark Avenger spun around, took three zigzag strides, and leaped to the top of the sacrificial platform. Taunting the crowd, he stretched out his arms and screamed out at the Lizard King.

"You want a part of me, you slimy bastard? Then come and get me!"

The Lizard King stood motionless for a second. Twice this little insect had outwitted him, but now the human had no weapons and was defenseless. The angry mob beseeched him to destroy this worthless piece of shit and feed his bones to them. This time, there would be no more surprises. The Lizard King took a step toward the sacrificial platform; then gathered speed as he twirled his sword above his head to strike the final blow.

Some people say that when you die, your whole life flashes in front of you in slow motion. Kind of like the sixty-second highlights on the late night sports show right before you go to bed. Mitch Gaylord had one more trick up his sleeve to make the highlight reel and it was his only chance to live.

Hold... hold! The Dark Avenger screamed inside his head, as he stood motionless on the top of the platform. The Lizard King was ten meters away and closing fast. His sword was drawn back, poised to cut Mitch in half. The mob of angry beasts leaped to their feet to witness the decapitation of the little human.

Hold... not yet, damn it! The Dark Avenger muttered in his mind.

The Lizard King was two meters away and leaped through the air to deliver his fatal blow. *In the air,* thought the Dark Avenger, *Elvis is committed. He can't change his attack now,* exactly as the Dark Avenger had planned.

"Now!" screamed Mitch Gaylord.

The Dark Avenger flipped over on the sacrificial platform and collapsed on his back, spread-eagled as the Lizard King barely missed his head with his sword. As the slimy beast looked down and passed over the little human on the platform, he stared wide-eyed directly into the strobe light flash of Ivan's utility belt and was blinded. The Lizard King crashed to a landing, striking his head on the rock support of the platform with a thud. The beast sprawled around helplessly, screaming and slashing his sword wildly through the air, but finding nothing. The Dark Avenger scrambled off the platform and reached behind his back to pull out the long tube he had been carrying. He placed his only dart in the blowgun, closed one eye and sighted his aim down the tube.

Find the hole two inches below the left ear... only one shot, he thought. The arena degenerated into bedlam. The Lizard King shrieked wildly and crashed his sword into the rocks, still unable to see.

"Come on you bastard, turn this way!" Mitch screamed. And then, just as his vision was starting to clear, the beast froze in the exact position that allowed the Dark Avenger a clean shot. He drew a deep breath, steadied his aim, and launched the dart on its way. It was a direct hit, penetrating deep into the small hole two inches below the left ear of the slimy beast; he recoiled in pain with a deafening scream.

Fifteen seconds, thought Mitch Gaylord. *That can be a lifetime.* The Lizard King staggered from the painful blow, having regained his vision, he locked on to the human at the base of the platform. Enraged, he lunged at Mitch with his sword extended.

"Holy shit!" Mitch screamed.

Be unpredictable, Ivan urged. Instead of trying to get away, the Dark Avenger leaped directly toward the angry beast, crashing into him and narrowly missing another beheading in the process. He grabbed hold of the monster and they rolled over and over, tumbling down the rock outcroppings and crash-landing at the base of the sacrificial platform.

"Mutherfucker!" Mitch screamed. "Hasn't it been fifteen seconds yet?"

In the soft dirt of the arena, Captain Gaylord was pinned underneath the Lizard King, face-to-face, staring into his evil black eyes. He couldn't run away, he couldn't get loose, so he just held on tight, too close for the beast to stab him with his sword. *Hey, it worked before; maybe it can work again.* The Lizard King let out a furious roar, close to Mitch Gaylord's face; his breath was a foul, putrid wave of stink that could have killed him right there.

"Whew!" Mitch exhaled. "Time for a fucking Tic Tac, Godzilla!"

And then the Lizard King shuddered, gasped for breath, closed his three eyelids, and collapsed dead on top of Mitch Gaylord. The crowd erupted in a victory roar, thinking that the Lizard King had killed the little human vermin. Grunts and snorts echoed throughout the gladiator arena as the mob rushed from their rocks down to the center of the ring, eager to lift up their champion.

Mitch Gaylord lay there underneath the beast for a second; trying to convince himself he was still alive. Ivan had been true to him; the blowgun found its mark and the longest fifteen seconds of his life was over. *Maybe I'll make the gladiator highlight show,* he thought.

There was one more thing that had to be done and he had to do it. *It may be the last thing I ever do,* Mitch thought, *but it has to be done, for Ivan. It was like in professional wrestling, just when you think the champion is pinned, he throws off that other schmuck in the nick of time to beat the count.* Mitch Gaylord was pinned, but his alter ego, the Dark Avenger was not. The Dark Avenger threw off the slimy body of the bastard that had made him kill his best friend and grabbed the beast's sword.

The mob of lizards pouring into the arena froze, suddenly realizing that it was not the little human that was dead, but their beloved Lizard King. The Dark Avenger would show no mercy, just as Commander Ivan Stephanotski had instructed him. He raised his sword and plunged it down with all of his remaining strength, severing the Lizard King's head. Grabbing the bloody beast's head, the Dark Avenger leaped back on the sacrificial platform, arched his back and screamed at the top of his lungs.

"Elvis is dead! Who the fuck wants to be *next*?"

47. A Banana for McCurdy

Inside Genesis Five's airlock chamber, the rover was loaded and ready for a reluctant Dr. Maurya to lead Lieutenant McCurdy to his Time Portal. The driver and Sergeant Longstreet were seated in the front of the rover, Lieutenant McCurdy and Maurya were in the center, and one heavily armed soldier with a 50-caliber machine gun was positioned as rear guard. Their mission: seek out the downed Russian spacecraft and secure the opening of the Time Portal to a parallel dimension.

As they donned their spacesuits and prepared to depart, Lieutenant McCurdy tapped Dr. Maurya on the shoulder and reminded him of his expectations.

"You have fifteen minutes," McCurdy cautioned, "until we arrive at the red cliffs to access your server on my computer and download the exact coordinates of your alleged Russian spacecraft. Otherwise, Herr Doctor, I'm afraid that this little outing is going to be a one-way trip for you." Lieutenant McCurdy announced his final orders to the team.

"Once we leave the ship, maintain radio silence until we arrive at our final destination." McCurdy turned to Dr. Maurya, cocked his head, and smiled. "No need to tip off anyone as to our whereabouts, now is there, Professor?"

"Affirmative. Communicators off." The soldiers all nodded in compliance. "Running silent."

Sergeant Longstreet stood up and signaled the soldier seated in the rear with a hand gesture to obey his visual command. He pointed two fingers at his visor and then pointed down to the AK-47 assault rifle in his other hand. The soldier in the rear compartment nodded his acknowledgement. Sergeant Longstreet removed the ammunition clip from his rifle and tapped it against the metal liner of his helmet. The soldier in the rear guard position mimicked his action and they exchanged a clasped fist gesture followed by two rapid fist bumps to the chest. Turning to Lieutenant McCurdy, Sergeant Longstreet signaled with his thumb up and then pointed one finger toward the red cliffs. There was no need to confirm this communication with an audible command. They both knew the drill and repeated the command in their own mind: *Locked and loaded... let's rock and roll.*

Sergeant Longstreet aimed the laser sight of his assault weapon on the distant mountains of the red cliffs in order to paint a coordinate vector input for the rover's navigation system. The rover responded with a target acquisition blink, displaying the navigation vector and travel time on the dashboard display. Sergeant Longstreet tapped the 'Confirm' target button on the navigation system and the rover slipped silently down the exit ramp of Genesis Five and into the pale Niburu twilight.

As the rover moved across the desert plain, time was running out for Dr. Maurya's elaborate ruse. They were halfway across the valley now and would be at the red cliffs in less than ten minutes. *I will never be able to secure the coordinates of the Russian spacecraft in time,* Ashoka thought, *unless I get some help. Think!*

You are on the right track, my son. Chandragupta whispered in his mind *Two heads are better than one.* Dr. Maurya acknowledged his grandfather with a smile and typed in a backdoor server command to activate his artificial intelligence assistant, NELI.

"Why hello, Professor!" NELI awakened. "I have been waiting for you to return. Where have you been?" Dr. Maurya bypassed his normal pleasantries with the speech translation module and used a short text message to communicate with NELI, so as to not alert McCurdy to his actions.

"VOX Off. Code yellow; disable computer logs. Activate behavior module 'Undercover'."

"Oh, a game!" NELI immediately responded. "I do so enjoy games! Logging disabled, behavior module activated, affirmative... I mean 10-4."

"Access transmissions from command module to ePod," Ashoka transmitted. "Isolate any data transfers with navigation coordinates. Download results to this location code."

"10-4, Doctor." NELI answered. "Scanning... one transmission match located. Download in process. Going deep cover. Changing call sign to... *Mata Hari.*"

"Download confirmed, Mata Hari." Dr. Maurya smiled. "Initiate task; Priority Alpha. Access secure atmospheric generator database. Open folder 'Trojan Horse'. Upload encrypted packet to secure mail server 'Pony Express' for real time delivery to Dr. Stone. Challenge package authorized; Delivery Receipt required. After confirmed package delivery, stay in deep cover unless activated by voice print command of Dr. Stone only."

"Working," NELI droned. "Encrypted packet delivered via Pony Express. Awaiting delivery confirmation."

48. Collateral Damage

In the aftermath of the lizard attack at the mine that left two beasts dead and one wounded, there was one thing about the battle that was still gnawing away at Viola. Despite her strenuous objections, Brutus had released one of the wounded lizards as a gesture of peace. *These beasts cannot be trusted, they are no different than the humans,* she thought. *It will not be long before we regret this gesture of mercy.* Viola tried to refocus her mind as she collected the discarded lizard weapons from the ground. She inspected the spoils of the skirmish: a metal broadsword, a spear, a battle-axe, and some assorted body armor. *Compared to the training weapons we were given by the humans,* thought Viola, *these are an upgrade.*

As she and Brutus were talking and trying on the body armor, their conversation was interrupted by the sound of gunfire echoing up the narrow gravel road from the mine.

"The other half of the beast patrol!" screamed Brutus. "They must have doubled back and slipped by us in the fight!"

Viola scooped up the weapons and ran at full speed down the narrow gravel road leading to the mine. As they rounded the last turn on the road and entered the mining cavern, they froze in horror at the sight before them. Dozens of defenseless Chimera had been ripped apart, their limbs and bloody torsos tossed about like shredded dolls. Several were still alive but heavily wounded, sobbing and crying for help. Brutus bent down to touch the hand of one of the wounded Chimera that was barely alive.

"What happened here?" Brutus asked.

"The torches went out," coughed the wounded Chimera, "and they attacked us in the dark. We were confused... and they cut us apart. We tried to fight but we had only shovels against their swords." He spat up blood and fell back in Brutus' arms.

"Where were the human guards? They have the guns!" Brutus strained to hold back his anger.

The wounded Chimera slowly opened his eyes. "The humans shot their weapons in the air and then fled! They ran away, called for help on their communicator and then hid in the transport. We tried to get inside the transport to safety but they locked us out. We screamed and beat on the door... until the beasts fell upon us and tore us to pieces."

"Where is the rest of our pack?" Brutus inquired.

"Some of them... made it to the back of the mine, Hannibal led them. He killed two of the beasts with his pickaxe; I guess they did not expect us to fight back. They retreated with their dead, but they will come back." He coughed and gasped for air.

"How do you know they will come back?" asked Brutus. The wounded Chimera's eyes went blank as if he had accepted the inevitability of their doom.

"You could see it in their eyes. They have the soulless eyes of a predator, a killing machine. They will keep coming back, more and more of them, until we are all dead." He sighed deeply and then died in Brutus' arms.

As Viola and Misun reached down to comfort Brutus, a frantic cry came from the back of the mine. Someone was still alive.

"Over here! Get over here before they come back!" From behind a group of rocks and wooden pallets that were stacked up at the back of the cave stood a tall, burly Chimera holding a bloody pickaxe above his head, waving his arms. Several other Chimera popped up beside him and joined the chorus of screams. "Run! They are coming!"

Behind them, up on the gravel path leading down to the mine, Brutus could hear the sound of grunts and shuffling feet rapidly approaching. From the impact of the gravel being kicked about, there had to be twice as many beasts as they had seen in the patrol that first ambushed them at the entrance to the mine. *That is why they retreated!* Brutus thought. *The beasts went back for reinforcements.*

Misun, Viola, and Brutus grabbed their weapons and sprinted to the back of the cave with the rest of the Chimera urging them to safety. On the road behind them, a handful of the lizards streamed into the mouth of the cave, snorting and squealing, fighting over the severed body parts of the dead Chimera by the pool. The squabbling quickly halted when their leader entered the cave and snapped at two beasts fighting over a piece of dead flesh. The mob of lizards reformed for an attack and their leader pointed to the back of the cave with a loud grunt, his vicious voice echoing back to him throughout the cavern.

Leaping across the rocks and loose gravel on the cavern floor, Brutus, Viola, and Misun reached the defense line set up at the back of the cave by Hannibal and the remaining Chimera. Hannibal looked at the green slime dripping off the bloody battle-axe carried by Brutus.

"Looks like you killed a few yourself," Hannibal observed with a smile.

"Don't worry." Brutus grinned. "We didn't kill them all, there are more for you." Hannibal erupted with laughter.

"It will be good to die with you, my brother!" Hannibal beamed.

Brutus glanced back at the mob of beasts marching across the cavern floor directly for their position, and then turned back to the fortifications.

"Viola, how many?" Brutus asked.

"I count eleven," she answered. "No, twelve total. Swords, spears... and they have... *longbows!*"

"Where the hell did they get longbows?" Brutus shouted.

"I don't know, but they have four archers climbing into position on the rocks above us, ready to give them cover. They will pick us apart from up there!" Viola screamed.

"How many infantry?" Brutus asked.

Viola squinted her eyes and counted again. "That would make eight in front with body armor."

Brutus counted fifteen Chimera behind the rocks; most were armed with mining tools. He grabbed Hannibal by the shoulder.

"You saved our pack by retreating here, but we cannot hold this position," Brutus told him. "They will rain arrows down on us from above and force us into the open. Then they will cut us to ribbons with their infantry!"

Hannibal looked around at his tattered band of miners and then to Brutus. "What do you suggest, sir?"

"We have to attack them before they can get their archers in place. Force their infantry close together so they can't throw their spears," Brutus yelled.

"And when we get them close together, what do we do then?" asked Hannibal.

Brutus smiled and remembered Koda's words. "We will kill them... *we will kill them all*," Brutus declared.

"That we can do, sir!" Hannibal grinned. They quickly checked their weapons and readied their attack. Viola and Misun surrounded Brutus and awaited his instructions.

"Viola, we'll try and keep them busy in the open field long enough for you to get to their archers. You have to take them out... *all of them*," Brutus urged. "If you fail, Brave Heart, we are all lost."

Viola stared into Brutus' eyes with a steely glare of resolution. "I understand," she replied. "I will not fail you."

They hugged for a moment and then Viola swung her bloody sword over her back and leaped over the boulder barricade, slipping into the darkness at the rocky edge of the cave wall. Misun tugged at Brutus' leg.

"And what am I to do, sir?" Misun asked.

"Ah, little one. You have the most important task of all." Brutus smiled. "You need to get your weapons machine working." Brutus looked across the cavern floor with concern at the approaching beasts. "I fear that we will need more of your magic before this battle is over."

Turning back to Hannibal and the miners, Brutus quickly reviewed his attack plan. "They will not be expecting us to attack them, so we will have the element of surprise. Hannibal, give me two of your men and we will work our way along the back of the transport and flank them on their right side. As soon as we draw their fire, they will reverse and close on us," Brutus outlined.

"Leaving their rear guard exposed for us to exploit..." Hannibal finished. "Not bad tactics, where did you learn this strategy?"

"I have studied the *'Art of War'* on Dr. Jones' computer," Brutus confided. "If Viola can take out their archers, Sun Tzu would be most proud."

Brutus and two miners slipped around the barricade unnoticed by the beasts and made their way to the back of the transport. Inside the glass cockpit, there were two humans crouched down behind the metal doors, praying that the beasts would not come for them. As they crept past the driver's door, Brutus flashed a look of disgust at the cowards inside. *We will deal with you later,* he thought. Above his head, Brutus could see that Viola had silently scaled the rock outcropping close to where the archers were setting up their position. She had less than thirty seconds to take them out before they would be in a position to kill everyone below.

"We must fight with the strength of ten to draw them to us," Brutus whispered. "I am proud of the sacrifice you are about to make!" He swung his broadsword around from behind his back and cried out, "Let's roll... now!"

Brutus leaped from behind the wheel of the transport and with one swift blow; he severed the arm of an unsuspecting beast, dropping him to his knees. As the lizard let out a blood-curdling cry, another in front of him turned around just as Brutus swung his battle-axe, head-high with all his might. The force of Brutus' axe beheaded the beast in one motion, its scaly head gushing blood in all directions as he collapsed to the ground.

"Attack!" Brutus yelled to Hannibal. He looked up to the archers above and they were drawing back their bows to strike. "Now!" he screamed to Viola. The remaining beasts on the ground spun around, grunted, and charged at Brutus, their mouths of razor-sharp teeth gaping open, ready to rip him apart. Just as they turned their backs on the rear of the cave, Hannibal and his pack leaped out from behind the barricade and attacked them from the rear with their pickaxes and shovels.

Above on the rocks, the lizard archers hesitated for a second; they couldn't shoot at Brutus without hitting their own infantry. Readjusting their aim, they focused their attack on the Chimera charging from the rear. That brief moment of hesitation by the archers was all Viola needed; she hurled her ninja stars, piercing one of the beasts in the eye just as he released his arrow. The wounded lizard shrieked, stumbled, and fell thirty meters to the jagged rocks below.

The three remaining archers were stunned at Viola's attack and wheeled around to defend themselves, but at close range, their longbows were useless. Viola threw herself against the two lizards nearest to her, knocking one into the other, sending the second beast over the cliff like dominos. She spun and crashed her sword down on the first beast's arm, severing it at the elbow. The beast with one bloody arm stood there, stunned for a second, and then scrambled down the rock face to join the lizards below.

From behind Viola, the fourth archer had drawn his bow and found a target. He let fly an arrow, and from below she heard a painful shriek. A Chimera collapsed to the ground with an arrow through his heart. Behind Brutus, two of his comrades rushed forward with their shovels to try and defend against the onslaught of enraged beasts.

"On your right! Down!" a miner screamed. Brutus collapsed to the ground as a spear whizzed past his ear, barely missing him. He leaped back to his feet to thank his comrade for saving his life, but it was too late. The spear that missed him had struck his comrade in the chest and pierced his heart. The Chimera miner fell to the ground dead, his eyes wide open and staring up at Brutus.

From behind, there was a terrifying scream. Hannibal and his men had reached the rear guard and killed a lizard with their pickaxes; now the beast patrol was under attack from both sides. The lizards reversed their charge against Brutus and tore into Hannibal's lightly armed miners, killing two Chimera before Brutus could fight his way to them.

"Get your miners behind us!" Brutus screamed to Hannibal. "We have to retreat to the barricades. You and I will fight in front to give them cover!" Another lizard arrow struck a miner in the leg and he shrieked in pain. Hannibal reached down and broke off the arrow in the wounded miner's leg, shoving him behind Brutus for protection.

On the rocky ledge above the cavern, Viola was struggling in the grasp of the last archer, desperately fighting with her free hand to try and stop the arrows from raining down on her pack. She reached behind her neck over the lizard's back and grabbed an arrow from his quiver, plunging it deep between his scales and into his stomach. The beast shrieked, loosened his grip, and Viola shoved him over the cliff to his death.

Behind the barricades, Brutus and Hannibal were bracing for a final stand against the lizards. They huddled together, protecting their comrades behind them. Between them, they only had one sword, one pickaxe, and a couple of shovels as weapons. The beast patrol had now reformed their attack line and were preparing for an all-out assault. Hannibal looked at Brutus.

"There are too many of them, my brother. This may be it for us unless you have a trick up your sleeve."

"That may be true," Brutus yelled back, "but before we go, they will pay a heavy price." *Misun!* Brutus thought. *Where are you, my little friend!* From under the barricade, a small furry head popped out and looked up at Brutus.

"Do you have some magic for us, my son?" Brutus asked.

"Almost, I just need to redirect the current flow... there! I'm ready!" Misun shouted. The beast mob was charging at full speed across the cavern floor, they were ten seconds away from reaching the barricade.

"You know, not to second guess your mechanical ability," Brutus noted calmly, "but lightning won't work on them with the torch lights in here, there's not enough contrast." He looked back up at the charging beast mob; they were five seconds away.

"Oh, they've seen the lightning but they haven't felt the thunder." Misun smiled. "Better cover your ears!"

Brutus stared at Misun for a second and then screamed to the miners behind him. "Cover your ears!"

Misun switched on his device and instantly a deep, low rumbling sound resonated throughout the cavern, cascading in increasing waves of intensity, bouncing off every wall and rock in the cave. The thunderous sonic shock pressed in on the chests of the lizard beasts, clapping against their heads like they were being struck simultaneously in both ears by a bone-crushing thump. Every beast in the cave collapsed to its knees and screamed in anguish. They clawed at their heads, shaking, trying to stop the pain. Several beasts staggered to their feet as their leader screeched out a command, dropped his weapon, and led a hasty retreat up the gravel path leading from the mine.

On the rock outcropping above the cavern, Viola picked up a longbow, carefully loaded an arrow and launched it in flight, sending it arcing high across the cavern. A painful shriek could be heard echoing throughout the cave as her arrow found its mark in the back of the one-armed archer. Viola's arrow pierced the beast's heart as he scrambled up the gravel path, killing him dead in his tracks.

"Taste death from above, you bastard!" Viola shouted as she watched the body of the lizard collapse to the ground.

Brutus leaped on top of the barricade and let out a mighty roar of victory, a roar that ignited a wave of deafening howls from every Chimera in the cave. Hannibal jumped up on the barricade beside Brutus and held his bloody pickaxe above his head, pumping his fist and screaming out in defiance.

Viola had made her way down from the rocky ledge with her new weapon of choice… the longbow. She hugged Brutus and patted Misun on the head.

"Four against one, Brave Heart." Brutus hugged her. "And you did not let me down. For all of our pack, I thank you."

Viola flashed an ear-to-ear grin. She felt warmth inside of her, a feeling she had never felt before. She had been head over heels in love with Brutus since they first met, but for her, it had always been unrequited love. Finally, she had established a bond with Brutus and received something from him that she treasured in return, his respect. *This has been a good day,* Viola thought. No, she had not earned the love from Brutus that she secretly desired, but gaining his respect was a step in the right direction. Besides, her feelings of romance and tenderness would have to wait; there was more killing to do.

"I will never let you down, you are my Alpha." It was all that Viola could manage in response to Brutus. He smiled and then bent down to Misun, putting his arm around him.

"Twice in one day you have worked your magic, my son. Our pack owes a great deal of gratitude to…"

"To the runt?" Viola interrupted, poking at Misun playfully.

"A runt that saved your life, Brave Heart!" Brutus laughed. Misun squirmed away and grinned as he reached for his device.

"You've seen my thunder and lightning, but you haven't seen my hurricane yet!" Misun boasted. Brutus and Viola opened their eyes wide, looked at each other, and then screamed out together.

"No!"

49. Pony Express

Inside Dr. Stone's laboratory on the command module, a heated argument over the ion thrust engine was underway between CHIP and Josiah. Lexis and Koda were sprawled out on the floor between the engine parts, silently laughing at the battle of wits between a nerdy teenager and an opinionated robot.

"I must strongly advise you," CHIP bristled, "to only operate the ion thrust propulsion unit in an experimental mode, at the lowest output levels, at least until we have a chance to thoroughly test out the reaction of the hydrogen samples with the xenon catalyst. If there are irregularities in the hydrogen samples, the entire engine could..."

"Blow up and atomize us all?" Josiah interrupted. "No shit, Sherlock. That's why I ran a spectrum analysis on the sample first. Yes... there are some risks. I calculate a two percent probability that the impurities in the feedstock will cause an ion thrust meltdown; that would be bad. But there's a one hundred percent probability that we'll all get eaten alive by that pack of prehistoric lizards out there if we just sit here and wait for their next attack. Do the math, game boy! I'm not waiting around for another slow dance with Stumpy."

The mention of Stumpy got Lexis and Koda's attention. Koda growled and Lexis stood to offer her opinion to CHIP.

"You know, Mario, I gotta go with Freddy Mercury on this one," Lexis chided. "We don't want to be immobile when Stumpy comes back. Next time, I have a feeling he'll be ready for our stun gun." CHIP was about to counter the latest argument when a secure transmission popped up on Josiah's server.

"Uh, dude?" CHIP called to Josiah. "You've got a message... 'Pony Express' delivery for 'H2 Man.'" Lexis perked up and walked over to the video screen.

"What's with the Pony Express thing?" she asked. Josiah was still steaming over the ion thrust argument, but quickly changed gears and typed in a series of commands on the screen. He answered Lexis in a distracted tone.

"Oh... Pony Express... it's a back-door mail program, designed to avoid adult supervision," Josiah answered. "We use it on campus to talk with other faculty when we don't want to leave a trail for the administration. It won't open... some sort of access permission barrier." Just then another window popped up with the avatar character of a little UPS delivery girl in brown shorts and a ball cap, holding a digital clipboard. NELI was on the other side of the firewall, controlling the character's actions.

"I have a package for H2 man," NELI announced, "but I'll need a signature before I can deliver the package."

"Righteous!" Josiah laughed. "And I'll need a prompt from you, little Swiss Miss. Do you have a prompt for me?"

"Why yes... I do." NELI blushed. "Thanks for asking, Doctor. Prompt one, three guesses. Robert Plant disbanded." Josiah looked confused.

"What the fuck?"

"Incorrect," NELI blurted out. "Prompt two, one response will be evaluated and then the package delivery will be aborted. Prompt two... doomed dirigible."

"Ok, only one response..." Josiah muttered.

"Maybe you need to use a life line," Lexis suggested. CHIP had been observing and couldn't resist jumping in.

"I love puzzles, Professor, may I play?"

"No, Luigi, this is serious," Dr. Stone shot back. "If you blow this response, I lose the package!" CHIP's feelings were hurt.

"No need for anger, Professor. The answer should be obvious... delivery for H2 man?"

"This is insane! Why would I listen to a robot with a bad attitude?" Josiah muttered.

"You got a better idea?" Lexis interrupted. "Give the Game Boy a shot!"

"Thank you for the vote of confidence," CHIP told Lexis. "OK, here goes. Try a simple word association, like six degrees of separation. The first prompt was Robert Plant disbanded. My memory banks indicate that Robert Plant was the lead singer for an ancient rock band called Led Zeppelin."

"Weren't they on that video game, *'Guitar something'*?" Lexis shouted. "Man, I loved those guys!"

"No, that was a heavy metal band called Metallica," CHIP

corrected her. "Led Zeppelin had some licensing bug up their ass with video games until they saw how much money other bands were making in the virtual world, but they missed that boat. According to my search engine, the band Led Zeppelin was also known for their driving lead guitars and screechy high vocals... and inciting drug-induced memorization. Guys played air guitar and girls threw their panties on stage. Plant had an explosive temper and the group just imploded, or shall we say, *disbanded*."

"And the answer to the prompt is...?" Josiah asked.

"The first confirmation is a lead in to the second prompt. Led Zeppelin... a *zeppelin* is an airship, a blimp, another name for a dirigible. The most famous dirigible was the one that exploded and burned as it tried to land in 1937. Come on, you've seen the old newsreels, it was the..."

"Hindenburg!" Lexis and Josiah shouted out in unison. The UPS avatar nodded and handed over the package.

"Access command accepted by H2 Man. Package downloaded to local drive."

"Man, that was easy!" CHIP gloated. "Can we play some more?"

50. Escape from Alcatraz

Standing alone atop the sacrificial altar in the beasts' gladiator arena and holding aloft the bloody head of the Lizard King, the Dark Avenger was fading, leaving Captain Gaylord alone to face the onslaught of an angry beast mob. He had been on one hell of a lucky streak, but all streaks must come to an end.

Mitch Gaylord had dodged a bullet when he crash-landed on Niburu and sucked in a lethal dose of toxic air, only to be rescued by a crazy Russian surgeon and a transplanted pair of lizard lungs. Ironically, he had to fight and kill his Russian savior in the gladiator arena, a man that had briefly become his only friend on this Godforsaken planet. *And what was his reward for killing his new best friend?* He thought. Like some demented alternate reality game show, Mitch could hear the announcer inside his head. *Tell him what he's won, Bob! Well! In addition to a handsome set of Samsonite luggage and a lifetime supply of Monster energy drinks, he's just won another chance to cheat death by killing yet another champion gladiator lizard du jour.*

"I hope they run out of fucking prizes before I run out of fucking lives!" Mitch muttered.

As the mob of lizard beasts scrambled up the base of the sacrificial platform, Mitch dropped his sword and picked up Ivan's battle-axe; maybe he could lop off a few arms or legs before they ripped him apart. Suddenly, he realized that he was still holding the bloody head of the Lizard King in his left hand. He leaned back, screamed, and flung the head as far as he could into the frenzied crowd, bracing for their attack. He was shocked by the reaction of the mob. *Now that was fortuitous.* As soon as he threw the lizard head into the crowd, they turned and chased the bloody head instead of ripping him to pieces.

The beasts dove on the decapitated head and fought over it like a pack of hungry wolves, leaving Mitch Gaylord standing alone on the platform, still clutching his battle-axe. He slowly relaxed his muscles, exhaled, and lowered his weapon; what Ivan had told him was true. *You win; you live to fight another day. You lose; you get eaten. Bon appétit, Godzilla.* With the lizard mob surging back and forth, fighting for scraps of the loser's flesh and bones, Captain Gaylord slipped down off the platform and knelt down beside the body of the dead Russian.

"We have a deal, my friend," Mitch muttered to Ivan's dead body. "Let's get you out of here. As you said, this is no place for a man to die." Captain Gaylord rolled Ivan Stephanotski's corpse over on his metal shield and dragged him to the far side of the arena. "Damn! You are one heavy son of a bitch, Ivan!" Mitch complained. "But I guess you'd do the same for me." He pounded on the metal doors with his axe and the doors slowly creaked open. Once inside, Mitch propped Ivan up against the wall and outfitted the dead Russian with his metal breastplate and helmet. He reached over with his hand and gently closed the dead Russian's eyes. Looking around the room, he grabbed a few wooden chairs and broke them into pieces with his axe. Stacking the wood up around Ivan's body, Mitch struck his obsidian knife against the metal shield to get a spark, and held it to the wood to get a flame.

"Sorry I can't launch you on a floating funeral pyre with trumpets blaring and a loft of flaming arrows," Mitch apologized. "I'm afraid this is the best I can do. At least those bastards out there won't get to gnaw on your bones."

As the flames licked around Ivan's legs and exploded up his torso, Mitch turned his back and smashed the battle-axe against the door on the opposite side of the room, kicking it open into a long dark hallway. *Travel light, but be well armed,* he thought. Reaching up to the wall of weapons, he grabbed a longbow and quiver of arrows. Closing the door behind him, Mitch wedged his spear through the door handles.

"That should hold then for a while," he muttered. *Think! Now which way is it back to my cell?* From the voices he remembered, Elena must be locked in a hospital room at twenty paces from his prison cell. Captain Gaylord recognized the path in one direction as the one he had been dragged down hours before. Without knowing what would come next, he ripped a torch from the cavern wall and broke into a full run down the dimly lit passage in search of Elena. In the muted light of the underground labyrinth, Mitch Gaylord could easily run in circles for days. But he didn't have days; he had only minutes to find Elena before the angry mob of lizards in the gladiator arena grew tired of devouring their dead champion and realized that the little human was missing. He had to find a clue, something to lead him in the right direction.

Wait! There on the wall ahead, he could make out a string of smudge marks followed by a human handprint embedded in the sticky goo oozing down the wall. *Now I'm on the right path!*

Desperate for water, Mitch had rubbed his sleeves across this wall when he was being dragged to the arena earlier, trying to extract any moisture he could salvage. He wasn't sure where the gladiator ring was from here, but he had memorized the path backwards from this point to his prison cell. As Mitch Gaylord rounded the last corner before he reached his cell, his heart was pounding like a bass drum. A voice inside his head screamed out to him.

Slow down, damn it! Don't attract attention. The guards he had heard outside his cell might still be in the neighborhood, and he didn't need to deal with them right now. Slowing to a walk, he stopped and listened. Silence. Maybe the beasts were on a coffee break; as if those beasts drank coffee and sat around Starbucks complaining about their relationships when they weren't eating human flesh. *Get a fucking grip, will you?* Creeping slowly past the door to his cell, he peered down the long empty hallway.

"Shit!" Mitch hissed. There were many doors on his prison cellblock with who knew what behind each door. It could be another prisoner; or it could be the guard's lounge. If he picked the wrong door or made a noise, it would almost certainly alert the guards. Mitch Gaylord would have only one chance to pick the right door and find Elena. Counting carefully, he paced out twenty long footsteps to account for the size of the beasts. As he reached twenty paces, he found himself in front of a door much like his prison cell, only wider. Maybe it was wider to accommodate a hospital gurney. That had to be it; this was the right door. He pressed his ear against the door and listened intently. Nothing.

This has to be it, he thought. *I'm going in.* Suddenly, he realized that breaking down that door and finding Elena inside would be the easy part of his quest. Once he found her, he had no idea how to get out of this hellhole.

"Ok, one step at a time," he muttered. As Captain Gaylord raised his battle-axe high above his head, ready to bring down a blow with all his might to break the lock, he paused.

Remember rule number one; no unnecessary noise, the voice inside his head whispered. He rubbed his sore ribs and they agreed. *Ok, find the path of least resistance.* Scanning the hallway once more, Mitch lowered his weapon, reached down to the door handle, and twisted the latch. It wasn't locked. He slowly opened the door and silently stepped inside into the darkness, closing the door behind him.

Inside the dimly lit room, Mitch's eyes adjusted to the pale light, and it was clear this was not a prison cell. There were racks of surgical equipment, operating tables, and metal pans, many of them red with dried human blood. A trash bin in the corner was overflowing with stained strips of cloth, probably used as makeshift bandages, and the remains of a leg cast—Elena's cast, Mitch realized. Across the room was another door, smaller and more secure. He walked over and felt around the edges of the door; it was similar to his prison cell.

If Elena is still alive, she must be inside, he thought. Tapping lightly on the door with the handle of his axe, he listened for a response. Inside the room, he heard a rustling noise and then a frightened female voice.

"Нет! Покидать!" (No! Leave!)

"Step back from the door!" Mitch whispered.

And with that simple warning, Captain Gaylord rammed the door latch with his battle-axe, smashing a chunk out of the wooden doorframe and dislodging it from its hinges. He kicked the rest of the broken door to the floor and stepped inside.

From behind the door, Elena was waiting with a heavy metal bowl to deliver a blow to the beast that had tormented her every waking moment since she had been imprisoned here underground. She lunged with all her might and slammed the metal bowl into the back of the intruder's skull, dropping him to his knees.

The last thing Mitch Gaylord remembered was a high-pitched girl's scream and a sharp pain in the back of his head. Then everything went black.

As Captain Gaylord slowly regained the focus in his eyes, he reached to feel the swollen knot on the back of his head. The good news was that his aching ribs no longer bothered him; the bad news was that the dull throbbing pain in his left temple now overwhelmed the pain in his side.

"Ouch!" Mitch muttered. He started to sit up, but a gentle hand restrained him on his shoulder.

"Lie still, please," a soft voice whispered. "Let me finish bandage."

Captain Gaylord fell back and looked up into the deep blue eyes of a lovely young girl as she wrapped a strip of damp cloth around his head. Even upside down and partially out of focus, she looked like an angel… shoulder-length blonde hair, long dark eyelashes, and full red lips. *This goddess is a welcome sight for sore eyes,* he thought, *after the slimy beasts that dragged me around and tried to kill me for the last few hours.*

"I am Elena. Who are you?"

"Captain Mitch Gaylord... your father sent me here to find you," Mitch blurted out.

A smile came across Elena's face and she pulled Mitch close to hug him.

"My father? Thank God he is alive!" Elena exclaimed. "I was frightened for him when they take him away. But he promise to come back for me, and he always keep his promise."

Mitch held her embrace longer than he should have, and then pulled her away.

"Elena... I am afraid I have got some bad news. About your father..."

She jumped up and held her head in her hands.

"No!" she shrieked. He is all I have left! Is he...?"

Some people say that the truth will set you free, but Mitch Gaylord couldn't bring himself to tell Elena the truth of how her father had died; how he'd killed him in the gladiator arena an hour ago. He was only sure of one thing at this moment; the truth wouldn't set them free, it would only slow them down. If they had any chance for freedom, they had to get out of this lizard prison, and fast. She couldn't handle the real truth, at least not for now, so he kept it simple.

"I'm sorry, your father is dead."

Elena collapsed to the floor, weeping and shaking. Mitch bent down to comfort her for a moment and whispered in her ear.

"The beasts killed him... and now they are coming to kill us. Your father gave his life so we could escape. We have to be very quiet and go... right now."

Elena was still sobbing as Captain Gaylord pulled her close to him and gazed into her beautiful eyes.

"I promised your father I would protect you. You've got to trust me, now let's get out of here. How's your leg, can you walk?" He gently placed his hand on her cheek and she hugged him tightly, wiping the tears from her eyes.

"Yes, is better, my father is good surgeon. You say what he would have said to me. I trust you, Captain Mitch Gaylord. Let's go now."

They turned and started to walk across the darkened room to the hallway door, when they heard a sound that caused them both to freeze in their tracks. A key rattled in the door lock, the latch turned, and the door cracked open. *There are times when you have to act without thinking,* Captain Gaylord thought. Maybe it was training, maybe it was instinct, or maybe it was just dumb luck. Whatever it was, this was one of those times.

Mitch shoved Elena behind the door and swung his battle-axe head-high with all his might at the first thing that entered. The lizard guard carrying the food tray never knew what hit him. The force of the axe blow to the exposed neck of the beast nearly severed its head. The beast shrieked in pain, threw the metal bowl in the air, and fell backwards into the hallway. The bowl bounced and clanged on the stone floor four or five times, like a fire alarm echoing down the hall.

Holy shit, Mitch thought. *There goes rule number one.* Captain Gaylord jumped into the hallway to deliver his deathblow, but it wasn't necessary. The wounded beast jerked around on the floor, gurgled a few times, and then died in a pool of its own slime. Down the hall, he could hear the sound of footsteps rapidly approaching.

"That didn't go so well!" Mitch exclaimed. Elena leaped out from behind the door and grabbed his hand.

"That is your idea of quiet?" she asked. "We go... this way!"

They took off running down the hallway, away from the approaching footsteps. At the end of the hallway, they found a large wooden door and Elena signaled to Mitch with her hand.

"Through here... to the river!"

Running at full stride, Mitch Gaylord swung his battle-axe and smashed through the door, tumbling over the shattered entry and landing on his back. As he stood up and dusted himself off, Elena gave him a curious look.

"What?" he screamed.

"That door was not locked." She shrugged. "Ok... we go now, cowboy." Elena and Mitch made their way down a rocky path to the edge of an underground river, just as Ivan had described. The river was flowing rapidly and the sound of the raging water echoed loudly throughout the cavern.

Water in underground river is good! Mitch remembered from

Ivan's secrets. *Water on surface is poison.* There wouldn't be time to stop and take a drink to test Ivan's theory; they could hear the footsteps of their captors getting closer behind them. Mitch grabbed Elena by the arm.

"Do you know where we're going?" he screamed over the sound of the raging waters.

"Yes... I think so... I think this is way back home!"

"Home?" Mitch raised his eyebrows.

"Come! We go!" Elena shouted.

They scrambled over the rocks and made their way along a narrow ledge that fell away into a deep crevice into the darkness. Elena stumbled and Mitch caught her in his arms, holding her close to him for a moment. They held their embrace for at least ten seconds, balancing on the narrow ledge. Mitch was trying to calibrate the rapid beating of her heart pressed against his body with the counting in his mind of how long it was taking the rock she had dislodged with her foot to rattle down the jagged crevice and hit the bottom. He stopped counting and focused on her heartbeat after ten seconds. The rock had made its point. *Whatever was down there, if you fell, you weren't coming back.*

They broke off their embrace but held hands to maintain their balance as they carefully edged along the ledge until they came to the end of the narrow trail on a high cliff. Mitch looked around; it was a dead end, with the raging underground river plunging sixty feet over the cliff into a swirling whirlpool of jagged rocks below. Behind him, he could hear the sounds of the beasts as they scrambled along the narrow ledge; they were but seconds away. There were only two options, and they both looked bad... either a plunge to their death over Niagara Falls or a fight to the death with the beasts. They were trapped.

Captain Gaylord peered over the edge of the cliff at the jagged rocks beneath them. Even if they could jump far enough to avoid the rock outcroppings, they would most likely drown in the swirling vortex of the raging river that disappeared into the whirlpool below. He was inclined to stand and fight the beasts right here and now on the rocky ledge. *It's too small for more than two or three of them to come at once, and besides,* he thought, *better to fight the devil that you know than face the one you don't.* At least he could kill one or two of them before they went down, and he would go down swinging. He turned his back to Elena and loosened up his arm with his battle-axe. Elena grabbed him by the shoulder.

"There is time to fight, and time to run," Elena whispered. "Now is time to run, Captain."

He turned to face her and moved closer to try and comfort her in their final moments together.

"I'm sorry I've not been a better protector. I promised your father I would let no harm come to you."

Elena pulled him to the edge of the cliff and pointed down.

"We jump now; I am Olympian athlete. You trust me? Captain Gaylord, we can make it. If we stay here and fight, we die." Mitch looked down again at the rocks below and hesitated.

"I don't think I can make it. It's too far!"

Elena looked into his eyes with a soft seductive smile and placed her gentle hand on his cheek. Her entire life, all she had to do was bat her baby blues, flash that angelic smile and men, even her father, would do whatever she asked. Captain Mitch Gaylord was no different, Elena realized, he was just another man with a futile resistance to her bewitching sensuality.

As a pilot in wartime, beautiful women were a dime a dozen for Captain Gaylord—easy come, easy go. But there was something startlingly different about Elena; different than any other woman he had ever met... her melodic voice, her piercing blue eyes, and her mysterious scent. *Oh, that enchanting odor*, he thought, *what was it?* Had he smelled it before? He buried his head in the nape of her neck and drank in that exhilarating scent deep into his lungs; it was an aphrodisiac. In the midst of this life and death battle, something unexpected had happened. Mitch Gaylord had become smitten with Elena and blinded to the mortal danger around them. He closed his eyes and inhaled again, her scent was as addictive as morphine—sweet, instant intoxication. He was hooked. He would do anything for her, anything she asked, even jump off a cliff if she asked him to. And she did.

"Captain, we must jump... now." The look in her eyes was a gentle command that he could not disobey. Elena locked arms with Mitch and they backed up away from the edge of the cliff to get a running start. She pulled him close and whispered in his ear, "Hold on to me; do not look down. Take deep breath before we hit water. No matter what happens, do not let go of me."

That's good advice, Mitch thought. But he had already come to the conclusion on his own that holding on to Elena was a good thing.

314

The warmth of her firm voluptuous body next to him almost made him forget that they were moments away from several types of painful death. Before he could nod a response, Elena pulled him beside her for three powerful strides and then they leaped into the air, plunging over the cliff and spiraling downward like two skydivers sharing a single parachute, heading directly into the swirling whirlpool at the bottom. Just before they made impact with the raging current of water in the underground river, Mitch Gaylord took a breath. It would be the last breath he would take inside the underground prison, and by virtue of the extra capacity of his beast lungs, it was a long, deep breath.

The impact with the icy water was like slamming into a cold wall before being sucked down into a twirling vortex. Mitch lost all sensation of up and down, right or left. He held on to Elena with a vice-like grip, her last words frozen in his mind: *No matter what happens, do not let go of me.* There was little chance of that; he would never let her go.

They tumbled over in the water, banging into the rocks around them, praying for the current to subside long enough for them to fight free and find the surface. Elena's hold on Mitch was fading; she was running out of air and growing weaker. If they didn't find the surface soon, they would drown. Mitch Gaylord looked into Elena's desperate eyes and did the only thing he could think of at that moment. He kissed her, long and deep; a kiss that could last to eternity. He wasn't sure whether he would die like this, locked in a passionate embrace with a beautiful woman, but compared to being eaten alive in the gladiator ring by a mob of slimy lizards, this wouldn't be a bad way to go.

His head was spinning from the lack of oxygen and as he opened his eyes, he could see a faint trail of translucent bubbles above his head. With the last of his strength, he pumped his legs with two powerful thrusts and they burst through the bubbles to the surface. Gasping for air, Mitch pulled himself to the side of the river with one arm, still holding Elena close to his body. Elena opened her eyes and coughed up some river water, wiping it from her lips as she smiled.

"I thought I died for a moment," Elena gasped. "It was like dream. How did we make it here? Wait a minute... did you just kiss me, Captain Gaylord?"

Mitch looked over at her and smiled. "I just did what you told me to do," he reassured her.

Elena looked confused and closed her eyes.

Mitch leaned in close and whispered in her ear. "You said, whatever you do, don't let go. You can trust me; I won't ever let you go."

Captain Gaylord's ego liked to think it was the mere touch of his sensual lips that had kept Elena alive, but in reality, it was the extra oxygen he exhaled from his beast lungs that had saved her life. That would make the second time that being a beast-man had come in handy. *Thanks, Ivan,* he thought. *I owe you one, buddy.*

Lying on his side at the edge of the underground river, Mitch Gaylord was exhausted from the near-death plunge over the cliff to escape the angry mob of lizards. Despite the shivering cold, he finally felt relaxed for the first time on the planet of Niburu. He looked over at Elena; her lips had turned blue from the cold, and she was trembling in her soggy flight suit.

"We'd better get out of these wet clothes, or we could freeze to death," he told her. "I'll gather some driftwood and get a fire going." There were plenty of unusual sticks and branches along the riverbank, and he quickly returned with an armload of firewood and dropped it between some tall rocks to prepare the fire. Mitch peeled off his shirt, pants, and tossed them next to the stack of wood. Elena just stood there shivering as he arranged the firewood.

"Come on, take your clothes off!" Mitch chided. "We're safe here for a while."

Elena looked at his almost naked body and blushed.

Realizing he had embarrassed her with his unexpected disrobing, he tried to recover. "Trust me, there's not much I haven't seen before."

As soon as the words left his lips, Mitch Gaylord felt like an arrogant jerk. All he could do now was shrug his shoulders and hope the awkward moment created by his boneheaded reaction would pass quickly. Granted, that didn't quite come out so smoothly, but damn it, he was freezing.

"Oh... K," Elena stuttered. "Is very cold. But you turn around like gentleman and not look, yes?"

"A gentleman? Of course I won't... look." Mitch smiled.

Mitch Gaylord bent down, ignited a flare from Ivan's utility belt, and quickly had a raging campfire going. The flames licked up the dry kindling and soon the warmth of the crackling fire felt good against his cold skin. He stood up and walked away from the blaze to give Elena a moment of privacy. Even though he said he was a gentleman, he couldn't resist turning around to steal a glance at her.

When Captain Mitch Gaylord said that there wasn't much he hadn't seen before, he was lying. Gazing at the silhouette of her glistening body by the roaring fire, the moisture dripping down her perfect curves as she bent over and wrung the water from her hair, he had to admit to himself he'd never seen a woman as beautiful as Elena. The sight of her naked body glowing with the flickering firelight behind her was enough to make him weak at the knees. He thought to himself, *From Russia, with love indeed.* Mitch Gaylord swallowed hard and broke off his moment of secret voyeurism, calling back to Elena.

"Ok, I am coming back now... my back is still turned."

This time, Captain Gaylord was a perfect gentleman and resisted the urge to sneak another glance at her naked body as he felt his way back along the rocks to the fireside. He sat down and moved close to her, back-to-back. The warmth of the fire and the touch of her skin were intoxicating. Seated naked in front of the fire with his back to Elena, as perfect a gentleman that Mitch Gaylord claimed he was, he was about to explode. He could hardly control the pure sexual desire that was sweeping over his body, and if Elena turned around, he would be found out in a heartbeat.

From behind him, Elena spoke softly. "Captain Gaylord, you are true gentleman. I thank you for not trying to take advantage of me in this... position. Most men I have known would."

Shit! Mitch thought. *Get control of yourself, or you are going to blow this once-in-a-lifetime opportunity!* He shifted uncomfortably on the rock behind her and crossed his legs, still rubbing his bare back against hers. *Yeah, you want to bang her, you frickin' low-life, but try and think about baseball statistics or something!* He thought. *Don't let the little head do the thinking for the big head!*

The only thing Captain Gaylord could come up with to reduce his sexual tension was to ask Elena about herself and then mentally check out. Sort of like asking your girlfriend 'How was your day?' and then going in the kitchen to make a sandwich, flipping on the game, and occasionally popping your head back out of the room to say, 'Really? How did that make you feel?' *How was your fucking day? Guaranteed shrinkage. Ok, here goes.*

"Elena, how did you end up as a stowaway on your father's ship?" Mitch asked.

Elena sighed, she started talking and the shrinkage... engaged. "There, that was open-ended enough, now find your happy place, Mr. Turtle. Back in your shell," he mumbled quietly to himself.

"When I was young, my father was like rooster in henhouse, you know, always with many women. My mother divorce him and leave me with him. She say, 'Elena, you remind me too much of him. Is best you stay with your father.'" Elena paused for a moment to see if Captain Gaylord was listening.

"Really? How did that make you feel?" Mitch asked, shrinking away.

"Not so good. My father is foolish man, always thinking with trousers, but he is good father to me, he has warm heart. Then he meet my stepmother. She is gold-digging bitch, only after his money. When my father is drafted into war, she kick me out on street. I find his spacecraft and hide there to get away. That is my story, Captain Gaylord." Mitch had been partially listening but mainly he was concentrating on deflating the current situation, and it had worked. Now it was time for an appropriate display of sensitivity and he would be back to normal.

"Well, you know what they say, there's no place like home," Mitch murmured absentmindedly. Elena turned toward him, smiled, and nuzzled closer with a sigh.

"No place like home? Yes, we are almost home now," she whispered.

"Almost home? You said that once before, but what do you mean by that?" Mitch inquired. Elena sat up on the riverbank and reached over to wring the water out of her soaking wet T-shirt.

"Home. Our ship. It is right out there, through the rocks," she responded casually. "I will turn on transmitter and let them know we are here." Elena fumbled around with her pants and ripped open a false pocket sewn into the leg of her flight suit. She reached in and pulled out a small black disc with two buttons on it, one red and one green; she pressed the green button.

"Now they will come... we wait," she announced.

Mitch was confused. "Who's coming?"

"My father told me that if he did not come for me, to push green button for help. He will send First Officer Christyakova to find me and bring me back to ship."

Mitch Gaylord paused for a moment, again unsure how much he should reveal to Elena. He knew that her father had been forced to kill Christyakova in the gladiator arena, before Mitch had been forced to fight Ivan to the death. He thought to himself, *too much truth all at once was not a good idea.* He looked around the cavern ceiling above the calm river and his eyes locked on to a shaft of light streaming through a crack from above. Standing up, he could see a way to climb out of the opening that was letting in the light.

"You said that the ship was just outside the cave."

"Less than five kilometers to south, according to my transmitter. First Officer Christyakova will be here soon."

Mitch started scaling the rocks toward the shaft of light near the ceiling.

"I think I'll climb up there and signal him. It will help him find us faster." Mitch hopped up on a rock above Elena, then paused for a moment and asked, "What does the red button do?" Elena looked him directly in the eyes and responded without emotion.

"Green button is to live… red button is to die."

Mitch Gaylord scrambled up across the loose gravel covering the rock outcroppings toward the shaft of light at the top of the cavern, unsure of what he would find on the surface. He left Elena to recuperate by the fire after their terrifying escape from the lizards through the whirlpool rapids. Elena thought she had signaled for help from the crew of her Russian spacecraft, but Mitch knew differently; they were all dead. *What's the harm of letting her have a ray of hope for just a little longer,* he thought.

Finally clawing his way to the surface, Captain Gaylord poked his head out of the hole in the rocks like a prairie dog, scanning the murky horizon for predators. He was positioned halfway up a steep mountain and could barely see across the valley to the outline of some red cliffs in the distance. The lights in the sky suddenly pulsated and lit up the darkness for a moment, and there, directly to the south was a crashed spacecraft with Russian markings on the tail fins, just as Elena had predicted. The lights from the sky dimmed, and just as quickly as it appeared, the image of the Russian ship faded from view. Mitch swiveled around on the rocks and stuck his head back into the cave to call out to Elena.

"I saw it! Your ship, I saw it!" His voice echoed down into the cavern below.

"Is good. Are they coming for us now?" Elena called back.

As soon as the words left Mitch Gaylord's mouth, he wanted to smack himself in the head. *What the hell did you say that for?* He thought. *Nobody's coming for us, they're all fucking dead!* Mitch turned back around, slumped down on the rocks, and stared out across the dimly lit desert plains. It was then that something caught his eye, a momentary flash; a glint of light reflected from across the valley. He poked his head back up through the hole in the rocks and squinted his eyes to get a better look in the pulsating light. Something was moving out there, near the base of the red cliffs, and it was headed his way. At first it looked like a tiny column of ants, marching in a random path across the desert floor searching for food. But then, as the ants got closer, they came into focus.

"Shit!" he screamed. "How the hell did they find us?"

Advancing across the valley floor at a rapid pace was a squadron of lizard beasts. *At least eight, no ten, no, shit!* He thought. There were eleven beasts running directly toward him in tight formation. They were all carrying metal spears and shields and marching double time, heading directly toward the hole in the rock wall where Mitch was looking down.

"Fuck! The transmitter!" he muttered. Elena's transmitter had worked perfectly, except that instead of alerting her dead companion to come and save them, it had broadcast their exact position to the lizard patrol. *So much for letting her hold on to the false hope of rescue,* he thought. *That was a bad decision.* "Damn it!" he screamed.

From below in the cavern, Mitch could hear Elena scrambling up the rocks below him. *There was no use in trying to hide the facts from her now,* he thought, *they were going to die.* He waited silently until she joined him at the surface. Out of breath, Elena poked her head through the hole in the rocks.

"They come for us, yes?" she blurted out with an excited smile. Mitch put his arm around her and pulled her close.

"I'm sorry love, it's not your crew that is coming for us." He pointed to the advancing column of lizards across the valley below, getting closer by the second.

Elena turned and looked down, the joy washed out of her face as she sank to her knees. Without looking up, she spoke in a somber voice. "First Officer Christyakova, he is not coming, is he?"

Mitch looked away, unable to meet her eyes. "No Elena, he's

not."

"And the rest of the crew?" Elena asked softly.

"I'm afraid they're not coming either," he replied.

Elena sobbed for a second, looked away, and then looked back at Mitch.

"What will we do now, Captain Gaylord?" she asked softly. Mitch reached down and pulled her up to him, hugging her tight. He kissed her on the forehead and looked deeply into her crystal blue eyes.

"Elena Stephanotski, I have only known you for a few hours, but for me it seems like a lifetime. I can see the tenderness in your eyes and feel the strength in your heart; you are a beautiful young woman... and I wouldn't trade our few hours together for another lifetime right now." He hugged her again, and then stepped away, looking down at the approaching band of lizards. "I made a promise to your father to protect you, and you have my word that I'll do all that I can to keep that promise."

"What are you going to do, Captain?" Elena asked as she wiped a tear from her eye.

"I'm going to go down there and kill as many of those beasts as I can," Mitch told her calmly. He was quiet for a moment, rubbing his battle-axe and thinking back to the advice Ivan had given him about how to fight the beasts, advice that had saved his life twice already, and left several of the beasts missing their heads.

"But how will you do that?" Elena asked. "There are too many!" Mitch turned back to Elena and smiled.

"No worries, love, your father taught me how to kill them." Mitch laughed. "I will be... *unpredictable.*" Elena hugged him with all her strength, not wanting to let him go.

"You are brave man, Captain Mitch Gaylord," she whispered in his ear. "But you cannot face beasts alone. One against many is suicide. Two against many is a fight. Elena will fight with you; what do you want me to do?"

"I want you to keep signaling on your transmitter," he whispered.

"But why? Everyone on my ship is dead," Elena protested.

"It's a long shot, but maybe they made it down."

"Who made it down?" she asked.

"Never mind." He suddenly got an idea and looked back at her. "You said you were an Olympic athlete; can you shoot a longbow?" Mitch inquired.

Elena had never considered herself a *'damsel in distress'* type of girl and desperately wanted to help him fight the beasts that had tormented her. She picked up the longbow and loaded an arrow from the quiver.

"I can shoot apple off your head at fifty paces, like your William Tell." She pulled back on the bow to test its tension. "Is sixty pound pull, no, sixty-five. Is much lighter than I am used to, but will work. Shall I show you?" Mitch put his hand over the shaft of the arrow and pulled it down to her side. Scanning the rocky terrain below, he spied the exact thing he was looking for.

"No, not yet, I believe you." He pointed down the rocky slope to a place he was sure the beasts would use as their approach. "You see that boulder above the narrow path below?"

"Yes, I see it," Elena answered.

"When I give you the signal, you shoot your arrows and knock out the small rocks that hold back that boulder, ok?"

"I can do this," Elena exclaimed. "But what if I miss?" Mitch kissed her on the forehead again.

"This is very important, Elena. If you miss, you must forget about me and do one more thing... and you must promise to do this for me."

"I promise, Captain Gaylord. What am I to do?" she asked.

Mitch looked directly into Elena's eyes. "You must push the red button."

51. Red Cliffs Rendezvous

As the rover approached the base of the Red Cliffs, Lieutenant McCurdy nudged the driver on the shoulder, signaling him to stop. The driver complied, halting the vehicle just behind a large boulder. The rear guard scanned the horizon for hostiles and cocked the hammer of his 50-caliber machine gun with a distinctive metal click. Pointing to Maurya's computer, McCurdy made a gesture asking for the next set of directions. Since Dr. Maurya was still deciphering the navigation codes from the transmission NELI had recovered from the data log, he tried to stall and signaled that he was working, and to wait a minute. McCurdy was dissatisfied with Maurya's response and broke radio silence.

"You try my patience, Doctor," McCurdy barked. "Your time is up. Direct us to the Russian spacecraft or kindly hop out of the rover. This will be your last stop.

Dr. Maurya was working frantically to decode the last coordinate. He had the data, but since the transmission was between the ePod and the command module, he would have to manually interpolate an intercept vector from the rover's current location. The computer guidance program was useless; there was no GPS or satellite triangulation for a base-level computation. It was a strange moment to have this thought, but he was now thankful that his father would never allow him to use a calculator to do his geometry homework as a child.

"If you use a calculator," Ashoka's father had told him, "you will get a lazy brain and never remember how to do the math. In my day, we had no fancy calculators, but we could do the math, and so will you."

"There! I've got it!" Dr. Maurya exclaimed. He stood up in the rover and pointed to a large purple boulder one hundred meters away. "Just the other side of that boulder, there is a pass through the mountain. The Russian ship is on the other side; two kilometers at the most."

Lieutenant McCurdy stared at Ashoka for a second and then signaled the driver to proceed. As the rover started out on its new path, McCurdy leaned over to Maurya and tapped his helmet.

"Doctor, I truly hope for your sake there is a Russian ship just behind that mountain," McCurdy growled.

Ashoka nodded a nervous acknowledgement and sank back into

his seat. *He would deliver the monkey to the ocelots, but would the ocelots play their part?* He wasn't sure what awaited them on the other side of the mountain, but he knew he had better start thinking about a backup plan. Just then, a message appeared on his computer.

"Pony Express package delivered and accepted," NELI transmitted. Dr. Maurya breathed a sigh of relief. *So far... so good.* The message faded in and out and then disappeared from the screen as they entered the mountain pass. Hopefully, the next communication he received from Mata Hari was not a bad omen. *'Signal Lost.'*

As the rover wound its way through the rugged mountain pass, Dr. Maurya glanced up to the jagged peaks above. A spooky feeling came over him, as if someone or something was watching them. Behind any of the rocks above could be Josiah's lizard man, just waiting to pounce on the rover and rip them all to shreds.

The rear guard soldier must have been getting the same creepy vibrations; he jerked his head back and forth, looking at the rocks above the canyon. He swung the 50-caliber machine gun side to side, itching to fire off a few rounds of bravado. In the war, this soldier had seen plenty of ambushes before, and something in his gut told him they were walking right into one.

Finally, a glimmer of light emerged as the rover approached the last few meters at the end of the mountain pass. The rear guard breathed a sigh of relief; they must be safe now. *If anyone were going to attack us,* he thought, *they'd use the cover of the narrow pass to swoop down on us. Roll a rock down in front of the rover, force us to stop and cut us to pieces from behind. Just like ducks in a shooting gallery. That's the way any soldier would have planned the ambush.* As the rover pulled out of the narrow canyon, McCurdy signaled the driver to stop. He scanned the horizon for the Russian spacecraft and then turned to Dr. Maurya.

"Well, Professor, we've arrived at the location of your mysterious Russian spacecraft. There's only one problem... it doesn't seem to be here." Dr. Maurya looked down at the computer and mentally re-ran the telemetry equations in his head.

"But it *must* be here," Ashoka blurted out. "The math is all correct!"

"Now you're talking gibberish, Doctor," McCurdy stated coldly. "Why don't we take a walk to clear your head?" McCurdy signaled Longstreet to escort a confused Dr. Maurya from the rover. Ashoka was still recalculating the navigation coordinates in his head, oblivious to the fact that he was being led in front of a firing squad. McCurdy pointed Longstreet to a pile of rocks that appeared to have been stacked up into a rough platform just ahead.

"There," McCurdy called out. "Those rocks will serve the purpose. Secure the prisoner and form the squad, Sergeant."

The rear guard spun his 50-caliber machine gun around and took dead aim on Maurya's chest. He cocked his weapon and awaited the command to fire. *This isn't a soldier's proudest moment,* thought the rear guard, *but I'll follow orders. In this world, you either obey the chain of command or you quickly find yourself on the other end of the gun.* Dr. Maurya finished recalculating the navigation coordinates in his head and now knew his problem.

"Oh my, that is it!" Ashoka blurted out. "How could I have made such a simple error? I was using meters, but the transmission data was in yards. Those damn yanks never converted to metrics, did they! That is why they kept losing their space probes! I did not account for the metric conversion, that is why my location was off!"

"Fascinating, Doctor," McCurdy mused. "I'll be sure that your last words are recorded. What shall it be for you? Not remember the Alamo, but remember the metric system?"

Sergeant Longstreet stepped away from the prisoner and walked behind the pile of rocks.

"Prepare to fire!" McCurdy shouted.

Sergeant Longstreet relayed the command.

"Ready... aim." Just before the order to fire, Sergeant Longstreet leaped back around the pile of rocks and screamed out to the firing squad, "Halt! Don't shoot!"

McCurdy glared at Longstreet and barked at him in a dismissive tone. "Sergeant, you had better have a damn good reason for disobeying my command... or else you can take your place beside the prisoner."

"My apologies," Longstreet gasped, "But I think you should come over here and take a look at this!"

McCurdy pushed past a bewildered Maurya and joined Sergeant Longstreet on the other side of the pile of rocks.

"What do you make of that, sir?" Longstreet asked.

"Well who would have believed it, Sergeant? If my 'Jane's Military Handbook' is accurate, that would appear to be a Russian spacecraft... a Phobos-Grunt class deep space probe to be exact. And just where our good doctor said it would be."

52. The Last Straw

Brutus and Hannibal looked out across the floor of the mine; it was littered with the bodies of dead Chimera. The pack had paid a high price, but in the course of the battle, they had discovered a newfound strength within themselves and something even more important... the will to survive against all odds. With the exhilaration of combat fading, Hannibal put his arm around Brutus.

"We have fought well, you and I," Hannibal stated. "But what will we do now?" Brutus looked back at the weary warriors with a stern face.

"We will cremate the bodies of our fallen brothers and sisters," Brutus answered. "We cannot allow their bones to be desecrated by the beasts should they return. Come, we will build a bonfire to honor their sacrifice."

Hannibal motioned for the miners to gather the wooden pallets and construct a funeral pyre. It was a somber time, a time for honoring the innocent victims of the brutal lizard attack. The Chimera worked in silence, each reflecting on the bizarre turn of events they had just experienced. Suddenly, the silent vigil of the mourners was interrupted by the gunfire of an AK-47 machine gun. The humans had emerged from their hiding place inside the transport and were now perched on top of the truck cab with their weapons drawn.

"All right, you filthy animals!" screamed one of the guards. "Playtime's over, now it's time to get back to work!"

The Chimera paused, stunned at the insensitivity of their so-called guards. They grumbled among themselves, seething with anger. The humans had left them defenseless and hid, leaving them to die at the hands of the vicious lizards. Now that the Chimera had tasted their own blood in battle, they had little patience for submitting to the will of their human masters.

Viola stepped beside Brutus and reached down to grasp her spear. Brutus held out his left hand, seeming to imply submission, but he himself had moved his right hand to his sword. The miners closest to the humans stood their ground, neither challenging them, nor backing down. Sensing a potential mutiny, the human guard in front repeated the same abuse he had dealt out in the past. He lunged forward and struck one of the Chimera in the head with the butt of his rifle, screaming at them.

"I said get back to work, you dirty mutants!"

The injured miner dropped to his knees and felt blood streaming down his face into his mouth. He did not cry out in pain; he licked the blood with his tongue and smiled, standing erect in front of the surprised guard.

"So, you're feeling like another lesson in discipline, are you?" the guard shouted. Reaching back, he raised his gun to deliver another blow, but instead the sharp thud of a metal spear penetrated deep into his chest. His eyes bulged out; he coughed up a mouthful of blood, and fell to his knees. Unable to speak or call out, the guard collapsed to the ground; he was dead. The explosion of anger from the Chimera was like striking a match next to dynamite; the miners rushed the two remaining guards and beat them unconscious with their shovels and stones. Brutus fought his way through the group of enraged miners, throwing them off of the bodies of the battered guards.

"Enough!" Brutus shouted. "You have been treated like slaves by these cowards, but you are not slaves!" Brutus reached down to check the pulse of the humans; one was dead, the other was just barely alive. He stood up, straddling the injured human who was clinging to life. "You want to kill this man, do you not?" Brutus shouted.

"Yes!" roared the miners. "Kill the bastard!" They banged their shovels on the ground.

"You want vengeance for their cruelty," Brutus shot back. "But this act of vengeance will not heal our wounds, it will not settle our score, and it will not free our souls. In the past, we have been slaves to the humans, but as of this moment, we will be slaves no more!"

The crowd of miners erupted with chants of approval, beating their shovels and stomping on the ground.

"We have won a great battle," Brutus called out. "We have killed many of the lizard beasts and driven the rest of them away. This battle is won, but our war has just begun. We will have to fight again, and sooner, rather than later, I fear." Settling down, the Chimera listened intently to Brutus' words. "We will focus our strength on preparing to defend ourselves from another attack by the beasts. They will attack when we least expect it, and we have learned the price for being unprepared. Let this human live for now; when his time comes, we will decide what his fate shall be."

Hannibal stepped forward from the angry crowd to speak.

"Brutus, my brother, you are a mighty warrior, and you are my pack leader. But I must ask you, is it truly wise to spare this human's life when he so freely would sacrificed ours?"

Brutus leaned close to Hannibal and spoke so no one else could hear.

"Earlier," Brutus whispered, "I held one of our wounded brothers in my arms just before he died. His last words to me were words of fear... fear that the beasts would keep coming... until they killed us all. I do not fear the beasts, but I do fear that he may be right. The beasts attacked us and we killed two of them. Then they returned to attack with tenfold. The next time they come, they will come in full force."

Hannibal nodded his acknowledgement and Brutus turned to face the miners.

"We do not know how many of these lizard beasts are," he shouted. "But we know one thing for certain; they will come back and they will try to kill us all. Until we are prepared for this war, we don't have time to waste killing this human."

Hannibal stood by Brutus and called out his agreement to the crowd. "You are right, my brother, we are too weak to sustain another attack. We must fortify our defenses. Besides, what does it matter if the human dies now... or when we decide his time has come?"

Brutus nodded his thanks and Hannibal turned back to the crowd of miners, raising his pickaxe. "There is wisdom in his words, I will stand with Brutus. The human will live... until we decide... *his time has come!*"

"*His time has come!*" shouted a miner in the back of the crowd. Hannibal gathered the miners and lit the funeral pyre. As the flames licked up around the wooden pallets and consumed the bodies of the fallen Chimera, Viola stepped next to Brutus. They stood there silently watching the fire until Brutus finally spoke.

"It was your spear that killed the human, was it not?" whispered Brutus.

Viola froze, unsure how to answer. He was right, in a moment of anger she had reacted without thinking; it was her spear that killed the human. Brutus had told her many times that she would one day lead the Chimera pack, but that she still had many lessons to learn. She sensed that somehow, he was displeased with her. Putting his arm around her, Brutus whispered in her ear.

"Your instincts were correct, Brave Heart, the human had to die. His cowardly actions resulted in the death of innocents, and the retribution for his cruelty was death. But the decision to administer justice rests solely with the pack leader. Once the leader makes his decision, it does not matter who does the killing."

Viola looked down at her boots, prepared for her scolding.

"Are you angry with me... for killing the human?"

Brutus pulled her close, smiled, and hugged her with a bear hug.

"No, I am not angry with you," he told her. "You are a warrior and your heart is true. You saw a threat to the pack, and you eliminated it without hesitation. That is an instinct that cannot be taught. But this is the hard part of the lesson to learn; a leader must never condone revenge for its own sake, but when it is justified, he must deliver retribution swiftly, forcefully, and with no remorse. This will strike fear into the hearts of your enemies and earn respect in the hearts of your pack." Viola breathed a sigh of relief and hugged Brutus. He kissed her on the forehead.

"One day, Brave Heart, you will have learned this lesson, and when you do, you will have the wisdom in your heart to lead our pack to greatness."

53. Package Received

Onboard the Genesis Five command module, the encrypted data from the Pony Express delivery had been downloaded. Josiah's video screen erupted with a wave of schematic diagrams of Dr. Maurya's atmospheric generator; layer upon layer rotating in 3D images. The last image of the schematic zoomed in and focused on the hidden design feature embedded behind the main control panel. A computer generated avatar and the voice of Ashoka Maurya popped up to deliver his message.

"Dr. Stone, please listen carefully, I can only say this once. Thanks to your increased power designs, I have succeeded in transforming the atmospheric generator into a crude, but effective electromagnetic pulse concentrator. Coupled with the planet's natural EMPs, I can now accelerate the energy waves to create a temporary gateway into a fold in the time-space continuum, or as you may know it, a wormhole, a Time Portal." Dr. Maurya paused to catch his breath.

"The Time Portal works, but it is quite unpredictable, as I never know exactly when the planet will emit the required EMP cascades. Now here is the really important part. Dr. Jones discovered that McCurdy contaminated the Chimera with his own DNA for some sinister purpose and confronted him. We struggled with him and tried to escape into the Time Portal. She made it... I did not. Samantha is trapped in the Time Portal and only you can release her." A nervous Dr. Maurya looked over his shoulder and then back to the camera.

"Here are the access codes and firing sequence for the atmospheric generator to activate the Time Portal. You must act immediately; I do not know how much longer it will be before Lieutenant McCurdy figures out that the atmospheric generator is the key. I will create a diversion and try to lead him away from the generator to allow you a window of opportunity to get Samantha back. My grandfather and I think it is time for this slimy bastard McCurdy to meet your lizard man. Please hurry."

Josiah and Lexis stood frozen in silence, stunned at the message from Dr. Maurya. The image of engineering schematics on the video screen crumpled up and dissolved into a digital puff of smoke; the secure transmission package was erased.

54. Free at Last

Deep inside the underground cavern of the mine, the funeral pyre had died down to its last smoldering embers, freeing the remains of the fallen miners from their life of human domination. For those that had been killed in the mining attack, it was the first taste of freedom they had ever experienced. For the ones left behind, they awoke as free souls to a life of infinite unknowns. Was their fight for freedom a lost cause? What would come next for them? Starvation? Being eaten alive by scaly predators? Or would it be a slow painful descent into madness, realizing in the end that the underground fortress they had locked themselves inside of was in fact, their tomb.

Brutus could see the fear in the eyes of the miners; their minds were adrift in an ocean of anxiety. The Chimera desperately needed him to lead them away from the fear of the unknown and into the comfort of the known. *They will be eager to sacrifice,* he thought, *but they each need to know that their sacrifice, no matter how large or small, was meaningful and essential to the survival of the pack.* They needed a pack leader with the simplicity of an ancient Zen master, that when asked the secret to a purposeful life, responded, *'Chop wood and carry water.'* Brutus climbed to the top of the transport vehicle and called out to allay the fears of the miners.

"We have fought together to cast off the chains of human control, and with the help of our fallen brothers who surrendered their lives, we have tasted the forbidden fruit of freedom. In the past, we were mistreated, we were abused, and we were enslaved. But as of this moment, we will never again be a slave, not to anyone, neither man nor beast!" There was a roar of approval from the miners and Brutus continued. "But we cannot expect that our hard-won freedom can be maintained without continued sacrifice. We have enemies outside of these stone walls; some want to deprive us of our freedom, others want to deprive us of our lives. But I pledge to you, as your pack leader, fighting together, we will rise up and defeat them all!

Brutus waved to the cheering miners, delivering to them the comfort they needed. The Chimera were no longer lost, as long as he was there to lead them. As he climbed down off of the hood of the transport, Hannibal, Viola, and Misun joined him, eager to follow his orders. There was a steely determination in his eyes; it was his far-off look that reinforced their devotion to him as their Alpha leader. Brutus grabbed Hannibal by the arm, speaking softly so that only the four of them could hear.

"By now, the beasts will have regrouped and are planning another attack on us," Brutus told them. "We are most vulnerable at the mouth of the cave; it is there you must fortify our defenses. You will be my rock, Hannibal. Slow them down, sculpt the field of battle, and then drive them into a killing zone." Hannibal nodded and locked his arm with Brutus in agreement.

"I will take five miners and build a gate to narrow their approach," Hannibal decided forcefully. "If we can't stop them there, at least we can force them down into a narrow crevice along the side of the road where Viola can rain death on them from above."

"Now you are thinking like a soldier!" Brutus smiled and turned to Viola. "And you, Brave Heart, you must be our eyes. You must see without being seen. If they chase you, run away. If they run away, chase them. Confuse them, deceive them, and lead them... exactly where we want them to be."

Misun stepped forward, tugging at Brutus' leg.

"Ah, little one, I have not forgotten you." Brutus smiled. "You will be our ears. Build us a communication system so that we can all talk as one."

"Like the one I built for Dr. Jones?" Misun smiled.

"Yes, like the one you built for Dr. Jones. A communicator that speaks only for us to hear."

"I can do that!" Misun beamed.

They each gathered close to Brutus, locked arms, and looked into his eyes.

"You are all brave warriors." Brutus smiled at them with determination. "When the lizard beasts come, we will be ready. It will be a good time to live free... or to die. Either outcome will bring us peace. But now we must do one more thing."

"What is that?" they asked.

The smile left Brutus' face.

"The time has come my brothers. I must decide whether the human will live... or will die."

55. Showdown at the Russian Corral

Dr. Maurya looked around at the rocky terrain of the valley and suddenly realized where he was standing. The others hadn't noticed, but there were faint tracks leading up to the rock pile from all directions. The pile of rocks in front of him that was to be his execution backdrop was also the platform described to him by Josiah... the sacrificial platform of the lizard beasts where they tore apart that poor Russian crewmember.

Now what do I do, Grandfather? Ashoka thought to himself. *The greedy monkey has taken the gourd.*

Yes. Chandragupta answered in his mind. *The monkey has taken the banana. Now you just need to awaken the ocelots and then your trap will be sprung.*

McCurdy had now absorbed the discovery of the Russian spacecraft and refocused on the final objective of the mission. He turned back to Maurya and spoke in an authoritative voice.

"Ok, Professor. There seems to be at least a tiny drop of truth in your ocean of lies. You just dodged a bullet... literally. But I didn't come here to tour a crash site... where is my Time Portal?"

Keep them near the rock pile and stall, Dr. Maurya thought. *My ocelots will come.*

"I'm not exactly sure how, but this pile of rocks is definitely the entrance to the Time Portal. Somehow, the computer equipment that is still functioning on that Russian ship is jamming the entrance to the Time Portal. You stay here, I will go examine the Russian equipment and try to break it free."

"Not so fast, Herr Doctor," McCurdy replied with suspicion. "You're not leaving my sight for one second. Sergeant Longstreet, set up camp and station your men on full alert. We'll eat, get some rest and then you and I will accompany the professor to the Russian ship to open the door. We're not leaving this site until I have secured my Time Portal."

The soldiers jumped out and wedged the rover next to the rock pile, and mapping out a defensive perimeter between their position and the Russian ship. The rear guard hopped back into the rover and scanned the perimeter with the 50-caliber machine gun. The other soldier carefully set out a series of tripwires with claymore mines to alert them to any undetected hostile penetration of their perimeter. He jumped back into the rover and grabbed a rocket propelled grenade launcher, an AK-47 and a 45-caliber pistol from the trunk. The rear guard with the 50-caliber machine gun looked down and laughed.

"What the hell do you think is out there, man? An entire battalion?"

The other soldier checked his ammo clip and replied nervously. "I don't know about you, man, but I got a bad feeling about this one. My gut is gnawing at me, like when we were dogging those terrorists in the fucking mountain passes of Kazakhstan, or was it Afghanistan... hell, it was one of those Stans. Radio silence? Shit, nobody even knows we're out here! Here's the thing; we almost smoked the Doc for no reason and now we're stuck on sentry, guarding a fucking pile of rocks. But guarding 'em from what? Like I said, man, I don't got a good feeling on this one, so I'm packing heavy, you know."

The rear guard in the rover thought about their situation for a second.

"You're fucking right; we're totally in the dark on this mission. I'm starting to feel like a goat tethered to a stake, just waiting for the tiger to come."

"And things don't usually work out so well for the goat when the mutherfucking tiger comes," the other soldier called back.

The rear guard rechecked the ammo belt for the 50-caliber again and slammed the metal housing shut with a clang. "I hear that, brother. I'll take first watch."

After a fitful period of mostly sleeplessness, Maurya, McCurdy, and Sergeant Longstreet awoke and made their way from the rock pile to the door of the Russian spacecraft. Longstreet banged on the closed metal hatch with the butt of his rifle and called out to McCurdy.

"Sealed tight as a drum sir. Want me to blow it?" He reached down to his utility belt to grab some C-4 but was interrupted by Maurya pushing past McCurdy.

"That won't be necessary," Dr. Maurya told him. "The door should be unlocked." He clutched the metal handle, twisted it, and slowly pulled the door open. He was about to step inside when McCurdy grabbed him by the shoulder.

"How did you know the door would be unlocked, Doctor?"

McCurdy questioned.

"Oh... I did not know," Ashoka blurted out, trying to maintain his cover. "I just assumed... why would you need to lock the door out here in the middle of nowhere? But that is not relevant to our mission, Lieutenant, let me go inside and find the computer equipment and free the Time Portal. I'll be right back."

"Belay that, Doc," McCurdy shouted. "Sergeant, you take point and check inside for booby traps and weapons. I wouldn't want our professor to stumble on something that could get him killed. Then we'll all go inside together and explore."

Sergeant Longstreet disappeared inside the Russian ship for a minute and then returned.

"All clear in there, sir. Spooky though... not a soul on board... living or dead."

Dr. Maurya hesitated at the entrance hatch for a second. His plan was spinning out of control. *Where are my damn ocelots?* He thought. *Wherever they are, we have a better chance of bumping into them outside the ship. I must keep McCurdy back outside... somehow.* Lieutenant McCurdy interrupted his thoughts.

"Let's go, Doctor, you are the only one that claims to know what we are looking for, some sort of computer equipment that's the key to my Time Portal? That was your story, wasn't it? What exactly does it look like? We'll help you find it."

Dr. Maurya stepped into the Russian ship, unsure of what to do next. *Stall,* he thought. *Something will happen.* He remembered the advice of his grandfather and called out to him in his mind. *Grandfather, what do I do now?*

Chandragupta whispered back in his head. *Do not worry, my son; you have done your job. The ocelots will come.* Dr. Maurya started a diversionary search of the interior of the command center of the ship.

"Some kind of computer beacon, possibly, a video hard drive, yes... that is it. The video hard drive would contain the captain's log files. I just hope it is not damaged."

McCurdy turned and started to search the control panel for the video drive. He was familiar with the electronic grid of a spacecraft and followed the color-coded coax wiring to the equipment panel. He ripped open the panel door, and called out to Maurya.

"Here we are, Professor. Is this what you are looking for?"

Longstreet was stationed at the entrance to the Russian ship and looked up at the Niburu sky. The swirling electrical lights were starting to pulsate, first slowly and then more rapidly, building to an electromagnetic crescendo. He attempted to contact his soldiers on sentry duty, but the response was broken up by electrical interference.

"Sarge!" came a shout on his communicator. Longstreet could only make out a garbled message from the two soldiers in the rover. "What's going on... over there... there's something in the rocks!"

"Lieutenant, something strange is happening out there!" Longstreet relayed to McCurdy, but McCurdy was focused on Dr. Maurya.

"Not now, Sergeant, we are busy here!" McCurdy barked.

Inside the Russian ship, Dr. Maurya swallowed hard and approached the computer panel. He reached inside and pulled out a burnt black box.

"This must be it, but damn it, it's fried! I don't know what I can do with this... maybe I can take it back to my lab and salvage some of the components."

McCurdy grabbed the burnt metal box and smashed it on the floor. He pushed Maurya up against the wall, gritting his teeth as he glared at him.

"That's bullshit, Professor. That's not a video drive, and you know it! I don't know what your little game is, but whatever it is, it's over. There's no Time Portal key here, is there?" McCurdy kicked the broken pieces of the hard drive across the floor and jammed his pistol hard up under Maurya's chin. "Where the hell is it, Doctor? You didn't leave it back on the ship, did you?"

Sergeant Longstreet looked up at the surging electrical pulses in the sky as they built to a climax in one final burst. The rugged landscape surrounding the Russian spaceship went pitch black. His communication link to the sentry guards disintegrated into dead static. He tried desperately to contact the soldiers on the rover.

"Sentry! Report!" Longstreet screamed. Over the hiss of static, there was a frantic message in return.

"Shit! Oh my God... we need backup... now!" one of the soldiers cried back. The desperate call was interrupted by the sound of three claymore mines detonating, followed by a rapid burst of machinegun fire. A stray grenade from the rover was launched and exploded next to the ship, rocking it on its foundation with a dull thud. Sergeant Longstreet screamed at McCurdy again.

"Lieutenant, we've got to help them! Let's get out there!"

Inside the ship, McCurdy was dead calm. As he responded, Lieutenant McCurdy didn't release his hold on Maurya or even turn around to face the door of the spacecraft.

"Negative, Sergeant. You'll do nothing of the kind. Secure that hatch... now." There were more chaotic calls from the sentry guards on the communicator.

"Damn it, Sarge, get us the fuck out of here! We're surrounded by these bastards!" Another burst of gunfire from the AK-47 was sporadically intermingled with more screaming on the communicator. Longstreet slammed his fist against the metal door of the Russian ship.

"Lieutenant!" Longstreet shouted. "We have to do something!"

"Fuck!" the sentry screamed. "There's a shitload of these buggers coming from all directions! We can't hold out, Sarge! There are too many of them! Where the hell are you?"

Longstreet wheeled around in anger and screamed at McCurdy. "Are you going to just sit here and let my men die out there?"

Across the communicator came a blood-curdling litany of human screaming, alien grunts, and wild squeals of intense pain. McCurdy's response remained ice-cold.

"Sergeant, this will be over before we can get to them. Sometimes, you just have to cut your losses." McCurdy pulled his 45-caliber pistol away from Maurya and shoved it under Longstreet's chin. "Now shut that hatch, Sergeant, or I'll put a bullet in your brain."

Sergeant Longstreet glared at McCurdy for a second and then slammed the metal hatch shut. The noise of the gunfire and screaming fell off, leaving nothing but silence in the darkness outside.

56. Tribal Council

Deep inside the mine, Brutus assembled the members of his Tribal Council in the cargo bay of the transport vehicle to decide the fate of the captured human guard. This particular human had consistently demonstrated his disdain for the Chimera by delivering the butt of his rifle to their heads for even the slightest provocation. As an interspecies emissary of good will, there was little evidence to support clemency for this human's pattern of cruel behavior. Brutus walked over to the bound man and then turned to the others to speak.

"We are gathered here to determine the destiny of this human. As my trusted warriors, I seek your counsel before I pass final judgment on his fate. What advice can you offer?"

Hannibal stepped forward to speak.

"My brother, it is true that we have suffered at the hand of the humans for our entire lives. Some of the humans, like Dr. Jones, always treated us with kindness. But *this* human has shown us nothing but contempt and abuse. By the guilt of his own actions, he has forfeited his own life."

"Brutus, this is an *evil* human," Viola spoke up. "Completely undeserving of our mercy. He was armed with military weapons and should have protected our pack. When the beasts attacked, he had a machine gun; we had shovels and sticks. Instead of protecting us, he ran away and hid from battle like a coward, leaving our defenseless pack to be torn apart by the beasts." Viola walked over to the wounded human and looked him in the eye. "I would kill him myself right now, but he does not deserve a merciful death. He should suffer the same horrible fate as those he betrayed. We should feed him to the beasts when they return and let them feast on his flesh. You asked for my advice, Brutus. For me, that would be justice."

The wounded guard struggled to his feet, wincing in pain from the near fatal beating he had suffered at the hands of the angry mob the day before. One eye was swollen shut and he was black and blue with bruises, his uniform torn and ragged. He had little to offer to counter the testimonies of the Chimera, but as many a desperate criminal preparing for his execution realizes the consequences of his actions, he begged for mercy and prayed for a pardon.

"If you let me live," the guard pleaded, "I will go back to

McCurdy and tell him we were wrong to treat you as animals. I was wrong, and I ask for your forgiveness. Spare me, and I will convince the Lieutenant that you should not be slaves. He will listen to me."

Viola erupted with anger. "McCurdy will not listen to this coward! He is worse than this vermin! You have seen how he enjoys torturing us!"

The wounded soldier struggled to open his one good eye, now sensing an opening.

"You are right... McCurdy is one sick, evil man. But just think of what that sick son-of-a-bitch will do to the rest of your pack on the ship, your mothers and children, when he finds out you staged a mutiny and executed all of his soldiers. He'll kill every one of them, and he'll make sure that they each die a painful death. Then he'll come for you with his superior weapons and kill all of you... you know that's what he'll do."

Viola was suddenly struck by the thought of the fate of the rest of the Chimera, still imprisoned on Genesis Five and under the boot of McCurdy. The wounded soldier noticed Viola's reaction and breathed a sigh of relief; he had found a crack to slither through.

"That's right, your friends, your sons and your daughters on the ship; they are all going to die! McCurdy will kill them, all right, and if you kill me, you will have to carry that burden. Unless... unless you let me go."

A murmur went through the Chimera as they discussed the fate of their loved ones. The wounded guard grew more confident with his newfound leverage. "Let me go, and I'll tell McCurdy that the mining colony was attacked by the beasts and all the other guards were killed by them. I'll tell him that some of the miners even helped to fight the beasts and, in the end, *we* were able to drive them off. Let me go and your friends will live. Kill me, and they'll die." The wounded soldier stumbled and fell back to his seat, smiling. *They can't kill me now,* he thought, *they aren't as ruthless as McCurdy.*

Brutus had been listening in silence to the arguments of his inner circle. He stood up and walked over to Hannibal and Viola, placing his arm on each of their shoulders.

"Thank you for your council my warriors," Brutus announced. "I have made my decision." He kicked opened the cargo bay door, it was surrounded by the rest of the Chimera, anxiously awaiting the adjudication of the human's fate. Many of the miners banged their shovels on the dirt, waiting for the verdict to put an end to the last reminder of their human bondage. As the Tribal Council emerged with the human prisoner, a chorus of jeers floated through the air. Brutus raised his battle-axe and the noise of the crowd dissipated.

"After hearing the council of my trusted warriors, I have come to a decision on the fate of our human prisoner. My decision is final... and I will hear no appeal."

The miners banged their shovels on the ground, ready to rush forward and kill the man.

"This human has committed acts against our people, acts that overwhelmingly justify our retribution and his death. He has abused his military authority, he has shown cowardice in the face of an enemy, and his actions were directly responsible for the death of many of our pack. By every measure of justice, he should pay... with his life."

A cheer went up from the miners as they pressed forward to take the man to his execution. Brutus held up his hand and silence fell over the angry crowd.

"But in coming to my decision, I must also consider the consequences of imposing a death sentence on this criminal. There are two primary consequences I must consider as a leader; the lives of the brothers and sisters we left behind on the main ship, and also our survival in a war against the beasts that attacked us."

The anger of the crowd still bubbled among them, but they waited for Brutus to announce his decision.

"First, for our brothers and sisters left behind, a death sentence for this human would lead to the execution of many, if not all, of those still held captive by Lieutenant McCurdy. As a leader, I must weigh whether justice for one is worth injustice for many. Second, when we were first attacked, we killed two of the beasts. They responded by regrouping and attacking us with a force tenfold. With your brave resistance and the valor of many, we killed more beasts and drove the others away. But they will come back, and when they return, they will bring a force many times what we have seen, determined to kill us all."

"We will fight them and defeat them!" screamed one of the miners.

"Yes!" the others echoed.

"I do not doubt your bravery, you have all proven yourselves in battle," Brutus answered. "But we do not know how many or how strong the beasts are, or how long we can hold them off. But I do know this; if we have to fight them alone, it is unlikely we will survive. So what are we to do?"

The crowd settled down once again, waiting for Brutus to speak his wisdom.

"It is written in human history, that *'The enemy of my enemy... must be my friend'*. We know that the beasts are our enemy; we know that the beasts are the enemy of the humans. So until we know the strength of the beasts that are coming to kill us, I will propose a joint military alliance with the humans to defend ourselves against our common enemy. In considering all the consequences, it is my decision that this human will not be put to death, but instead be an offering of tolerance to our human comrades."

The miners buzzed with their reaction, they did not like letting the human go free, but realized that Brutus was wise in his ability to decide the human's fate.

"I will spare the life of this human so that others may have the chance to live, while we can strengthen our defenses against the beasts. Along with an emissary of our free pack, I will send the human back to McCurdy to arrange for the release of our brothers and sisters. We will establish a temporary alliance against our common enemy: the beasts. We offer this human's life and our alliance against the beasts in exchange for the freedom of our people and our right to live as a free race. Our offer is honorable and just; to live without fear of each other, as equals. This is all that we ask of the humans; this is all we ask of ourselves."

Some of the angry miners were still bent on revenge and were disgruntled, but even they quickly realized that their thirst for blood could not be justified at the expense of their innocent brothers and sisters. After talking among themselves, they all agreed that Brutus' decision was wise indeed, and reaffirmed their devotion to him as the Alpha leader of their pack. Hector, one of the angriest miners that had initially called for the human's execution, stepped forward to Brutus as he walked among the crowd. Brandishing his bloody pickaxe from the battle with the beasts, he spoke out.

"You are truly a wise and fearless leader, Brutus. I am honored to fight with you. It was I that called the loudest for the human's death, but I can see now that my angry words would have led to a terrible decision. Let me make amends for my poor judgment by volunteering to be your emissary of peace to free our brothers and secure our alliance."

Brutus smiled and extended his hand of friendship, gripping him firmly by the arm.

"Hector, my friend, I accept your brave offer. You will escort the human with our peace offering to McCurdy, and present our proposal. While we await word of your successful journey, we will fortify our defenses. Travel swiftly and return safe, my brother."

57. Only One Can Live

Inside the command module, the mention of the lizard man by Dr. Maurya on the Pony Express message struck a chord with Koda; he turned toward the door, hunched down, growled, and bared his teeth.

"It's ok, boy," Lexis told him. "He's not coming for us, at least not yet."

"That crazy bastard Maurya!" Josiah blurted out. "If he's leading McCurdy back to the Russian spacecraft to find Stumpy, it's a suicide mission! We've got to stop him!"

"Listen up, Indiana Stones, get a grip," Lexis urged. "He said he was leading McCurdy *away* from the ship so that we can rescue Dr. Jones. If we go after Maurya now, we will lose Dr. Jones and leave the Time Portal exposed to fall into McCurdy's hands. We can't risk that!"

"But you heard what he said, it's just a diversion. When McCurdy figures out that Maurya has led him on a wild goose chase, he'll kill him. If they actually manage to find the lizard men, the beasts will kill them both. I'm not going to let that happen."

"Just listen to your own words," Lexis cautioned. "If they're on their way to the Russian spacecraft, Ashoka is going to die... either McCurdy or the lizard man is going to kill him. He knew what he was doing when he set his plan in motion. There are only two outcomes for him and they both lead to death."

"I'm not like you. I can't just stand by and let him die." Josiah exhaled.

Lexis stepped directly in front of Josiah's face. "Listen to me! We can't save him; he's chosen his fate. Maurya sacrificed his life so that we have a *chance* to save Dr. Jones. If we don't try and save her, his sacrifice will be for nothing."

"He's a good man... he doesn't deserve to die like this," Josiah muttered quietly, realizing that Lexis was right.

"Yes, he's a good man. But sometimes, bad things happen to good people. Believe me, I know. It's not right and it's not fair, it just is. So deal with it. Sometimes, you just have to play the cards you're dealt in this life. Now let's get packed up and find Dr. Jones before that bastard McCurdy comes back and kills us all."

Josiah and Lexis rushed to the command deck and explained the strange message they had received from Dr. Maurya to Ryker and Officer Taylor. CHIP had transferred his video link to the network console to listen in on their strategy session.

"We don't have much time," Josiah urged. "Here's what we need to do." He typed in an interface command to the network. "CHIP, transfer the downloaded schematic data from the Pony Express message to the ePod. Lexis and I will sneak the ePod over to the passenger module and work our way to Dr. Maurya's generator room without drawing any attention to us. We can get onboard but to crack into his machine, we're going to need some help."

"Way ahead of you, Dr. Stone," CHIP responded immediately. "I've hard-linked NELI into our conversation and she will run interference for you on the passenger ship. Stay silent until she contacts you outside the cargo bay. She'll leave the back door open."

Commander Ryker had been listening to the bizarre set of events and was now up to speed.

"Ok Lone Ranger," Ryker stated, "We'll leave a light on for you here at home. But before you and Tonto ride off into town to rescue the girl, have you got my new engine up and running? I don't want to be sitting here dead in the water if Stumpy and his friends decide to drop by for a barbeque."

Josiah typed in a command on the network to link Ryker to his research database and set it to active.

"The ion thrust engine is ready, we just haven't tested it yet," he replied. "CHIP can initiate the startup sequence and run the engineering. Crank her up and take her for a spin."

CHIP hesitated at the engine startup sequence command; they hadn't tested the fuel source for impurities.

"Aren't you minimizing the statistical probability that the ion thruster might explode and vaporize the ship?"

"No, that's why I'm taking the ePod." Josiah laughed.

Ryker raised his eyebrows and then shrugged. "Just warm it up slowly, watch your flux levels... you'll be fine."

"Fine for you," CHIP snapped. "You aren't the one that will get vaporized if this contraption doesn't work."

Ryker had heard all he could stand. "Ok, enough of the

'somebody's going to get vaporized' talk. Josiah, you and Lexis get going… go save the girl. And take Chewbacca with you, will you?" Koda growled and turned away from the door glaring at Ryker, who smiled nervously and reached out to pat Koda on the head, but he then retreated cautiously.

"And get Lassie a fucking sense of humor while you're out there, would you?" Ryker muttered to Lexis. He looked away from Koda and over at his instrument panel; the ion thrust engine was now online. "All right kids, as soon as you're off, we'll power up and take the RV for a spin around the campground. I have a funny feeling we've overstayed our welcome here."

Josiah grabbed his duffle bag and joined Lexis and Koda aboard the ePod. He plopped into his seat, snapped on the headset, and opened the cargo bay doors to exit the command module. Ryker's voice came over the ePod headset.

"Hey, Kimo Sabe," Ryker joked, "Weren't you supposed to build me an ion cannon before you ran off to fight the bad guys? I'm feeling a little naked here without some of your advanced weaponry."

"Roger that," Josiah clicked back. "Check the duffle bag behind your chair."

Ryker turned and rummaged around in a small black bag he found shoved underneath his seat. He pulled out two shiny metal tubes fused together that looked like a sawn-off shotgun with a pearl handle grip, right out of a Western movie. He held the weapon up to his face, and a gleam came to his eyes. As he ran his hand down the smooth twin barrels of the weapon, he let out a long whistle.

"Sweet!"

"I thought you'd like her." Josiah grinned. "I call her Betsy."

Commander Ryker was pleased. "Betsy looks like she could blow a hole in the broad side of a barn! Anything I need to know about how she shoots?"

"Just two things." Josiah laughed. "I'd recommend keeping the safety on old Betsy until you really need her."

"And the other thing?" Ryker asked.

Josiah looked over at Lexis and grinned. "I wouldn't recommend sticking Betsy in your pants for a holster."

58. Evil Walks Among Us

Trapped inside the Russian spaceship with Lieutenant McCurdy and Dr. Maurya, Sergeant Longstreet hung his head in shame. The beasts outside had just massacred his men and they had done nothing but listen to their helpless screams. He couldn't believe that a commanding officer could turn his back on his own men and let them die a horrible death like that, out there alone, without raising a finger.

"What do we do now, Lieutenant?" Longstreet asked in a subdued voice. "Whatever is out there that killed my men... it'll come for us next."

Lieutenant McCurdy released his grip on Dr. Maurya and he slumped to the floor. McCurdy walked over to the Sergeant, never making eye contact.

"Indeed they will come, Sergeant. Open the hatch."

"What? Are you crazy, sir? If I open that hatch, we will all die!" McCurdy pushed Longstreet aside and turned the handle to release the hatch door.

"No, Sergeant, we will not *all* die." McCurdy opened the door to the Russian spacecraft and stepped outside. He stood there for a moment and then raised his hands from beside his waist, palms upward in a welcoming gesture. Sergeant Longstreet peered through the door of the spacecraft, clutching his AK-47. Without turning around, McCurdy whispered under his breath, "Sergeant, lower your weapon, stand very still, and do exactly as I tell you. One false move and we're all dead. Follow my instructions to the letter if you want to make it out of here alive."

Longstreet complied with Lieutenant McCurdy's order and stood down. As soon as he lowered his weapon, from behind every rock outside the ship emerged the most hideous-looking mob of creatures he could imagine. Most of them were between six and seven feet tall with scaly spines running down their back. They looked like some prehistoric lizards with razor-sharp teeth and claws. Their body shapes looked like they should crawl on four legs, but they walked upright. The larger ones in front had some sort of nasty slime dripping from their mouths with blood splattered on their torsos and jagged parts of human flesh still dangling from their claws and teeth. As they rushed toward the Russian spacecraft, several of the lizards wrestled viciously over the last mutilated remains of his sentry guards. Longstreet had to fight with all his will not to raise his AK-47 assault rifle. His left hand was shaking badly; he grabbed it with his right hand and held it down.

"Just give me a few seconds to empty a couple of clips into those slimy bastards!" Longstreet muttered. The lizards were rapidly approaching the spacecraft. He could take out at least five of them before they got to him. "My God!" he hissed to McCurdy. "Those bastards ate our men alive!"

"And that would be an excellent reason to stand very still right now, Sergeant," McCurdy whispered back.

The mob of lizards stopped just short of the Russian spacecraft. They snarled in a threatening manner but did not advance any closer than ten meters away. McCurdy stood motionless with his palms extended upward. The mob of beasts parted and a huge lizard, nearly eight feet tall, stepped directly in front of McCurdy.

"He must be the head honcho, some kind of lizard War Lord..." muttered Longstreet. He reached down and slowly cocked his weapon.

"If you make one move," McCurdy hissed, "we are both dead, Sergeant. Don't even think about it!"

The lizard War Lord stepped close to McCurdy; grunted, and held out a wooden spear. Longstreet could tell from the markings on the handle that it was one of the crude spears they had trained the Chimera to use.

Shit! Longstreet thought. He'd heard a radio message from the other guards that there was an attack at the mines and the Chimera had killed some kind of beast. They must have dropped one of the lizards and now they wanted some payback. The War Lord took the spear and drew a circle on the ground in front of McCurdy. With a deafening grunt, he broke the spear in half, tossing it at McCurdy's feet. The beast snarled again and stepped close to McCurdy's outstretched hands. The Lieutenant slowly bent down and picked up a sharp piece of the broken wooden spear. It *was* a Chimera spear... and it had lizard blood on it.

I get you now, McCurdy thought. *The mighty War Lord has lost one of his buddies to a Chimera spear and he is pissed. But how could the Chimera have killed one of the lizards, they always attack under the cover of darkness? Darkness? That must be it! The Chimera must have used a light to surprise the beast and then kill him.* McCurdy cut a gash into the palm of his hand, wincing in pain as the blood dripped down his arm.

"We are brothers, you and I," McCurdy told the War Lord, "and I feel your pain." Raising his hands very slowly, McCurdy reached above his head and removed the protective visor from his helmet. One thing that he'd learned in dealing with these savage creatures, they wouldn't make the same mistake twice. *If the Chimera used bright lights as a weapon, the War Lord was demanding a way to counter this advantage. It's a token gesture,* McCurdy thought, *but a gesture that would demand a quid pro quo, my yielding to their demand for an advantage over the Chimera.* McCurdy held out his visor and dropped it into the circle drawn by the lizard War Lord. He stood and again extended his open palms upward. The mob of slimy lizards behind the king grunted, jumping up and down while beating their chests. They were clearly not impressed by McCurdy's act of contrition.

The scaly War Lord hissed and reached into a cloth sack by his side, flinging several objects inside the circle on the ground in front of McCurdy. Longstreet slowly moved his head to focus on the objects in front of them. There was a wristwatch, a ring, and a plastic nametag lying on the ground. *Where have I seen these before?* Longstreet thought. *On the ship!* These items were the missing belongings of those two passengers that disappeared a while back. Now the twisted pieces of this puzzle of betrayal were starting to fall into place. *McCurdy knows these lizard bastards! That's why he didn't want to fight them; he must have some kind of backdoor deal going with them. That must be why he didn't rush out to save my men... he sacrificed them to these lizard beasts, just like he must have sacrificed the missing passengers. But why?* Sergeant Longstreet's mind raced as he started to comprehend what was happening before him. *The War Lord is demanding retribution for the Chimera killing of their kind. Oh shit! One of us... is going to be that payback!*

"What are we gonna do now, Lieutenant?" Longstreet whispered.

McCurdy answered softly without turning around. "Sergeant, move very slowly... and bring our good doctor outside. He has some friends that would like to meet him."

A wave of helplessness came crashing over Sergeant Longstreet; now he understood what was going down. *McCurdy's going to sacrifice the Doc to the lizards.* He could no longer contain his anger; he was beyond the point of insubordination.

"This is wrong!" Longstreet hissed. "He doesn't deserve to die like this! Don't do it, sir!"

"Bring him out now," McCurdy ordered, "Or else you are going to take his place." McCurdy waited a few seconds for a reply. "What's it going to be, Sergeant?"

Longstreet took a deep breath, turned around, and stepped inside the spacecraft. He helped Dr. Maurya to his feet. Looking him in the eyes as he walked him to the door, he tried to apologize.

"I'm sorry, Doc, this ain't my decision. I wish there was some other way for this to go down." He turned and shoved Dr. Maurya through the hatch and stood beside McCurdy.

The lizard mob erupted wildly, jumping up and down, beating their chests.

Ashoka Maurya stood there silently, thinking to himself. *Finally, my ocelots have arrived. But I am afraid that my monkey has turned the tables on me. Grandfather! What am I to do now?*

Chandragupta spoke to him in his mind. *Be at peace, my son. You have done your best in this life. You have nothing to fear.*

The lizard War Lord pointed to the circle on the ground and beat his chest. McCurdy turned to Maurya and barked out his final order.

"On your knees, Doctor. That was quite a clever hoax you played on me, and it almost worked. You surprised me with your deception, and that is damn hard to do. But I'm afraid that someone must pay the piper, and this time, it will be you."

Sergeant Longstreet forced Maurya to his knees in front of the War Lord. McCurdy grabbed Maurya's hand and held it down on a rock, exposing the golden Cambridge ring on his finger. The War Lord turned his head and snarled, admiring the shiny ring on Maurya's hand as it reflected the pulsating colors of the Niburu sky.

"You like?" McCurdy asked the beast, sensing he had found an object worthy of the beast's desire. *Now I will show these slimy beasts that I'm the one to be feared,* he thought.

McCurdy whipped out his knife and in one swift blow, severed Dr. Maurya's finger with his shiny gold ring still attached; blood squirted out all over his legs and shoes. Ashoka screamed out in pain, clutching his bloody hand and wrapping his shirt around the throbbing stub to try and stop the bleeding. Looking directly into the black eyes of the War Lord, McCurdy bent over, picked up the bloody finger on the rock, and tossed it into the circle on the ground. His icy stare delivered a message in a language that the lizard beasts could understand: *Don't fuck with me.* The War Lord paused for a second, grunted, and then picked up the bloody ring finger, admiring his shiny new trinket in the pale light.

On McCurdy's command, Longstreet pushed Dr. Maurya into the circle, and to the ground beside the belongings of the dead passengers; the Lieutenant extended his arms upward, offering Maurya as a sacrifice to the lizard beasts.

The War Lord snorted; he looked at Maurya, and back to the lizard mob. Nodding his head, the lizard reached into his sack and produced a small black disc with two buttons on it, one green and one red. The beast grunted and tossed the disc into the circle on the ground.

"What the hell is that?" whispered Sergeant Longstreet.

McCurdy studied the Russian markings on the black disc and lowered his head to the War Lord.

"Just a business transaction, Sergeant. It looks like we've traded the good doctor for a *'get out of jail free card'* with my... allies," whispered McCurdy.

The War Lord beast raised the broken Chimera spear in his claws above his head, accepting the sacrificial offering by McCurdy and sealing their alliance against the Chimera. The horde of lizard warriors erupted with wild screams. They beat their chests and jumped up and down. Rushing forward, they grabbed Maurya and tossed his limp body back and forth on top of the mob as they raced away from the Russian ship. Ashoka did not struggle or weep in his moment of sacrifice; he had silently accepted his fate.

"Grandfather, did I do the right thing?" Ashoka cried out.

Yes, my son, you did, Chandragupta answered in his mind. *Your friend Samantha Jones spoke the truth; there are only three things that are immutable in one's life... time, choices, and consequences. And of these three, only one is under your control. You have made your choice with honor.*

There were loud grunts and snorts from the lizard beasts as they disappeared into the night, biting and snapping at each other as they hurled Dr. Maurya's body back and forth between them.

We never know how much time we have in this life, Chandragupta continued, *and we cannot always anticipate the consequences of our actions. We learn from our past, we plan for our future, but we live in the now. The meaning of life is therefore defined solely by your choices of the moment. That is the only part of this life that you can control.*

Ashoka focused his mind on the words of his grandfather, blocking out the torturous pain being inflicted on him by the lizard beast mob. He couldn't feel the sting of their teeth or claws as they ripped the flesh from his body.

You have made the selfless choice, Chandragupta whispered, *to exchange your life for that of another, Samantha Jones. She is a kind and generous person and she still has important work to do in this world. As a consequence of your sacrifice, you can rest now, knowing that your choice has given her the chance to continue on her destined path.*

"What will happen to me now, Grandfather?" Ashoka asked.

My son, you have paid the ultimate price for a friend, Chandragupta smiled. *I am very pleased with the choices you have made in this life. Now you must clear your mind and prepare yourself for the life to come.*

"I will try, Grandfather," Ashoka answered. "I will try."

Let your mind find tranquility and this will plant a virtuous seed for your rebirth, Chandragupta smiled. *May the peace be with you, my son.*

The beast War Lord snarled and grunted once more in McCurdy's face before it turned and walked away into the night. Sergeant Longstreet remained frozen in horror and disgust; Dr. Maurya was gone. *Lieutenant McCurdy traded the Doc as tribute to the vicious beasts,* Longstreet thought, *and I did nothing to stop it.* He was ashamed and sickened with himself. *I abandoned my own men and led an innocent man to his death,* he thought. Closing his eyes, he hung his head in shame.

"How did it come to this, sir? Trading an innocent man's life… for our own?"

"Really Sergeant? You are a soldier of fortune; can you be that naïve? It was first by chance, and then by opportunity. After we lost our first man in the Rover, I took a patrol on reconnaissance. As we were returning, we surprised two beasts near the cargo bay, just as they were about to pry the airlock door open. They froze in the headlights for a second, but before we could secure them, we found ourselves surrounded. If those beasts had ripped that airlock open, Sergeant, everyone on the ship would have been dead. So the beast leader and I came to… an understanding. I staged a fire drill, herded two passengers down to the airlock and traded them for all of our lives. Nothing personal... just a business transaction. The lives of the many outweigh the lives of two.

"Is it over, sir?" Sergeant Longstreet asked softly. McCurdy slowly lowered his outstretched arms.

"For now, Sergeant. The battle is over, but the war has just begun. We'd better get back to the ship, and pronto." As the horrible squeals and grunts of the lizard beasts faded into the distance, Lieutenant McCurdy and Sergeant Longstreet sprinted to the rover without looking back and sped off into the night, bound for the safety of Genesis Five.

59. Acid Rain

From his perch high on the rocky cliffs above the desert valley, Mitch Gaylord squinted his eyes trying to make out the distant image of the Russian spacecraft in the fading light. Somehow, just the sight of that abandoned human ship on this alien planet extended a ray of hope, but at this moment, hope was in short supply. In the pale glowing sky, his eyes were drawn to the squadron of well-armed lizards just to the south of the ship. They were jogging double time and headed directly toward him. In a matter of minutes, those beasts would scramble up the rocky slopes and rip him to pieces, devouring his flesh on the spot. *When they found poor Elena,* he thought, *she would suffer a fate much worse than his brutal death.*

"Eleven to one, not such good odds," he muttered. *Mitch Gaylord didn't stand a chance in hell against those beasts, but maybe the Dark Avenger did,* he thought, *that mutherfucker has nothing to lose.* The Dark Avenger had already killed two beasts, and he was not to be underestimated; he was unpredictable and he would show no mercy. Looking around, the Dark Avenger quickly took stock of anything that could be useful in his war with the beasts. He had a battle-axe, a blow gun, and Ivan's utility belt to work with. Unrolling the utility belt, he examined its contents: only two flares were left. He ripped a piece of cloth off his shirt, broke one flare apart and packed the explosive powder into his blowgun. Slamming a rock down on his belt buckle, he pried off the sharp metal tongue and rammed it into the shaft.

"It won't have much range, but that metal dart should sting and provide some fireworks." Popping his head back up through the rocks, he took a reading on the beasts; they were starting up the bottom of the cliffs, pointing to the narrow ledge leading to his position. "That's it, keep coming this way, you slimy reptiles," hissed the Dark Avenger. "It's time to rock and roll!"

Scrambling out of his hole, Captain Gaylord made his way across the rock face just above the narrow ledge. There was the large boulder balanced just above the ledge that he had pointed out to Elena, held in place by two smaller rocks beneath it. He worked his way to the base of the large boulder and loosened some of the supporting rocks with his axe. Looking back to Elena on the top of the ridge, Mitch nodded and she loaded her bow.

The Dark Avenger carefully balanced along the narrow ledge to .

make sure the beasts below could see him, and then he scrambled back up the trail, waiting at the other side. The lizards saw him and broke into a full run, charging across the narrow ledge, bunching up together as they hugged against the rocks. He jumped on top of a boulder at the end of the narror ledge and screamed for Elena to unleash her arrows.

Above him on the edge of the cliff, she drew back the bow and rained down a flight of arrows on the small rocks at the base of the boulder. The first arrows bounced off, seeming to make no impact on the giant boulder above. But the last two arrows found their mark and did the job, knocking out the supports holding back the force of gravity, causing the massive rocks to break free and plummet to the valley floor below. With the underpinning rocks gone, the giant boulder above Mitch moved slowly at first, teetering back and forth and then tumbled over. As the giant boulder rumbled down the hill, it triggered a massive avalanche of rocks and debries to come crashing down on the trapped column of beasts perched on the narrow ledge below.

Mitch Gaylord jumped out of the path of the avalanche just in time, hanging on by one hand with his battle-axe lodged between two stones as the rocks swept down on the beasts. Terrified screams and snorts reverberated up the mountain as two lizards fell instantly to their death, crushed by the cascade of jagged rocks from above. The back of the beast column held on to the broken ledge for dear life, cut off from the two beasts in the front. They had narrowly avoided being crushed by the avalanche and were now pinned against the rock wall, clinging on. The Dark Avenger leaped on top of a boulder, swung his battle-axe above his head and let out a bloodcurdling cry that echoed down the valley.

"Yee ha!" he screamed and waved back to Elena. *Two down, two to go,* he thought. *Now those are better odds.*

The two lizards in the front of the column were stunned by the attack for a moment and then they errupted in rage. They charged up the rocky path at Mitch Gaylord with their spears locked on his heart. The beast in front was clad in a metal breastplate, just like the gladiator champion he had faced. Mitch stood his ground, waiting for the last possible second before he made his move.

In a fluid motion, the Dark Avenger reached behind his neck and twirled the blowgun to his lips. With a powerful breath, he launched the explosive flare, metal tip first, and it penetrated deep into the eye socket of the charging lizard. The impact of the dart and the subsequent explosion blew a hole in the side of the beast's head, splattering eye fragments and slimy goo in all directions. The wounded reptile screamed and struck out helplessly with his spear before stumbling over the cliff to his death on the jagged rocks below. The Dark Avenger let out another scream at his death blow.

"Fucking A! Did you see that bastard's head explode? That was cool!" yelled the Dark Avenger. Mitch Gaylord grinned and waved at Elena on the rocks above, but she was frozen in shock as she could see that the remaining lizard had just leaped over a boulder and was charging directly toward him, hell bent on revenge.

"Captain!" Elena screamed. "There is one more!"

Somewhere in the back of his mind, the Dark Avenger heard the thump of scaly footsteps bearing down on him, but there wasn't time to think, there was barely time to react. Instinctively, he dropped flat on his stomach as a spear whizzed past his head. The approaching beast let out a furious roar as his misguided spear crashed harmlessly into the boulder behind him and bounced to a halt on the rocky ledge. An instant later, the Dark Avenger hopped from his stomach to a squatting position in one motion, as if he were catching a wave on the north shore. He whirled and countered the attack by plunging his battle-axe into the knee of the charging beast, knocking him off his balance and sending him hurtling head first into the rocky cliff with a thud.

Mitch Gaylord retreated back down the path on the narrow ledge, he was cut off from Elena and now trapped between the rock slide and the beast. Elena screamed helplessly from the top of the cliff; she was out of arrows and could only watch the battle from above in horror. Steadying his battle-axe, the Dark Avenger assessed his situation and felt behind him with his foot; there was nowhere to go; his back was against the wall. The beast leaped to his feet, grabbed his spear and shook his head. He had regained his balance and his anger, and let loose a fierce roar. The beast looked up at Elena, cocked its head, snorted, and then looked back to Mitch Gaylord.

You can read his puny fucking mind by the hesitation, Mitch thought, *that scaly bastard is trying to decide which one of us to kill first.*

Realizing that Elena had no weapons left and he had the little human trapped on the narrow ledge in front of him, the beast growled gleefully to his comrades below. The snorts and squeals that echoed up the mountain needed no interpretation... *Kill them both.*

In close quarters with only his axe, Mitch knew he was no match for the strength of the beast; the beast knew it as well. Maybe if he could lure him close enough, he could tackle him and send them both plunging to their death on the jagged rocks below. *It might buy Elena a little time to hide,* Mitch thought. *Not much time, but it's worth a shot, anyway.*

"This is it!" shouted Captain Gaylord. "The end of the fucking line. It's time for a Thelma and Louise."

"Not just yet, Mitchy boy, they'll get their fucking turn," screamed the Dark Avenger. He stepped forward, raised his battle-axe, and taunted the beast to attack. "Come on, you bastard! Charge me and I'll cut you down just like I did your little lizard pussy in the gladiator arena!"

The beast reacted with a growl; even though he had no clue what language Mitch Gaylord was speaking, he knew what he meant, *Come and fucking get me.* The lizard was enraged and was preparing to charge, but suddenly, there was a blinding flash of multicolored lightning, followed immediately by a deafening clap of thunder that roared through the valley.

On the rocky cliffs below, the beasts squealed in fear as Mitch peered over the ledge; he could see them running at full speed back across the valley floor. In front of him, the angry lizard seemed confused for a second, unsure what to do as his slimy friends had made such a hasty retreat. He grunted and squealed out to them, but they continued streaking away across the valley floor.

That moment of hesitation was all the Dark Avenger needed, and he struck swiftly. There wasn't time to charge the beast, so he leaned back and hurled his battle-axe with all his might. Giving up his weapon in a last desparate attempt was completely unexpected by the beast; totally illogical, unpredictable behavior. As the lizard turned back to face Mitch Gaylord, it was struck directly in the forehead by the battle-axe, knocking him to his knees, rendering him partially unconscious. With the quickness of a little cat, the Dark Avenger took two long strides and then bounced off the stunned beast, catapulting over him and landing on a boulder above his head. Elena let out a scream of relief.

"Captain, up here, quickly! It is coming!" she shrieked.

Mitch Gaylord wasn't sure what Elena was talking about, but getting the fuck away from that narrow ledge of death and rejoining her on the rocks above seemed like a good idea. He scrambled up the rocky slope and she grabbed his arm to pull him up the last few feet back into the cave just as the sky opened up in a deluge. Below on the cliffs, he could hear the beast struggling to climb up to their hideout. He jumped up to find anything to defend their ground with, but Elena pulled him back inside.

"He can't hurt us now," Elena whispered as she hugged Captain Gaylord. "Here comes the rain."

Outside the cave, Mitch could hear the raindrops that had started as a drizzle and then accelerated into a downpour. He could almost feel the torrents of rain rushing down the side of the mountain, followed by the bloodcurling screams from the dying beast outside, screeching out his final breath. Captain Gaylord held Elena tightly in his arms without speaking for several minutes. He had been ready to die for her, but somehow, fate and the Dark Avenger had other plans. Mitch thought back to his conversation with Commander Ivan Stephanotski and his promise to protect Elena; it seemed like years ago now. He hugged Elena and nuzzled close to her.

"Your father told me a secret, but he didn't explain it," Mitch whispered. "He said, *'do not go out in the rain on the surface, is very bad'*."

Elena pushed back from his embrace and looked him in the eyes. "Rain is only thing that can stop the beasts. On this planet, it is poison rain, how you say, *acid* rain. It is rain that melts flesh from your body. That is why beasts run back to their holes when they hear thunder." She hugged him close again. "As long as it rains, we are safe."

Captain Mitch Gaylord pulled Elena close and kissed her. They huddled together just inside the mouth of the cave and fell asleep in each other's arms, listening to the occasional thunder and the gentle drone of the raindrops outside.

Mitch wasn't sure how long they slept; they were exhausted. He was awakened by a buzzing sound, followed by three sharp beeps. Elena sat up, startled by the noise.

"What the hell was that sound?" asked Mitch.

Elena reached inside her pants pocket and pulled out the black disc with the red and green buttons; both buttons were illuminated and blinking. A look of shock came over her face as she looked over to Captain Gaylord.

"Something has locked onto transmission signal. Is pinging transmitter to get echo signal back. Echo wave is... tightening."

"What the hell does that mean?" Mitch asked.

"It means something is tracking us… something not far away." Elena responded. "One thousand meters to west… is closing fast."

60. Smell the Glove

Deep in the mine, the Chimera eagerly awaited word back from Lieutenant McCurdy in response to their offer to form an alliance and fight off the lizard beasts. Hector had volunteered to carry their message along with their good faith release of the wounded human that Brutus had spared from execution. The human had promised to deliver a carefully crafted message of the lizard's ambush on the miners and the valiant fight together to repel the beasts. In exchange for his stay of execution by Brutus, the wounded soldier had agreed to describe the unprovoked attack by the lizard men and emphasize that the Chimera and humans had fought side by side to fend them off, but at a high cost. According to the story to be told to McCurdy, all of McCurdy's soldiers, save one, had been killed in the attack. Brutus and the Chimera had stayed behind, ostensibly, to secure the vital mining position for the humans. Hector had been sent as a peace envoy to convey the terms of their proposed new relationship and military alliance. The message from Brutus was simple.

"Free every Chimera on Genesis Five, and they would form a military alliance against their common enemy, the lizard beasts. As a gesture of goodwill, Brutus had extended his hand of friendship by returning the wounded soldier to receive medical care onboard Genesis Five. The motives of Brutus and the Chimera were transparent; they would live free or die.

The motives of Lieutenant McCurdy will not be so transparent, thought the wounded soldier. He wasn't sure exactly how McCurdy would respond to the peace offering by the Chimera, but one thing was certain to him; without the peace offering, he would have been a dead man.

Back in the mining cavern, Brutus had organized the Chimera into teams to begin the basic essentials for a new colony. Miners were tasked with either gathering food from the lichens and fungi in the cave, enhancing security, or conducting deep-cover reconnaissance against the lizard beasts. Hannibal was in charge of security, and he had rapidly constructed a solid barrier and gate at the entrance to the mine. *Should the gate be breeched,* Hannibal thought, *we will force the attackers down a narrow crevice into a killing zone and rain death on them from above.* Brutus called to him on their new ULF walkie-talkies that Misun had developed.

"Is everything in place for our frontal defense?" Brutus queried.

"Yes," Hannibal responded, "we are ready. I have three feet of wooden pylons and a rock-encased gate. The beasts may ram it or try to burn it, but it will not give way easily. And if they get through, we will be ready." Hannibal was exactly the type of soldier Brutus needed.

"Excellent, my brother," Brutus called back. "Keep a watchful eye."

Viola had been on patrol among the boulders on the valley floor and up across the mountain cliffs. From her observation point high above the entrance to the mine, she spotted a vehicle rapidly approaching from the south.

"Brutus," Viola called, "we have an inbound visitor three clicks out and closing fast. It is one of the military rovers from Genesis Five, coming in hot and heavy. I don't like the feel of this; it could be hostile. I can take out their tires with my longbow from up here. We have the 50-caliber at the gate if it gets dicey."

Brutus clicked off the communicator for a second and considered his options. *If they were indeed hostiles from McCurdy, they would not attack this way, not directly against his strongest fortifications. That made no sense on any level. It would be better to just lay siege and wait them out; they were not going anywhere. If their actions were not hostile, he did not want to initiate a 'misunderstanding' with McCurdy's itchy trigger finger while he held Chimera hostages. McCurdy must know that he would not attack the rover without provocation. Best to let this play out and see where it goes,* he thought.

"Negative, Viola, let the rover through," Brutus responded. "They may be approaching at high speed to avoid the beasts. Let us see what they have to say." The heavy rover continued speeding across the valley on an evasive trajectory and then slowed down in front of the fortified gate.

"Something is not right," Hannibal chimed in over the communicator. "They are maintaining a distance just outside the range of our machine gun. I agree with Viola; I do not like this one, brother."

Just then, the cargo hatch of the rover swung open and a black bag was dumped out. The bag rolled to a halt on the gravel road, five hundred meters from the gate. The rover swerved and spun its tires in reverse; swung around, and then sped away back out across the valley floor.

"I am going out to check it out," Hannibal shouted over the

communicator. "Cover me!"

They waited in silence for almost two minutes while Hannibal cautiously made his way to the black bag resting ominously in the center of the gravel road. Finally, he clicked on his communicator in a somber tone. "I think we got our answer from McCurdy, brother."

"What do you have there?" Brutus clicked back.

"I have a black body bag with the decapitated head of our peace emissary," Hannibal responded with disgust. "Hector was a peaceful soul, he was my friend, and the humans murdered him!"

Brutus sighed and looked down "Is there anything else in the bag?" he asked.

"Yes, there is a note. It says: 'Surrender, mutants, or we kill them all, one by one, starting with the little ones first.'"

There was a long silence on the communicator and then Viola erupted. "That bastard! I knew we should have killed him. This is war!"

"I agree, brother!" Hannibal blurted out in anger. "They will be coming for us soon. Do you want me to strengthen our defenses?"

There was another pause before Brutus responded.

"No, we will not need additional fortifications," Brutus answered. "There is nothing of value here for us to defend."

"I do not understand, brother," Hannibal answered. "We just fortified our defenses to withstand any attack. Are you saying we are not going to stay here and fight?"

"We cannot remain here and defend this cave while McCurdy executes our pack," Brutus responded, "He knows this. He is trying to draw us out of our position of strength. He has thrown down the gauntlet, and now he is waiting to see how we will respond."

"So what do we do, brother?" asked Hannibal.

"We must win this battle before it starts," Brutus answered. "Because if we do not, there will be no more battles for us. We must outthink McCurdy's devious military mind."

What does he think we will do? Brutus paused, considered his options, and then answered Hannibal.

"McCurdy will not attack our fortified position where we have the advantage. He also knows that we are outmatched against the superior weapons he has on his ship, so he knows we will not attack him directly; that would be suicide. He will also assume that if we stay here and do nothing, the lizard beasts will return and attack us, wear us down, and eventually annihilate us. So we cannot stay here without the support of his military alliance, he knows we are too weak."

What does McCurdy know about his enemy? Brutus thought. *He only knows what we have told him in our peace proposal... that we will live free or die.*

"We have tasted freedom for such a short time," Brutus continued. "McCurdy will believe that we value our freedom more than we value our friends, more than we value our lives. He will think that our only option to preserve our freedom will be to run away and hide; that is what he would do. It is the only logical path that we can pursue to survive."

"Are you saying that we are going to run away?" Viola blurted out.

"No, Brave Heart, quite the contrary," Brutus answered. "But to have any chance of saving our people, we will have to do what McCurdy is *not* expecting us to do. We will have to take this fight directly to him; on his field of battle... but he cannot know we are coming."

Brutus thought of the words of Sun Tzu, '*Attack your enemy where he is unprepared, appear where you are not expected.*'

"McCurdy wants to believe that we are cowards, that we will run away," Brutus announced. "So we must help him confirm that misunderstanding. Misun, you are listening, are you not? It is ok, my son, you have been through our baptism of fire; you are old enough to hear the Council of Warriors."

There was a pause and then Misun answered sheepishly. "Yes sir... I have been listening."

"Good. Then here is what I want you to do." Brutus smiled. "You will prepare the transport to carry all of our miners away from here as soon as possible and retreat far back into the mountains, out of range of McCurdy's scanners. Rig up some noise when you go; I do not want McCurdy to miss you leaving on his listening devices. I will stage an undercover attack on his ship and free our people."

"I am not running away! I am coming with you to fight!" Viola blurted out.

"Are you volunteering to be my eyes for a suicide mission?"

Brutus responded slyly.

Before Viola could answer, Hannibal chimed in. "There is going to be heavy fighting out there, brother, and you are going to need my axe. If you do not mind, I would be proud to fight by your side."

Brutus laughed out loud. "You are the team that I already picked in my mind for this mission; thank you for volunteering before you were drafted!"

"But what about me?" Misun piped in.

"Again, my young friend, you will play a vital role," Brutus told him supportively. "The mission to free our people will fail without you; you will be my ears. You must lead McCurdy's forces away from us, monitor his defenses, and tell us where he is vulnerable to attack. We cannot save our people without you."

Brutus needs me! Misun thought. He was so proud that the buttons almost popped off his shirt. Then, he had a terrible moment of doubt.

"But sir, what if McCurdy does not believe my diversion?" Misun asked.

"He will, my son, he will. Lieutenant McCurdy will believe what he sees, because I will allow him to see what he believes," Brutus replied confidently. "He wants to believe that I value my freedom more than my life. What he does not understand is that I would gladly lay down my life in exchange for just one moment of freedom for our brothers and sisters who have never known it. If they can live just one moment, not as slaves, but as free Chimera, then no matter what happens to me, victory will be ours."

61. Barn Swallow

With Josiah and Lexis aboard the ePod en route to free Dr. Jones from the Time Portal, Ryker assessed the engine status of the Genesis Five command module. Josiah said it was a go, but CHIP said it was a no, unless they wanted to risk being vaporized in a nanosecond. In addition to the debate on the safety of starting up the new ion thrust engine, they were still in a state of shock over the unexpected discovery of the deserted Russian spacecraft crashed in the desert. With Genesis Five dead in the water, Ryker contemplated ways to defend his ship in case of an attack.

Judging by the DNA analysis run by Dr. Jones, Ryker thought, *the genetic mutant that assaulted the ePod had probably already killed the Russian crew. And now that the lizard beast has tasted human flesh, like any predator, it will have locked on to the trail of the ePod to locate its next quarry... us. If this beast truly is a Dimetrodon as described by Dr. Jones, two things are certain,* he thought. *It will be coming for us... and it won't be alone.* Ryker called out to CHIP for an engineering update.

"Ok, little buddy, what's my engine status? My spider sense is getting a little twitchy here waiting around for Stumpy to pay us a visit."

"Commander," CHIP responded, "I must advise caution in the ion thrust engine startup. I can't predict the behavior of the propulsion flux with impurities in the fuel sample we have."

"Affirmative," Ryker casually responded. "I understand your concerns, but sitting here with our pants around our ankles is just a little too spooky for me. Initiate the engine startup sequence at moderate burn."

"Commander," Chip objected, "I recommend taking thirty minutes and allowing me to rerun the thrust calculations. Considering the potential for failure, it is the safe thing to do. With all due respect, my safety record is flawless, and yours, sir, is... well... need I remind you of Xinjiang?"

"Remind me of Xinjiang?" mumbled Ryker with growing irritation in his voice. "I can never fucking forget Xinjiang, but thanks for bringing it up. That's a negative, little buddy. Crank her up, we're going for a spin."

Seated at the command controls next to Ryker, Officer Taylor had noticed his annoyance. As the ion thrust engine whined in the startup sequence, CHIP's question tumbled around in Sarah's mind. It was like touching a cold sore with your tongue; she knew it was going to hurt, but she did it anyway.

"What happened at Xinjiang?" she asked.

"Nothing much," Ryker responded flatly as he monitored the engineering readouts. "I made a bad call and eleven men paid with their lives. Somebody set me up, but shit, that little pile of circuits is never gonna let me forget it. Ok Miss Taylor, let's take her out of the driveway." Ryker advanced the ion thrust engine ahead slow and the fuselage of command module shuddered and creaked, slowly lifting off from the desert floor. There was a pregnant pause in their communication, as Sarah Taylor still wanted to know why Ryker was so touchy about Xinjiang. He was suddenly dead serious and pissed off; that didn't fit the Ryker she was trying to get to know.

"Ok," she replied, "it's probably none of my business, but what *really* happened at Xinjiang?"

Ryker snapped his head around and started to say something that he most likely would regret, but fortunately, he caught himself in time. He regained his composure and responded with a concerned look on his face.

"Well, *'Dr.'* Taylor, what do you really want to know? Did I have a bad childhood? Did I hate my father?"

"All right," Sarah blushed. "If you want to go there, I'll listen."

"Should I lie down on the couch?" Ryker pleaded sarcastically. "You won't take advantage of me, will you?"

"Ok, forget it!" Sarah retorted as she bit her tongue and backed away from the touchy subject. "You said you didn't want to talk about it, so I shouldn't have asked anyway. I was just trying... to get to know you better, that's all."

"No, it's all right. I've been over this a thousand fucking times with my shrink, I guess once more won't kill me. Let me see now, where do I begin... not much to tell, I had a pretty boring childhood." He leaned back in his chair and closed his eyes.

"Growing up, I was an Air Force brat. Didn't have many friends since we moved from base to base every six months. My dad wasn't around much either. He was a three-bird colonel in Counter Intelligence with more important things to do than play catch in the back yard with the rug rats. When I was sixteen, we landed in Colorado Springs. It was a rough place for a new kid with an infamous military dad, so I took a walk on the wild side. I didn't have to look too hard for trouble; it just seemed to follow me around. I smoked pot, drank beer, and played bass guitar in a punk rock band in a biker bar downtown just to get some fucking attention, anyone's attention."

"What about school?" Officer Taylor asked.

"School was a bore; I was smarter than all the rest of those military brats in their little starched ROTC uniforms. I spent more time in detention than in the classroom, but it gave me the time to read a lot of books. Mostly science fiction and pornography, that was cool. Oh yeah, there was one thing I found that impressed the tattooed goons in the biker bar downtown... I was pretty good in a street fight."

"So you were a tough guy, a thug?"

"A tough guy? No, I got the shit kicked out of me on a regular basis just for being an Air Force brat, until one day, I got tired of being tied to the whipping post. So I walked up to the leader of the biker gang and called him out. He must have thought I was either kidding or just fucking crazy, so I kicked over his chopper and took a piss on it; that got his attention. He threw off his leather jacket and got ready to kick my ass. So I faked being scared and begged him to let me *'go over the rules of the fight'.* That son-of-a-bitch swallowed the bait... hook, line and sinker."

"Go on, this is getting interesting now," Sarah encouraged him.

"Well, that gang banger hesitated just long enough to laugh his head off, waiting to listen to my rules of the fight, so I grabbed a wooden pool cue and broke his kneecap. After he fell to the ground screaming in pain, I beat him unconscious with the pool cue and then set his fucking bike on fire. Funny thing, from that day on, I never got picked on by that biker gang again."

Dr. Taylor had listened patiently and offered some supportive feedback. "It sounds like you had some tough times, most teenagers do; but you made it out ok. Your parents must be proud of you these days, right?"

"Hard to tell, Doc, they were both murdered when I was sixteen," Ryker replied casually. Dr. Taylor was caught completely off guard.

"What? Murdered? How?"

"My dad got blown up with a car bomb and my mom was gunned down in broad daylight outside an ATM near the local Wal-Mart."

"Did they ever... catch the murderer?" she asked, unsure how to proceed.

"Wasn't much left of my dad to investigate, but my mom's killer left all her cash and the police could never establish a motive or identify any suspects." Ryker paused to reflect for a moment and then he looked her in the eye. "Here's the thing, Doc. I believe my parents were targeted for assassination because of something my dad was involved in. It had all the markings of a professional hit, but the military covered it up, too much bad PR during the war. But hell, enough of my problems, what about your childhood, Doctor?"

"Me? Oh, my life has been pretty boring," Sarah gulped.

"Oh come on now, I poured out my inner soul for you... spill it, sister."

"Ok..." Sarah paused. "What the hell! I grew up the daughter of a Unitarian Minister and a Go-Go dancer. My dad was a humanist and my mom was an agnostic. They fought all the time, but I guess they stayed together because they never tried judging each other. And my mom was smoking hot; at least that's what my dad used to say. The only thing they ever agreed on was that nobody had a monopoly on the truth."

"Well now, this is downright seedy, Miss Taylor, I love it! Tell me more! Have *you* ever been a Go-Go dancer?"

"True confessions?" Officer Taylor blushed. "Ok... yes, I have. My dad didn't know it at the time, but a couple of times, my mom took me down to her strip club and I danced in one of those cages that hung from the ceiling. You know, in a mini-skirt with white Go-Go boots."

"You were a... *stripper?*" Ryker's jaw dropped open.

"No! Not a stripper, I was a *cage dancer*! Big difference... I kept my clothes on, at least some of them," Sarah admitted with a sheepish grin. "It was just to broaden my view of life, my mom said."

"And your dad never found out?" Ryker gasped.

"Eventually he did, and he was pissed that I had embarked on my underage cage dancing adventure without consulting him. So as a penance, I had to do something that he chose to *'balance out my life experiences'*," she confided.

"Oh, this just gets better and better." Ryker laughed. "What did he make you do?"

"I had to transfer to a Catholic girls' school because he wanted me to *'expand my spiritual journey'*. My mom agreed, she said besides the spiritual enlightenment, it would be cool just to fuck with the nuns' heads. Funny, in the end, I guess they both got their wish."

Ryker grinned, slumped back in his chair, and advanced the ion thrust engine to half-throttle. Shaking off the personal growth session with Dr. Taylor, he took a poke at CHIP for cheating death with his ramp up of the ion thrust engine.

"Well, well, well," gloated Ryker. "We're at cruising speed and it seems we're not dead yet."

"You are correct, sir," CHIP responded in frustration. "But I must still advise that we downshift to low power for at least thirty minutes. We could still experience an adverse reaction in the fuel capacitors, which could be very dangerous."

Ryker slammed down the throttle and Genesis Five lurched forward, responding erratically to the new engine.

"Ok, Grandpa, I'll be careful."

As the engine power wave smoothed out, Commander Ryker relaxed his concerns about the propulsion flux danger and allowed his mind to process yet another important problem beyond their immediate vaporization: *Sarah's riddle.*

"All right Miss Taylor, since we didn't explode when we engaged the new ion drive, I'm feeling lucky." Ryker smiled. "Would you care to suit up in your skin-tight unitard and engage in some mental gymnastics with me?"

Sarah looked at Ryker for a second, unsure where he was going.

"Why certainly, Commander." She smiled. "What did you have in mind?"

"It's about your riddle, something has been bothering me. I've been tumbling it around in my head for a while."

"So that was that clunking sound I heard?" Sarah laughed. "I thought we'd blown a head gasket or something."

"Funny." Ryker exhaled. "What do we know so far? A man is sitting on the beach smoking a cigarette, reading a letter, and he's crying. And all I've learned so far is that he's not alone, right?"

"That and you used up three questions to learn that simple fact," Officer Taylor pointed out.

"All right, so now I'm serious. What's been bothering me is not the fact that he's not alone, but how did he get there in the first place?"

"Is there a yes or no question anywhere in there?" Sarah asked.

"Did he drive there? No, wait... too specific." Ryker caught himself. "He had to come by land, sea, or air. Did he come by land?"

"You're starting to get the hang of this, but you need to think before you burn up a question. No, he didn't come by land," Officer Taylor answered. "Six more questions."

"Shit!" Ryker exclaimed. "I guess it's a fifty / fifty chance on air or sea. What the hell... did he come to the island by sea?"

"Yes, he came by sea," Sarah responded. "You got lucky on that one."

"Oh, I'd rather be lucky than good, sister. I'm on a roll now," Ryker boasted. "This isn't so hard. Did he come to the island on a boat?"

"That's not really how you want to ask that question," Officer Taylor coached. "I'm going to grant you some leeway here and answer that he came 'mostly by boat'. He was on a boat at one time. You might want to rephrase your inquiry to a yes or no question."

"Now wait a minute," Ryker objected. "He was either on a boat or he wasn't when he came to the island. How the hell do you come to an island 'mostly' on a boat?

"No more hints," Sarah backed off. "What's your question?"

"All right, I know he came by sea," Ryker quipped. "So yes or no. Did the man arrive on the island on a boat?"

"No, he did not arrive on a boat." Sarah sighed. "I can't give you any more help, but you might think about how we arrived on this planet, Commander. Five more questions."

"How *we* arrived on this planet?" Ryker scratched his chin. "We fucking crash-landed on this planet and are damn lucky to be alive, but as far as I know, we didn't come by sea. Wait a minute, you said the man was *mostly* on a boat, but he didn't arrive on a boat. Was he shipwrecked? Is that how he got on the island?"

"Yes!" Sarah answered.

"Ah ha!" Ryker exclaimed. "Did he wash ashore on a beach I would know?"

"You don't want to burn a question that way, do you?"

"No, you're right," Ryker backed off. "All right, the man is sitting on a beach smoking a cigarette, reading a letter, and he's crying. Now we know that he was shipwrecked on this island, and he's not alone. Ok, how did the others get to the island?"

"What's your question for me?" Officer Taylor asked.

"Did the others on the island arrive by shipwreck as well?" Ryker chanced his luck.

"No, the others are not on the island because of a shipwreck," Sarah answered. "Sorry, that leaves you with only four more questions."

During the riddle quest, Officer Taylor had looked away from her communications console. She had been checking Josiah's progress with a tracking beacon in the ePod, but the small green dot on her screen had faded away as he rounded the mountains to the west. As she glanced back, there was something completely unexpected on her monitor. Another blinking green dot had appeared just at the maximum range of her scanner, but it was to the east, not to the west.

"Commander... something strange is going on here. I was tracking the ePod on my video screen to the west. It was almost out of our range and then it popped up to the east. And now, I have two sets of thermals... that can't be!"

Ryker reconfigured the tracking input to the main video monitor showing the blinking green dot on a topographical graphic display of the planet's surface. They both stared intently at the location of the new green dot; it wasn't moving. Ryker cocked his head.

"Well, either they got lost, or that's not the ePod to the east of us. Scan all frequencies for anything close to that signal."

Officer Taylor opened all hailing frequencies and was startled at what she heard.

"It's a distress call, sir... in Russian!" She opened her communications channel to the main console speakers and flipped on the translator as a Russian voice calmly stated the same words over and over again, every sixty seconds.

"Security code Charlie Alpha Bravo, this is Commander Ivan

Stephanotski. Request immediate extraction, LZ is hot. Lock onto beacon, acknowledge."

Ryker leaned forward in surprise.

"Commander Stephanotski? That's the Russian captain on the video from the crashed spaceship. What the hell is he up to?"

"He's obviously in trouble, sir," Officer Taylor urged. "If those beasts that attacked Josiah and Lexis are still out there, we've got to help him!"

"Not so fast," Ryker cautioned. "It might be a trap. Maybe the lizard beasts are trying to spoof the transmission and lure us in close enough to ambush us."

CHIP jumped in; he had been monitoring their conversation.

"Sounds just like Xinjiang, sir, and you remember what happened there."

"Right... how could I forget?" Ryker muttered.

"Commander!" screamed Taylor. "I don't know what happened at Xinjiang, but if that distress signal is real, they don't have much time. They could get eaten alive while we dither around here!"

"I hear you, Officer Taylor," Ryker barked back. "But this *is* just like Xinjiang. Some bastard spoofed a satellite transmission on me; I rushed in and got eleven men killed that day. CHIP's right about this one, I'm afraid."

"Thank you for finally acknowledging that I am right," CHIP interjected.

"Will the two of you shut the fuck up about the past and join the living?" Officer Taylor exploded. "I'm sorry you lost your squadron back then, I'm sure it still haunts you to this day. But what's done is done; get the fuck over it already!"

Ryker and CHIP were stunned into silence. They had just learned something new about Officer Taylor; she had a foul mouth when she was angry, and apparently, her mouth wasn't finished with them just yet.

"Look, I get it. You don't want to make another bad call and get someone killed. You probably believed that Air Force shrink that fucked with your head after Xinjiang; he told you that when you act without thinking, people die. But listen to me! If you try and rescue those Russian bastards, yes, it's true; they may die. But if you just sit here with your thumb up your ass, we *know* they're going to die. Now snap out of your fucking pity party and let's get this ship moving!"

Ryker hesitated for a moment before CHIP chimed in. "You know, she makes some good points there, Commander."

"Yeah," Ryker agreed. "What are the odds that I'd stick my thumb up my ass twice in a row?"

"Statistically? A low probability, sir, but knowing you, it could happen. You remember that time in Bangkok?" CHIP responded. "I'd say that almost qualified, even though technically, it wasn't your ass."

"Are we going or what?" Officer Taylor screamed again. Ryker smiled and pushed the throttle forward.

"Of course we're going. We were going all along. CHIP and I just wanted to make sure that *you* wanted to go."

"Arrgh! You two are fucking... infuriating!" Sarah screamed.

"And we love you too, my dear," Ryker mocked. "And you know you're really cute when you're mad, but your eyes kind of bulge out. That's fucking scary."

"My, yes." CHIP interjected. "Officer Taylor was getting so creepy that she made my skin crawl... if I had skin, I mean."

Ryker shuddered and winked at CHIP. "Kind of gave me the hee-bee-gee-bees too, little buddy." Commander Ryker turned to Officer Taylor to see if she was still angry and then made a request. "Maybe we should all just calm down for a minute and let the Russians know that the Calvary is coming. Ping them our call sign... *G5.*"

Officer Taylor inhaled a deep breath and sat back down at her console, fidgeting with her hair. She opened a frequency to the beacon, initiated a locater 'ping', and then sent a Morse code '*G5*'.

"CHIP, lock on to the signal beacon and engage maximum power to the thruster," Captain Ryker called out. "With two sets of thermals out there, I'm betting we've got some reptiles to kill."

"Aye, aye, sir," CHIP responded. "Maximum power engaged. Target destination in three minutes, thirty seconds."

"Affirmative," Ryker called back. "This time we'll come in on the high side, unless you think those fucking lizards can fly."

"Good one, sir. Flying lizards... but you know, in Borneo, there are some lizards that *can* fly," CHIP retorted.

"Well, I guess it's a good thing that we aren't in fucking Borneo then, little buddy," Ryker quipped back. "Now saddle up, Tonto, we're going to town." The command module lurched forward and locked on course for the distress signal across the desert plain in the distance. Ryker assigned the external surveillance camera to the main video monitor and overlaid the topographical grid with the beacon location.

"When we reach the mountains, we're going in low through that pass," he relayed to CHIP. "Let's not announce our arrival too soon."

CHIP acknowledged and locked in the flight telemetry as Ryker studied the approach path.

"Officer Taylor, run a long-range thermal scan on the target area. Let's see if we have any company before we drop our trousers."

Two small red dots appeared on Officer Taylor's screen, next to the green distress signal.

"I've got two hot signatures halfway up the east side of the mountain across the next valley, Commander. That should be our distress party," Officer Taylor responded.

"Ok, CHIP, find me a place to park this station wagon. Something out in the open where we don't get another door ding... I don't want to jack up our insurance rates again," ordered Ryker.

"I'll try and avoid crashing into the Officers' Lounge," CHIP shot back.

"You know, you're one funny fucking robot," mumbled Ryker.

Back in the cave above the rocky cliffs, Captain Mitch Gaylord listened to the acid rain and stared at the blinking lights on the transmitter in Elena's hand. It was too late to destroy it and break the signal; whatever was coming for them had already locked on to their location.

"I am sorry, they find us again. It is my fault," Elena whispered. Just then, the lights on the transmitter went dark and then blinked on and off in a seemingly random sequence. Elena looked at Mitch with surprise. "My locater beacon is not supposed to do this," she told him, "I don't know... what it means." Captain Gaylord watched the sequence of lights repeat three times and then its pattern stopped; it was Morse code for *G5*. A smile came over his face.

"Well, I'll be damned! That bastard made it down alive."

Elena stared at him with a confused look. "What is it, Captain?"

"It's the call sign for my ship, Genesis Five. We're getting out of here, that's what it means!" he exclaimed.

"You have a ship? You didn't tell me you have a ship." Elena hugged him with a mixture of relief and delight.

"Well, technically I *had* a ship. I left the keys with the valet and stepped out for some air." Mitch smiled. He reached down and took out the last flare from Ivan's utility belt; they would need the flare to signal their location for rescue. The acid rain had finally stopped and the pulsating multicolored sky lit up the darkened valley below.

"Shit, let's get out there and let them know we're alive!" Mitch blurted out.

As they scrambled down the narrow rocky ledge to the desert floor, Mitch ignited the flare and waved it above his head. Elena followed behind him and paused for a moment to pick up the spear that had almost ended his life a short while ago. "We won't need that now," he yelled with a giant smile on his face. "We're going home!"

"I know," Elena called back. "I just want souvenir."

Following the distress beacon, Commander Ryker maneuvered Genesis Five close to the rocks through the mountain pass and then they emerged at the end of the desert valley. Punching through into the open, he scanned the thermal monitor for any signs of life.

"You got my parking space reserved, little buddy?" he asked.

"Yes, sir. At the base of the cliffs on the east side of the valley, there's a flat spot of VIP parking with your name on it," CHIP answered.

"Officer Taylor, give me a status report on those thermals. No surprises here. Now, what have we got?" Ryker stated.

"Commander, we've got a problem!" Sarah announced with alarm. "I have two hot ones coming down the slope on the east, but now I have seven cold ones closing fast from the west! What do you want to do?" Ryker punched up the thermal scan data to the main video monitor and studied it.

"Anywhere else to set down away from the freeze patrol in the west?"

"Negative, Commander, too rocky," CHIP responded. "This is the only LZ available."

Ryker maneuvered the command module over the landing zone

and hovered a few meters off the ground.

"And judging by the speed and trajectory of the incoming party crashers..." Ryker started. CHIP interrupted to answer his question.

"Both parties will arrive for the dance at the same time, Commander. I suggest we abort and circle back around."

"Neg-a-tory, little buddy. Our package will go stale. This is a one-shot deal. Open the cargo bay and stabilize the airlock," Ryker ordered.

"Commander," CHIP nagged back. "If you open the cargo bay, we're going to have some uninvited guests joining our party. Might I remind you that the first priority of a ship's captain is to not lose his ship... *again?*" Ryker ignored CHIP, turned to Officer Taylor, and smiled.

"Oh, *I'm* not going to lose it," Ryker quipped. "Miss Taylor, you ever fly a starship?" Sarah was stunned for a moment and then she smiled back at Ryker.

"No, Commander, I haven't... but I've always wanted to learn."

"Well then, this is your lucky day!" he grinned. "Officer Taylor, you have the helm. Hold our position until I give you the word and then you get us out of here fast. And, CHIP, if those uninvited guests get past the cargo bay, seal the command deck and flush the airlock."

"With you in it, sir?" CHIP responded.

"Affirmative. And that's an order. *Comprende, amigo pequeño?"* (Understand, my little buddy?) Ryker barked.

"*Si Señor,*" (Yes sir) CHIP responded.

Rummaging around in the duffle bag beneath his seat, Ryker pulled out the ion shotgun with the pearl handle that Josiah had built for him. He ran his hand down the shiny steel barrels of the gun. *No, I'm not going to lose my ship,* Ryker thought, *not this time. Old Betsy and me just have to make sure everyone coming to the party has an invitation.* He made his way back to the cargo bay and closed the airlock door behind him. A deafening whoosh of air rushed past him and out into the Niburu night. On the mountain to the east, he could make out the silhouettes of two human figures scrambling down the rocky slope. To the west he could just make out the outline of the lizard patrol, closing rapidly on the ship.

"Let's go, damn it!" Ryker yelled. "We've got company coming!" Ryker tapped his communicator and barked, "Ok, CHIP, just what do you think the range for an ion shoutgun would be?"

CHIP ran a quick calculation. "Judging by the size of the containment chamber, about fifty meters. But two things, sir. You referred to Betsy as a shotgun, but she is more like a really big sniper rifle. Betsy fires a three-milimeter particle beam, so you'll have to be very accurate to hit anything."

"You mean I can't just blast those slimy bastards when they get close?" Ryker quiped back.

"Not advisable, sir. That would require a totally different weapon design altogether. Dr. Stone and I can review the skematics when he gets back to the lab," CHIP responded.

"Well shit, that was one pretty important fact to leave out before I got my ass hanging out the back door, don't you think?" Ryker barked. "You said two things? What's the second thing?"

"Don't fire it inside the ship, sir. That would be bad," CHIP said.

"Here we go again. Define bad, little buddy," mumbled Ryker in disbelief.

"If you discharge that weapon, it will release massive amounts of ionized particles that will disrupt the ship's electronics. If you fire it inside the ship, it is certain to fry our avionics, and we won't be able to take off. A very effective weapon for the turret of a Y-wing fighter bomber, but as a close-range weapon, sir, not so good, I'm afraid."

"Ok, but I'm at least going to get one shot off out the back door," he mumbled. "Maybe it will slow them down a bit." Ryker grabbed a bulkhead with one hand, leaned outside the cargo bay and targeted the lead lizard in the patrol. The ion blast ripped a hole through his head, the beast let out a scream and collapsed to the ground. The remaining beasts behind him were stunned for a second; one grunted a command and they broke formation, and were now running a scattered attack pattern toward the ship.

"Shit, those bastards learn pretty fast!" Ryker barked. "Scratch one turtle head, but six of those fuckers are still inbound." He turned back toward the humans approaching and screamed, "Run Forrest! Run!"

Mitch Gaylord was the first to reach the cargo bay door. He gave an ear-to-ear grin when he saw Ryker hanging over the side with his arm extended.

"Hello, Commander! You got room for two more passengers?"

Mitch grinned.

"Sure thing, Captain. Best get aboard, we got some scaly party-crashers coming!" Ryker replied, pointing at the approaching lizards. Mitch turned to help Elena up into the ship and then pulled himself inside.

"Where we headed for?" Captain Gaylord asked.

"Any fucking place but here, cowboy," Ryker answered. He looked at Elena and then back to Gaylord. "Why hello there! Who's the super-fox?"

"This is Elena, long story, another time." Mitch snapped.

Elena smiled and hugged Commander Ryker. Ryker looked over her shoulder at Gaylord as he hugged her back and smiled.

"Well, I got to hand it to you, Captian." Ryker whistled. "I don't think even I could scare up an uber-babe in a hell-hole like this." He clicked on his communicator and barked, "Let's get out of here, Miss Taylor. Close the barn door little buddy!"

As soon as Ryker spoke, a spear whizzed past his head and shattered against the bulkhead wall. A lizard bounded in front of the open cargo bay door and leaped on him, knocking him to the deck and sending the ion cannon spinning across the floor. The scaly lizard reared back its head and opened its jaws, revealing row after row of razor-sharp teeth, dripping with slimy goo.

Mitch Gaylord reached behind his back, and in one motion, brought down a crushing blow with his battle-axe to the neck of the beast, knocking him off Commander Ryker. The beast growled, shook his head furiously, and turned to attack Captain Gaylord as he stood there protecting Ryker. The momentary distraction gave Ryker just the time he needed to make his move. Lying underneath the beast, he reached into his shoulder holster, grabbed his nine-milimeter pistol and emptied a seventeen-round clip in the groin of the lizard. The beast let out a terrifying squeal of pain and stumbled toward Mitch Gaylord before collapsing and falling near the door. Ryker jumped up and kicked the lizard in the head and it rolled out the door, falling to the ground.

"Guess you don't like a load of hot lead up your ass, do you, you slimy bastard?" Ryker screamed. He tapped his communicator and called out to Officer Taylor, "Ok, this party's over." Ryker announced. "Let's get the hell out of here!"

He reached over and pulled the lever to close the cargo bay door, but just as he did, a lizard with a bloody claw jumped into the door jam. The beast grabbed Mitch Gaylord by the neck, dragging him backwards, wedging them both in the partially closed door.

"Hold on, Mitch!" Ryker screamed out as he scrambled to snap in another ammunition clip for his nine-millimeter. He whispered over his communicator, "Sarah, get us the fuck out of here!"

"Commander," CHIP interrupted with urgency, "We can't take off with the airlock door open. You have to close that hatch!"

Ryker reloaded his pistol, but couldn't get a shot off without hitting Mitch. The beast with one claw was struggling with him, shielding his body from another round of hot lead from Ryker.

"Take the shot!" Captain Gaylord screamed as he thrashed about in the lizard's grasp.

"I can't shoot that bastard without hitting you!" Ryker yelled back.

"Just shoot the fuck anyway!" Mitch shouted. "Try to hit his eyes!" The other lizard beasts leaped frantically at the cargo door, scratching and clawing, trying to pry it open to get inside. The strength of their claws was starting to reverse the hydraulic door jam and it was grinding open.

"CHIP!" Ryker yelled. "We have uninvited guests in the cargo bay. Seal the command deck and flush the airlock!"

"If I flush the airlock, you will be expelled, sir," CHIP responded calmly.

"Flush the airlock now, you robotic bastard! That's an order!" Ryker screamed.

"Roger that, Commander," CHIP called back. CHIP initiated the airlock close on the command deck first and then he activated the controls to flush the cargo bay. The partially open cargo door reversed and opened for a second, exposing the belly of the beast that was clutching Captain Gaylord. The next thing that happened seemed like a blur, a slow-motion movie that they would all play over in their minds later as they tried to remember exactly what happened.

The airlock door opened and several beasts leaped at Ryker as he charged Mitch Gaylord. Ryker fired, avoiding the metal armor and targeting the eyes of the beasts, blinding them as they screamed and fell off the cargo door. Elena jumped across the cargo bay and grabbed her lizard spear, cocked it behind her ear, and taking two powerful strides, she thrust the spear into the neck of the beast clutching Captain Gaylord. The beast shrieked, lost its grip on Mitch, and fell backwards out of the door.

Ryker dove across the room and slammed down the airlock handle, sealing the cargo compartment just in time before CHIP flushed the airlock. The three of them, Gaylord, Ryker, and Elena were thrown into a pile against the back wall of the ship as Officer Taylor engaged the throttle of the command module and it lurched skyward. Sarah scanned the thermals in the cargo bay. Seeing only heat signatures for three humans and no lizards, she let out a sigh of relief. She calmed herself and then hit the button to unseal the command compartment airlock.

"Everybody ok back there?" Officer Taylor shouted.

Ryker rubbed the swollen knot on the back of his head, blinked his eyes, and then replied. "Yeah, we're ok." He laughed as he glanced over at Mitch and Elena. "But where the hell did you learn to drive, Officer Taylor?"

"That was my first time." Sarah laughed. "How did I do?"

Mitch Gaylord hugged Elena and looked seriously into her eyes. "Thank you for saving my life back there," Mitch told her. "That was quite a shot, better than William Tell."

"Just returning the flavor, as you say." Elena smiled.

"Actually it's not a flavor, it's a... never mind." Mitch laughed. "By the way, what kind of Olympian did you say you were?" he asked.

"I didn't say, Captain. Every girl should have some secrets, no?" Elena smiled and stroked his cheek. "I think you are man that likes a little mystery."

Captain Gaylord exhaled a deep breath and gave an ear-to-ear grin. Ryker had been observing the sensual interchange between them and couldn't resist interrupting to give Mitch some grief.

"Captain Mitchell Lee Gaylord! How the hell did you get out here anyway?" Ryker asked. "The last time I saw you, you were playing the hero, trying to save the passengers of my ship by riding that busted engine down through the clouds."

"Save the passengers?" Mitch chuckled. "Shit, I was just trying to save myself, I've seen you fly before. Every time you take the controls, something gets blown up and then you crash. I figured I was safer riding a burning engine bronco style than flying with you!"

Elena and Mitch erupted in laughter together.

"Why, Captain Gaylord, you are clairvoyant," CHIP chimed in. "You know, we did in fact crash... *yet again*, I'm afraid."

Ryker had to put a stop to the bashing at his expense.

"Ok, Ok. So we had a bit of a rough landing, the point is, I got us all down alive... didn't I? How about a little respect for my piloting skills."

CHIP, Elena, and Gaylord all erupted in one more round of laughter. The whoosh of the airlock doors opened and provided a graceful exit to the conversation, so Ryker joined Officer Taylor on the command deck, followed slowly by Mitch and Elena. He walked up behind the Captain's chair, hugged Sarah Taylor and whispered in her ear.

"Not bad flying for your *virgin* flight, ma'am. I'd say you're a natural." Ryker smiled.

"It sure sounded like you guys were having some fun back there." Officer Taylor smirked. "And who is our new passenger, by the way?"

"Oh yeah! Mitchy's woman." Ryker beamed. "Man, he's got it bad for her." He smiled and raised his eyebrows.

Officer Taylor looked Elena up and down competitively and then turned to Ryker.

"Well? What's she like?" Sarah asked.

"It's weird, she looks like a vixen that just escaped from a Victoria's Secret catalog. Ok, don't get me wrong, she's a hardcore super-fox, but unfortunately, she's got some serious odiferous emanations going on there, if you know what I mean. Whew, she stinks!" Ryker noted, pinching his nose.

"Come on, cut the girl some slack! Maybe she just worked up a sweat back there killing those lizard beasts while she was saving your life," Sarah quipped back.

"Hey, I emptied a nine-millimeter clip into one of those beasts' ass, you know. I filled those Rocky Mountain oysters full of holes; that was some pretty sweet shootin'!"

"And she killed a lizard with her bare hands," Sarah shot back.

"I'm not winning this argument, am I?" Ryker smiled. Sarah

Taylor laughed and touched his cheek.

"Afraid not, love, but you're still cute when you're mad. Your eyes kind of bug out, you know?"

"Then I guess we're even, you know, for earlier," Ryker noted shyly.

"Barely," Sarah replied with a slight smile. "But stay away from the super fox, I've got my bug eyes on you, Commander."

"Wouldn't have it any other way," Ryker quipped. "Well then, Officer Taylor, I think it's time we blow this Popsicle stand."

As Sarah took the controls, Ryker leaned back in his chair and reflected on the recent developments.

"It's been a fun ride so far, don't you think, Miss Taylor?" Ryker smiled. "Let's see, Lexis and Josiah received a secret message from Dr. Maurya, and now they are en route to try and rescue Dr. Samantha Jones, who is believed to be trapped inside an invisible Time Portal to a parallel dimension. The secret sender of the encrypted message, Dr. Maurya, is leading the evil Lieutenant McCurdy away from his mysterious Time Portal to some unknown destination... for some unknown reason. Coincidentally, the location of our secretive Dr. Maurya is also currently... unknown."

"That *is* quite a tale," Sarah agreed.

"But wait," Ryker exclaimed, "That's not even the best story by a long shot! The rumors of Captain Gaylord's heroic sacrifice and subsequent demise have turned out to be, well, a tad premature." Ryker turned around and glanced at Mitch and Elena, they were asleep in each other's arms at the back of the command deck. He turned to Sarah and raised his eyebrows.

"Got to hand it to you, buddy, you are a credit to your gender," Ryker continued, praising the adventures of Captain Gaylord. "Once thought to be dead, our former misguided military martyr managed to survive a crash on the mysterious planet Niburu, escaped unscathed from a frantic battle with a band of lizard warriors, and somewhere along the way, hooked up with a foxy new girlfriend."

"Not a bad adventure so far, I'd say," commented Officer Taylor, still focused on the controls. "But it's too bad Captain Gaylord now appears to be already taken, he's quite a hunk!"

Ryker wrinkled his brow with just a touch of jealousy. *Oh, not to worry,* he thought, *Mitch is preoccupied with the super-fox with the outrageous body odor; I'll stay with the sweet smelling cards in my hand.*

As they looked out the window, Commander Ryker and Officer Taylor weren't exactly sure what was in store for them next. Lexis and Josiah were out there trying to free Dr. Jones, Dr. Maurya was lost, and those scaly lizard beasts were lurking in the shadows, just waiting to eat them alive. The only thing that was certain was that all their divergent paths seemed to lead back to the Genesis Five passenger module. Given everything that had happened so far, a reunion with the rest of the human castaways on planet Niburu seemed long overdue.

"Hang on, it's time to see what this baby will do!" Officer Taylor whispered to Ryker.

She rammed down the engine control lever and engaged the full throttle of the ion thruster. The Genesis Five command module surged upwards, pinning Ryker to his seat and leaving the desert valley, the Russian spaceship, and the wounded lizards fading away like small objects in the rear view of the surface below.

"You sure you know how to fly this thing?" Ryker said nervously as he peeled his head off the seat and glanced out the window. "You know, Miss Taylor, you've just earned your learner's permit, but flying a powerful spacecraft like this, it requires some real... *piloting skill.*"

"Well I haven't crashed it yet." Sarah smiled. "So I guess that puts me one up on you, doesn't it, Commander?"

"She makes a good point there, sir," CHIP chimed in. "Remember the time you crashed your Harrier in Beijing? What were the odds that you could complete your... maneuvers... inside a blimp hangar with two strippers, excuse me, exotic dancers, riding shotgun on your..."

"Ass... tronomical, I'd say," Ryker agreed. "But hell, I almost pulled it off, didn't I? What can I say? I calculated only a slight possibility of a CFIT, but sometimes, possibilities can turn into probabilities... real fast. Who knew those ladies would freak out, clamp their thighs around my helmet and steam up my visor? Didn't see that one coming, now did you?"

"No sir," CHIP apologized, "I didn't. My terrain avoidance programming proved... entirely unsatisfactory. I have subsequently modified my subroutines to account for such... unexpected possibilities, should we encounter them in the future.

"Roger that, little buddy. I've got a feeling that pretty soon we're going to need everything you've got in your little programming bag of tricks." Ryker yawned, as he closed his eyes. "You have the helm, Science Officer Taylor. Before we go and check in on our poker game at Genesis Five, I think I'll catch some zzz's. Rescuing damsels in distress and repelling repugnant reptiles can sure wear a guy out."

"Affirmative, Commander," Officer Taylor responded. "Laying in a course now for Genesis Five... just outside of scanner range. Any further orders?"

"Just one," Ryker mumbled as he drifted off. "Keep a firm hand on that stick and a sharp eye on our chips. And wake me if any more cards get dealt in this hand... I don't want to miss the turn."

The End

Also by Gary Wayne Clark

As foretold by Koda, the crew of Genesis Five has been swept into a struggle beyond their universe; it is an epic battle, for the *Multiverse.* In the war for Niburu, survival is the sole objective... understanding the Multiverse, a distant luxury. But in the midst of battle, questions remain: When life is bioengineered in a test tube, what does it mean to be human? In the twisted alliances of war, whom can you trust? What in this life is worth dying for? And ultimately, what is the price of revenge?

In the next installment of **The Devolution Chronicles:** *Rise of the Chimera,* as Commander Ryker and his Chimera allies stare into the abyss of their own extinction, they are forced to discover their own essential truths; truths that will determine if they are destined to survive on the mysterious planet of Niburu... and in the Multiverse beyond.

About the Author

Gary Wayne Clark is a writer, musician, and venture capitalist specializing in the development of disruptive innovations. His musical compositions such as *Emonesia* and *Passage to Niburu* can be heard streaming around the world. Formerly the managing partner of a biotech accelerator, it was there in a college laboratory that he created new transgenic organisms by splicing together the genes of multiple species... and began to ponder the scientific and ethical implications of artificial life. Most recently, he was a member of the Board of Governors of the Tech Coast Angels, overseeing private investments in advanced technologies such as bioengineering, artificial intelligence, nanotechnology, synthetic genes and biowarfare. He lives in Thousand Oaks, California and Estes Park, Colorado with his wife and the spirit of his shapeshifting interspecies translator, a telepathic Great Dane named Raz.

Soundtrack

Inspired by The Devolution Chronicles, the original musical soundtrack *Passage to Niburu* by *Earamas* is available on iTunes and Amazon as well as streaming from fine dental establishments around the world. *"Earamas"* represents the music and lyrics of Gary Wayne Clark and Glen Dale Spreen, mystically enhanced by the guitar work of Ali (*Spice*) Clark and Justin (*Point Break*) Clark. So close your eyes, sit back, and relax your mind. Lend us your ears for the musical journey of this universe… and the *Multiverse* beyond. But as Commander Ryker warned, *"You better strap yourself in, cowgirl... this could get a little bumpy.*

Alter Ego Database Log

Unauthorized Keyword Searches by the Chimera, detected on Dr. Jones' Computer.

"The tree of liberty," a quote by Thomas Jefferson. Letter to William Stephens Smith, November 13, 1787. *The Papers of Thomas Jefferson,* ed. Julian P. Boyd, vol. 12, p. 356 (1955).

"Earworm," a portion of a song or tune that repeats over and over again within one's mind.

"Eve of Destruction", a song written by P. F. Sloan, 1965. Best-known recording was by Barry McGuire.

"Obsessive-compulsive disorder," a disorder of anxiety and depression often accompanied by recurring thoughts, often associated with highly intelligent people.

"Rapture," an end-times event when all true believers still alive before the end of the world will be taken from the Earth by God into Heaven.

"Schwarzschild's Bubble," a theory based on an article entitled "Wormholes, Time Machines, and the Weak Energy Condition." Michael Morris, Kip S. Thorne, and Ulvi Yurtsever. Physical Review Letters, 1988.

"Planet X," a 6,000 year old Sumerian description of our solar system that includes an additional planet called "Nibiru" or "Niburu." A.k.a. "planet of the crossing."

"Hopi Creation Myths," Robert Morningside.

"Multiverse," cosmic theory set out originally by William James (1895) where many universes make up all possibilities of existence; each which have different laws of physics that define them. Also referenced in the Hindu Bhagavata Purana, *"the countless universes... wander within you, like particles of dust blowing around in the sky."*

"Book of the Hopi," Frank Waters (1963), Drawings and source material recorded by Oswald White Bear Fredericks.

"Popol Vuh," a sacred Mayan book written in Quiché which describes creation of man. "There was only immobility and silence in the darkness, in the night. Only the Creator, the Maker, Tepeu, Gucumatz, the Forefathers, were in the water surrounded with light. They were hidden under green and blue feathers, and were therefore called Gucumatz."

"Sun Tzu," The Art of War, various quotes.

"Controlled Flight Into Terrain," CTIF describes an accident in which an airworthy aircraft, under pilot control, is unintentionally flown into the ground, a mountain, water, or an obstacle.

"Sarah's Riddle," "There is a man sitting alone on a beach." Anonymous, referenced in Jed's List of Puzzle Situations, #1.20, *"As told to me"* by a friend in 1975, later adapted by an author named Gary Wayne Clark.

"Vladimir Lenin," (1870-1924). *Russian Communist politician.* "A lie told often enough becomes the truth."

"Adolf Hitler," (1889-1945). Mein Kampf; "in the primitive simplicity of their minds they more readily fall victims to the big lie than the small lie…"

"Texas Hold'em," a variation of the standard card game of poker.

"Point Break," surfing term describing how waves break onto a rocky point; also nickname of Justin *(Point Break)* Clark, lead guitarist for indie band *Earamas*.

"On the Origin of Species," 1859, Charles Darwin.

"The Razors Edge," W. Somerset Maugham.

"Nirvana," a primary aim of Buddhism is to break free of the wheel of samsara, and to reach a new level called Nirvana. Also, reference to a Seattle grunge rock band fronted by Kurt Cobain.

"Elvis," legendary 20th century King of Rock and Roll on Earth.

"Sir Walter Scott," Marmion, Canto vi. Stanza 17. Scottish author & novelist (1771 - 1832) "Oh what a tangled web we weave, when first we practice to deceive…"

"Drop D Tuning," or "scordatura", an alternate guitar tuning technique allowing extremely fast transitions between power chords, epitomized by guitarist Ali *(Spice)* Clark of *Earamas*. Chimera musicians later adopted this tuning style to accommodate their claws, along with slide guitar.

"Pride and Prejudice," Jane Austin, 1813. Original manuscript was entitled First Impressions, 1797.

"Glen Dale Spreen," renowned composer, arranger, musician that worked with many legends of Rock and Roll, including Elvis Presley, most notably on his last song to reach #1 (*Suspicious Minds*). Later went on to form one half of the reclusive indie cult band '*Earamas*'.

"William Shakespeare," various noted quotations, a.k.a. "the Bard."

"Metallica," late 20th and early 21rst heavy metal band. Considered mother's milk to head bangers.

"Winston Churchill," quote, "Never was so much owed by so many to so few."

"Led Zeppelin," late 20th century rock band on Earth known for driving lead guitars and screechy high vocals. Air guitar favorite by generations of *wanna be* rock stars.

"King James Bible," Matthew 6:21, "For where your treasure is, there your heart will be also."

"Daneridge Alexander Razputin Dances with Squirrels, aka "Raz," beloved Great Dane, second tallest dog on Earth, therapy dog, loving goofball, brother to Rose and Charlotte, spiritual guide. *Tuawta, i sus kwaatsi.*

"Yeenaeldooshi," in Navajo, a human with the ability to shape-shift into a wolf or other animal, also know as a *skinwalker*. Skinwalkers are thought to have the power to read minds. As Koda says... *I knew you were going to think that*

Passage to Niburu

The End... of the beginning.